# CROWNS

# NORTH QUEEN

## NICOLA TYCHE

COLUMBIA RIVER
PUBLISHING

COLUMBIA RIVER PUBLISHING
Vancouver, WA 98685

First published in the United States

ISBN: 978-1-959615-01-9

Cover design by Saint Jupiter
Edited by Kate Studer
Edited by Hanna Richards
Proofread by Lauren Riebs

*For Shaun. Without you, this story
would have never been told.*

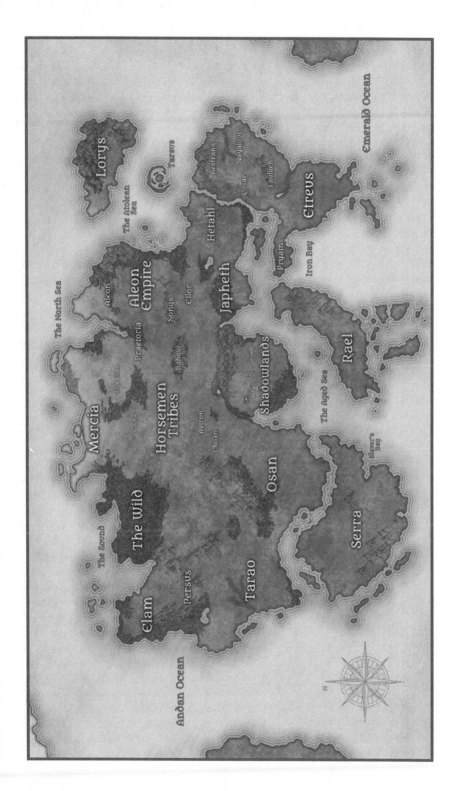

# NORTH QUEEN

# CHAPTER ONE

Consciousness came like a dream, bending the mind as dreams often do. Her eyelids fluttered under an icy weight, and she struggled to focus her vision against the blur that fell across her face.

Where was she?

She blinked back the cold of snow and drew a sharp breath as she made out the shapes of needled treetops against the sky. How did she get here?

Her pulse quickened as she sat up with a start to find herself in the middle of a winter forest. Trees rocked softly in slips of wind, and dry snowflakes danced through the air.

What was this place? Where was she?

The hair rose along the back of her neck as an icy trickle ran up her spine.

*Who* was she?

A rush of panic coursed through her veins. She tried to stand but stumbled as a throbbing pain inside her head caught her on the rise, threatening her fragile balance. She pressed her fingers against her temples. What had happened? As she breathed, the ache subsided. Her eyes cleared, but her mind didn't. Why couldn't she remember?

She glanced around. The eyes of the aspens stared back at her, watching; the wind swept whispers around her. Fear pushed back the cold. The rush of blood pulsed in her ears. Her body told her to run. But from what? And to where?

*No.* She couldn't let panic take over. Her mind would come back—she only needed to give it a moment.

She drew in a deep breath to calm herself as she surveyed the forest around her. Several inches of snow sat on the ground, but only a light dusting covered her. She hadn't been here long. Frozen tears stippled the corners of her eyes, but she was lost for their cause. She struggled for reason against her clouded mind.

"Calm down," she told herself. "You're a grown woman. Pull yourself together." But telling herself to calm and actually calming were two different things. Still, she managed to keep the second wave of panic at bay.

She brushed her long icy-blonde tresses back from her face and combed the trees as she turned her attention back to her surroundings. The snow held only her own footprints, and they ended abruptly a few steps away. How had she even gotten here? It was as if she'd been dropped from the sky. And she was alone. A pang of fear twisted in her stomach again, but she pushed it down. That wouldn't help.

Movement startled her, and she jumped to find a winter fox peering out from deeper within the trees.

"Hammel's hell," she said breathlessly. "You scared me."

His white coat blended with the snow, and his black-tipped ears flicked back and forth. A fascinating beauty with an unnatural pull hung about him, and his bright, golden eyes looked back at her with a deep curiosity. For a moment, she forgot about being lost—but only for a moment.

He gave a chitter and trotted off between the trees. *How peculiar.*

But her mind didn't stay with the fox for long; she had more pressing matters. She skimmed the trees as her pulse picked back up, and again, she resisted the urge to run. There was nothing to run from, and nowhere to run to, but that settled her only slightly.

She shifted her attention to herself. The cool blue of her dress, layered under a smoky-white cloak, matched the winter world around her. Her sleeves ran long over the backs of her hands. A delicate chain hung from her neck, and she reached up to feel a round pendant at her chest. She ran her fingertips over its braided edge as she looked closely at the raised image at its center: a winterhawk. Surely it meant something, but what?

Turning back to her surroundings, she spotted a break in the woods and headed toward it. When she reached it, she found herself looking out over the rolling hills of an open meadow, where clusters of trees sporadically broke the sea of white. The brightness of winter flashed harsh against her eyes, and she squinted.

She searched for signs of a village or town: a road, tracks in the snow, smoke against the sky—anything. But only winter lay as far as the eye could see.

A chitter sounded behind her, and she turned to see the fox again. He gave a small snort.

"You're back, are you?"

What did he want? He trotted off into the forest, as if beckoning her deeper into the trees, but then stopped to look back over his shoulder. He twitched his tail, seemingly in agitation.

"What are you doing?" she called. His presence gave a welcome distraction from the threatening panic over her situation. "Can't you see

I have problems of my own?" She sighed, but as she eyed the animal, a small smile came to her lips. "Are you here to help me, little fox?"

He cocked his head at the sound of her voice and then flitted off again, light as the snowflakes around him.

*Funny little thing.* Did he want her to follow him? She shook her head. That was silly. She ran her eyes along the edge of the forest and then back to the meadow. The meadow seemed her best option; she'd have better visibility and possibly a better sense of direction.

She glanced back to see the fox again. He cocked his head to the side once more and flicked his ears.

"Do you want to come along?" she asked, nodding toward the meadow. "I'd appreciate the company." Gods knew this furry distraction was the only thing keeping her from losing her last sliver of calm.

He skirted back into an icy thicket at the base of a large tree, peering at her from within.

Talking to a fox was silly. Pretending the fox had a rational mind and understood her was silly. But he was cute, and she supposed she could allow herself a little silliness to help lighten her circumstance.

"Are you sure you don't want to come?"

He didn't move from the thicket.

She shrugged. "All right. Well, goodbye, little fox." She gave him one last smile and then stepped into the open winter.

Now, away from the forest and the shield of the trees, she shivered as the wind bit at her skin. She pulled up the thick hood of her cloak, but it did little to warm her. Her eyes stung, and her fingers ached from the cold.

Her pace slowed in the deeper snow of the open meadow. Twice she stumbled on hidden rocks. Perhaps following the tree line along the forest might have been better.

She couldn't control her shivering now, and she forced her eyes and mind on only her path ahead. The first cluster of trees wasn't much farther, and it would be a small reprieve from the gusts of icy air. Her legs burned as she pressed on. She reached the small grouping of trees and huddled against the rough bark, rubbing her arms underneath her cloak to spur some warmth. How had she managed to get herself in the middle of a frozen forest? Where had she come from? Her dress was well made; she seemed properly put together. Surely she hadn't been out long, which, she hoped, would mean someone would be looking for her and might soon find her.

"You look lost," a gravelly voice called.

She jumped and turned to see a burly man leaning against a knotted pine. He wore a frayed winter jacket lined in matted fur and a dagger belted around his waist. His unkempt hair fell unevenly over his grimy brow, and he gave a grin of rotting teeth. He rocked his weight off the tree and lumbered toward her.

A shiver ran down her spine. "Oh, I'm fine," she said, trying to hide her unease with a polite smile. Her mind raced for defenses. "I lost my horse on my morning ride, but I know my brothers are looking for me and will be along soon."

He scratched at the motley hair on his unshaven cheek and slid his gaze down and back up her body. His grin widened. "What a coincidence," he rasped. The snow crunched under the weight of his footfalls as he stepped closer. "My brothers should be along soon too. And they'd love to meet you."

Her heart pulsed faster. Escaping would be difficult in the open. She swallowed the panic rising in her throat. She needed to keep her wits about her.

"I'm sure they're lovely, but I should be on my way." She backed up slowly, positioning herself to flee, but he lurched forward and grabbed her wrist, stopping her escape.

"I can't let you do that."

"Get your hands off me!" she demanded, trying to pull away from him.

He gave a grisly chuckle.

She fought his hold, striking out with her free hand, but his thick layers thwarted her defense. He pulled her closer, and the putrid smell of his breath—a vile, rotting stench—filled her nostrils. She whipped her hand up and raked her nails across the exposed skin of his face. He reeled back, growling in pain, and she sank her teeth into the flesh of his fingers. He lost his grip, and she wrenched away.

Everything within her screamed to run—this time with reason.

She sprinted back toward the forest. Her heart raced, coursing energy through her and giving her a burst of speed. His raged curses rang heavily close behind, and she feared she might not make it to the trees. Her lungs stung with each icy inhale; her legs begged her to stop. But she pushed herself harder, coughing for breath as she ran.

His growling huffs grew fainter, and she finally dared to peek back. She had gained a bit of distance from him. He was fast for his size, but she was faster. Her body tired, slowing, but her fear kept her going. She couldn't feel her feet and worried about falling—she *needed* to make it to the forest. Almost there, she racked her mind with what to do next. The snow would give her position away. She would have to outrun him.

She glanced back again and, to her horror, caught sight of not only her assailant but three more men a little way behind him.

Reaching the tree line, she charged into the wood. As she fled deeper into the forest, it grew quiet behind her. Had he stopped? Was he waiting for his friends? She looked around desperately. Her body couldn't run anymore, and the high-branched evergreens gave little opportunities to climb and hide. She couldn't see her pursuers, but the sound of their voices told her they had joined up at the edge of the forest.

She paused as she raced through her options. Suddenly, the small fox appeared again, sitting calmly on a fallen tree.

"You again," she said, panting as she looked around and tried to rationalize a plan. "Any help would be greatly appreciated," she added. His ears perked as he watched her.

*Stupid*, she scolded herself. Now wasn't the time to be talking to a fox.

She picked up her pace again, fleeing farther into the wood. Lighter snow made her trail less noticeable. She saw a ridge ahead and sprang toward it. A frozen stream lay below, sheltered from the snow by its banks. Her pulse raced as her chances of eluding her pursuers grew marginally better. She slid down onto the ice, trying not to disturb the snowy bank too much, and made her way along the frozen water, but it still didn't hide her. If they made it to the stream, they'd see her.

She noticed an alcove carved out along the stream's bank. Although it was small, it would conceal her. If she was lucky, she could wait until they moved on. She crept into the hollow, pulling her skirts tightly around her and trying to quiet her labored breath.

The forest stood quiet. She waited. No one came. She waited longer. Still, she heard nothing, but she knew better than to venture out.

A branch snapped nearby.

Her heart beat heavily in her chest. A wave of fear washed over her, and she cursed her choice to hide. She should have kept running. Now she could only wait and hope they wouldn't find her.

"Where are you, lovely?" a sickening voice called. "I know you hear me."

"Alke, we shouldn't be in here," a second voice replied. "It's not worth it. We should just leave her."

"Shut your face, you coward! I'm not leaving without that wench."

She bit back a cry rising in her throat.

"There's much worse than me in this forest," he called to her. "Be smart, come out."

His companion snickered.

The air grew quiet again. She strained her ears, but she heard nothing. Still, she waited. She wasn't foolish enough to think they'd gone. Her legs cramped in the tight confines, but she didn't dare move.

Suddenly, a hand reached down and grabbed her arm. She let out a scream as he dragged her from her hiding space.

"Gotcha," the brute wheezed, this time holding her at arm's length to stave off her defensive attack.

"Let me go!" she cried, twisting against him.

His companion, looking just as disheveled, chuckled beside him, but there was no sign of the other two. Where were they?

"We got her!" her captor bellowed over his shoulder, and she realized the others had stayed at the edge of the wood. They gave a few celebratory calls and urged their friends to hurry out as he dragged her back toward them.

"Let me go!" she shouted again as she struggled, desperately fighting against him, but she couldn't match his strength. He gave a raspy chuckle and pulled her along.

"Alke," the second man called from behind them, but her captor dragged her on, too enthralled with his catch.

"Alke!" The man's voice came more urgent now, enough to pull even her attention.

The man that held her looked over his shoulder with a snarling glare. "Shake off, man. Come on."

But something was wrong. His companion didn't move.

"Bullo, come on," her captor snapped, growing impatient.

But the man still didn't move. His lips trembled.

"Bullo?"

The man pulled a dagger from his belt with shaking hands and brought the blade to his own neck.

She paused in her fight to free herself as a creeping dread snaked through her.

Her captor's eyes widened. "Bullo, what are you doing?"

Bullo's face strained, his veins bulging at his temples. "Alke!" he cried to his friend in terror. "Help me—"

But the blade cut off his words as he sliced into his own flesh. She gave a terrified gasp but held back a scream. Bullo sputtered as he choked for air. Blood sprayed down the front of his matted furs, falling to the ground and coloring the surrounding snow. He staggered forward, then collapsed with a gurgle onto the forest floor.

"Bullo!" her captor shouted, and moved toward him. Then he stopped suddenly. He let go of her wrist, but she stood frozen, too terrified to run. He looked back at her as his face twisted, his eyes widening with fear. "Witch!" he snarled.

She stumbled back. He bared his rotting teeth as he pulled his own dagger from his belt. She took another step back, shaking her head. What was happening?

"Witch!" he bellowed.

His fellow men yelled to him from the tree line, their voices urgently calling him to get out of the forest, but they didn't enter. Why didn't they come?

He raised his dagger, and terror ran through her. He blamed her, and he was going to kill her.

"No, please!" she cried.

They both let out a scream as he swung the dagger inward on himself and plunged it into his own stomach. He fell to his knees, and she staggered backward.

"Witch!" he screamed, then he pulled the blade from his belly and swung it again, sinking it back into his gut. She covered her mouth and watched in horror as his screams died, and he fell forward onto the forest floor, soaked in his own blood.

"Alke!" the two men bellowed from the tree line. "Alke! Bullo!"

But they still didn't enter.

Her weeping breaths were uncontrollable now.

The air fell quiet. Had the others fled? The man named Bullo had been afraid—but of what? Whatever had killed these men would surely come for her next. She waited, her tears freezing on her face.

But nothing came. Quiet sat around her, broken only by the sound of her ragged breath.

A faint rustling made her jump, and she turned to see the fox sitting on a stump. He cocked his head.

A terrifying thought hit her. "Did you do that?" she whispered.

*No.* That was ridiculous. But if he didn't, what did? The animal flicked his tail, waiting.

She stood, shaking from the cold or from terror. Maybe both. As she stared at the dead men, her fear urged her to flee, but she was on her own, and she needed a weapon. Bullo's lifeless hand still clutched his bloody dagger. She approached cautiously, almost fearing he'd spring back to life. Sneaking forward, she grabbed the dagger by the blade so as not to touch him, and then scrambled backward in a hasty retreat. It was sticky with his blood, and her stomach turned. She wiped as much as she could on the frozen ground and then looked back at the fox.

"This is madness," she whispered shakily, "but I'm out of ideas. If you want me to follow, then lead on already. Take me away from here."

He leapt forward, finally happy at her compliance, and she followed after.

# CHAPTER TWO

She followed the fox north, breathing deep the winter air to calm herself, but calm wouldn't come. Blood still stained her hands. Fear still stained her mind. What had happened to the men in the forest would haunt her. But what *had* happened?

She eyed the fox warily. He had been there...

He trotted alongside her, stopping to pounce on anything that resembled something to play with, or a tasty snack.

"You seem to be taking this entire situation rather well." Her voice still shook slightly. "Better than I am."

He batted the tip of a stick above the snow with his paw and then skirted to the next.

"I mean, you didn't run away. You don't even seem... bothered, really."

Because he was a *fox*, with a twilight of memory, and he probably didn't even care. And yet...

She narrowed her eyes at him. "You can see how that might make one question... your involvement..."

The animal darted under a thicket at the base of a tree and shuffled around before barreling back out of it. He didn't even seem to remember she was still there, much less able to overpower the minds of her attackers and force them to kill themselves. It was a ridiculous notion, and she quickly pushed the thought from her mind. But if it wasn't the fox, what had come for those men? And why hadn't it come for her?

And now here she was, following this fox—admittedly not the wisest idea, but he was all she had at the moment. He was all she knew. And he helped settle her.

"If you're here to help me, perhaps you could do something useful? Maybe dig me a burrow to sleep in?"

He seemed oblivious to her now.

She gazed up at the fading afternoon sky. "A warm burrow, with a fire and fur blankets." She would need shelter soon. And food. "Maybe you could find me something to eat? Or lead me to a castle with a warm bath and a feast of roast and honeyed bread?"

He cocked his head. She would have smiled if she weren't trying so hard to quell the panic rising inside her.

"You're cute. But I'm beginning to think you're lost too." She scanned the trees around her. It didn't seem she would find shelter anytime soon, and she shivered as the cold sank into her core. She pulled the hood of her cloak up, covering her head for more warmth. "I'm ready for that burrow now."

The animal ignored her and sniffed around a large rock. She pursed her lips as she tried to not let desperation overwhelm her. It was foolish to have followed a fox. She wasn't any closer to improving her situation, and the day was fading. Fear crept back inside her, and tears threatened.

"Don't be so dramatic," she whispered to herself as she turned her attention to what to do next. The protection of the trees kept the wind at bay. She could build a fire for warmth, and she reminded herself people didn't starve to death right away. Her nerves started to settle.

Suddenly, the fox stopped. He crouched low, flicking his ears forward, then back. His nose tested the air, and her pulse quickened. He flattened his ears against his head with his hackles raised, let out a low growl, and then turned and raced back the way they'd come.

She clenched her stolen dagger tighter as her fear resurfaced. Two ill-intentioned men still lurked about. Had they returned? She stood frozen, listening and scouring the trees for any movement.

All was quiet.

She was alone.

She let out her breath. Flighty fox, she thought, feeling foolish to have believed he was leading her somewhere. She'd wasted precious time.

Just then, a sound caught her ear. She stopped, straining to hear from which direction it came. It echoed through the forest again—a rustling thud—closer now, and she peered through the trees. Spotting movement, her heart leapt to her throat. Her eyes narrowed, focusing.

An animal.

A horse.

A horse with a rider. A man. Drawing nearer.

She ducked low and sidled up to a large tree, but she wasn't exactly hidden. The best she could do was to not draw attention and let him pass unaware. She clutched the dagger tighter and praised herself for taking it.

The rider drew closer, and she slunk back out of sight and waited, listening to the hoofbeats of his horse. As they grew louder, she placed him only a few yards away. A little longer and he'd be past her. She backed around the tree to stay hidden, but her shoulder caught a small branch, and its echoing snap broke the quiet of the forest.

The hoofbeats stopped.

Her heart raced.

The sing of steel made her shudder as he pulled his sword from its scabbard, and she braced her back against the tree. Her mind screamed for her to run, but her body threatened to forfeit. She didn't have the energy; he would catch her.

With animals in the forest, the sound could have come from anything—if only he'd believe that. She prayed he'd move on. Waiting felt like an eternity.

She strained to listen, but she could barely hear over the hammering of her heart in her ears. Had he gone?

Slowly, she peered around the other side of the tree. Her heart stopped when she saw the horse.

It stood without its rider.

She made a hasty retreat backward but gasped as she collided with a figure behind her—a figure very firm. And very male. Whirling around, she stumbled, but he caught her. She wrenched herself away and whipped her dagger to his neck.

He didn't move to counter. Instead, he held his arms out, with his sword pointed down, yielding.

"I don't want any trouble." She tried to sound as fierce as she could.

His eyes widened as he drew in a breath. "Norah?" he whispered.

Did he call her a name? Was it *her* name? Her chest tightened. Did she know him?

She pulled back the hood of her cloak as she took a step back, with her arm still outstretched and threatening to use the dagger. They only stared at each other.

His blond hair was short, but not too short. His square jaw held the shadow of a beard as it tapered to his chin, although she could tell he was a man typically clean-shaven. He wore light armor over a thick jacket—he was a soldier of some sort. His fitted breeches met polished boots, and silver trimmed his scabbard. He wasn't like the men who had chased her before. And there was something about him...

He took a step closer, and she moved back, gripping the dagger. "That's far enough!" she warned.

His face twisted in confusion. "Norah?" he said again. He took another step toward her.

"Stop!" she demanded, holding the dagger in front of her. "Don't come any closer." He was already too close.

He looked at the blade and then back up at her. "Don't you recognize me? It's me, Alexander." His eyes held the glint of a tear. "Norah, it's me."

No recollection came as she studied him. She had no memory of his face, his concerned brow, his eyes. No memory of his name. Yet he seemed to know her...

Relief flooded her, but she clutched it back. She wasn't having the best of luck in meeting trustworthy strangers in the forest. He held his hand up in pause, then slid his sword back into its scabbard without taking his eyes off her. She softened her stance but didn't lower the blade. A handsome face didn't make one trustworthy.

"You know who I am?" she asked, still guarded.

"Of course," he said with a broken breath. "I'd know you anywhere."

"And who am I, exactly?" If he called her a witch, she'd stab him.

His brows drew together. "You don't know?"

If she knew, she wouldn't be asking, but she bit back the snap of words on her tongue. Emotion glazed his face, bringing a stir of her own. Her heart raced as she shook her head.

He hesitated but then asked, "And you don't know who I am?" His voice came even softer.

She shook her head again. "No."

He winced and then looked to the ground for a moment. Then he swallowed.

"Who am I?" she pressed.

His eyes found hers again, and they burned a brilliant blue. "You're Norah Andell... of Mercia, the Northern Kingdom."

*Norah Andell.* A name strangely familiar to her, yet not. Slowly, she lowered the dagger.

"I've been searching for you." He gazed down at her hands, and his brow creased. "You're bleeding. Are you hurt?"

Chained in her bewilderment, she didn't move as he swept forward and took her hands in his, but his touch made her jump. "Um, no," she said, pulling away. "It's not mine." He was so close to her now. Dangerously close. But he didn't feel dangerous. He felt safe, and...

*No.* She didn't know this man. Then something caught her eye. The breastplate of his armor bore a raised emblem—*a winterhawk*—the same as the pendant around her neck. She reached up to her chest and clasped her fingers around it. "Who are you?"

His brow dipped. He paused before saying, "I'm Alexander Rhemus, lord justice to the queen regent. Norah, she's been waiting for your return. We all have."

That didn't make sense. "The queen regent? Why?" Why would a queen regent be waiting for her?

"Because you're her granddaughter."

Her pulse quickened. Her granddaughter? She shook her head. "No, that can't be right." A granddaughter of a queen wouldn't be wandering alone in a forest. "That can't be right," she said again.

"I tell you the truth, but, Norah"—he glanced around them—"we should go. I can explain everything on the way, but right now, we need to get out of the Wild."

She took a step back. She wasn't going anywhere with him. Not yet. "How did I get here?"

He shook his head. "I don't know."

Her eyes narrowed. "Then how did you know where I was?"

"I didn't, exactly," he answered with a tilt of his head. "I've been searching for what I saw in a vision."

She raised a brow. "You saw a vision, and you just got on a horse and came to find me in the middle of a forest?" No rational person would do that.

"Not just any forest—the Wild. But yes."

She didn't know what that meant, but that was the least of what she needed answered. "That's madness."

"But... you're here," he countered. "And we really do need to go. It's not safe here."

She took another step back. "Why?" As far as she was concerned, the forest was keeping her safe from random strangers.

"The Wild isn't kind to those who trespass."

Was that what had happened to the two men earlier? Yet it hadn't done anything to her. Maybe this was a ploy to get her to go with him. If she was who he said, how had she come to be wandering alone in a forest, anyway? Perhaps she'd run away. Maybe she didn't want to go back. She bumped up against a tree behind her.

"How long have I been gone?" She couldn't have been out very long. Her dress wasn't too soiled, aside from her fall, and her hair hung untangled and neatly kept.

He pushed out a scant breath, baffled. "You remember nothing?"

She swallowed the lump rising in her throat. "No."

He stared at her. "You've been gone three years."

Her breath quivered, and she gripped the tree behind her to steady herself. "Three years?" She shook her head. That wasn't possible. How could one, especially the granddaughter of a queen regent, just disappear for three years?

He looked around them again. "Norah, please. We have to go." He reached out his hand. "Will you let me take you home? Your grandmother's at the castle."

*Castle.* She glanced around for her fox. Her thoughts had been in jest, but perhaps he really had been leading her to a castle. Better than a burrow.

"We won't arrive until tomorrow," Alexander told her. "But there's an old homestead we can reach before dark. It's not much, but it's shelter with a place for a fire."

She still fought the uncertainty, trying to take everything in and searching for clarity on her situation. But she did need shelter and a fire. And still, there was something about him...

"Norah," he pleaded, "you do know me. You may not remember yet, but I do. And your people do. They've been waiting for you a very long time."

*Her people.* She knew he meant it in reassurance, but it brought only more anxiousness. So much responsibility. If people were truly waiting for her, they'd expect something from her, need something from her, and what could she give if she couldn't remember?

And could she trust this man? She shifted, glancing at the winterhawk emblem on his breastplate again, then the gilded handle of his sword. He certainly wasn't the same as the foul-intentioned men before. It was almost nightfall, and it had started to snow. She couldn't see another choice. She'd have to trust this stranger—this stranger who knew her. Slowly, she nodded.

With a small exhale of relief, he led his horse in front of her and reached out his hand. "May I?"

She eyed him warily. "I can manage."

The corner of his lips turned up, and he gave an obliging nod.

She felt Alexander's eyes on her as she climbed onto the horse. Her dress made her efforts less elegant than she'd hoped, but she managed to settle sideways into the saddle, with the dagger still in her hand.

The animal, a trained warhorse, stood steady, but Alexander held it like he trusted nothing. He waited until she gave him a nod. Then, with a final look around, he led them back the way he'd come.

# Chapter Three

She didn't know him...

Alexander led his horse past the tree line, out of the thickly wooded forest, and north into the snow-covered hills. A small sense of relief filled him to step out of the Wild and away from its dangers, but it was short-lived. He'd rather face those dangers than accept the circumstance before him now.

*Three years.* Three years he'd waited for the day he would see her again, and she didn't even know him. A pain gripped his chest, but he fought to ignore it. Later. He'd deal with it later, after he got her to safety. After he got her home.

Leaving the forest, she pulled her cloak tighter around her and grew even smaller in the saddle of his giant destrier, like she was reluctant to leave. Her eyes swept warily across the open hills, as if she didn't know she was crossing into safety. As if she preferred to stay in the most dangerous place in the world.

Something had happened to her. The blood on her hands...

"Will you tell me what happened?" he asked.

Her lips parted, and she looked down at the dagger she held. Then she swallowed.

"Whenever you're ready," he added. It had obviously been traumatic for her. His chest tightened. He should have come sooner. If only he'd known.

At least she wasn't physically hurt. In fact, far from it. She looked well taken care of. Had she been in the Wild all this time? No—that was impossible. So where *had* she been, and how did she end up in the Wild?

He couldn't keep his eyes from wandering back to her as he led his destrier through the hills. He was so afraid it was all a dream, afraid none of it was real. When he glanced back to find her watching him, he forced his gaze forward again.

"How did I come to be lost?" she asked, finally breaking the silence.

He glanced back at her. He still couldn't believe he'd finally found her. Her question... He forced his mind to focus. Where to start? There was no easy answer, but he had told her he'd explain, and she was waiting. "We were at war," he said. "Your father took you away. Somewhere safe."

She straightened. "My father?"

"King Aamon." One of the greatest kings Mercia had ever known.

"You'll take me to him?"

His heart fell for her, and he stopped. "No, Norah." He'd been dreading the day she would learn of this. "He died in the war, shortly after you left, in the Battle of Bahoul."

She stilled, and her throat moved with a struggled swallow. She'd been close with her father. Perhaps it was merciful that she didn't remember right now. Despite that, there was no mistaking the sadness in her eyes.

"I'm sorry," he said softly. "He was a good man and a great king, and he loved you very much."

She cast her eyes down, but at nothing in particular. When she raised them, they were glistening. "And if my grandmother is queen regent, then my mother..." Her words trailed off.

"She died in childbirth. You never knew her."

She quieted. Anger coursed through him—how cruel fate was to give her loss before she'd even found herself. How cruel the gods.

Slowly, he started them forward again.

"How do we know each other?" she asked.

He wavered at her question, looking back at her from the corner of his eye. He couldn't yet accept being a stranger to her, but he forced himself to answer. "We've known each other since we were children. I'm the son of Beurnat Rhemus of Northridge—Beurnat the Bear—who was lord justice and right hand to your father. My family has served Mercia and the crown for twelve generations." He looked back at her. "It's in my blood to protect you and the realm."

That seemed to settle her slightly. He was glad he could give her some sense of comfort.

Their pace slowed in the deeper snow, but he pressed on with greater urgency. They needed to make it to the homestead by nightfall, before the darkness and true cold set in on them.

"Am I alone, other than my grandmother?" she asked.

"You have a cousin, although you don't know each other well. No other family."

He glanced back and caught the hint of a frown on her lips. "But you're not alone," he added. "There will be many to help you. Your grandmother's a strong woman who has great wisdom and the respect of the people. She'll guide you, along with the members of the Mercian Council. And"—he paused—"you'll have a lord justice."

Her brows drew together. "And what's a lord justice?"

Only his life's duty. But he gave a small smile. He wasn't offended. "A justice provides counsel and commands your armies. Executes your will. A justice is your right hand."

"Will that be you?"

He'd introduced himself with that title, but... "I'm justice to the queen regent, who holds Mercia in safekeeping until your return. After your coronation, you'll select a justice of your own choosing." And he wasn't so bold as to assume she'd choose him, especially not now.

The sun had set and only its fading light remained. A wave of relief filled him when he finally spotted the small house in the distance.

"Have you any family?" she asked.

A smile came to his lips. "I have a younger brother, Adrian. You'll see him at the castle again—or meet him, rather," he corrected himself. "He's missed you."

"It sounds like we were close?"

He nodded. "You were very much like a sister to him. He'll be incredibly happy to see you."

"I imagine it will be hard for him that I don't remember."

His steps slowed, and he swallowed. His own heart suffered the same. It *was* hard. The hardest. He pushed down the pain and forced a smile. "Even if you *did* remember him, you wouldn't recognize him. He's nineteen now, almost twenty, as tall as I am, and training for the guard."

"How old am I?"

"Twenty-five."

"And you?" She shifted in the saddle, as if suddenly feeling her questions too prying.

"Twenty-nine," he answered readily. He would tell her anything of himself, especially given that she knew everything about him already. Or she used to...

She pulled her lip between her teeth, the way she did when she was puzzling something. "Did you really believe I'd come back? After all this time?"

He shot her a look of surprise. "Why would I not?"

"Three years I've been gone. I could've been dead."

"But you weren't. And we didn't know it would be three years. Each time I searched for you, I thought I'd find you. But the days turned to months, and the months turned to years."

"You've searched for me this entire time?"

Alexander glanced back at her again. "Of course I have."

Their eyes caught, and he couldn't look away this time. Her mouth parted slightly, and she drew in a breath.

His heart beat faster. Did she remember something?

But she broke the hold and looked across the hills. "Why did my father take me away? You said we were at war?"

He didn't answer immediately. He'd tell her anything, but he feared some of it might be too much, too soon. "I know you have a lot of questions," he said over his shoulder. "But I should leave some of these answers to your grandmother. She'll want to share them with you herself." And it was better that way. Some things he didn't want to talk about—tried not to even think about.

It was near dark by the time they reached the homestead.

"It's no place for a princess," he admitted, "but it's shelter. We'll continue on at first light."

He brought the horse in front of the small stacked-stone house and turned to Norah, offering his hand. She accepted it and slid to the ground. He stared at her hand in his for a moment, holding it. The pause felt too long, but he couldn't let her go. Her fingers trembled, and he realized she was shivering. He needed to get her warmed.

He pulled her toward the house. "Let's get you inside."

The homestead was quaint, open, and bare beyond the necessary amenities. Alexander worked quickly to build a fire in the hearth on the far wall and motioned her closer. "Here. Come by the fire."

She neared, flexing her fingers that were still stained with blood. She'd said it wasn't hers. What had happened to her? He wanted to ask again, but he stopped himself. He'd let her settle more.

"I need to see to my horse," he said. "I'll be back in a moment." He didn't want to leave her, but the animal needed care. There was a small outbuilding behind the house that would provide shelter.

Alexander made quick work of it, putting the destrier in a stall and blanketing it with a cover that hung near the door. He broke the top layer of ice that had formed in the water barrel and tossed into the stall a half bale of hay that had been stacked in the corner. He'd leave some coins for the kind soul who kept the homestead stocked for travelers.

He returned to the house with his leather packs and a bucket of snow. When he entered, the sight of her stopped him in his tracks all over again. Norah sat by the fire, holding her hands out to catch its warmth. She glanced back at him. Her blue eyes danced with the light of the flame.

Alexander caught himself staring and pulled away, finally closing the door against the cold. He held up the bucket. "We can melt this," he told her. "It's not exactly a washbasin, but you can clean off your hands."

She gave him a small appreciative smile and worked on melting the snow while he put more wood on the fire. She didn't wait for it to warm before she plunged her hands in, rubbing them harshly to scrape off the blood and dirt.

Alexander watched her. "Where did you get that dagger?" he asked. Now able to see it better, he noted it wasn't a high-quality blade.

She scrubbed the last of the blood from her skin. "I took it from someone." She cut him a look that told him he'd be sorely mistaken if he expected her to give it up. He almost chuckled. He would never.

"A drifter?" he asked.

Her brow quirked in confusion.

"There are men who have no home," he explained, "but venture about, harassing people they run into and causing chaos. Their numbers have grown over the years. They've become quite a problem."

"Sounds about right," she mumbled.

"Is that where you were all this time?" he asked. "With drifters?"

She frowned. "Do I look like I've been with drifters?"

Was she offended? He shook his head quickly. "No. You look beau—not like you've been... No. No, you don't." It was a weird stumble of words, and heat rushed to his cheeks. She watched him as he watched her.

She flexed her fingers again against the heat of the flame. He was desperate to ask her more, but he didn't want to push her. Fortunately, he didn't have to.

"I came across a man, much like you described," she said. "He and three others chased me into the forest."

Alexander shifted his weight, and a fever of anger rippled over his skin. He couldn't help himself, and he asked, "What happened?"

She shook her head. "I'm not entirely sure. Two... um..." She struggled with the words as she clutched her hands together, and his heart lurched. What she must have gone through...

She rocked forward a little, then back. "Two, uh... they... killed themselves."

*Killed themselves.* In front of her. And she was still obviously shaken. He wanted to move closer, to take her hand, to comfort her, but he couldn't. He was a stranger to her—the best thing he could do right now was give her space.

"The other two ran off," she continued. "I can't explain it, but it was horrific. The most terrifying part was that... they didn't want to kill themselves, but it was like they had no control. One of them kept screaming that I was a witch."

She swallowed, shifting under his eye. "But I'm not a witch," she added quickly. Her voice dipped, betraying her lack of confidence in those words. She shook her head with an unsure shrug. "I don't know what happened. And I thought whatever killed them would come for me, too, but it didn't. So, I took the dagger because I had nothing else, and I was following a fox through the woods when you found me."

His brows drew together. "You were following a fox?"

"I'm not mad," she insisted.

"No, you're not mad," he assured her. "And I know you're not a witch. The Wild is home to the faeries, or spirits, whatever they are. It's said that they protect it with a kind of power, one that lets them take over the mind of anyone who enters, make them do things, harm themselves or others. Everyone knows the stories like the one you tell now."

"And you still came?" Her blue eyes stared back at him.

He was caught in the snare of her gaze again. "There's nowhere I wouldn't go for you, Norah," he said softly.

Her lips parted slightly, and her breath caught. He couldn't look away. Finally, she pulled back and broke the spell. "The fact we're talking about faeries at all is utter madness," she said.

He gave a small smile. "Then maybe you are a witch."

But his joke fell flat, and she only blinked.

"Forgive me," he said. "That was meant in jest."

"And it was funny. I'm just..." She let out a breath.

"You're tired, and you've been through a lot. You should eat." He reached over to his pack and pulled out some salted meat and bread, along with a wineskin, and handed them to her.

They sat on the floor by the burning logs, soaking in the warmth of the flames. He adjusted another log with his sword. "I'll hunt for us in the morning."

"It's fine, really. I'm appreciative just for this," she said, lifting the meat in gesture and then finishing it. He held out his bread roll, and a small smile escaped from her as she took it. He offered his meat as well, but she politely shook her head.

"I know you want it," he said.

"Thank you, but I'm full."

He knew she wasn't, but he didn't press. He watched her for a moment and smiled, then folded the meat back in the cloth instead of eating it and tucked it into his pack for her later.

"You shouldn't carry a drifter's dagger," he said as she finished the last of the bread. "Here." He pulled a knife from the sheath on his calf, tucked inside his boot, and held it out for her. "This suits you better."

She reached out and took it. The blade was shorter, and the hilt fit her hand better. It was his favorite knife, custom made and well taken care of, unlike the rusted drifter's dagger with open seams along its handle.

He pulled off his calf sheath and held it out to her as well. "Put this around your leg, inside your boot, with the knife where you can easily reach it."

She slipped the blade into the sheath and stared down at it in her hands. When she raised her eyes again, they locked with his. "Thank you," she whispered.

He shook his head. "No need to thank me. It's my duty."

Even in the dim light of the room, the storms of her blue eyes pulled him in, holding him. "We should get some rest," she said.

Yes. Rest. Alexander rose and pulled open the second pack. He shook out a rolled pad over the meager bed. "You sleep here. I can't promise comfort, but it's clean. I'll be by the door."

Norah gave a small nod. She settled in, creaking the bed frame with every movement. He pulled a chair to the door and sat with his sword unsheathed and resting across his knees.

But as she lay, she didn't close her eyes. She only stared at the ceiling. "What happened?" she asked finally. "I have to know. Why did my father take me away?"

He sat quiet. This wasn't a short story, and not one of the first he wanted to welcome her home with.

"Tell me," she pressed.

Alexander let out a long breath. "We were at war, and they were coming for you." He paused. "Your father feared your capture, and so he took you. Far. Somewhere safe."

"Who was coming for me?" she asked.

"These aren't stories to tell in the night. You're safe, Norah. There's so much to remember, to learn. There will be plenty of time." But he knew his answers only drew more questions. "Rest," he said. "There will be more tomorrow."

Finally, she closed her eyes. After a time, her breaths came longer and deeper. He relaxed in the chair, but he wouldn't sleep. Not until he safely got her home.

# Chapter Four

Norah woke to the sound of a crackling fire. She pulled the blanket higher around her neck and nestled into its warmth. It smelled of pine and soft leather, comfort and refuge—a familiar smell, a smell she'd always loved. She smiled as she blinked her eyes open. But unfamiliar stone walls looked back at her, and her smile faded.

Where was she?

Memories of the day prior flooded back, and she sat up with a start. The blanket that covered her spilled down into her lap, and she saw it wasn't a blanket at all, but Alexander's cloak.

She glanced around the empty room. Where was he?

Sunlight poured in from the small window onto the bed and across the floor. Her racing heart slowed. She eyed the cloak again as she drew her fingers across it, all too aware of the sense it had given her.

The door opened, and Alexander stepped in with more firewood and something else in his hands. The smell made her stomach rumble. She pushed off the cloak and stood, straightening her dress and brushing her hair back from her face.

His eyes caught hers, and he paused, simply looking at her. His lips parted. "Good morning," he said finally.

Even though he'd spoken only two words, his voice held a strange familiarity.

"Good morning," she replied.

He broke from her gaze. "I hope you slept well. Are you hungry?" He held out a hand of freshly cooked meat with flatbread wrapped in linen. "There's water by the fire."

"That smells amazing, thank you," she said, taking the food. "And I slept surprisingly well."

Alexander refueled the fire and then sat on the edge of the hearth. He held his food in his hand but didn't eat it.

Norah tried to keep her eyes from him as she ate, wary of the lure of his gaze and of the stir it caused inside her. "Yesterday you said you saw me in a vision—what was it?" she asked, refocusing herself on getting more answers. "How did you know to come for me?"

He shifted back on the hearth. "It was the last vision seen of you, three years ago, right before you left. We didn't know what it meant at the time, but after you disappeared, we suspected it was a clue as to where you were. You were in the middle of a forest, with trees all around you, dressed as you are now." He paused. "And your hair was... bright, shining. As it is now."

She raised her eyes to his and found herself caught in the snare she had tried so hard to avoid.

"I've searched every forest this kingdom over," he said, "well into Aleon and south into the lands of the Horsemen tribes. The Wild was the only place I'd stayed clear of. Until now."

She gave him a small smile. "Because of the faeries?"

"Because men don't return from there."

Norah bit her lip, feeling her jest poorly placed.

"It was the last place I thought I'd find you," he added.

Well, it *was* the last place he found her, but she kept that joke to herself. This wasn't a joking matter. She'd seen firsthand the dangers of this land of no return. She pulled herself free of the shackles of his eyes and finished the last of her meal. "I still doubt that I'm the person you say."

He offered her his meat and bread.

She shook her head. "I've had enough, thank you. You eat." He hadn't eaten his food the evening prior. She suspected he'd saved it for her.

"You *are* Norah Andell. I wouldn't mistake you, no matter how much time had passed." He settled back, finally taking some of his own food. "Wait until you return home. You'll see."

*Home.* That word seemed so distant right now.

"Speaking of, we should go." He smiled. "Your grandmother has no idea she's going to see you today. And Catherine Andell is not an easy woman to surprise. I'm very much looking forward to it."

Norah couldn't help but smile at the sense of his genuine excitement. But inside, her stomach twisted at the thought of meeting her grandmother.

*Catherine.* The name held no recollection. Yes, she expected the woman to be surprised, but this might not be the surprise she was hoping for—her lost granddaughter with no memory of herself or those who knew her. Norah turned her thoughts to their arrival, and the weight grew heavier in her stomach. People had been waiting a long time for her return; she wouldn't be what any of them were expecting, and likely not what they hoped for. There would be people she'd be expected to know, expected to care about. People that cared about her.

They left the warmth of the homestead and continued on their way, with her riding and Alexander again leading the horse. They'd make better time both riding, but the suggestion seemed too forward, and she couldn't muster the courage. They traveled mostly without conversation, but he glanced back to check on her often, as he had the day before.

At midday, they stopped for a meal of salted meat and more bread. Norah looked over the powdered hills of snow and wondered how much farther until they reached the castle.

"Mercia is just beyond those hills," Alexander said, pointing in the distance, as if reading her mind. His eyes met hers, and he smiled. "It's beautiful."

Norah forced a smile, but her stomach sat heavy. She tried to imagine her arrival. What would she say when she saw her grandmother? Would she recognize the woman? Would Norah be a disappointment to her?

"Here," he said, handing her a wineskin. "This will help calm your nerves."

She raised a brow. "Is it that obvious?"

He tipped his head to the side with a smirk. "A little. But you should be excited. You'll be surrounded by people who love you and have waited for this day."

"Alexander," she said, looking into his eyes, "I'm trusting you." It wasn't a statement; it was a plea.

His face grew serious. "I'll be by your side," he promised. He offered his hand, and this time she took it. He lifted her to the saddle and then took up the reins and led the horse forward. They continued on, and Norah sipped from the wineskin as they went.

As they reached the final peak, she gasped. A large city sprawled from the base of the hills to the northern coast in the distance. On an island off the mainland, a castle stood with its turrets and spires sharp against the sun-filled sky.

"Mercia," Alexander said as he looked back at her, his eyes shining. "Home."

"It *is* beautiful," she whispered.

"People will know who you are the moment they see you. Are you ready?"

She was nowhere near ready. She shifted in the saddle. "Do I look ready? No dirt on my face or sticks in my hair?"

He smiled. "No dirt or sticks. You're beautiful."

She couldn't help but smile back.

Alexander led his horse down and through the city. People gathered along the sides of the streets as they saw them, murmuring to each other with increasing excitement. As she and Alexander passed, the crowd followed them. Shouts rang out, and Alexander looked back at her with his eyes bright.

People came in flocks now. She looked at all the faces; there were so many of them. Some were laughing, some were crying, some were merely watching in astonishment. A deep fear seeded itself inside her. She hadn't entirely believed Alexander before... but what if she really was the princess? It all seemed very... impossibly possible now...

Just then, a bell rang out from the castle.

"Now everyone knows you're here," Alexander said.

They made their way to the bridge that connected the mainland to the castle's island. Tall stone arches rose from the frozen waters, as if placed there by the gods. It was hard to believe this was the work of men. Streams of helmed soldiers poured out of the castle gates and lined either side of the bridge. Norah looked at them in awe as Alexander led her through and into the large courtyard inside the castle walls.

They stopped at an empty fountain in the center. He reached up to her, and she let him help her to the ground. A flash of white caught her eye, and she looked up to the banner of the winterhawk in the sky.

"White is the color of Mercia," he explained. "The winterhawk is your father's—your—sigil." His blue eyes danced with excitement. "Welcome home, Norah." He moved to lead her toward the castle.

"Alexander," she called, stopping him.

He paused. "Yes?"

"Be near." She needed him near.

"Always," he promised.

Throngs of people flooded the courtyard from the terraced buildings surrounding the castle on the isle. Alexander led her through, moving slowly to keep her close. He summoned more guards, who closed in around them. Norah reached for his hand but then stopped herself. The want came so naturally, and it surprised her. They reached the stairs to the entrance, and he halted abruptly, pulling her from the thought.

Norah looked up to see a woman approaching, flanked by her guard. She was older, elegant and regal in a dark navy gown. Brown furs lay bulked around her neck and lined the hood of her cloak, but there was no missing the striking white hair peeking out from underneath. She floated down the stairs with magnetic beauty.

Alexander stepped forward. "Queen Regent." He bowed. "I—"

But she moved past him, as if not seeing him, and not hearing him either. Her gaze was locked on Norah. She pulled back the hood of her cloak; the green pools of her eyes were filled with wisdom and the cautiousness of disbelief. She was slightly shorter than Norah but held a regal stature—the poise of power. Beauty graced her face with her high cheekbones, her bright eyes. Age respected this woman. She stared at Norah for a moment, her expression giving nothing away.

Norah bit the inside of her lip. Was this where everyone would discover she wasn't who they thought? Perhaps that was better, anyway—to get it out of the way early and save them all from embarrassment later.

But then the woman's lip trembled. "Norah," she breathed. "Oh, my dear. You've finally come home."

Or they would just continue with this insanity. Norah couldn't move.

The queen regent reached out, brushing a lock of Norah's hair with her fingertips, and tears sprang from her eyes. She let out a silent cry and embraced Norah, pulling her close.

Norah drew in a sharp breath. Her own eyes brimmed. Even though she was still lost to herself, this woman made her feel found. She let herself accept the warmth of the embrace, the warmth of love. Her fear, her anxiety, her worry, all stopped for a moment. She needed this embrace, and she let herself have it.

Stepping back, the regent's eyes darted over her, taking her in. "How long we've waited for you to come home."

Norah forced a smile, trying to quell her own emotion. She couldn't find the words to speak.

"Queen Regent," Alexander started again.

"You must be so tired," she said to Norah. "Come. Come inside."

"Catherine," he said again, stronger now, finally pulling her attention. He leaned in close to her and said in a low voice, "She has no memory."

The woman's brows drew together. "What?"

He shook his head. "She doesn't know herself, or you." He paused a moment before he said, "She doesn't know me."

The regent looked at Norah in shock. "How ever did you find her?" But she didn't give him time to respond. "No matter," she said as she took Norah's hand. "Come, child, let's get you inside. We'll figure it all out."

Norah looked at Alexander, and he gave her a nod as the regent pulled her toward the castle. The oversize doors swung open, and the woman swept through, with Norah following behind. As the doors closed, they drowned out the sound of the crowd.

Relief settled over her, now that she was away from the masses. She didn't like the attention, but she quickly forgot the crowd as they passed through an expansive hall and then several smaller hallways. She marveled at the polished stone of white and light and the intricately sculpted busts that sat between the arched windows. Everything around her was so... bright, as if made from the sun itself. She glanced behind her to see if Alexander still followed. And he did.

They reached a chamber and entered, startling a young maid inside.

"Rebecca," the regent called to her, "start a bath."

The woman stood for a moment, then her eyes widened. "Princess Norah!" she exclaimed, and bowed quickly.

The title still unsettled her, and Norah shifted under its weight. Rebecca beamed as she stared, then she caught herself and broke away to prepare a bath.

The regent turned to another servant. "Something to eat for the princess. And wine. And water."

Norah didn't think she could eat; her nerves had the best of her, and her stomach, but the servant left before she could refuse. She let her eyes comb over the room with its fine tapestries and ornate furniture. Light spilled through the tall windows on the west wall. It was beautiful and overwhelming. A castle, the finery, the servants—surely she didn't belong here. She glanced back at Alexander, who remained at the door, not stepping inside. He gave her a reassuring smile.

The queen regent stopped and took her hand. "Are you all right, child?"

She pushed out a breath, fighting an unexpected wave of emotion with all the strength she could muster. "I'm sorry. This is all a bit much," she managed to get out.

"I'm sure it is, but we'll sort everything out. It will come back to you."

Or it *wouldn't*. She didn't want to think about that possibility, though. Not right now.

"What do you remember?" Catherine asked.

Norah shook her head—what did she remember? "I woke in the forest, like this." She motioned to herself. "I was lost for a time." How much detail to share? She didn't have the energy and didn't want to relive it. "Then Alexander found me." She looked back at him.

"Of course he did," the queen regent said, letting her gaze rest on him with a warm smile.

He gave a bow. "I'll leave you, Queen Regent." To Norah he said, "Welcome home, Princess Norah." He was more formal now, and more serious. She didn't like it.

"Thank you," Norah said. "For everything. And don't tell me it's your duty."

He lingered a moment longer, a silent confession he didn't want to go, then he gave a small nod and left her to the queen regent.

"Lord Justice," the regent called, "one more thing." She swept out of the chamber and into the hall after him.

Norah heard their voices in the hall but couldn't make out what was being said. She stood, drawing her bottom lip between her teeth. Perhaps she should just wait, or...

The woman named Rebecca stepped back into the room from the side chamber. "Your bath is ready, Princess Norah."

*A bath.* A bath would be good. Her mind reeled with the increasingly likely possibility that she might truly be a princess—she just needed to focus her mind on one task to hold herself together. She turned toward the bath chamber.

"By the gods, child," her grandmother said as she came back into the room.

Norah paused and turned back to her.

"I know you must be tired, but let me look at you." She clasped Norah by the shoulders and gave a smile that trembled with emotion. "How I wish Aamon were here. You're the image of your mother." Then she caught sight of the pendant around Norah's neck, and her eyes welled. She brushed it with her fingertips. "He gave this to you on your last birthday that we celebrated. The winterhawk belongs to Kelos, god of protection and vanquisher of evil. It's the sigil of the Andell crown. Your crown."

Norah brought her hand to the pendant and glanced down as she tilted it between her thumb and forefinger. Perhaps it had been Kelos watching over her. Alexander had found her in the middle of a forest—seemingly unbelievable, without some divine intervention. And the matching winterhawk on his breastplate was the only reason she'd agreed to go with him.

Well, the *main* reason.

The other being... there was just something about him...

The woman let out an emotional breath, snapping Norah back to the present. "Let's get you washed," her grandmother said, "and then we'll see you fed." She and the maids shuffled Norah into the bath chamber.

Before Norah could protest, they stripped her of her cloak and dress. She barely had time to squirm from her undergarments as she was shooed into the tub. Despite the initial feeling of invasiveness, a strange familiarity at being bustled about hit her, and the warmth of the water washed any remaining objections away.

"Rebecca, Serene," the queen regent said to the maids, "I'll take it from here."

The two women curtsied and left as Catherine draped a robe over a settee and sat beside it. "I still can't believe you're home."

Norah couldn't either. Why couldn't she remember? How could twenty-five years of her life have been taken from her? Would her memories come back? A slight panic welled again at the thought of them not.

"Now that you're back, everything will be set right," Catherine said.

Norah didn't even know what that meant, but it sounded daunting and only added to her growing anxiety. "I don't even know what I'm doing here."

"That will pass, my dear. Your memories will return, but until they do, we have to take care. I want no one to know of your condition."

"Wait. What? Why?" She couldn't keep this a secret for long.

"Your circumstance is complicated enough. And we can't risk anything jeopardizing your path."

"What path?"

"Don't worry about it right now. We'll get you cleaned and rested and fed. Your memories will return, and we'll sort through everything."

How could this woman be so calm about this? "How are you so sure?" Something within her snapped. Norah shook her head. "I can't keep this a secret. I don't know anyone, I don't know myself, or how I should be or what I should say. I don't even know what to call you. I've woken up in this world with all these expectations, and everyone's going to quickly discover I'm a fraud." It was hot in the bath now. Too hot.

"Oh, child," the regent said as she clasped Norah's shoulder. "Somewhere inside, you have over twenty years of ladyship ground into you. I saw to it myself. And all young rulers know nothing. No one will think you're a fraud. You're Evanya's daughter, and my granddaughter. There's no doubt."

But Norah had a lot of doubt.

The woman picked up a jar of bath salts and scooped a handful into the water. "Let's start with simple solutions. You may call me *queen regent*, as is appropriate in public. My name is Catherine, as I'm sure you've gathered by now, which you may call me privately. Or you may call me *grandmother* if you're comfortable with that. I'll no longer be queen regent after your coronation—a day I look forward to very much. It's not right for a kingdom to be without a head for so long."

A knot formed in her stomach. "My coronation?"

"Of course. Now that you've returned, you'll be queen. I've only been queen regent in your absence."

Norah shook her head again. She couldn't be queen. She knew nothing of this place, of these people; she knew nothing of ruling. "I can't be queen," she said. No. *No*, she couldn't do this. She swallowed. The air was suffocating. "This can't be right. I shouldn't be here." She reached for the towel and moved to rise.

Catherine clasped her shoulders firmly, stopping her and forcing Norah to look at her. "Child, I know this is overwhelming, terrifying even. But you're strong. You always have been. And I'm by your side, and I'll guide your every step. For now, we'll take one thing at a time. You will get through this. Do you understand?"

Norah drew in a breath. The regent's words were firm, sharp even, but not uncaring. It was what Norah needed to stave off her panic. Ever so slightly, she nodded—not a nod of agreement, but a nod of settling.

The woman's hands softened, but still held her.

*One thing at a time.* She could do one thing at a time, with Catherine beside her. And Alexander. *One thing at a time.* "I think I'd like to call you grandmother."

Catherine smiled. "I'd like that."

# Chapter Five

Inside his chamber, Alexander hung his belt and sword on the wall and pulled off his armor, but it wasn't the weight of the steel plating that had been sitting heavily on him.

He played it back in his mind—seeing her in the forest, calling her name. The sting of her not knowing him hurt more than any battle wound.

So many ways he'd imagined how their reunion might have gone. Mostly joyous. Sometimes he imagined her angry with him, perhaps still hurt, but in each dream, he'd held her in his arms again. But for her to feel nothing... He hadn't imagined that.

Perhaps it was better this way. Things could never be as they were before, but now it was as though he'd truly lost her, and he didn't think he could bear it.

Alexander lumbered toward his bed. His legs didn't feel like his own. He sank down with a grimace, then he covered his eyes with his hand. It had been a long time since he'd shed any tears, so long he couldn't remember when. But they flowed freely now, and he let them come.

He hadn't been able to keep his pain hidden from Catherine. She'd raised him; she knew him like her own blood. And while the queen regent loved him, he'd seen the warning in her eyes. No doubt she would see this as an opportunity for Norah to start new. She would try to convince him to do the same. But that wasn't possible.

And he'd have to find a way to support Catherine. She'd spent more than twenty years preparing Norah's free spirit for the obligations of the crown, but now everything was gone, and what had taken twenty-five years would need to be rebuilt in days—another feat he wasn't sure was possible.

A knock on the door pulled him back, and he straightened, collecting himself. Alexander ran his hand over his face, wiping away his emotion, and rose to answer. He opened the door to find the captain of the guard.

Caspian nodded in greeting but paused as their eyes met. Alexander suspected he saw the remnants of his sorrow, but the captain graciously offered no mention of it.

He stepped back into the room, leaving the door open for Caspian to enter. Alexander wasn't one to show emotion, and few men other than Caspian had seen him outside his calm and pensive nature. They'd fought together, bled together, won together, lost together. They were more than comrades, more than friends. They were like brothers. Still, Caspian wasn't one to pry, but he knew what Norah's return meant to Alexander, and he needed to know the situation.

"She doesn't remember," Alexander said, not entirely confident in his voice.

Caspian shifted back. "She doesn't remember what?"

"She has no memory, Caspian. She knows nothing. Not Mercia, not herself." He paused. "Not me."

Caspian's eyes widened.

But Alexander didn't want to linger on it. He couldn't without emotion threatening. "Brief her core guard," he said, "as well as her maids. They'll need to help her. The queen regent was clear—no one else can know. Not even the council. She's fought too hard to protect Norah's crown in her absence. We can't risk losing it now."

"That won't be easy. We'll have to keep the princess from them."

"I'll let the queen regent manage that," Alexander said. Then he frowned. They'd have to keep her from quite a few people. His mind turned to his brother. Adrian would want to see Norah as soon as he learned of her return, but he'd suspect something right away. Alexander would have to find a way to keep him from her for a while too.

"I've sent messengers to the outer reaches, calling all forces back," Caspian said. "Except for our men in Bahoul."

Alexander gave a small nod. The mountains—they'd need to keep men there to hold them. When the Shadowlands learned of Norah's return, it would only be a matter of time before they came for her. *Again.* "Send the Ninth to join them." Another thousand men in Bahoul would mean a thousand men less at the capital, but if the Shadow King attacked, Bahoul would be the first line of defense. Caspian nodded, and then he paused. "What about Aleon?"

The mention of their eastern ally made Alexander stiffen, but he pushed the twinge aside and took his belt and sword from the wall. "I'll send word to Aleon that the princess has returned. And then I'll go to the seer. Perhaps her return has brought new visions."

"I'll take care of the message to Aleon," Caspian told him. "You go see Samuel."

Caspian knew his struggle; he knew the bitterness that the thought of Aleon brought, and Alexander clasped his shoulder appreciatively. Then he buckled the belt of his sword and set his mind to the seer.

He didn't bother with a cloak as he passed through the castle and outside toward the gallery house. He'd made this walk many times over, each with the same hope. But today was different. Norah had returned.

Alexander strode over the cobblestone street to the gallery of the seer. While it was connected to the castle, it was only accessible from the outside. He pushed through the doors and sidestepped the paintings strewn throughout. It was growing more difficult to weave through to the back gallery where he knew the old man would be. As expected, he found Samuel at his easel, hunched over and working on his craft. Alexander's pulse quickened at seeing the seer at work. A vision must have come.

"A vision? You've had one?" he asked anxiously, not bothering with a greeting.

Samuel bobbed his balding head up in surprise. "Hmm?" In seeing Alexander, Samuel pushed his glasses back up the bridge of his nose. "Oh, it's you," he gruffed.

"You've had another?" he pressed the old man. "Of the princess?"

Samuel scowled, turning his attention back to his work. "Boy, you've been asking me that for years, and for years I've told you—"

"She's returned."

Samuel stopped, glancing back up at Alexander. "What did you say?"

"The princess. She's returned. Did you not hear the bells?"

Samuel wrinkled his nose and waved his brush. "Those damn bells ring all the time."

Alexander drew in a deep breath, trying to summon his patience. "Well, she's returned. Surely you can see something of her now."

The old man drew his brows together and shook his head, then set his brush down. "No. I've seen nothing of her."

Alexander sighed. The last painting of Norah was the image of her in the forest. It had come just before she had left, three years ago. When she'd disappeared, the visions of her stopped. Now that she'd returned, he hoped the visions had too. Samuel's gallery held only a few paintings of her, all of which had been completed before she'd disappeared. Alexander knew every detail, every brushstroke, especially of the painting that had made Norah's father take her away: the image of the enemy that would come for her—the Shadow King. The vision of her capture.

War. Death. That had been her fate, the fate her father changed by taking her to safety, wherever that might have been.

Then there were the images of himself. But those he put from his mind. "What are you painting then?" he asked Samuel.

The old man snorted. "Nothing you care to see."

Alexander moved around the easel to look over the old man's shoulder, and he sighed. *Not again.* "What is that?"

"What does it look like?" the seer asked with an edge of annoyance. "I've been painting long enough that I consider myself quite good at it."

Alexander stared at the painting on the easel. It was a village in flames. The dead littered the streets, the houses had been destroyed. And in its center stood Alexander. But his image didn't show fear. It was as though he relished the destruction. His image stared at him from the canvas with the want of war in his eyes, like the others Samuel had painted of him over the years.

Alexander sighed. Years ago, paintings like this had bothered him to obsession, but the visions of himself never came to be. He used to ponder every detail, trying to understand their meaning. Now they only served to annoy him. If it wasn't for the truth in the visions of others, he would have thought the old man a charlatan.

He looked closer and scowled at the black ink marking the skin on his neck in the painting. Dark patterns swirled just under his jaw. "Why must you always paint these markings?" he asked the seer.

"Boy, I've told you a hundred times, I only paint what I see," Samuel snapped. Then the old man snorted. "And is it only the markings that bother you? Not the wave of destruction you cause?"

"That's not me, Samuel," he said, irritated, but not *too* irritated. Samuel had stopped showing others the paintings of him, so he didn't have to keep defending himself.

"If it's not you, then why do you care if there are markings?"

Alexander let out a long breath and turned back toward the door, his interest waning. "You'll send word if you see her?"

The old man waved him off with his brush. "As I always say I will."

# CHAPTER SIX

Norah stood by the window in her chamber, unsure if it was night or morning in the darkness. The winter sun didn't rise with the start of the day—it came later and set sooner. Despite the pristine white of her room, the linen and draperies of light and silver all looked black. She stared through the glass of the window, out into the abyss of more darkness. Much like her memories.

She had tried to sleep. Her body begged her for it, but her eyes couldn't close, her mind couldn't rest. Was this life really hers? It couldn't be. It felt... not right. None of it was right. But she couldn't shake the one thing that felt... a little less not right...

The one thing that felt familiar...

No—she couldn't let her mind fall into that trap, and she pushed Alexander from her thoughts.

Time passed slowly. She was almost contemplating attempting sleep again when Rebecca whisked into the room. The maid greeted her with a warm smile. "Oh, Princess Norah, you're already awake!"

The ring of the title in her ears made her wince, but she forced back a polite smile. "Yes, um, I was up early."

"The queen regent will be here soon, as will the dresses."

*The dresses*? Norah raised her brows in surprise. The fittings hadn't been finished until well into the evening prior. And there would be more than one? "So soon?"

"Yes, of course." The girl's smile grew broader. "The seamstresses have been working on them all night."

*All night*? How were the dresses so important they required midnight making? It seemed so... unnecessary.

"Are you hungry?" Rebecca asked.

Norah forgot the dresses. "Starved," she answered eagerly, a smile finally coming to her lips. The mere mention of food made her stomach rumble. Her maid's eyes widened. Was that not what she'd expected? Norah bit her lip. "I mean, just a little hungry. But not that much. Normal hungry. As one normally is in the morning." She pursed her lips between her teeth and scolded herself. *Stop*. But she couldn't. Everything came so awkwardly.

Rebecca fluttered back out of the room to get breakfast.

Norah made her way to the bath chamber but stopped when she caught sight of herself in the mirror. Her eyes, large and expansive, were the color of a stormy sea and stared back at her over the highs of her cheekbones. Her icy-blonde mane twisted wildly around her. When she'd seen her image the day before, it hadn't surprised her. She knew her face.

"You can't erase all of me," she whispered to whatever had stolen her memory.

The sound of voices and her chamber door opening pulled her attention.

"Norah?" Catherine's voice rang out.

Norah stepped out of the bath chamber to find the queen regent, followed by Rebecca, who was carrying a plate of fruit and cheeses.

"Grandmother," she greeted.

"How did you sleep, child?"

"Well, thank you," she lied.

"Wonderful. We've a busy day ahead of us. You'll be seeing the council today."

Norah nodded. Yes, *good*—her council. "And they'll help me figure out what to do until my memories—"

"No," Catherine said sharply.

No? "Wait, why not?" She was drowning merely in her thoughts of stepping into this life, into this world, and the reality would be so much harsher. She needed all the help she could get.

"I told you, no one must know of your condition."

*Condition.*

As if it were a sickness. Perhaps it was, but—

"We only have to present you," Catherine said, "and I'll make it as quick as possible."

Her heartbeat rose to her throat. Why didn't Catherine want the council to know? Alexander had said they would help her. Why couldn't they know?

Catherine set about the room, pulling out various drawers of dressers and chests and looking through them. "You probably won't even say more than a few words—"

"W-Wait," Norah stammered, "I can't meet the council like this. They'll discover me. I haven't even been back a full day yet. I have no idea what I'm doing."

"I'll take care of that," Catherine replied with a nod.

How? "You just want me to pretend?"

"Precisely," the queen regent answered back as she laid three necklaces on the vanity, eyeing them with a tilt of her head. The woman had clearly missed her sarcasm.

In her state of total astonishment, Norah almost laughed. "*How*? I literally know nothing—no people, no history. I barely remember the name of this place, and nothing of myself! You have to give me more here. I—I need to know my story, what's happened... just... something." *Anything.*

Catherine stopped. "And that's why I've come early." She took Norah's hand and led her to the settee, sitting them both down. "Listen to me. All of this will be very sudden for you. But we don't have much time, so you'll have to learn as quickly as possible."

Norah nodded. She could learn quickly. Hopefully. Her eyes caught sight of the plate Rebecca had brought in with cheeses and fruit. She'd kill for the pear looking back at her, but she forced her attention back on her grandmother.

Catherine drew in another breath, as if organizing her thoughts on where to start. Perhaps she did have time to get the pear.

"We are at war, Norah."

And Norah stopped.

*Are.*

Alexander had said *were*.

"We've been at war with the Shadowlands for ten years. The Great War, it's called. And we've been waiting for you to return, to end it."

Norah blinked. She hadn't heard correctly. "I'm sorry, what?"

Catherine folded her hands together. "You'll unite the kingdoms against the Shadowlands, and you'll end it. For good."

"Um... I didn't quite expect you to start with that. Um..." She stood. A *war*. She'd been anxious about the expectations of her before, but a war raised the stakes, and her pulse. She rounded the small table where Rebecca had set the plate, and she grabbed the pear. Not to eat—she wasn't hungry anymore with her mind on war—but she wanted to have something to hold in her hand, something to fiddle with, to calm her.

War.

She flexed her nails against the pear, but not hard enough to break its skin.

*War.*

Then she took a bite.

Catherine watched her, giving her a moment.

So... *war*. It would have been nice to start first with her mother and father, but she supposed they could start with the war. She swallowed the bite of pear. "Why are we at war?"

"This is not a short story."

"You said you came early."

Catherine sighed. "Mercia's been a longtime ally and friend of the Aleon Empire," she explained. "Aleon used to consist of six kingdoms ruled by the High King Horath. However, ten years ago, as Horath lay on his deathbed, he split the kingdoms of the empire between his three sons: Gregor, Phillip, and Aston."

Six kingdoms sounded like too much for any one man, anyway. And all this seemed perfectly reasonable, unless Norah was expected to remember all these names. She took another bite of her pear.

"But," Catherine continued, "Gregor, the eldest, although given the richest of the kingdoms, Japheth, felt robbed of his birthright. He killed his youngest brother, taking the second kingdom of Hetahl as well. He needed—and still needs—the remaining four kingdoms of Aleon from Phillip to restore the full empire. When he tried to take them, your father stood as Phillip's ally. This was the start of the Great War."

Norah struggled to swallow the pear as a sudden lump rose in her throat. That anyone could kill their family for power was a monstrous thing. Inhuman.

Rebecca whisked back into the room with a wine decanter and two chalices. Norah hadn't realized she'd even gone anywhere. The maid left them on the small side table beside the settee before seeing herself out of the room again.

Wine with breakfast... *odd*. Norah set her attention back to the conversation. "So, what do Aleon and Japheth, this war between Phillip and Gregor, have to do with the Shadowlands? And Mercia, and me?"

"Aleon and Mercia stood together, and so Gregor needed an ally," Catherine explained. "He joined together with the Shadowlands."

"So, it's Mercia and Aleon against Japheth and the Shadowlands?"

Catherine nodded. "Exactly. But Phillip will manage his brother Gregor. You must focus on the Shadowlands. The Shadow King is a greater evil, and he'll do everything in his power to see you dead."

Her stomach twisted. "Why?" It was a little extreme, to want someone dead.

"The visions have shown it. You'll take the Shadow throne, purging his darkness from this world."

Norah pulled her bottom lip between her teeth, not knowing what to make of her grandmother's words. She didn't want anyone's throne. She wasn't even sure if she wanted her own. "You sound so certain of this."

"I am. It was a powerful vision, Norah—seen by seers across the kingdoms. The Shadow King joined with Japheth soon after, with a vengeance. He'll stop at nothing to change his fate, and he almost did. Many times he's attacked, and many times your father drove him back, but three years ago, another vision came—a vision of your capture, and of the Shadowmen breaching our defenses, flooding into Mercia, and killing the council. That's when your father took you away, to keep you safe."

A chill ran down her spine, and Norah sat back on the settee beside her grandmother again. "But... they didn't end up breaching Mercia."

"Pay attention, child," Catherine said shortly.

Norah frowned. She was paying attention.

"It was a *vision*. It hadn't yet happened. But your father refused to take chances, and by taking you away, he changed your fate."

But that only raised more questions: Where had her father taken her? What place would have been safe if Mercia wasn't? And how had she lost her memories?

Catherine took her hand. "And while your father was successful in driving the Shadow King back deep into his hell, he still lives. It's why you must keep your course, Norah. You mustn't take chances either. You'll become queen and wed King Phillip of Aleon as planned, to keep the alliance strong."

Norah's heart stopped, and her head jerked up at her grandmother's words. Her nails pierced the skin of the remaining pear in her hand. "Wed? As in, marriage?"

Catherine pursed her lips. "That's what *wed* means, yes."

She knew what *wed* meant, but it couldn't mean that for her. "I can't be married." She didn't even know herself, much less know someone else enough to marry them. She struggled for words in the chaos overwhelming her mind. "I've never even met this Phillip. I don't love him. What if I don't even *like* him?"

"You *have* met him. Many times. And you do like him. But whether you like him doesn't matter. What matters is the future of Mercia and the strength of our kingdom. Only with Phillip can you defeat the Shadow King." Catherine paused. Then she said, "There are other things of which you must be aware. Mercia is in a dire position. We're still early into winter, and we've not enough food to sustain our people. Aleon sends provisions in goodwill, as they have for the past three years, but it won't be enough, and it won't continue without a marriage."

The weight in her stomach grew to a pit—a pit that her very being was falling into, flailing, and drowning.

Wine would be good now. Norah's hands shook as she dropped her pear on the tray, poured herself a chalice, and drank. Deeply. Everything she knew of life had been born in the last two days. She'd only just arrived in this strange kingdom she was to call home and was already a pawn in a game she didn't understand.

"And," Catherine continued, "with this marriage, you'll become queen of the new Aleon Empire."

"So, there's a new one now?" Of course. But she didn't want to be queen of the new Aleon Empire. She didn't want to be queen of Mercia. She didn't want to be a queen at all.

Catherine's frown deepened. "I know this is difficult for you, stepping into a life you don't remember, but it carries a great obligation, and I beg you to take it seriously."

Her grandmother's words sobered her. She swallowed as she set her chalice back on the table. "I do take it seriously. It's just very difficult to absorb everything, especially a surprise marriage."

"This marriage has been long in the making, with many marriages between Mercia and Aleon in our history. I myself am from the Aleon kingdom of Eilor. Your mother was from Songs."

Norah poured more wine into her chalice and took another drink.

"Mercia is a kingdom of honor," Catherine said, "and joins Aleon in cause. We share the same values, the same beliefs, the same language. An alliance between our two kingdoms is an essential one, for each fortifies the other. It's why Phillip has been so patient. But the council isn't patient and shoves the option of your cousin's hand at him at every turn. Now that you're back, they'll be eager to see you crowned and wed in short order."

Norah's head reeled. She suddenly didn't feel very well. Just then, the chamber door swung open, and ladies made their way in with dresses, fabrics, and trays of glittering accessories.

Catherine stood and pulled Norah to her feet. "It's a lot, I know, and as I said, you'll have to learn quickly. But you're strong, and I'll help you sort everything out."

The queen regent turned and worked through the array of dresses before she settled on one of her liking. Norah found herself amid a flurry of activity as servants rubbed her skin with scented oil, helped her into a deep-ruby gown, brushed out her hair, and powdered her face. But she barely registered what was happening.

*Married.* She was to be married. She could barely remember her own name and she was going to be married to... Wait—what was his name?

"So, we'll see the council this morning," Catherine told her. "There's no avoiding it, but you needn't worry. It's merely to present you and share your return."

"Will Alexander be there?" Alexander was... safe. And known. And she needed something safe and known. She wanted him by her side. Right now.

"You must use his proper title, Norah."

His title. She nodded blankly. What was his title? *Lord justice.*

Her grandmother sighed. "I can assure you that he'll never be far from you, but put the lord justice from your mind and focus on the council. I'm sure they'll have questions about where you've been, and we'll have to navigate through them carefully, but I'll keep it as short as possible. Just remember to..."

Catherine's words blurred into an echo inside her mind, and Norah's stomach knotted. She didn't want this: not the weight of it all, not the marriage, not the dress or the scented oil, and certainly not the necklace that her grandmother held up to her.

She stumbled backward and caught herself against the wall. The room swirled around her.

Catherine paused. She set the necklace down and took Norah's hand, steadying her. "Take a breath," the woman told her, and she did.

The room steadied, and so did she. Norah looked up to find Catherine staring back at her with a deep sadness in her eyes. Her grandmother pulled her closer and brought her hand to Norah's cheek. "I'm so sorry, my darling. I wish I had more time to prepare you for this. The weight of the world is on your shoulders, I know. Your life is not your own, and I understand how difficult it is to come to terms with that. But you must do exactly as I tell you. So much depends on it—you, your people, all of us. Do you understand?"

Her mind understood, but her heart still wavered.

"I'll be by your side every step of the way," Catherine said.

And Norah found herself nodding, just not exactly in agreement.

Nausea rippled through Norah as she stepped out of her chamber and into the large arched hall of white and light. Perhaps she'd had too much wine. Or not enough. The sun reflecting off the marble nearly blinded her, but she walked, unseeing, in more ways than one.

She envied the woman who had stood at the window in the dark only a few hours earlier, before she knew of this Shadow King that wanted her dead, before she knew she'd be wed to a stranger. As if waking up as heir to the crown and with no memory wasn't enough. Her grandmother walked briskly beside her, like this was all normal. Was this to be her normal? She looked back over her shoulder at the guard that followed close behind. Was this her life now?

As they turned a corner, she spotted a familiar face waiting at the end of the hall, and suddenly, the weight of it all seemed to lighten.

*Alexander.*

Their eyes locked as she approached. And his stare...

"Princess Norah," he greeted her with a bow once she reached him.

"Lord Justice," she replied. Using his title felt awkward to her, but he gave a small smile, and it settled her. "Am I overdone?" she asked sheepishly, glancing down at her gown. It was a rhetorical question. She was entirely overdone.

"Not at all," he assured her. "You look... very regal."

"I should. All this took an absurdly long time."

His smile widened.

"Good morning, Lord Justice," Catherine greeted him with a sternness in her voice.

Alexander snapped to with a quick bow, and Norah looked on in amusement as she suspected he hadn't even noticed her grandmother.

"Good morning, Queen Regent," he replied to Catherine. "I trust you've rested well."

"As well as all this excitement would permit."

"The council waits in the judisaept," he told them.

The queen regent looked at Norah. "Remember what I told you, and you'll fare just fine."

Norah's pulse quickened. Catherine had run through what to expect and how to respond to the council while Norah had been shoved into her dress and powdered like a ball of dough, but she still drew in a nervous breath. Remembering wasn't her strong suit at the moment. Catherine had told her to keep silent about her memory loss, but she still didn't understand why. Surely people would figure it out right away. She tried to push her fear from her mind and followed after her grandmother.

The judisaept was a smaller room than Norah had expected, given the stature of the castle she'd seen so far, but it was no less splendid. Carved beams ran along the walls and between the stone, reaching to the ceiling. In the center hung a large iron chandelier holding candles within delicately blown glass flutes. Underneath sat a rectangular table, with beautifully scrolled trestles. Large shields adorned the walls. They weren't made for decoration, as each of them bore the marks of battle.

Around the table stood four councilmen, who bowed as she entered.

"Princess Norah!" called the man to her right, coming forward. "Welcome home!"

Edward, maybe, based on Catherine's description. He was a shorter man, pale and balding, and about the same age as her grandmother. He was thin, except for a slightly protruding belly not entirely hidden by his council robes. His facial features were sharp—especially his nose and chin—but his face wasn't unkind. He reached out and took Norah's hand, which he promptly brought to his forehead as he bowed.

Her heart raced as she forced a smile and tried to appear calm. Could he feel her clammy hand shaking? He seemed oblivious. Everything her grandmother had told her evaded her mind, and all she could do was pretend normalcy.

"Councilman Edward," Catherine replied, "is she not the image of her mother?"

"Indeed, she is." He pulled Norah forward, extending his arm to the rest of the councilmen. "The gods smile upon us."

The councilmen all bowed again, clapping their hands, and Norah swallowed back the lump in her throat.

"And the gods favor upon the lord justice for bringing you back to us," he added with a nod to Alexander, who had taken a position on the side of the large table.

Alexander bowed his head stiffly, shifting under the attention. "As was my duty," he said. His eyes locked with hers again and held her. Was duty all it had been?

Edward turned back to her. "You must first tell us, Princess, where you've been all this time."

Norah's attention turned to his question, and her breath caught in her throat. Of course that would be their first question. Her heart beat faster.

"Councilman Edward," Catherine said, "there's so much to discuss, but I see Councilmen James and Elias aren't with us?"

"They're in Damask, and we expect their return in two days," Edward answered. "We'll assemble the state then."

*The state*? Norah didn't know what that meant, but it didn't sound like something she would look forward to.

"The princess's return is a serious matter," Catherine said firmly, "and requires our full council. We'll not discuss it without them."

Norah could already see the skill with which her grandmother handled these conversations. She couldn't imagine doing the same herself.

The councilman paused with a crease in his brow, but then he nodded. "Uh, yes, of course."

Norah let out a silent breath of relief.

"There will still be celebratory festivities, yes? To present her?" another councilman asked. He was about the same height as Edward, but double the width, and wore a thick cover of white, short-cropped hair. Norah couldn't match him to the names and descriptions her grandmother had run through. Henricus, maybe? "Everyone will be expecting to see her," he added.

Catherine gave a smooth smile. "Arrangements have already begun for tomorrow evening."

"Very good."

Edward turned back to Norah. "Well, there's much to discuss, Princess, but for now, welcome home once again. We look forward to our state and to hearing of your time away from us."

Before Norah could respond, Catherine put her hand on her arm. "Councilmen, if you'll excuse us, there's still much we have to tend to."

The men all gave respectful bows as Catherine pulled Norah toward the door. Norah glanced over her shoulder and caught Alexander's eyes, but a councilman called to him, pulling his attention from her.

"Marvelous, dear," her grandmother whispered as they stepped into the large hall and away from the judisaept. "You did better than I'd expected."

Norah frowned. "But I didn't say anything."

Catherine patted her hand. "Exactly."

Norah wasn't sure how she felt about that, but her mind was too consumed with other things to care much. "What's a state?" she asked.

"A state is a meeting of the council to work on resolutions for the challenges our kingdom faces. We discuss many things: matters of the purse, alliances, war, trade, pirates—"

"Pirates?"

"Yes, troublesome thieves. Any kingdom with a fleet suffers their raids. And Mercian fleets carry some of the most valuable trade in the world—Mercian steel."

So the council solved problems. Alexander had said the council would help her, so why didn't her grandmother want them to know of her circumstance? "How long will we keep my memory loss from them?" she asked.

"As long as we can," Catherine answered shortly.

"But that can't be long." Not long at all. The council's first question had left her stumbling.

Her grandmother eyed her sternly. "We can't risk anything that might delay your path to the crown or keep you from getting it at all."

That only raised more questions, but ones she knew she couldn't ask now, so openly. Her mind turned to other curiosities. "You said I have a cousin. Will I be seeing her soon?"

Catherine's gaze snapped back to her. "A second cousin," she said warily. "Evangeline. She'll present herself to you at the homecoming celebration, but you'll do well to keep her at a distance. There are those who would love to see her on your throne. Not everyone has been as patient for your return."

Evangeline on the throne? Perhaps that wasn't the worst idea. *Evangeline.* She'd likely be a better fit. The title even went better with her name. Queen Evangeline. It rhymed, as though planned. Queen Norah—it sounded like a vegetable when said fast enough.

"If she could do a better job..." Norah mumbled.

Catherine stopped and turned abruptly, making Norah almost run into her. She pulled Norah close, speaking in a hushed whisper. "Listen to me carefully. There are people who are hungry for power and will use whatever means necessary to get it. But this is *your* throne. *You* are the daughter of King Aamon, *you* are the rightful heir and the one who will unite the kingdoms and defeat the Shadowlands. Do you understand?"

What happened to one thing at a time? And what did she mean by *people who are hungry for power*? Within Mercia? Her heart pulsed. She didn't think she could manage another challenge.

"Now the council will push to have your coronation as quickly as possible," the regent continued. "I'll also insist on it."

"Wait, what?" Norah shook her head. "Why? You're obviously doing a wonderful job as queen regent." She hadn't even been able to wrap her mind around pretending to have her memories. This was all coming too soon. It was too much.

"The council will want to see you wed quickly to King Phillip, for which they'll want to crown you first. This works in our favor. Until then, you'll say nothing of your memories."

That sounded like a terrible idea. "I can't—"

"We'll not talk of it now." Catherine hushed her as Alexander emerged from the judisaept and made his way toward them.

Another objection sat on Norah's lips, but it slipped from her mind as her sight set on him.

Catherine sighed as she squeezed Norah's hand. "Don't worry, child. We'll get it all sorted. But right now, I must tend to some things. The guard will see you back."

"Queen Regent," Alexander called, coming up behind them. Catherine turned. His eyes, a deep cerulean, caught Norah's, and he gave a small bow of his head. Then he broke and turned to Catherine and said, "I'd like to introduce the princess to the captain and the rest of her guard. She needs to be familiar with them."

Catherine looked at Norah warily and pursed her lips. Then she sighed. "Very well. You'll see her directly to her chamber after."

He nodded.

"I mean it," Catherine pressed. "Don't linger about."

"Of course," he assured her.

He turned back to Norah.

And Norah smiled.

# CHAPTER SEVEN

"This way, Your Highness," Alexander said. He extended his arm down the mainway.

She cringed inside. "Please don't call me that." She could bear it in public, but not here when it was just between them.

"Princess Norah."

She grimaced. "Not that either."

"I have to."

She was afraid he'd say that. "Always?"

"Not always," he assured her. Then the corners of his mouth turned up. "When you're queen, I'll call you *Your Elegance*."

She shot him a heavy-browed eye of disbelief. "That can't seriously be a title."

He chuckled. "It is. And you thought it was ridiculous before too."

She stopped, desperate for the thoughts she'd had when she'd been herself. He'd known her. "Tell me more of what I thought before."

Alexander quieted. His eyes held a wisp of sadness, as if those old thoughts haunted him. Then the corners of his lips turned up, and the sadness disappeared. She wondered if she'd seen it at all. "You thought the king's title was better."

"Which was?"

"Regal High."

"That *is* better." Why didn't the queen get a powerful title?

"Would you rather be called *Regal High* when you're queen?"

"I'd rather not be called any of it."

He chuckled again, and she bit her lip. She should be more careful with her words. Catherine would be beside herself if she heard her say that.

"I know," he said.

How much did he know about her? He opened his hand and motioned them to continue, and they started again down the hall.

"My grandmother doesn't trust the council," she said as they walked. Why didn't she? They were her council, there to *counsel*.

"Your grandmother trusts no one."

Norah raised a brow. "She trusts you."

He shrugged with a smile. "Sometimes."

They turned down another hall, where several small groups congregated, and Norah slowed. The voices fell, and all eyes were on her. Her chest tightened, and her stomach puddled.

"Do I know these people?" she whispered. The threat of panic crept up her spine and tickled the back of her mind. Would they expect something of her, for her to do something, to say something?

"You know most of them. But no one will speak unless you speak to them first. So, we'll just walk through."

The men bowed, and the women curtsied as Norah and Alexander passed. Everyone was smiling. Not acknowledging them seemed pretentious, and Norah found herself nodding with genuine courtesy.

Alexander gave her a small smile as they left the hall. "People are going to love you."

She'd done absolutely nothing. "Why?" They turned down another hall, one that opened to the outside along a columned sidewalk.

"Because you see them."

How could she not? The acknowledgment felt strange, but Alexander didn't give her time to mull it over before he muttered something unintelligible and suddenly grabbed her arm.

"What..." she started, but couldn't finish her sentence. Wide-eyed, she let him hastily pull her back inside, down a hall, and into a small arched alcove of a doorway. He tested the door within its frame, but it was locked.

"I'm very sorry about this," he said in a hushed voice, "and it's highly inappropriate, I know." He waved the guards to keep walking, then he glanced out from their hiding place.

"What... what are you doing?" she asked.

"We just need to wait a moment," he whispered. He leaned over and cast another glance down the hall.

The alcove was small. Very small. He held her gently by her upper arms as they stood tucked in the tight space. She jerked her hand to his chest, as if that would put a barrier between them, but it only seemed to link them, to draw them closer.

"W-Why?" she stammered breathlessly.

"I know I said no one would speak to you unless you spoke to them first," he whispered, "but there are... a few in court who might not abide. And I'd like to avoid one of them right now."

"I thought I saw her!" a high-pitched voice called out.

Norah locked eyes with Alexander, and he tilted his head with a raised brow, as if his point had been proven. She didn't argue. To avoid people who knew her, people who might discover her, she was fine with hiding. She'd rather avoid everyone.

They stood, so close, waiting. He'd been carefully peering out from the side, but as he glanced down at her, he stopped. Her hand still sat against his chest, and she stared at it. She should pull it off. *Off.* But she didn't. Underneath, his heart thrummed against her palm. It's rapid beating matched her own. So close they were. He stood still as a statue, but his warmth seeped into her, through her. It wrapped around her. It was the familiar warmth of a familiar body, the familiar beat of a familiar heart.

"I think it's clear now," he whispered.

He dropped his hands from her arms, and she pulled back her own hand, but still they made no move to leave. So many questions sat on her lips—questions she wasn't brave enough to ask. Finally, he stepped out from the alcove and back into the hall, breaking her from the invisible hold.

Norah smoothed her dress as she stepped out beside him, but her heart still raced. She glanced at him, and he looked as if nothing had happened. Had she imagined this connection between them? Or dreamed it, perhaps. Her cheeks flushed. Maybe there'd been nothing at all.

"This way, Princess," he said, motioning back down the hall and putting some distance between them, both physically and with his tone. Her cheeks grew hotter. She'd certainly imagined it.

They resumed their walk, back the way they'd come to the exterior doors and down the sidewalk. Alexander cast a wary eye as they went, watching for other inconvenient visitors. "I'm taking you to meet Caspian," he said, "the captain of the guard."

*Excellent*—something different to focus her mind on.

He paused for a moment and motioned behind her, where she once again found two men from her guard.

"This is Titus and Liaman—two of several men you'll see regularly." She hadn't realized they'd picked back up behind them. Had they seen her and Alexander duck into the alcove? Of course they had. *Not awkward at all.* "You have the best swordsmen in Mercia by your side," he told her.

She swallowed uncomfortably but followed Alexander's lead in pretending it didn't happen. "Then I feel very safe," she said with a nod to the soldiers. "Pleased to meet you."

"Your Highness," they said in unison, bowing their heads. She squirmed under the address. Liaman looked younger than she, almost boyish, but he moved with an aged grace. Titus was a large man, larger even than Alexander, and had certainly known a battle or two. His head was shaved, and he had a hint of a beard. A jagged scar lined his jaw, and one broke the arch of his right eyebrow.

Alexander continued, and she followed. As they made their way toward a gated building, a man stepped out to meet them with two soldiers at his flank. When he reached Alexander and Norah, he brought his fist to his chest in salute.

"Your Highness," Alexander said. "I present Captain Caspian Frey."

Caspian was handsome in an honest way. He was a kind-looking man with a generous smile and blond hair like many of the Northmen. He looked to be about the same age as Alexander.

"Captain Frey," she greeted him.

He smiled warmly as he bowed. "Your Highness." He then opened his arm to the men behind him. "Allow me to present Aaron and Daniel." Each man bowed his head as his name was called. "With Titus and

Liaman, these men make up your core guard. You'll never be without at least one of them."

"Thank you," she replied, although it came out as more of a question.

"These men are all aware of your situation, and will help you acclimate," Alexander told her. "You can ask them anything."

Norah gave an appreciative nod. *That* she was truly thankful for, although she'd wait just a bit before she peppered them with questions.

Caspian gave her another bow. "We'll leave you to your business. Welcome home, Your Highness."

"Thank you... Captain." The titles still challenged her.

Caspian and the two soldiers left them to their walk.

Alexander turned to her. "I should get you back."

*Right.* She stifled a rising groan at the thought of returning to her chamber. "I suppose so." They started back toward the castle.

As they walked, her eye caught a large, majestic building with brightly hued stained glass threaded together with elegant tracery stretching to its peaks.

She stopped in her step. "What's that?"

"The library."

It was beautiful, sitting squarely and centered by a pointed arch over heavy wood doors. A vaulted walk with carved pillars lined its perimeter, and a tower in the back stretched toward the sky.

"It houses the largest collection of knowledge in the world," he told her. "History, philosophy, all modern works of science and study—it's all here. Everything about Mercia and beyond."

"It's beautiful." She smiled, forgetting everything else for a moment. "Can I see inside?"

Alexander hesitated, looking toward the castle, no doubt mulling over his promise to her grandmother to promptly return her.

"Just a look," she pressed.

He sighed. "I suppose a quick look won't hurt."

She grinned.

Alexander waved the guard to stay outside as they walked through the carved double doors.

Norah gasped as she looked around at the magnitude of books that lay shelved to the ceiling. "It's incredible!"

"When the visions foretold the Shadowmen would invade Mercia, your father ordered all the books and scrolls to be taken to Aleon for safekeeping. It took over ten thousand men."

The mention of Aleon made her stiffen. She wanted to ask him about the marriage, but that seemed too personal now. "Is Aleon safer than Mercia?" she asked instead.

"Not necessarily, but the Shadow King didn't have his destruction focused on Aleon."

No, it had been focused on her. Norah bit her lip and turned her eyes back to the shelved books.

"Your father had every intent to change the future, but he wasn't one to take risks. He always said knowledge was the most important thing in the world, besides you. After we took the mountains of Bahoul and drove the Shadow King back deep into the Shadowlands, only then did we know it was safe to bring everything home. And it was safe for you to come home."

She clasped the pendant around her neck, running her thumb over the winterhawk. "My grandmother said the Shadow King will still come for me."

His eyes burned a deep blue, then darkened like the ocean. "He'll try."

She swallowed. The thought of a dark foe coming for her rattled her. It more than rattled her—it scared her.

"But I won't let that happen," he assured her.

She nodded. She hoped so.

He caught her arm. "Hey"—he called her eyes to his—"I would never let anyone hurt you. Ever."

The promise in his voice... It was personal, beyond duty, beyond sworn loyalty.

He let go of her and continued walking through the library. "Thousands of years of work are kept within these walls. We spent many hours here when we were young, reading, studying." He stopped, growing somber, and touched a leather-bound book on the shelf. "This one you loved."

"What is it?"

"A story—told in a collection of poems." He pulled it from its place and held it for her. The darker dye of the leather had been worn through to the tanned softness underneath; the evidence of many readings. "It holds your favorite poem."

"Do you know which one?" Silly question—of course he wouldn't.

Alexander grew quiet, looking down at the book. Then he slowly opened its laced pages. He selected the passage, its final stanza, but his eyes found hers as he spoke the words.

*"Sleep now, love, and wait for me*
*For in time, it will come to pass*
*That I will follow after, wrapped in rest beneath the earth—"*

*"Together, my darling, at last,"* she whispered, finishing. Emotion rippled through her—a familiar longing, an ache deep within. She knew

it. She knew this, knew the words and the feeling and meaning. She knew the story.

Alexander stood frozen, staring. His lips parted. He stepped closer. "You remember?" he breathed.

She nodded with a shaky breath. "I know it."

"What else?" he asked, eager now. "Anything?"

But her excitement fizzled. *No.* Nothing else had come. No memories, not even the memory of actually reading the book, only the knowledge of it. Slowly, she shook her head.

He swallowed, straightening and stepping back, as if collecting his fallen hope. "It's all right," he said. "It will come."

"Unless it doesn't."

Now she could see it—the sorrow. But then he snatched it back quickly, hiding it behind a wall. "It will," he said with a face of perfect reassurance.

She looked through his words. What was he hiding behind that wall? Then she paused. "You know my favorite poem by memory?"

The countenance of perfection fell, and he swallowed. His lips parted, and his breath quickened. "Norah, I—"

The doors of the library swung open behind them, and she turned to see a man step inside. When his eyes found them, a large smile split across his lips, and he started toward them. His height, coupled with the shape of his face and jawline, gave him away almost immediately: Alexander's brother. Adrian.

Alexander had said they'd been close. Act close... smile, she told herself.

And she smiled.

"Norah!" he called with a hearty laugh. His pace didn't slow as he drew closer, and her heart beat faster. He moved to embrace her, but Alexander's hand snaked out and caught him with a friendly clasp on the shoulder, halting the young man under the guise of affection.

"Adrian," Alexander said as he pulled his brother closer to him and looked at Norah. It was a subtle effort to introduce him.

Adrian looked at Alexander, clearly confused. Then he found a bit of formality, no doubt from his brother's chastising eye. He smiled awkwardly as he bowed. "Princess Norah," he said with a slight stiffness.

She wasn't sure how to respond. "Lord Adrian."

Adrian's brow creased. Her words felt wrong as soon as they rolled off her lips. But he was a lord, wasn't he? Too formal, maybe? *Damn it.*

He gave a puzzled nod, but his smile quickly returned. "I almost didn't believe it when I heard. You're back."

"I am," she said. She was indeed back. And standing awkwardly. She glanced at Alexander.

Adrian's mouth opened to say more, but Alexander interjected. "Speaking of getting you back, we should go," he said to Norah as he returned the book to the shelf from where he'd taken it.

She sensed Alexander's unease with his brother, and Adrian's confusion. Catherine had been very pointed about keeping her memory loss a secret. It would be hard for her with people who knew her well, and she imagined it would be hard for Alexander to keep it from his brother too.

"Of course," she said, smiling politely at Adrian.

As they stepped out of the library, the wind brought a shudder, and Norah pulled up her cloak. The Northern Kingdom, Mercia was called. It felt very northern.

"I'm surprised my brother has you out in this cold," Adrian told her.

She smiled. "It's not Alexander's doing. I kept him out. The building was beautiful, and I had to see it."

His brows drew together, and Alexander winced.

"Just to see what might have changed," she added quickly.

Adrian chuckled. "A building that's stood for a thousand years won't have changed much in the past three."

"No, I know. I meant the books." She swallowed. "To make sure..." They'd been taken to Aleon for safekeeping and returned, hadn't they? "To make sure they were in the right place." What was wrong with her? She needed to stop talking.

Alexander shook his head faintly, and she knew. "I should probably get back," she said breathlessly.

"Yes, you should," Alexander said.

A servant approached. "Your Highness," he bowed politely to Norah and then turned to Alexander. "Lord Justice, the queen regent requires you."

Alexander looked at Norah, then back to the servant. "I'll come."

"She waits in her study," the servant said with a bow, and left.

His eyes found Norah's. "I have to go. Your guard will see you back."

"Where else would you like to go? I can take you," Adrian offered.

"You have your duties," Alexander cut in. He turned to Norah. "Titus and Liaman will see you back to your chamber."

"Can my duties not wait, brother?" Adrian asked. "Surely the princess—"

"No," Alexander cut him off firmly, taking Adrian aback and silencing him. "The princess needs to return to her chamber." He turned to

Norah. "Your Highness," he said with a bow of his head. He gave Titus a nod and then left to find the regent.

Norah looked at Adrian apologetically as she started back toward the castle. He picked up alongside her.

He glanced at Norah. "Do you mind if I at least walk back with you?"

"Not at all," she said with a small smile. What else would she say?

"I still can't believe you've returned," he said as they walked. "Where have you been?"

"Adrian," Titus gruffed, and the young man glanced back at the guard in confusion.

Norah's pulse quickened. That was the question on everyone's mind. "It's complicated. I'm really just trying to get settled right now."

He nodded. "Of course."

Norah felt a pang of sympathy. He seemed kind and genuinely happy to see her. He just didn't understand, and neither did she.

They reached the castle and entered from a side door, and Norah found herself disoriented at the intersecting halls.

Adrian stopped. "I am glad you're back, Norah. There's so much I want to ask you—there are so many things to talk about, but"—he eyed Titus with a puzzled brow—"I guess that can wait for now. I can see you later, though?"

She swallowed and smiled. "Yes, of course."

This was where he clearly intended to part, but he lingered. His eyes narrowed. "Do you know where you're going?"

The question shook her. Of course she didn't know where she was going, but that would be a dead giveaway. "I was... just deciding if I might stop by the kitchen to get something to eat before I went back to my chamber."

The side of Adrian's mouth twitched. "Why would you go to the kitchen?"

Because that was where the food was. But... a princess wouldn't go get her own food. Norah bit the inside of her lip. *Damn it.*

"Liaman," Titus growled, "run ahead to the princess's chamber and have her maid fetch something to eat."

The younger guard hurried down the hall to her right, and Norah silently praised Titus's quick wit.

"Just looking for another reason to be out and walking, I suppose," she tried to explain. "But I guess I should get back. It's good to see you again, Adrian."

He gave a small bow of his head with a polite smile, but a line still stretched across his brow.

She turned down the hall that Liaman had chosen and tried not to exit too quickly as she felt Adrian's eyes still on her. When he was out of sight and earshot, she glanced back at Titus. "Thank you. That wasn't going well."

"Not well at all," he replied.

She frowned. He clearly wasn't the reassuring type.

# CHAPTER EIGHT

The sun set and rose again before Norah felt like a day had even passed. Perhaps it was the overwhelming amount of information Catherine and Rebecca tirelessly pressed upon her—what names to remember, how to act, how not to act, what to say, what not to say, how to move. Perhaps it was because she was dreading the upcoming celebrations. She didn't feel like there was a reason to celebrate yet. The Mercian princess might have returned, but she wasn't herself.

Rebecca pulled the lacing of Norah's gown tight as Norah watched blankly in the mirror. Emerald silks edged in gold rippled around her.

"Are you all right, Your Highness?" her maid asked, finishing the lacing and smoothing the fabric.

Norah glanced at her maid in the reflection and forced a small smile. "Of course." But she wasn't all right. She was being stuffed into a dress again to show herself in front of people she didn't know and pretend to be someone she wasn't.

Rebecca fastened a matching emerald necklace around Norah's neck and added stringed jewels to her ears. "There. You're beautiful."

Norah found her reflection in the mirror again. Her loose tresses hung freely over her shoulders. Her high cheekbones were kissed with color under the bright blue of her eyes. She felt beautiful, and she couldn't help a small smile.

"Are you ready?" Rebecca asked her.

She wasn't ready, but she stepped out of the chamber and into the hall, where her guard was waiting. "Where's my grandmother?" she asked them.

"The queen regent is in the great hall," Titus said with a small bow of his head. "I'll take you to her."

"Is Alexander there?"

He briefly hesitated but nodded. "He is, Your Highness."

A heat tinged her cheeks at her question, realizing it was probably obvious that Alexander lingered on her mind, but that was quickly forgotten as her thoughts turned to seeing him again. She followed Titus through the halls, down the stairs, and past the throne room, to where the great hall brimmed with music. She slowed when she saw Catherine walking toward her.

"Oh, my dear," Catherine said with an approving smile, "you're beautiful. Come, come. Everyone's waiting. Now, this should ease you back into things. It's quite informal. I'll announce your arrival, and we'll take our places at the front of the hall. Throughout the evening, I'll announce any lords and ladies who wish to extend their congratulations so you can receive them. You may accept a dance, if invited. Don't bother with food; you'll need to speak. We'll dine privately later."

It seemed the opposite of informal, and Norah's stomach rumbled at the mention of something to eat. She was hungry, and a mouthful of food seemed a perfectly acceptable explanation for not speaking to people, but she turned her attention to the night ahead. Her heart raced as she tried to remember everything her grandmother had run through.

Catherine herded her to the heavy oaken doors, and Norah drew in an uneasy breath as the captain she'd met earlier pulled them open. Paneled tapestries stretched from the ceiling to the walls and draped down to the floor. Hundreds of candles flamed brightly in the tiered chandeliers and corner candelabras. People filled the room, dressed in fine gowns and jewelry. Yes, so *very* informal.

"Welcome home, our Princess!" Catherine's voice rang out, and it was met with deafening clapping. Norah followed Catherine's lead to the front of the hall, with her guard and captain close behind.

"Be ready, my dear," her grandmother whispered as they turned to face the room.

Almost immediately, an older man approached with a young woman beside him. He was the same height as Norah, with a moderate build and his graying-blond hair meticulously combed back. His embroidered doublet had cuffed shoulders, no doubt to augment his stature. Around his waist he wore a thin belt from which hung an even thinner sword. Norah wondered if the blade was even real. Her stomach knotted. Surely this was the worst part of being a princess—talking to people. People she didn't know.

"Lord Allan," Catherine greeted as he neared, "and Lady Evangeline."

*Evangeline.* Her second cousin, whom her grandmother had warned her about. Norah had pictured her... differently—not at all like the warm face smiling back at her, the rose-colored cheeks beaming, the blue eyes shining. She couldn't have been more than sixteen or seventeen. She curtsied as the man next to her—Lord Allan, her father—bowed.

"Princess Norah," he said, "we're so happy for your safe return."

She found herself doubting that, based on what her grandmother had told her and the stiffness radiating off him, which was very unlike his

83

daughter beside him. The series of responses that Catherine had prepped her with evaded her mind. She glanced at her grandmother, who gave a prodding lift of her brow. "Um, thank you, Lord Allan. It's... so great to be home." She finished with a nod, hoping that was enough.

His lips smiled, but his eyes didn't. "We'll leave you to the evening. Welcome home, Princess Norah," he said. He looked at Catherine. "Queen Regent." He bowed again, and Evangeline curtsied beside him.

The exchange seemed mercifully short and surely more for onlooking eyes than anything else. Norah copied Catherine as she gave a nod. That was what she was supposed to do, right? Nod at a bow?

"Excellent," Catherine whispered to her as Lord Allan and Evangeline departed. "Now smile."

Norah forced her lips into a smile as her eyes swept the room. So many people, and not all of them happy about her return. And so many expectations. Her anxiousness grew.

"Here, have some wine," Catherine said as she handed her a glass provided by a servant.

*Yes.* Wine. Norah took a long drink from the glass, and it was promptly refilled. She took in a breath, feeling a little better, and then drank deeply again.

"But perhaps not all the wine," Catherine added as she pulled the glass from her hands. "And try to smile with your whole face, child."

She did her best to put on a cheerful face as another well-wisher came forward to greet her. The wine threatened to come back up, but she swallowed it down. She just needed to make it through this evening.

She stood through what felt like eternity—smiling, nodding, thanking the warm welcomes. One after another they came, and just when she didn't think she could bear it any longer, blue eyes met hers.

She stopped and smiled—a real smile this time.

"Queen Regent," Alexander smartly greeted Catherine first, and her grandmother nodded. Then he turned to Norah. "Princess Norah. You seem to be managing the evening quite easily."

That wasn't how she would describe it, but none of that mattered.

"Have you eaten?" he asked.

Catherine cast her a stiff glance.

"I'm really not hungry," she told him.

He stepped up beside her, turning and looking out across the hall. "Now, I know that's a lie," he said quietly, so only she could hear.

She held back a smile. It was a lie. She'd wreck a garden for something to eat right now.

"This is about the time you'd tell me you'd wreck a garden for something to eat right now."

Norah jerked her head to him, her eyes wide.

"Should I steal you something?" he asked, his eyes gleaming.

It was all she could do to keep from laughing.

"Norah," Catherine scolded.

*Right.* She was here with a purpose. "I'm sorry, I..."

Her words dropped as a poignant melody filled the hall, and she stopped. She knew this song. Norah turned and stared at the string orchestra as they played the familiar tune. A wave of nostalgia rippled through her, leaving her light-headed.

"Are you all right?" Alexander asked, stepping forward and ever so lightly catching her arm.

Her mind blurred.

"Norah?" Catherine asked. Her voice was distant.

"I know this song," she breathed. "I know this dance."

Alexander leaned closer. "You remember 'Allameade'?"

"*Allameade.*" Yes, that's what it was called. She nodded and glanced at Catherine, who stared back at her, wide-eyed.

"Do you remember anything else?" he asked, eagerness growing in his voice.

She shook her head and closed her eyes, listening. "Just the dance, the music. I know it." She opened her eyes and smiled at him. Before Catherine could object, she grabbed his arm. "Come with me," she said breathlessly as she pulled him to the center of the hall amid others dancing, who readily made way.

They stood for a moment, facing each other. She bit her lip at his humble unease, trying to hold back a laugh, and then bowed, inviting him. He hesitated, then returned the bow, accepting.

They brought their right arms up together in a twist, but not touching. Their eyes met as they circled one another and then changed arms. For someone who seemed so reluctant, he knew the movements well, she mused. She did too.

He held his arm out to the side as she moved in a series of steps around him, through the story of the song. They carried themselves in the arrangement across the floor. He slipped behind her and curved his arm around her, but he was careful to keep ever the faintest of space between them. That was the challenge of this intricate dance: two people unable to touch, unable to truly be as one. She drew her arm across her chest between them, reaching back and stroking the air, down the length of his arm, then out to her side.

They moved in unison, losing themselves to the melody and in their closeness to each other. She turned in step to face him as he reached up and brought his palm so close to her cheek she could feel the warmth of his hand. Still, he didn't touch her. His eyes burned with a wild intensity and stirred something wild inside her.

The song ended, and their closeness left her breathless.

His lips parted—a question seemed to linger on them—but he didn't speak it. Instead, he took her hand and bowed, placing a gentle kiss on the back of her fingers.

"Well done, Your Highness. Thank you for that. It was a pleasant surprise." Then he straightened, his formality returning, and Norah realized all eyes in the room were on them. His voice came quieter now. "I should see you back to your grandmother."

Her head felt light as he swept her back to the company of the regent, who cast her a disapproving eye.

"Your Highness," Alexander said to Norah with another bow of his head. "I hope you enjoy the rest of your evening." He gave a small bow to Catherine. "Queen Regent." His eyes again locked with Norah's in a gaze that haunted the shadows of her mind. Then he took his leave to the other side of the hall.

"*When invited*, Norah," her grandmother chided in a harsh whisper. "You can't just go fluttering about and pulling men in to dance."

But Norah paid no mind to Catherine's chastisement. Her heart raced. She had been here before. Even though she had no memory, she knew the dance to "Allameade." She knew the bright light of Alexander's eyes.

Her heart beat even faster.

She knew the feel of his lips on her skin.

# CHAPTER NINE

Alexander made his way toward James's chamber, taking the stairs two at a time. The councilman had been in Damask when Norah had returned, and it surprised Alexander he'd arrived back so quickly. Damask was two days' ride away. James had to have left as soon as the bird's message had arrived, then ridden through the night. Perhaps that shouldn't be a surprise. The entire kingdom had been waiting for Norah's return.

The seer had painted the vision of Norah in the forest before her father had taken her. Alexander hadn't known what it had meant then. He hadn't known she'd be lost to him. It was only after King Aamon had died, taking the secret of her location with him, that James thought the painting was a clue to finding her. More than that, James had believed it was part of Alexander's destiny to bring her home. Alexander had wanted to believe that, so much that he had dreamt about it night and day.

For three years, he'd searched the forests throughout the kingdom, and even those beyond Mercia's borders. For three years, he'd returned alone. Until he had ventured where no men dared to go, the land from which men did not return—the Wild. He should have gone sooner, but it was a place he truly hadn't expected to find her.

But he had.

A deep pride swelled within him as he walked the long hall. There had been so many times he'd doubted, so many times he'd feared failure and that Norah would be lost to him forever. And he'd feared disappointing James. No one could take the place of Alexander's father, the great Beurnat the Bear, but James had always been like a father—guiding him, coaching him, loving him, even.

Alexander caught himself and cast his pride aside. This wasn't his accomplishment. This was his duty, his obligation to both Norah and Mercia, his promise to his father and to James. He could be happy and grateful, but he couldn't be prideful.

He reached the councilman's chamber and knocked on the door.

"Enter!" James called.

All the councilmen of Mercia had servants, all except James, who viewed them as being excessive. He minded himself, dressed himself, and even upset the kitchen staff by making food at times. He was a selfless man, which made his counsel invaluable. Alexander desperately wanted that counsel now, but Catherine had been firm. No one, not even James, was to know about Norah's condition. It had even been difficult to convince her to share it with the guard, and even then, she'd limited it to the core guard. But he understood. The regent wouldn't risk anything that might keep Norah from the throne. Without her memories, Norah was even more vulnerable. Catherine was only trying to shield her granddaughter from those she didn't trust. And Catherine trusted no one.

It was a challenging balance between Catherine and the council—the council had given her the regency and had the power to take it away, yet Alexander's vows as justice were to the queen regent only.

As Alexander stepped inside the chamber, James emerged from his cabinet, washed from his ride in and donning a fresh councilman's robe.

"Ah, Alexander," he greeted. "I came as quickly as I could."

Alexander nodded. "I'm glad you're here."

"Is it true?" the councilman asked him. "Is it really her?"

"Yes." Alexander paused as the words caught thick in his throat—the words he'd feared he might never claim. "I found her, James. It's really her."

"Where?"

"In the Wild."

The older man reached out and clasped the side of Alexander's neck. "You've done it, my boy. You've done what I always knew you would."

Alexander's emotion brimmed, making it difficult to speak. He only nodded.

James took a deep breath and walked to the window, letting himself digest the news. "So, the time's finally come." He turned back to Alexander. "Where has she been?"

Alexander paused, then shook his head. "The queen regent has been waiting for you to return before answering that. There's much to catch up on, and she wants the full council present."

James humphed, almost to himself. "I want to see her."

"The queen regent is still getting her settled," he said quickly. Norah wasn't ready to meet James yet. Unlike the other councilmen, James had been close with King Aamon and Norah. He'd know she was different, that something was wrong, like Adrian already suspected, he was certain.

"I'm sure she'll wish to discuss her selection for lord justice once she catches her breath," Alexander told the councilman, hoping to move him past the effort to meet with Norah now. His statement was true. Norah would be expected to seek James's advice on her selection. Although Alexander had dreamed of the placement for himself, he didn't dare expect it. His father had groomed him for it, to follow in his footsteps, but the position of lord justice was one of great power. Only the queen and the combined council stood above it, and Alexander didn't presume himself worthy... or ready. There were others, great men who'd served King Aamon, men far wiser than he. The only reason Alexander held the position now was because of Catherine's distrust for everyone else.

"Has the coronation date been set?" James asked.

Alexander's head jerked up. "No. Not yet. Do you really mean for it to be so soon?"

"Of course. Her return sets everything in motion. Has word been sent to Aleon?"

Alexander's chest tightened. He nodded. Caspian had seen the message off. Within the next few days, the news would reach King Phillip, who would no doubt expect what had always been promised—the seal of their alliance. *A marriage.*

The council would be eager for this marriage, but first they'd see Norah crowned queen. Alexander had hoped she'd have some time. He had hoped *he'd* have some time.

"Good, good." James nodded. "I'd like to see her right away. I'll speak to the queen regent."

Alexander gave a respectful bow of his head. A lord justice didn't bow to councilmen, but James was different.

The councilman reached out and clasped Alexander's shoulder. "Well done, my boy. Your father would be proud."

The emotion returned with James's words. He certainly hoped his father would be proud and that he'd brought honor to their family. He wished his father were there now.

Alexander stepped from the councilman's chamber and headed to find Catherine. He'd need to inform her of James's intent to speak with Norah, so they'd both be prepared.

"How is James?" a voice called from a side hall as he passed.

A silent groan rolled in the back of his throat as he stopped and turned to find his brother. He'd been avoiding Adrian, and he was sure it hadn't gone unnoticed. Adrian's face didn't carry its usual grin. And Adrian didn't have the slightest interest in James, Alexander knew.

"Tired, but well," Alexander answered.

Alexander continued forward, and Adrian fell in step beside him.

"And how are you?" Adrian asked.

He pushed a long breath from his lungs. "The same." His brother could read him better than anyone. No matter how stoic Alexander's face, Adrian always knew how he felt. Now was no exception, especially not after the strange interaction with Norah, but he had neither the time nor the energy for Adrian's questions.

Adrian caught him by the arm, bringing them both to a halt. "You're not well. Why, brother?" His voice was soft and concerned.

"As I said, I'm tired." It wasn't entirely untruthful, although if he were to close his eyes, no sleep would come. It wasn't weariness that weighed on him.

"Why are things different?" Adrian pressed. "Why is she different?"

Alexander searched for the words that might appease him. "She's been gone three years. Of course she's going to be different." But Alexander knew that explained nothing. There were no words that would quell his brother's suspicions. Adrian was too smart for his own good sometimes.

"What about you?" Adrian asked. "Are you different now too? The way you speak to her, the way you act." He paused, looking around and dropping his voice low. "Like there was nothing."

A flash of anger ran through Alexander. Adrian was too free with his tongue. "Watch your words," he warned, but he knew his brother only questioned out of concern for him, out of love. He softened. "Things are different now. She'll be queen in a matter of days."

Adrian shook his head. "What aren't you telling me?"

Alexander clasped Adrian's shoulder. "I've told you all you need to know. Please, don't make my work harder."

Adrian's face fell. He conceded, nodding.

Alexander squeezed his brother's shoulder and then went to find the regent.

# CHAPTER TEN

*Darkness hung around her, but Norah wasn't afraid. Her lips pulled back into a smile as she slipped on her dress. The fabric clung to her damp skin. She grasped behind her to tie the lacing, but gentle hands took over, and she let them. Her heart pulsed warmth into her cheeks, and she reached up and swept her hair to the side, feeling the cool air tease the flesh of her neck. The last tie was made on her gown, but she lingered. A warm breath from behind her rolled over her shoulder. Her skin prickled. Then, ever so soft, lips brushed her skin. She let out a small gasp as her head fell to the side, and warmth pooled deep inside her stomach. She turned—*

Norah blinked her eyes open as she lay under a wave of confusion. She sat up with a start, pushing back the thick quilts, and realized she was in her chamber. She'd been dreaming, although it didn't feel like a dream.

It was morning, but the sun hadn't yet risen. Rebecca would be in soon to wake her. She slipped out of bed, still breathless from her dream, and splashed water on her face from the basin. Her mind turned to the night before—the dance with Alexander, his nearness, his lips on her skin. Then she scolded herself. Alexander should be the last thing on her mind.

As expected, Rebecca swept into the room with a tray of biscuits and tea. "You're an early riser, Your Highness," she said with a smile. "I hope you slept well."

She hadn't, thinking of the dream, although she wouldn't be terribly upset if it were to happen again. Her cheeks flushed, even at her own private thoughts.

"The queen regent said she'll be in after midday meal," Rebecca told her as she pulled out a gown for Norah to wear.

Norah's brow tensed. That was a long way away. "What will I do until then?"

Her maid helped her into the gown and said, "There are several things I can bring you, Your Highness: drawing things, books, needlepoint."

*Needlepoint?* That sounded terrible. None of those things appealed to her. "Do I have to stay in my chamber?"

"Well"—Rebecca paused as she pulled the gown tight and fastened it—"the queen regent said she'd be here after midday meal."

Yes, she'd already said that. Norah wriggled inside her gown as Rebecca tightened it, situating herself as comfortably as she could, as if comfort were possible. Then she brushed her hair back from her face. "All right, I can be back before then."

Rebecca gave a small grimace. "I don't think the queen regent would be pleased." She pulled a brush through Norah's loose tresses and fastened the hair back from her face with floral pins.

Norah frowned. "Did she *say* I had to stay in my chamber?"

The maid wavered. "Not exactly."

Norah sighed. "I can't stay in here all the time, locked away."

Rebecca looked at her with sympathetic eyes.

"What about the library?" Norah asked her. The book of poems—she'd been wanting to return for it. She didn't need her maid's permission, but she recognized the value in an ally.

The maid hesitated but finally caved. "Then you can't take long. It wouldn't be good if she were to come and you weren't here."

Norah grinned. "I won't be long at all."

Rebecca grabbed a cloak and draped it over Norah's shoulders, and Norah slipped out into the hall.

Her guard shifted when he saw her, clearly not expecting her to go out anywhere.

"Your Highness," he said, "you should remain in your chamber."

"Good morning, Titus," she said, smiling sweetly. "I'm just going to the library to bring back some books." She turned on her heel before he could object again, knowing he'd have no choice but to follow.

She traced her way back down the halls from what she remembered. She wasn't too concerned with getting lost; Titus would help her if needed. As she stepped outside, she slowed. Where she expected to find the cold emptiness of early morning, she instead found people were already bustling about. For a moment, her confidence wavered.

Norah tucked her chin and kept forward, as if focused on important business. Alexander had said no one would address her unless she addressed them first, so she just wouldn't address them. *Easy enough.* But her self-assurance fell flat as she remembered that wouldn't work on everyone. She would just go to the library and back. Quickly.

But as she reached the end of the pillared walkway, a familiar face came around the corner.

Adrian. *Damn it.*

He was as tall as Alexander and carried himself with the same poise. Norah felt that he was older than his years, and she had to remind herself he was only nineteen.

"Princess Norah," he greeted her. His eyes were the same as his brother's, piercing, but more expressive.

"Adrian," she greeted him, smiling to hide her unease. He was just the kind of person she'd hoped to avoid. She was certain he already suspected something was off.

"How are you settling?" he asked.

She drew in a breath, pushing aside her anxiousness. "Well, thank you." He watched her curiously, and the silence pressured her to offer more. "I'm just going to pick up a few books."

He smiled politely.

She glanced back at Titus. He returned her gaze with a wary eye. She moved toward the library, looking for a natural break, and her pulse quickened as Adrian picked up alongside her.

"Is it strange to be back?" he asked.

"Yes, it is," she answered honestly. "Does it feel strange to have me back?"

"It does," he said, and Norah appreciated his honesty too. "But I'm sure in no time this will feel like home again."

It was hard to imagine Mercia feeling like home—a place that was so foreign now. "I'm sure," she mumbled.

"I imagine you'll—" He stopped as a small group of women walked by. One woman in the group locked eyes with Norah, and excitement flashed across her face, but she said nothing. Norah shifted her attention back to Adrian. What was he saying? Why had he stopped?

He glanced at Norah, then watched the group of women as they passed, before turning back to her. "Do you not want to say hello to Lady Jane?" he asked, his brows drawing together.

"Um"—the woman looking at her must have been Lady Jane, and Norah searched her mind for answers—"my grandmother asked that I settle in before catching up with anyone." She tried to give a jesting smile. "I probably shouldn't even be speaking with you."

Adrian smiled back, but his eyes burned an inquisitive, brilliant blue. "That's too bad. Jane's missed you, you know."

"And I, her." Norah swallowed back the choke of a lie in her throat. "It's been a long time."

He nodded, eyeing her closely. She shifted under his gaze.

"Her mother will be happy to see you too," he said.

"And... I look forward to seeing her as well."

He wasn't smiling anymore. "Except Jane doesn't have a mother."

*Nine hells.*

"You don't remember Jane?" he asked.

Norah fumbled for words. "I'm a little overwhelmed with everything. Of course I remember. I just wasn't thinking."

But his eyes told her he didn't believe her. "Why are you so different? And did you not know your way around the castle the other day?"

"Adrian," Titus warned from behind her.

Her heart raced in her chest. "Um..."

Titus stepped between them. "Enough."

Adrian wasn't swayed. "Do you not remember? Do you not know?" His voice came more urgently now.

Titus grabbed him by his tunic and pushed him backward.

"Why do you call me Adrian?" he called.

"Wait," Norah said to Titus, and the guard reluctantly paused. "Leave him be."

Titus released him, and Adrian drew nearer to Norah again. He swallowed. "Do you not remember me, Norah?"

This was why Alexander had wanted to keep him away. She couldn't hide her secret from the people who knew her well. It was too obvious. She cursed herself. She should have stayed in her chamber.

"You don't, do you?" he pressed. "You don't remember."

Her heartbeat pulsed in her ears. Titus stepped forward again, but she stopped him. "Leave him," she said. She looked back at Adrian. "You've discovered me." The admission took a weight off her shoulders—the weight of a lie, but it was short-lived. Now he knew, and she wasn't sure what to do about that.

He swallowed. "Do you remember my brother?"

Her silence answered for her.

"He said you were different."

She couldn't lie anymore. "I am different."

Adrian took a step back as the weight of the circumstance settled over him. "Do you remember anything?" he asked.

Titus shifted uneasily as she shook her head. "Alexander and my grandmother have advised me not to share my condition. Obviously, I'm doing a very poor job of that right now. I'd appreciate it if you would keep it to yourself."

"Of course." His voice came low and soft now. "But why don't you remember?"

That was the answer she was so desperate for. She let out a long breath. "I don't know. But I'm trying to find out. I'm reacquainting myself, seeing if anything stirs a memory, if anything might be familiar."

He nodded with a solemn frown. "Forgive me," he said softly. "It wasn't my place."

"There's nothing to forgive." She looked back at the castle. "I should get back." Then she paused. "Hey—what did I used to call you?"

He hesitated, and she wondered if he was reluctant now that she was a stranger to him.

"Adri," he said finally. "You always called me Adri."

His voice held a touch of sorrow. Her loss of memory was not only making it challenging for her but also hurting those she had been close to, those who cared about her.

"I'm sorry," she whispered. Her eyelids grew heavy under the sting of emotion. She turned back toward the castle.

"What about the library?" he asked.

"Another time," she said. She'd already done enough for today.

# CHAPTER ELEVEN

Norah sat on the chaise in her chamber, a needlepoint canvas in her lap, but her eyes were on the gray skies outside the windows. She hadn't told Rebecca what had happened, about running into Adrian and that he'd discovered her.

Out of all things, her not remembering Alexander seemed to have upset him the most. There was a brief knock on the door. Rebecca moved to answer, but Catherine swept in before her maid reached it.

"Ah, there you are," her grandmother said when she saw Norah, as if she'd been looking everywhere.

"Here I am," she said, glancing at Rebecca to see if the maid would mention her outing. But Rebecca only smiled at her.

"Councilman James has requested to see you," Catherine told her as she picked up the hairbrush from the vanity and waved Norah over. "Rather persistently, I might add. He won't wait for the state. I can't hold him off any longer."

Norah sat at the vanity as Catherine dragged the brush through her hair. "Norah, of all the councilmen, James was closest to your father, and to you."

"Then he can help me manage whatever is going on with my memories. He can help me sort things out."

"No," Catherine said. "If he has concerns, he'll most certainly discuss them with the other members of the council, and we can't have that. Not yet. No, you must approach this with care. But don't worry, I'll be right by your side, and I'll help guide the conversation."

While Norah didn't like the idea of people speaking for her, she'd much rather have Catherine handle these conversations, and she took some reassurance in that. Nevertheless, apprehension grew in her core. She wasn't having the best of luck in maintaining appearances. Catherine raked the brush through another section of her hair, and Norah winced. She was beginning to think it didn't need brushing as much as her grandmother needed something to fill her hands.

"You must greet him warmly," Catherine told her. "You were very fond of him as a girl."

"All right, I can give him an embrace when I see him, and—"

"What?" Catherine grimaced. "That's exactly what you won't do."

Norah bit her lip, feeling sheepish.

"It's not proper. So no, you won't *embrace* him, but you will call him James. Others will see it as a slip, as will he, but it'll represent the relationship you had."

It seemed so odd, but Norah supposed she could understand that. Adrian hadn't used her title, and they had been close. And it wasn't lost on her that when they were alone, Alexander had called her by her name.

Catherine's voice brought her back. "As queen, you'll need to select a lord justice. And you'll need to do so quickly. No doubt James will raise it with you. You'll discuss three names with him: Lord Bosley, Lord Branton, and Lord Semaine."

Norah wanted to object to the coronation again, but the mention of choosing a lord justice drew her mind. "You don't think I should choose Alexander?"

Catherine's eyes met hers in the mirror's reflection with a fierceness. "You should not."

"Why?"

"You're a clever girl," Catherine said firmly, as if that answered her question. "But you must choose quickly. Seek James's council; it's what he'll expect, and it will hold his attention. Just make sure it's one of the three. Lord Branton should be your top choice, although the other two are satisfactory if James feels strongly."

Norah couldn't ignore the sinking feeling in her stomach. Why shouldn't she pick Alexander?

"Come," Catherine said, satisfied with Norah's hair, which looked no different than it had before. "James will be looking for your audience, and I can't delay him anymore."

She followed her grandmother as they made their way toward the throne room. Norah said the names of the lord justice candidates over in her mind. It wasn't the first time she'd heard them. Catherine had introduced her to each of them at her return celebration: Lord Bosley, Lord Branton, Lord...

*Damn it.*

Panic swelled inside of her. This was an important introduction, and she felt too rushed and ill prepared. James would see right through her.

James and Alexander were waiting when they arrived. Alexander stood fixed, but his gaze caught hers. She wondered if Adrian had told him about their conversation. She broke from his invisible hold and tried to push him from her mind to focus on the task ahead.

"Princess Norah," James greeted her, stepping forward and sweeping up her hand in his. He was tall and thin, balding on top, and old enough to be her father. His eyes held a deep affection. "Welcome home, my dear."

"James," she said, reaching for as genuine a smile as she could manage. She caught a glint of a tear in his eye, but he cleared his throat.

"Though years belated, let me express my sorrow for the loss of your father. He's greatly missed. As you've been."

Norah nodded, unable to speak. Her father had died in the war while she'd been gone. Was she expected to be mourning him? She wished she could remember him so that she could. But she did mourn everything she'd lost. "Thank you," she replied. "It's still difficult to speak of him." That was truthful enough.

James squeezed her hand in understanding. "There's so much to cover since you've been gone. And with your coronation fast approaching, I can understand that you might still be in shock of it all."

Norah let out a relieved breath. Finally, someone who seemed to understand, at least a sliver.

"You probably don't feel ready for this," he said.

If he only knew...

"Is anyone ever truly ready?" Catherine asked.

He gave a small nod, thinking. "Might we go for a walk?" he asked Norah.

"Um..." she said uneasily, looking back at her grandmother.

"James," Catherine said, trying to intervene. "Edward is looking to set up a state now that you've returned. You'll have ample opportunity—"

"Yes, I look forward to it," he said, giving her a bow of his head. "But I would like to speak to the princess now." He turned back to Norah. "Shall we?"

Norah glanced back at Catherine, who she knew couldn't do much more. "Of course," she replied uneasily. She tried to steady her breath as she walked with James out of the hall.

"All this must be quite overwhelming," he started.

She couldn't help a small smile. She appreciated his empathy. "It is," she admitted.

"Where have you been, Norah?"

She continued walking, trying to not let his directness intimidate her. The sun was setting over the castle, casting long shadows through the hall.

"I can't share that, at least not yet," she said, as confidently as she could manage.

"And why is that? Is there no longer trust between us?"

Her mind searched for words. She wished she'd been better prepared. "My father wished to keep it a secret. Secretly." Keep a secret secretly? *So stupid.* She cursed herself.

James's eyes narrowed as her heart beat in her ears. "Is that so?"

She shifted. "Yes."

"And when will you be able to share this *secret* secret?"

Norah cleared her throat. "Soon. I hope." And she did hope.

James nodded with a pondering frown. "It's interesting."

She frowned. "What is?"

"When you lie."

Her stomach tumbled.

He stopped and turned toward her, his eyes holding her captive. "You always seem to have a valiant reason, as I'm sure you do now. But you *are* lying."

Norah's breath caught in her throat, and she nearly choked as she swallowed. She couldn't bear his gaze, but she couldn't turn away.

"Will we leave it at that?" he asked. "Or will you tell me what's really going on? I care for you very much, Norah. Will you not let me help you?" He waited for an answer.

If Catherine was afraid he'd tell the rest of the council about her memory, he'd certainly tell them she was lying. She might as well come clean. And he did seem to care for her; she felt as though she could trust him.

"I don't know where I've been," she finally admitted. "Alexan—the lord justice found me in the Wild, where I'd been lost, but everything before that day is just... gone."

James's brow dipped, and his lips parted slightly before he drew them into a frown.

"Along with all my memories," she added, "of everything and everyone." She didn't know what else to say. Her heart raced.

"Hmm." His frown deepened.

Norah sighed with a small shrug. "Adrian discovered me as well. I'm finding I'm not very good at hiding anything."

"You never were. We'll figure out how to manage that."

Her heart skipped a beat, and a wave of hope ran through her. "You believe me? And you still support my coronation?"

She stood under his heavy gaze, feeling the threat of his condemnation, until he finally said, "An Andell with no memories is still better than a gullible teenage girl and Lord Allan's influence on the throne. Although, I'm not sure how many councilmen will share that view."

It wasn't quite the endorsement to bolster her confidence, but it was better than she'd feared.

He paused. "Who else knows?"

"Ummm... Adrian, Grandmother, and my guard. And Alexander, of course. Grandmother was adamant we tell no one else."

He nodded. "She's right. Listen to her, Norah. She knows how this game is played."

It didn't feel like a game, at least not a fun one.

"We'll have to move up your coronation," he said. "As soon as possible."

Her chest tightened. "Wait, no"—she shook her head—"now that you know, you can help me. We don't have to rush into this."

"On the contrary; time is of the essence now. It has to be before the state. The council, particularly Edward, will want to meet with you first, but there's absolutely no way you'll make it through a state meeting without revealing yourself and your situation."

Was that really so bad? "What would happen? Will they not support me as queen?"

James paused, mulling over her question, and then said cautiously, "I fear they won't if you give them a reason not to."

"Why?"

"Evangeline has a legitimate blood claim to the throne, and she'll do as she's advised." He locked his eyes with hers. "That's always been the concern with you, Norah."

Her eyes narrowed. "So, they'll look for a reason to give Evangeline the throne over me because they fear I won't do as I'm told?"

"That's not what I said."

"It sounded pretty close."

"Even so, who do you think will make the best decisions for a kingdom?" he asked sternly. "A young girl who knows nothing, or a council with the wisdom of generations?"

Norah stepped back, her mouth open, but no words would come out.

James's face was firm, and his mouth was pressed thin. "While we don't always agree, those on the council carry Mercia's best interests in their hearts. We make decisions for the good of our kingdom and the good of our people. Now, I will support you, Norah. I will help seat you on the throne, but you must *listen* and take it seriously. Do you understand?"

How else does one take a queenship if not seriously? She nodded, although she wasn't entirely sure what she was agreeing to. Was this a commitment in exchange for his support? She didn't know if she even wanted his support. Would Evangeline on the throne be such a bad thing? But she didn't have the time to ask him. Or the courage.

"What of your selection for lord justice?" he asked, pivoting the conversation. "The crown is heavy, and you'll tire with a kingdom on your shoulders. You must choose your lord justice wisely."

Yes, that's what she needed help with—a justice. "I was looking for you to help me with that. I wanted to discuss a few names with you: Lord Bosley, Lord Branton, and Lord... Seymour."

He raised a brow. "Lord Semaine?"

Norah cursed herself. At least he already knew her secret. Otherwise, that would have been yet another giveaway.

"Choose Alexander," he said firmly.

"W-Why?" she stammered in surprise.

"Why would you not?" he tossed back.

It was a fair question. One she had asked herself. He was justice now. Catherine had chosen him. Why shouldn't *she*? She gave a small shrug. "It's just a big decision, and it needs to be right."

"Do you feel it's not?"

"It's not that." She paused, searching for words. "I've only known him for a few days."

"My dear," James said with a rich warmth in his voice, "you've known him your entire life, and there's not a man alive more committed to his duty or more loyal." He paused. "You know, when Catherine selected him, the council worried he was too young and not ready. I worried that myself. But his father had prepared him for this role since he was a child, and over these past three years, he's done a damn fine job at it. He's kept this kingdom safe. His words are wise and true. He even manages to persuade Catherine at times, and that alone is a god's feat."

Norah couldn't help a small smile. That did seem like a god's feat. Her heart warmed. Alexander sounded exactly like the kind of man she should choose. "But what about the others?" she asked. "Like Lord Branton." She couldn't go back to her grandmother without at least one more name.

"No others. Choose Alexander, Norah. You asked my counsel, and I'm giving it."

It wasn't counsel that Catherine would be happy with.

"I guess I just need to think about it."

"You had better do it quickly."

Norah nodded, with a heavy stomach.

He paused again. "So... you remember nothing of your father?"

While she didn't feel the pain of his passing, the tragic void wasn't lost on her. She shook her head.

"It's a shame," he said sadly. "He was a great man."

"I want to remember him. I'm trying."

He nodded. "Then I suppose I'm not too insulted you hold no memory of me either." But deep lines of sorrow creased his brow. This was the hardest part—the pain of loss felt by the people who had cared about her. Suddenly, his eyes narrowed. "Did Catherine tell you to drop my title and just call me James?"

She pulled her lips between her teeth and winced.

"Oh, she's good," he said with a gruff. "Well, let's get back. I'm sure she's beside herself. Just do me a favor and wait until I'm gone before you tell her I know about you."

Norah couldn't help a small smile again. It lightened her spirit. They found her grandmother and Alexander in the throne room, and both turned abruptly as they entered, looking to see how the conversation fared, no doubt.

James turned to Norah. "Welcome home, Your Highness. Enjoy these last few days, for everything is about to change." He bowed to Catherine, then left the throne room.

Alexander followed James into the hall with a deep anxiousness in his stomach. The councilman had given no indication that Norah's secret had slipped, but he was a difficult man to read at times.

"No memories?" James said finally as they walked, eyeing Alexander with a raised brow.

Alexander snorted. *Of course.* "She told you." He shook his head. "She's not very good at secrets, is she?"

"I'm surprised by you, Alexander. Did you think I wouldn't find out?"

He expected this. "Of course not. But, James, I gave my word, and I'm committed."

"That you are." The old man pushed out a long breath. "Quite a mystery, though, isn't it?"

It was a mystery, one that Alexander was desperate to solve. But he also needed to focus on the future. "Will you help her, James?"

"I will, so long as it helps Mercia."

"Are they not one and the same?"

James turned to Alexander, a seriousness coming to him. "No, they're not."

# CHAPTER TWELVE

Norah followed Catherine to her chamber. She wasn't sure the woman could contain herself until they got there. She wasn't exactly looking forward to sharing that she'd told James about her memory loss, especially after Catherine had explicitly told her not to, and that Alexander was still her only consideration for lord justice. They reached the chamber too soon.

"How did James feel about Lord Branton?" Catherine asked as soon as the door closed.

Norah's heart raced. "He knows," she said with a frown. "He knows I'm not me, that I don't have my memories." It was best to get it out of the way.

"You told him?" Catherine asked, alarmed.

"He saw right away I was lying. There wasn't much I could do. But he's going to help me."

"Does he plan to tell the council?"

She bit the side of her cheek. That would have been a good question to ask. "I don't think so," she said slowly. "He asked me who all knew and said you were right: I shouldn't share it. He also told me to listen to you."

Catherine's eyes widened. "Did he now?" She straightened. That puffed her up a bit. "Let's hope he does the same," she added with an edge. "Norah, you have to be more careful."

How could she possibly be more careful? She'd have to not speak at all.

"Now, what did he say about Lord Branton?" her grandmother pressed again.

Norah's stomach knotted at the next wave of disappointment to deliver. "I have only Alexander to consider."

"You know that's not an option. You were supposed to discuss Branton."

"I did," she insisted. "I don't understand why Alexander's not an option. I don't know anyone else," she added, exasperated. "He wouldn't talk about any of the names you gave me. Branton, Bosley, Seymour—he didn't like any of them."

"Lord Semaine." Catherine sighed. "Oh, Norah, no wonder he discovered you."

"Well, he figured me out well before we even talked about names." And really, what did she expect?

"Don't worry, we'll solve this," her grandmother said flatly. "You'll choose someone else."

"Who? I just said I don't know anyone."

"There are many options. You'll settle on someone."

Norah felt a flash of frustration. Her grandmother wasn't listening. "All right, let's see, there's Adrian—"

Catherine snorted. "Don't be silly."

"Caspian." Norah counted the second name on her fingers.

"That's enough."

"These are literally all the people I know," she said. "Will a councilman do? Oh"—she brought a third finger—"there's a girl named Jane."

"Now you're just being ridiculous," Catherine snapped, but then she paused. "You saw Jane?"

"Um... kind of." She did *see* her.

Catherine's face turned an even paler shade of white. "What did she say? What did *you* say? Gods, that girl has a mouth on her. Just what we need."

Norah gave a smirk. "Actually, I didn't speak to her."

"Thank the gods," Catherine said with a sigh. "I'll have to set expectations better with the guard. We can't rely on courtesies for avoiding conversation."

"Oh, yes." *The guard.* "And add Titus to my list of people," Norah said as she held up four fingers. "And Liaman. There are more guards, but I forget the rest."

Catherine pursed her lips.

Norah looked at her grandmother squarely. "I'm not going to be able to keep this up for long. Adrian figured me out as well."

Catherine let out an exasperated huff. "Adrian knows? Norah! At this rate, the whole kingdom will know!"

"What do you expect?" Norah snapped back, her own desperation lashing out. "I'm not going to be able to fool everyone! These are smart people who've known me for a long time. They know something isn't right." Norah put her face in her hands, letting the cold of her fingers take away the heat from her cheeks. "I have to get my memories back. I have to find out what's blocking them."

Norah glanced up to find Catherine staring at her with an expression she didn't understand. Her eyes narrowed. "What?"

"I have an idea," the regent said.

Norah raised a brow, waiting. "Ummm... normally when people say something like that, they follow it up with the actual idea."

Catherine shook her head, breathless by whatever sudden thought had come to her. "Tonight. I have to do something first. I'll come back tonight."

Norah gaped at her, thoroughly confused. "Wait. What's your idea?"

"No time!" the regent said as she swept out of the room. "I'll see you this evening."

Norah snorted in disbelief.

Alexander sat in his study, looking through a stack of parchments, yet not reading them. He couldn't seem to keep hold of his mind. His thoughts kept returning to her—Norah.

He told himself what he always had: she had a path, one that would save Mercia, a path that he couldn't interfere with. But when she was near, it all came crashing back. The way she smiled, the way she laughed, the way she used to look at him. *Used to.*

"I thought I might find you here."

He looked up to see his brother.

Adrian smiled as he leaned against the doorframe. He stepped into the study and crossed the room. "You probably haven't eaten all day," he said as he put a plate with a pear and a biscuit in front of Alexander.

Alexander sighed, leaning back in his chair and giving a small smile at the pear. "Thank you," he said. Alexander loved his brother. They were very close; they had been ever since Adrian moved to the castle to be with him after their mother died. Adrian had been young, and her death had hit him hard. With their father busy with the duties of being lord justice, Alexander played the role of both parents and managed Adrian's studies while he himself trained. Where he fell short, there was always Catherine, who tended to them both as her own. In fact, Adrian took to her much like she were his own grandmother, as Alexander did as a child, although Adrian seemed to get away with more than Alexander ever could.

But now it was Adrian who often looked after Alexander. Adrian glanced around for a wine pitcher. "Do you want a drink?"

"No. Thank you." He could use some wine, but he had more work to do yet.

Adrian moved around and dropped into the wingback chair in front of the desk. "Are you all right?" he asked.

He couldn't answer that. "It's been a long day."

Adrian sighed, and Alexander knew he wasn't happy with his response. Adrian saw through him.

"Are you sure you're all right?" Adrian pressed.

Alexander closed a book that was open on the side of the desk. "Why do you keep asking me that?" He knew Adrian could see Norah was different. At least he didn't know—

"Because she doesn't remember you."

Alexander's eyes shot up, locking with his brother's. "What did you say?"

"Norah. She doesn't remember you. Or anyone else here."

The breath left his lungs. "She told you?"

Adrian bobbed his head to the side. "After I guessed." His voice softened. "Why didn't you tell me?"

Alexander sighed and rose from the desk. "The fewer people who know, the better."

"But I'm your brother," Adrian argued. "I can help you."

"You can help me by doing as you're told," Alexander said shortly.

"You should've told me. Why didn't you?"

"Catherine wouldn't permit it." He looked at the desk as he reached down and leaned his weight on it. "And I couldn't. You would... know what it meant, and I can't take another face looking at me... with pity."

They sat in silence.

Adrian finally broke the quiet. "To be fair, I have a much better pity face than Grandmother," he said, trying to lighten the air.

Alexander let out a snort, accepting his brother's effort. "Everyone has a better pity face than Catherine."

Adrian smiled.

They sat in the quiet, letting the ease return between them.

"Are you going to tell Norah?" Adrian asked.

Alexander sobered. "You can't call her that anymore. Things are different now. You must use her titles."

"Will you tell her?" he asked again.

Alexander shook his head slowly, staring at the three-candle holder on the desk. One candle had burned to the bottom, and as its flame died, a line of smoke trailed up until it disappeared into nothing.

"What if she remembers?"

Alexander shrugged. "What if she doesn't?" Then their story would be like the candle.

Adrian's eyes narrowed. "You don't want her to?"

He didn't want to talk about this. "It's not about what I want. It's about what's best for her right now. And what's best for Mercia."

"You should tell her," Adrian pressed.

"I don't have the right!" Alexander snapped, momentarily losing himself.

Adrian fell quiet.

Alexander drew in a long breath, calling his patience back. It was only because his brother loved him that he pushed as he did. He softened. "It's better if she forgets," he said quietly. "That part of her life, anyway. It's better if you forget too."

Adrian sighed. He stood and started toward the door, then he paused. "But will you be able to forget, brother?"

The answer haunted him.

# CHAPTER THIRTEEN

Norah's silk shoes fell silently on the stone as she made her way through the halls from her chamber toward the dining room for dinner. She glanced over her shoulder at her guard behind her. They always felt closer than they were. Especially Titus. Underneath his serious brow, his stern eyes were always on her.

She shifted her focus back in front of her and paused in surprise as she saw Catherine hurrying toward her.

"Come, child," the queen regent said as she grabbed Norah's hand and pulled her back toward her chamber.

Confusion muddled her mind. "Are we not going to eat?"

"Later. You're tired now."

Except Norah wasn't tired. She was hungry. But Catherine's tone told her to go along, and she did. She glanced at Titus as Catherine practically dragged her along. He gave no reaction at all; he simply followed.

When they reached the chamber, Catherine closed the door behind them, leaving Titus and Aaron outside. "Get your cloak. We're going to meet someone."

Norah raised a brow. "Who?"

"Someone with a special gift." Catherine pulled Norah closer, lowering her voice to a whisper. "You know of seers? Those who can see visions of the future? Well, there are rare people, travelers, seers with a greater power—one that allows them to journey into the minds of others."

Norah's heart skipped a beat. "Can someone with this power help me remember?"

"I don't know. But if they can, wouldn't you want them to try?"

"Of course I would." It shouldn't have even been a question.

Catherine grasped Norah's hands. "It's important no one knows of this visit, not even Alexander."

"Why?" Norah was growing tired of secrets.

"Travelers are forbidden in Mercia. Many believe their power to go into one's mind is the work of great evil, of dark magic."

"Is that what Alexander thinks?"

Catherine snicked her tongue against the roof of her mouth. "Hardly. But he wouldn't approve of us flitting off in the night to meet an unlawful mind worker."

It amused Norah that her grandmother would worry about what Alexander did or did not approve of.

Catherine led Norah through the bath and into the cabinet chamber. "Where's your cloak?" she asked, but pulled it from a hanger before Norah had a chance to answer.

Norah wrapped the cloak around her, then took a second one that Catherine held out for her.

"Take this one for me," the queen regent said.

Her brows drew together in confusion, but she didn't have time to question her. Catherine pulled up the center rug and opened a hidden door beneath with a small staircase leading downward.

Norah's eyes widened in surprise. "What's that?" she gasped.

"A hidden passageway. All castles have them. It's how you snuck around when you were younger. You always had your guard on alert." She looked back at Norah. "And don't think that big bald one has forgotten."

*Titus.*

"Now, go to the bottom of the stairs and wait for me. I'll meet you there."

Catherine herded Norah down into the stairwell. Once Norah was clear of the door, her grandmother closed it again, then flopped the rug back over the top.

Norah turned back to the stairs, holding the railing carefully as she made her way down into the darkness. How strange to find herself here, but her lips curved into a smile. Catherine was showing herself to be quite the free spirit as well. Norah felt even closer to her.

She did as she was told and waited for her grandmother at the bottom of the stairs. It wasn't long before she saw the faint light of her grandmother's lantern approaching from a side tunnel. Once she reached Norah, she took the extra cloak and wrapped it around herself.

Without a word, Catherine led her through a series of cold, dark passageways, winding and weaving, before they finally emerged onto a cobblestone street.

"Stay close," Catherine said. "I'll not have you lost in the city."

*The city.* Norah felt a wave of excitement. She hadn't been able to explore the city yet, having been limited to only the castle on the isle.

"How will we get across the bridge?" she asked.

"We already are, my dear."

Norah's pulse quickened, and she looked around to get her bearings, but the connected buildings along the street limited her sight.

"This way," Catherine called, and swept forward under the cover of darkness. Adjoining houses lined the narrow streets, and they moved quietly so as not to draw attention. The queen regent was fast, floating through the streets, and Norah almost had to run to keep up with her. They turned down a side alleyway and followed the rowed homes until they finally came to a door. Her grandmother gave two knocks, and they waited.

The door creaked open. A woman, Catherine's age, looked out.

"Esther," Catherine greeted her.

"Catherine." The woman smiled and opened the door, inviting them in. Esther was taller than Norah's grandmother, and thin but with a round face. She wore a simple, green linen dress, and her long white hair fell over her shoulder in a thick braid.

Esther gave Norah a warm smile and bowed her head. "Princess," she greeted. Then she turned to Catherine. "I'll get Nemus."

Norah followed her grandmother in, pulling off her cloak and waiting patiently. She looked around. It was a modest home, made warm by the handmade quilts and candles.

A few moments later, Esther emerged from the back room with an older man, who Norah suspected was Esther's husband. He was tall, but the hunch in his back made him only slightly taller than his wife. His short, white hair matched his short-cut beard, and he wore a light brown tunic over his darker brown trousers.

"Catherine," Nemus greeted her warmly. "Princess Norah, we were so happy to hear of your return."

Norah gave a small nod, noticing their informality with her grandmother. They were friends.

"Nemus, we need your help," Catherine said. "We have a burden we share in the strictest of confidence."

"Of course," he answered, his white brows dipping together.

"While Norah has returned to us, her memories didn't come with her. We have to find a way to bring them back."

He looked at Norah in surprise. "No memories?"

Norah shook her head. It felt strange to be so open about it now.

Catherine let out a breath. "I thought you might be able to help."

He nodded. "I can try. Come."

Nemus ambled over to a small nook and took a seat cross-legged on a large woven floor pillow. He gave Norah a nod and motioned her to sit on a pillow across from him. She settled awkwardly in her dress.

He pulled a quill and penned ink markings down his forearms, his lips moving in silence as he drew circles, lines, and interwoven triangles, designs she'd never seen before. Then he reached out and poured wine into a small bowl and set it down in front of him. Nemus pricked his finger with the tip of a blade, letting a few drops of blood fall into the bowl. He breathed silent words over the mixture and held it out for her.

Norah raised a brow. Surely he didn't mean for her to drink it.

"Do you want me to see?" he asked at her hesitation.

She swallowed. *Perhaps not anymore.* But then, reluctantly, she nodded. "Yes."

"Then you must drink," he told her.

She glanced up at her grandmother, and Catherine gave her a reassuring nod.

Norah shuddered back her aversion and accepted the bowl, taking a deep breath before drinking. The wine was tart, and the thought of blood mixed within made her stomach queasy. She forced it down and handed the bowl back to Nemus.

"Close your eyes," he told her.

She complied, pushing out a breath and dropping her eyelids closed.

"Go inside your mind," he continued. "Imagine yourself sitting in a room."

She imagined herself as she was now, sitting on a floor cushion in Nemus's home.

"You must see it in your mind," he told her. "The room. Do you see it?"

Norah focused on the visual. "Yes," she said.

"Don't be alarmed," he told her.

Why would she be alarmed? There was a faint flutter around her, and suddenly she saw a man before her in her mind. Norah startled, and Nemus chuckled.

"Happens to everyone the first time." He was younger, much younger, and he gave her a small smile.

"Is this how you are in this world?" she asked him.

"I am however I want to be." His words were different now, not heard by her ears but from inside her head. "I project into your mind, and I can control how you see me."

"Are you able to be someone else?" she asked from inside.

Nemus frowned. "If I know the intricacies of their looks, yes. But I prefer being myself." He glanced around, noting that the room was his own. "This looks familiar," he told her, and she gave an awkward smile.

He reached out his hand. "Come," he said. "Let's walk around, shall we?"

She took his hand and stood, and suddenly the cushions they had been sitting on were gone. Norah looked around the room and noticed a series of doors. There were more than there had been before. He motioned to one, and they went to it. He pushed it open, and they stepped inside. It was her chamber in the castle.

Nemus turned, looking all around him. "It's been a long time since I've seen the castle, any part of it. This is your room today?"

She looked at the ornate bed and the west-facing windows. "Yes."

He nodded. "Let's try another." He led her back to the door they had come through, but instead of opening back up to the room in Nemus's home, it opened into the small homestead that she and Alexander had sheltered in before coming to Mercia, where she'd slept on the bed by the fire while Alexander kept watch by the door.

The walls fell away now, and she followed Nemus through what seemed to be stages of her memories. One after the other she saw: meeting her grandmother, meeting the council, Alexander taking her through the library.

Nemus shook his finger at the lord justice and sighed with a crease in his brow. "That boy is everywhere in here," he said as he looked around her memories.

Norah couldn't help the small giggle that escaped her. Nemus looked young, but he had the vexation of an old man.

"He's been a large part of my time back," she admitted.

"And in your long-term memories, judging by the clarity."

In her memories... Where?

He looked around again, and Norah noted a wall with another door. Nemus reached out to push it open but was met with resistance. A look of confusion flashed across his face, and he pushed on the door more firmly. It still didn't move.

"What's wrong?" she asked.

"It won't open."

*Obviously*. "Why won't it open?"

He looked at her. "It's *your* door. *You* put it there."

"What do you mean *I* put it there?"

"Mind workers can't put things into your mind like this, not permanently." He sighed. "Let's try together." They both reached out and put their weight against the door, but it wouldn't budge.

Suddenly, Nemus fell to his knees, as if something had struck him. He disappeared from her mind, and Norah opened her eyes. They were once again back in Nemus's home, sitting on the cushions.

Her eyes widened at the trickle of blood falling from his left nostril. "You're bleeding!"

"What happened?" Catherine gasped as Esther moved quickly to Nemus with a cloth.

He wiped his nose and took a moment before looking back up at Norah. "Nothing to worry about. I just used a little too much energy. I'll be fine."

"Are they there?" Catherine asked. "The memories?"

"Well, something's there, but it's blocked." He looked at Norah. "By her, I think."

Norah glanced at Catherine, then back to Nemus. "How do I unblock it?"

"I don't know," Nemus said as he wiped his nose again with the cloth. "I don't have enough power to help you."

Norah looked at her grandmother as a wave of disappointment washed over her.

"We understand," Catherine said. "Thank you for trying, Nemus."

"Wait," Norah said with a start. She wasn't leaving without getting as much information as she could. "You're a seer of visions too?"

"I see them, yes."

"Are you the one who saw me taking the Shadow throne?"

He shook his head. "No. Others have, but I have not. Seers may see the same visions, or they may not. No seer sees all visions."

Norah frowned and looked at her grandmother.

"But," he said, drawing Norah's eyes back to him, "I saw the vision of your capture. And the breach of Mercia. It was I who showed your father."

Norah's breath came in quick clips now. "Are you able to show them to me?"

"Norah, we've asked enough already," Catherine pressed her. "And these are old visions, changed visions—ones that will never come to be. Your father saw to that."

But that wasn't enough. "Still," she said to Nemus, "can you? Please?"

Nemus nodded. Norah heard Catherine sigh, but she ignored it.

They both closed their eyes again, returning to the room inside her mind. He motioned to the front door and led Norah outside into the darkness. But they were no longer in the city. Mercia was gone, and in its place lay shadows of rocky hills. Her mouth hung open as a large army passed silently through the night. Between their ranks rode an ominous figure on top of a destrier. He looked more wraith than man, floating through the darkness wearing a horned helm and bladed shoulder armor. Draped across his horse in front of him lay a lifeless young woman. Norah couldn't see her face, but her breath wavered at the long tendrils of snowy hair that fell down the side.

"Is that me?" she whispered.

Nemus gave a nod. He held his arm out, and the army fell away.

They stood inside the courtyard of the castle—the castle of Mercia. It was daylight now, but men cloaked in darkness surrounded them, with their faces covered. These weren't Northmen. In the center of the courtyard stood gallows, with three ropes hanging from the beam above. Three men were led toward them, and she recognized Councilman Edward among them.

Norah watched in horror as her councilmen were ushered up in single file, pushed along by a monster of a man. This man was different from the vision before but equally haunting. He wore nothing on his arms and torso, as if he were invincible. His skin bore dark ink patterns, and his face was covered in a wrap, from which only his eyes showed. Edward screamed words she couldn't hear, but she could see the terror in his face as the ropes were looped and tightened around the men's necks. The monster executioner nodded, and the floor fell out from underneath their feet. Norah covered her mouth to hold in her own scream. Two of the councilmen hung limply, their necks immediately broken, but Edward squirmed at the end of his rope.

Norah couldn't watch anymore, but she couldn't look away. She could only stand in horror. A cry escaped her lips. Finally, as if a sliver of mercy existed, the monster of a man pulled a dagger and ran Edward through with the blade. Then, he turned, and the dark pools of his eyes looked right at her. Seeing her.

Norah gasped and opened her eyes with a start, shaking and struggling for her breath. They were in Nemus's home again, sitting on the floor. Catherine was by her side, taking her hand and holding her steady.

"Are you all right, child?"

Norah swallowed back the fear in her chest, inhaling deeply to keep from vomiting. That was the breach Catherine had warned of—the Shadowmen taking her, taking Mercia, and bringing death to them all. Her eyes found Nemus again.

"That's why your father took you and hid you away from the world," he told her.

Norah waited a moment for her breath to come back to her. "And you can't see where he took me?"

"I cannot."

"Is there another like you? Someone with more power?" As she said the words, they sounded rude in her ears. She hoped he didn't take it that way.

"You'll find only seers in Mercia, not travelers. I know none like me." His voice held a hint of sorrow. "I'm sorry."

"So, my father, he changed the future?"

He nodded.

"Can you see what happens now?"

Nemus shook his head. "I have no control over what the Eye shows me, but there have been no visions of you since you left, by any seers, that I'm aware of. Perhaps there's a shield over you, like seers have, a shield that doesn't allow the Eye to see you or know where you are. I imagine this relates to your memory loss."

"Who could have put this shield there? Another seer?"

Nemus shook his head. "I don't know who would have that kind of power."

# Chapter Fourteen

Catherine led them back through the streets toward the tunnels. Norah followed blindly, her mind racing. The vision of her councilmen would haunt her. And this shield—whatever blocked her from being seen in visions—who had put it there? Nemus had said he didn't know who would have that kind of power. If she could figure out how to remove it, would it bring her memories back?

They made their way quickly through the tunnels in the dark. Norah was amazed Catherine could remember the way. "How do you know all these passages?" she asked.

"I've been here a long time, my dear. And I've had many secrets to keep." They turned down another hall, and Catherine stopped. She felt the pockets of her gown.

"What is it?"

"Gods," Catherine muttered. "My key, the one for my own chamber. I've left it at Nemus's."

"Oh, that's all right, we can go back."

"No, no. I'll go. If you follow this walk two halls down, you'll see the stair on the right to your room."

"Wait." Absolutely not. No. *No.* "I can't go by myself."

"Oh, Norah, you'll be fine. I can't go back out through your chamber, anyway. The guard has already seen me leave. They think you're alone inside. Be sure to straighten the rug on the top after. I don't want anyone finding that door."

"What about *me* finding the door?" Walking through dark tunnels wasn't what she wanted to be doing. At all.

"Don't be dramatic. As I said, you're perfectly fine. No one knows of these tunnels but me." But she lingered for a moment. "I'm sorry about tonight, Norah," she said softly. "I really thought this would work."

Norah had hoped it would work too. She shrugged. "We'll keep trying."

Catherine patted her on the arm. "That we will. I'll see you in the morning, my dear."

With that, Catherine turned and disappeared into the darkness, leaving Norah holding the small lantern. She sighed and then turned down the tunnel toward her room.

It was difficult to see, even with the lantern, which barely lit the space in front of her. Fear rippled through her. Not from the dark—she wasn't afraid of the dark. She feared failure, disappointing those who cared about her and letting down her people and her kingdom. How could she be queen if she knew nothing? How could she make good decisions for her people when she didn't understand? And how could she fight an enemy she didn't know, especially an enemy like the one she saw tonight?

She paused when she noticed a hall, then cursed under her breath. She hadn't been paying attention. Did she already pass one, or was this the first? Surely she would have noticed if one had come up sooner. She kept going.

When she came to another hall, she turned and took it down to the end, where she found the stairwell. *Finally.* She held the rail as she climbed the stairs, but when she got to the top, the door wasn't above her head as before. It stood in front of her. She was at the wrong door.

Norah cursed under her breath. Maybe if she went back one hall? But what if she had passed two? She had walked quite a way while distracted by her thoughts. She glanced at the lantern. The candlewick was near its end. What she didn't want to do was get lost looking for a secret door with no lantern at all. She pursed her lips. Where was she now?

Her stomach knotted at the thought of returning to her chamber from the outside—where Titus stood. She supposed it wasn't the worst thing that could happen. It would be just like old times?

She turned the knob to the door as quietly as she could. It opened with no resistance, and she peeked through. A breath of relief escaped her. An empty room. She ducked out of what appeared to be a closet on the outside, then closed the door behind her. Everything was fine—she'd just figure out where she was and make her way back to her chamber.

Norah slipped out into the hall, appreciating the quiet of her silk shoes. It was late evening now, and she wasn't expecting anyone about, but she'd rather make it back to her chamber without anyone seeing her. There would be less to explain.

Light spilled out from a room ahead, and she slowed. She wasn't sure what room it was; she hadn't been in this hall before. When she reached the open door, she sidled along the edge of the frame, leaning forward just enough to peek inside. It was a study. Her heart beat faster.

Alexander sat at his desk, reading through several documents. The candle to his right dropped a trail of wax down its side—he'd been there for a while. He sighed as he put one parchment down and then picked up another.

She couldn't help herself. "What are you working on?" she asked.

He looked up in surprise, and a hint of a smile came to his lips. He rose from his chair. As his mind seemed to put things together, his brow creased. "Where did you come from?" he asked.

She stepped inside the study and shrugged. "Just walking."

His eyes ran over her cloak. "Outside?"

*Hammel's hell.* "Just around the castle. I... was cold." She bit her lip. That definitely sounded like a lie.

Alexander raised a brow.

She drew closer, and his eyes followed. She took a seat on the wingback chair in front of the desk, and he slowly sat back down. His face had a warm familiarity, and she struggled to separate whether it was the comfort of their new friendship, or something more. She spied a biscuit and pear on a plate on the corner of the desk, and her stomach grumbled. She hadn't eaten anything since Catherine had taken her to the seer. "Are you going to eat that?" she asked.

He glanced at the plate. "No. Are you hungry?" His brow dipped. "Have you not eaten?"

"I wasn't hungry earlier, but I just realized I am a little now." She grabbed the pear off the plate.

"I'll get you some food. Don't eat that. Adrian brought it hours ago." He moved to stand.

"No, it's all right," she said quickly. "The pear's fine."

He sighed and gave a small smile. "I'll have to make sure we do a better job taking care of our queen."

His words sat uncomfortably in her ears. *Queen*. She swallowed. She had no business being queen.

"Are you all right?" he asked. "Have I said something?"

She turned the pear in her hands, brushing her fingers over the smooth skin of the fruit. She wanted to tell him about the visit to the traveler, about seeing the visions, but Catherine had said not to. "My grandmother says that the council will push for my coronation right away." She drew her eyes back up, searching for confirmation.

He nodded. "It's true."

"How soon?"

"A few days."

A wave of panic washed through her. "A few days?" She wouldn't even know her way around the castle properly within a few days. How could she be ready to be queen and stand against a monster the likes of what she'd seen tonight?

"I know it seems soon," he tried to assure her, "but you'll figure things out. You always do."

Norah snorted in frustration. "I can't even figure out how to keep my memory loss a secret. Did you speak to Adrian?"

Alexander nodded calmly. "He told me."

"Talk about someone figuring things out. Well... he did. So did James. I hadn't even said three sentences, and James... told me I was lying. Which I was." She closed her eyes, silently cursing herself.

"Don't fault yourself for Adrian and James. I should have told them. There was no way they wouldn't have known something was wrong. They know you too well."

She shook her head. "It's more than just that. I can't do this."

Alexander leaned forward with his forearms on the edge of the desk. "Norah, you're going to be a great queen."

"You don't know that," she said, standing and bumping back the chair. "I have no idea what I'm doing."

Alexander moved to speak, but then stopped. The corner of his mouth curved into a slight smile. He rolled the documents in front of him into a leather binding and rose from the desk. "Come with me."

His sudden pivot in the conversation made her brow dip with suspicion. "Where?" she asked.

"I want to show you something."

She hoped it didn't involve navigating back through a series of dark tunnels. Her gaze met Alexander's. He offered his hand.

To hell if there were tunnels. She slipped her hand in his, and his skin warmed hers. It felt nice, and right.

He led her out of the study but paused in the hall. "Wait," he said. "Where's your guard?"

Norah twisted a little. "They... might... be back at my chamber door."

"Back at your door?" His brow furrowed. "You're alone? How did you slip out?"

She shrugged as she pursed her lips to the side. "Quietly?"

His jaw tightened, and the blue of his eyes burned brighter. Norah found herself not entirely annoyed at his concern. In fact, she wasn't annoyed at all.

"Never mind for now," he said. "Come on. We'll discuss this later."

She couldn't help a small smile.

Alexander led her through several halls, which were lit only by the dim glow of candles in chandeliers. Their shadows danced against the stone.

It was the first time he'd taken her hand, but he held it so naturally, like it belonged to him.

They came upon a guarded door, and Alexander nodded to the soldier, who stepped aside. He pushed it open and looked back at her, giving her a reassuring smile.

Through the door was another long hallway that led to another structure of the castle. They walked through the arched stone, finally coming to the hallway's end. Ahead of them, the hall spilled into a vast, round chamber, with a glass ceiling dropping moonlight into the great room below.

"Watch your step," he told her as he started down a spiral staircase to the bottom. His fingers tightened around hers to offer support.

"What is this place?" she asked.

"You'll see."

As they reached the bottom, she noted large openings carved into the walls. Each opening held a stone sarcophagus. *Tombs.* They were tombs. And there were so many.

"Is this supposed to lift my spirits?" she asked, raising a brow. "I share how I feel woefully inadequate, and you bring me to a room full of tombs?"

Alexander chuckled. "No. I mean, yes, it is supposed to lift your spirits. Although now I can understand how this might seem very odd." He gave her hand a gentle pull. "But I want you to see something."

She let him pull her farther into the chamber.

"This place is called the Hall of Souls. It's the tomb of the kings of Mercia," Alexander told her. "And queens."

Despite being in the home of the dead in the darkness of night, there was a beauty to it. Intricate carvings lined the walls between the cists.

In the center of the room were stairs to a small platform with a singular tomb that seemed to gleam under the rays of the moon. Inset in the stone were thick strips of wood engraved with scenes of battle triumphs.

"Here, look," he said, leading her up the center stairs to the sarcophagus in the middle of the chamber. "Only the kings and queens of Mercia have come here, with the occasional stealthy lord justice." His face held a smirk.

She smiled back.

He reached out and put his hand on the foot of the cist. "This is the tomb of King Hagen, the original great king of Mercia, who built this kingdom many generations before you. Put your hand here," he said, touching the engraving at the foot.

She reached out and felt the wood inset. It was smooth, almost polished.

"What do you feel?" he asked.

She shook her head. "Nothing. It's... smooth."

He took her hand and moved it further to the side. "And here?"

His touch was distracting, but she forced her mind to the carving. "Um... not as smooth?"

He nodded, his golden hair catching the moonlight from the windows above. "Think of how many men must have come here to ask King Hagen for strength, polishing this wood smooth with only the touch of their skin. How many hands does that take? How many touches?"

She moved her fingers back to the polished engraving, feeling its smoothness, to where her father must have touched and his father before him.

"See, Norah," he said softly, "you aren't the only one who's thought yourself lost."

The calm of reassurance settled her, and she looked at him. "Thank you," she whispered.

Alexander's lips parted to say more, but then he stopped. She glanced down at her hand, still in his. It fit so perfectly, warm, protected, and safe—the way he made her feel.

"I should get you back to your chamber," he said, finally breaking the spell.

*Right.* Her chamber. She felt a wave of disappointment, and it surprised her. She forced a nod, and he led her back the way they had come.

As they walked back to her chamber, she saw Titus's posture shift before they even reached him. Seeing her outside—he hadn't expected this.

"Sorry," she mouthed to the large guard as they reached the door. She turned back to Alexander.

"Good night, Your Highness," he told her. His formality had returned.

"Good night, Lord Justice." She turned back toward her chamber. "Sorry," she whispered again to Titus as she slipped past him and inside.

# CHAPTER FIFTEEN

The door to Norah's chamber swung open. "Rise, child!" Catherine said as she swept in. "Quickly!"

Norah sat straight up in bed. Daylight shined through the window. Had she really slept until the sun had risen? She wiped her eyes. She'd slept—she'd actually slept. And it felt amazing.

"Quickly!" her grandmother pushed again as Rebecca hurried in with a dress.

Catherine's tone quashed Norah's restful satisfaction. Why quickly? "What's going on?"

"The council has called a state now that James and Elias have returned. I thought we'd have more time, both James and I pushed, but no. It's today."

Today. Her pulse picked up. Today—*no.* "I can't meet with the council today." She wasn't anywhere near ready for the state. She still didn't entirely know what that meant, only that they would ask questions—questions that she had no answers for. They'd want to know where she'd been, and while Catherine had come up with a response that she'd rehearsed a hundred times, it still didn't sound true. Because it wasn't. And then when they discovered her...

She didn't want to think about that. She *couldn't* think about that and keep control of her nerves.

"Don't worry, my dear," her grandmother said, seeming to read her mind. "I'm still queen regent. I'll lead us through. Everything will be fine."

But she didn't believe that. Even James wasn't confident she'd fool the council—he'd told her so directly.

Catherine practically ripped Norah's nightgown from her just as Rebecca swept around with a corset, tying it and pulling it tight before Norah could adjust for her breath. The gown came over her head, from her maid or her grandmother, she wasn't sure. Not that it mattered. She just needed it on. Panic flowed through her veins, and being rushed didn't help. She forced her mind back to the question the council would ask her first—where she'd been...

"Remember, you'll say you've been kept well by a secret ally, one that wishes to remain secret," Catherine said, as if reading her mind. "Instead of focusing on the past, I'll drive our conversation to the present and the future. We'll talk about your marriage to Phillip."

Norah stiffened. She'd rather tell the council about her memory loss.

Catherine tugged the fitted gown straight, then pushed Norah to the vanity and pressed her abruptly down in the chair. She pulled the brush from Rebecca's hand and raked it swiftly through Norah's hair. "By now, Phillip will know of your return."

Norah winced, more from his name than the speedy, aggressive hair brushing. This man she didn't know—the man she was expected to wed.

Her grandmother swept back the sides of Norah's hair with floral pins. "We'll hear from him soon, and it shouldn't be hard to occupy their attention with that—it's what's most important, anyway."

Norah's mind reeled. With every fiber of her being, she rejected the notion of this marriage. Her soul clawed against the obligations that chained her and against the path she couldn't choose for herself. Or perhaps she could choose, but there was the weight of so many looking to her—of so many lives depending on her. Turning her back to them would break her. And she found herself feeling the same as she had with James—there was nothing she could do but agree. Nothing she could do but follow. At least for now.

Catherine swept a cloak over Norah's shoulders and pulled her toward the chamber door, and she went. Her guard picked up behind them as they started down the hall, as if herding her toward her future. She swallowed even though her tongue sat dryly in her mouth. *Pretend.* Pretend to be the person she was before. Look the part. Play the part. *Pretend* the best she could.

They exited the castle through the double doors to the outside and walked along the courtyard toward the judisaept. The winter air was cold, and Norah shuddered, but she welcomed it. Anything to distract her spiraling mind.

Beside her, Catherine slowed, and Norah followed her gaze to something on the other side of the courtyard. She squinted against the icy air but couldn't make out what or who it was through the throngs of people gathering.

"What is it?" Norah asked her.

"I don't know," Catherine said, but she'd stopped. Castle guards broke from their posts and hurried toward the crowd.

Suddenly, a scream ripped through the growing masses. Norah's guard swept around her. Another scream sounded, but not one of fear—one of anguish. Norah started toward it.

Catherine caught her hand. "What are you doing?"

"Something's happened—I have to see!" And she pulled her arm from her grandmother's grasp.

"Your Highness," Titus called from behind her, but she ignored him and strode toward the crowd. He followed after with his sword in hand.

She drew closer. The crowd surrounded a large wagon, pulled by four horses caked with dried mud and dirt. The animals stood still, weary and spent from their journey. No one drove the wagon, but it was stacked high with what appeared to be grain sacks in the back, stained in browning crimson. One sat open on the ground, but she couldn't see what was inside. A woman was crying with her arms outstretched toward the wagon as a man pulled her away.

Suddenly, Alexander was in front of her. She jerked in surprise as his arm came out, halting her. "Norah," he said, low, "go back to the castle. I'll be there in a moment."

But she didn't want to go back. "What's in the sacks?"

"Norah." He clasped her arm, gently but firmly, and tried to move her back toward the castle.

"What's in the sacks?" she pressed again.

"Just go back. I'll be there in a moment, and I'll tell you then."

"You'll tell me now," she demanded. Her patience was waning, and she wouldn't leave until she knew what was going on.

His mouth tightened. "We expected the Shadow King to attempt to retake the mountains of Bahoul again, especially if he learned of your return. It's a critical stronghold that used to belong to the Shadowlands. I sent another thousand men for reinforcement."

That still didn't answer her question. "What's in the sacks?"

His lips thinned. "The men I sent. Their heads."

Nausea swept through her as she glanced back at the wagon and its horror-filled cargo. The heads of a thousand men. She wavered. His hand tightened around her arm.

"Go back inside," he said. "I'll come after I've dealt with this."

Titus stepped forward, offering his own arm, but she pulled away from both of them and turned back toward the castle, numb with shock.

Catherine stood just behind her with Edward, James, and two other members of the council.

"Lord Justice!" Edward called out, and hurried after Alexander. The other two councilmen bowed to Norah and followed after.

Catherine reached out and clasped Norah's hand. "It's all right. Everything will be all right."

Norah shook her head, her mouth hanging open. "No, it's not. None of this is all right." She felt James's eyes on her and cast him a desperate gaze. "Are we to discuss this today too?" As if the myriad of other topics weren't enough. As if she wasn't already near breaking. And still she had to face the council. In a matter of moments. She wasn't ready. She couldn't do this.

He shook his head. "No. The state's been postponed."

It was the smallest of mercies compared to everything else, but still the relief of it almost brought tears to her eyes.

"To prepare for your coronation," James added. "You'll be crowned tomorrow."

Norah's heart stopped, and her lungs turned to stone in her chest. She couldn't draw in a breath. "I can't be crowned tomorrow."

"This works in our favor," James said.

"Favor?" she stammered breathlessly.

"We don't have the luxury of time, and this puts pressure to pull the coronation forward before the state. Pressure we need. Things will move quickly now. You must be ready."

"Of course I'm not ready!"

Catherine hushed her and pulled her toward the castle. "Not here," she said sternly.

Not here, not in public. Not that it mattered, with everyone's attention on the wagon of severed heads. Her stomach threatened to rebel. She needed to get away from the courtyard, and she let Catherine pull her back toward her chamber.

No sooner had the door closed when her grandmother said, "Do you see now?"

Norah scoffed in astonishment. "*See*? I see that you'll have me slap a crown on my head so I can hurry and marry! And that's the only thing on all of your minds, not the thousand heads in our courtyard, the heads James says are in our favor!" Her voice came nearly at a scream now. "In what mad world would that be considered in our favor?"

"It helps secure the crown before your ignorance loses it," Catherine snapped back. "And perhaps now it will open your eyes! This is only a token of what the Shadow King has done, and what he will do. You don't want to marry? Well, I don't want a kingdom of severed heads!"

Her grandmother's words silenced her. She didn't want a kingdom of severed heads either.

"Norah, Aleon has the largest army in the world."

"To help me take a Shadow throne I don't want?" She shook her head. "I don't even want this one."

Her grandmother snatched her arm and pulled her close. "Don't ever say that again. Not ever. Not even behind closed doors. Do you hear me?"

Norah drew in an uneven breath, then another. Her desperation was talking for her, and she couldn't let it.

"It's not about wanting the Shadow throne," Catherine argued sharply. "It's about stopping a great evil. It's about saving yourself and your kingdom. And I don't mean evil in simply a vile sense, Norah. He's true evil incarnate. The Shadow King made a pact with Darkness, a pact that required his own heart."

Her eyes narrowed. "A man can't live without his heart."

"He's no longer a man. And out of his pact with Darkness, he was given a demon to command his armies. The blood of men gives this demon strength. It does the bidding of the Shadow King, and in return, it gains the souls of the fallen. And now, the Shadow King has the power to corrupt this entire world and bring death to us all."

Norah's skin prickled. And he was coming for her...

Catherine's hold on her hands softened. "I don't say these things to scare you, child."

It was a little too late for that. Norah swallowed.

"Come. I have to show you something." Still holding Norah's hand, Catherine pulled her out of the chamber and down the hall to a side door leading outside. Norah silently begged that they weren't headed back to the courtyard.

They weren't, and she let out a sigh of relief. She let Catherine lead her down a cobblestone side path to an adjoining stone building with no windows. Her grandmother pushed open the door without knocking, and Norah followed her inside.

They stood in the middle of what appeared to be a sitting room, but all around them were paintings. Hundreds of them. Panels of stretched canvas stood upright and were stacked against the wall, balanced on chairs, and piled high on a center table.

Norah maneuvered slowly through the images, following her grandmother. There were so many—mainly of war but some of celebration. Some were of individuals; there were countless faces.

"Samuel!" Catherine called as they worked their way back.

An older man with thick glasses dressed in a sand-colored tunic and matching trousers appeared in the doorway of an adjoining hall, leaning heavily on his cane. "Ah, Queen Regent," he greeted Catherine. When he saw Norah, he gave a wobbly bow of his head. "Princess Norah. A very unexpected but very welcome surprise."

"The painting," Catherine told him. As if there were only one.

"Ah. Yes, yes." He waved his cane for them to follow as he hobbled through a door and into a back room.

"Which painting?" Norah asked her.

"The only one that matters." Catherine started after the seer.

Norah followed them to the back room. It was much like the first and also had paintings stacked against the walls. This room had more furniture, which, like the room before, seemed to serve only to hold more paintings.

"Are all of these visions?" Norah asked.

"They are," he said as he made his way toward the back.

Norah let her eyes pass from painting to painting in the room of visions. She didn't know what to make of them. Images of death and carnage surrounded her: castle ruins, fallen men, blood pooling in the streets. And in every image of destruction, there was a dark, monstrous man with a horned helm—the Shadow King.

"There," her grandmother said, and she pointed to a large painting against the back wall.

Norah stopped and stared at herself. It was an image of her sitting on a throne of night, with a crown atop her head. She wore white, the color of Mercia, but this wasn't the throne of Mercia.

"It's the Shadow throne," Catherine told her. "Do you see now? You'll take it. You'll overthrow the Shadow King."

Norah could only stare. She almost didn't recognize herself; this woman looked strong. Powerful. Like a queen. It looked nothing like how she felt right now. Her soul still shook from the courtyard, and her mind was still foggy with the day's horror. This woman in the painting wasn't her.

"This can't be me," she breathed.

Catherine clenched Norah's hand tighter. "Of course it's you, my dear. It will be you. Fate's written it."

# CHAPTER SIXTEEN

The day of Norah's coronation came with the sun, and Alexander sat in his chamber polishing his boots. He brushed them meticulously, trying to keep his mind from the thoughts that threatened to consume him. Today Norah would be crowned queen and would be one step closer to marrying King Phillip. They needed Aleon, but that didn't make supporting the marriage any easier.

A knock rattled the door. Before he could answer, Adrian stepped inside. Of course he'd come.

Adrian grinned. "Today's the day, brother."

Alexander raised a brow, but he knew what his brother was referring to. "You don't know that." Sometimes Adrian was too positive.

"What?" his brother scoffed. "Of course I do. You're going to be lord justice. Really this time."

Alexander shook his head as he wrapped the boot brush back in its cloth. "No. The decision hasn't yet been made, and there are others far more qualified than I."

"Like who?"

"Many." Catherine would have put forward a list of names. He suspected the decision would be Lord Branton. The Mercian lord had been a field general before he lost his sword arm in the war, and he'd been a trusted voice to the late King Aamon. His opinions sometimes differed from the council, which was a good thing. He was a good man, and Alexander could respect that decision. He pulled on one boot and then the other. "And even if she has decided, she most likely wouldn't announce it today."

"Councilman Edward said it's customary to name the lord justice on the day of the coronation."

"Councilman Edward has seen exactly one coronation. That hardly represents *customary*."

"Alec," his brother pressed, "get excited! This is real. It's going to happen. I *feel* it." He looked around. "Where's Jude?"

Alexander had sent his servant away. "I wanted to prepare alone."

Adrian shrugged. "I'll help you."

Alexander couldn't help a smile as he rose from the bed. Adrian picked up the polished breastplate from the table and lovingly gave it a wipe with his sleeve before positioning it on Alexander's chest and buckling the straps carefully. Alexander stood as Adrian finished, watching in the cheval mirror. This had been his father's armor. He remembered exactly how his father had looked wearing it. He looked very much like his father now.

Their eyes met in the reflection and Adrian smiled. "Father would be proud of you, Alec," he said, seeming to read his mind. "I am."

Alexander's eyes welled, and Adrian hugged him. Alexander held his brother close, treasuring the moment. Then he cleared his throat as he collected himself and clapped Adrian on the shoulder. "Thank you, brother."

Adrian handed him his sword, and Alexander buckled the belt around his waist.

"Are you ready?" his brother asked with a grin.

*No*, but he nodded, and they stepped out into the sunlit hallway.

They made their way through the crowded castle and toward the throne room. Well-wishers clapped him on the back as he walked through the crowd of people. The lords expected him to be named lord justice. He never considered himself an ambitious man, at least not the way most men were, but he had always hoped to follow in his father's footsteps one day. He'd hoped it was his destiny. Of all the visions Samuel had painted of him, none showed him as the lord justice. But then, they never showed someone else either.

Alexander left Adrian in the mainway and stepped into a side hall, finding the room where Norah was privately waiting. He paused for a moment, watching her. She was beautiful, as she always was, and she took his breath, like she always did. She was dressed in white, the color of Mercia. Ornate silver trim lined her gown, which was long with delicate beading. Her hair was pinned up, with loose curls swept back in twisted braids.

"Norah," he said softly. He should have bowed, but he couldn't take his eyes off her.

She turned and let out a breath. "Alexander. I'm so glad you're here. I'm a nervous wreck."

He couldn't help a small smile. "You needn't be. Remember, you only say two words. And I'm pretty sure you can say anything and it won't matter. In fact, your grandmother may speak for you."

The corner of her mouth turned up through her pursed lips. "So I'm just to stand there and look the part?"

"Well, you do look... very much a queen."

She glanced down at her gown. "I suppose that's the intent."

Time was slipping away from him. "Shortly, I'll be calling you Queen Norah."

"As long as it's not *Your Elegance*."

"Your Regal High," he said, and it finally pulled a real smile from her. Gods, he loved that smile.

"It isn't the ceremony I'm worried about," she said. "I'm not ready."

Neither was he. "No one ever is."

She let out a wavering breath.

"Norah," he said. She looked up at him. "It's not about remembering now. Leading people takes heart, and you've always been the heart of this kingdom. Follow yours, and you'll know what to do."

She pursed her lips into a fragile smile and nodded. "That's exactly what I needed to hear right now," she whispered.

He hoped he could give her some reassurance. If she could only see what he saw in her...

Her eyes moved past him and over his shoulder. He turned to see Catherine. "Queen Regent." He bowed. She gave him a nod, but her stern eye cued his leave. He looked back at Norah and gave her a reassuring nod. "When we speak again, you'll be queen." He gave her a small bow and slipped out of the room.

Norah's eyes trailed Alexander as he left to give her some privacy with her grandmother before the ceremony.

"Look at you," Catherine smiled, clasping her hand. "So much like your mother."

Her mother. *Evanya*. Had she felt the same when she'd married Norah's father? Had she been afraid? Unsure? Worried about disappointing everyone?

"Here," Catherine said, pulling out a velvet box. "I have something for you. You'll be crowned with this during the coronation, but I wanted you to see it first."

Norah removed the top, and her breath caught. Inside sat a gold crown. Carefully, she lifted it from the box. It was heavier than it looked. She ran her fingers over the smooth base, and then up the shaped floral-like edges.

"These represent lilies," Catherine told her, touching the top shapes of the crown. "They were your mother's favorite flowers. Your father would have them brought from Aleon for her." She smiled sadly. "She was taken from us before the crown was completed, but he had it finished, intending to one day give it to you. He would have loved to see this moment."

Norah's lip trembled. "It's beautiful," she breathed.

"Like its queen," her grandmother replied, with tears in her eyes.

Norah threw her arms around her grandmother, hugging her close.

Catherine squeezed her back. "They're with you now, child. And so am I."

Norah took a step back and nodded, unable to speak.

Her grandmother took the crown and put it back into the box. "Now, everything's ready. You needn't fret about anything. And tomorrow, we'll meet with the council and decide on your lord justice. Someone we trust implicitly."

Her stomach twisted. There was only one person she trusted implicitly.

Catherine smiled. "For now, one thing at a time, my dear."

But it was never one thing at a time. Norah swallowed down the lump rising in her throat. If she could just get through this ceremony...

Her heart raced. James had come earlier that morning, giving her the reassurance she had so desperately needed, guiding her toward what she already knew she needed to do. Still, it was hard, and she clenched her hands to keep them from shaking.

"Come now." Catherine smiled. "It's time."

Norah peeked through the double doors to the throne room and felt faint. So many people were inside, surely over a thousand. Her corset and stiff gown did little to help her catch her breath.

"All right, just as we rehearsed," Catherine directed, prodding her into place. "Yes. You'll stand out of sight as I enter. I'll walk to the end. They'll open the doors again, and then you'll come."

Norah nodded as she drew in a deep breath. She could do this, she told herself.

"Smile, my dear," her grandmother told her. "This will be the first time many have seen you. If it helps, keep your eyes on me as you walk."

Norah nodded again, and Catherine hugged her tightly. The doors opened, and she waited to the side as the queen regent walked regally down the center of the hall, toward the dais. The guards again closed the doors, and Norah positioned herself behind them. Servants ran quickly around her, adjusting her gown and making sure everything was in place.

Time seemed to stop, and she wrung her hands nervously. How long could it possibly take for one to walk to the dais? Was Catherine stopping between each step?

Then the doors swung open, and she wished them closed again. Murmurs rippled through the crowd, and she swallowed as she tried to keep herself calm. Never had she seen so many people—it was more than she thought she'd seen just moments before.

"Your Highness," her captain, Caspian, murmured from the side. She glanced at him, and he nodded.

*Walk*. She was supposed to walk.

Slowly, she stepped forward. She took one step, then another. Down the center of the hall she walked—slowly, but all too fast. Her heart raced, and sweat beaded the back of her neck as she clenched together her frozen fingers. Norah looked for her grandmother, but there were too many people. She made her way between the masses on either side, focusing on the red floor runner in front of her.

Focusing.

Following.

Following the red. Dark red.

Dark red like the stained sacks in the back of the wagon in the courtyard. She walked the trail of blood.

Her mind roiled through the past several days, from waking in the forest to this moment. Waking from nothing. Into nothing. Remembering nothing.

Now she was about to be crowned queen. Then she'd wed a man she didn't know—a man, a mortal. She'd unite their armies of mortals. And then she'd face an enemy beyond mortal men.

And the painting. She knew Catherine had shown it to her to give her courage, but it didn't give her courage. It scared her. She didn't know that woman looking back at her—that woman who would take the Shadow throne. What if she couldn't be her? Perhaps the woman she used to be could have. But not *her*. Not *now*.

She slowed.

Everything was happening too fast, and the moment hit her. Hard. The throngs of people were so close. *Too close*. There were so many. *Too many*. The hall seemed to grow smaller. Each step she took came slower, yet faster—shorter, but longer.

She couldn't do this.

She couldn't breathe.

And she stopped.

Whispers breezed through the crowded hall. All eyes were on her—as were their expectations, their judgements. And she could only stand there. She combed the front for her grandmother, but she couldn't find her. She couldn't move.

Then she saw Alexander.

He stood just to the right of the dais, close to her chair. Near to her—where he promised he'd always be. He waited, straight and formal, but his smile was warm. He gave her a reassuring nod.

Air filled her lungs. She could breathe.

His hands were at his side. One flicked open. So subtle, but she saw it. And it called her to him.

She could do this, and she stepped forward again.

Her steps came easier.

His smile grew, and so did her courage.

As she reached the front, the high priest held out his hand, taking hers, and helped her step up. An ornate chair stood in the center of the dais where she turned and sat, just as she'd rehearsed, or rather, as she thought she'd rehearsed. She didn't know anymore. Every rational thought—every instruction she'd been given, every piece of advice—abandoned her now. She could only sit and hope it was right.

The priest held his arms high. "We assemble in the hall of our great kings, whose wisdom we call upon, and under the eyes of our gods, whose favor we seek, to crown Mercia's new queen."

Norah glanced at Alexander and found him staring back at her. He didn't move, but the air between them carried his strength to her—strength she drew in. Her eyes drifted to her grandmother, whose gaze sat firmly on Alexander. She prayed he didn't look to see the regent's daggered glare. But his eyes were only on her.

"You are charged with the protection of our people," the priest said, "of our lands, of our traditions, of the values that are the very foundations of our souls."

Her heartbeat drowned the rest of the priest's words. She was sure he said something about the gods, probably another responsibility as queen. A prayer, maybe. She couldn't focus.

The priest pulled her crown from the velvet box and stood before her, bringing her attention back to the ceremony. He placed it on her head. A servant held the sacred scepter, which the priest took and placed in her right hand.

"Rise," he told her.

Norah stood, holding the scepter tightly, and looked out across her people. *Her people.* The priest draped a long robe over her shoulders. Had that been part of the rehearsal? She wasn't sure. It didn't matter. She was cold, and it helped.

"Do you vow to govern the people of Mercia, to lead them, protect them, serve them, and deliver judgment and justice according to our laws and our customs?"

Her heart pulsed in her chest. Heat flushed through her. Hot. She was too hot now.

"I vow," she managed. She'd spoken the two words Alexander had mentioned only a few moments before. Of course, he expected no more.

"And so, you are named Queen Norah Elizabeth Andell, Regal High, and may the gods guide your hand for the strength of our people."

*Regal High*. A king's title. Her eyes shot to Alexander, and he winked at her. How had he...

Cheers rang out from the crowd, and she looked across the hall. There were so many smiling faces, so many people depending on her. So much responsibility.

And she wavered.

The responsibility—she was queen now.

She was *queen*.

Norah wanted to sit down again, but with all eyes on her, with the sacred scepter and the coronation robe, she could only stand and do her duty.

She had a responsibility—and she'd never been more certain. There was nothing James had told her that morning that she hadn't already known. Her eyes found the councilman in the front, not far from her grandmother. He gave a nod.

Norah raised her hand, bringing the people to silence. Her heart beat like it would break from her chest, but her voice came steady. "My first act as queen shall be to appoint my lord justice."

She breathed deeply, refusing to look at Catherine. She already knew the icy gaze she'd find. "Alexander Rhemus, come forward."

The priest gave a nod, extending out his hand for Alexander to approach. Alexander stepped in front of her. His eyes burned a brilliant blue.

"Kneel," she told him, following the sequence James had walked through with her.

Alexander dropped to his knees and held his hands out, palms up. His face was calm, but there was an exaggerated rise and fall to his chest. This was his moment, the day he followed the path of his father. The emotion pulsed from him.

"Alexander Rhemus," she said, "I appoint you lord justice of Mercia, high commander, proxy of the Queen, and protector of Mercia and her people."

Not a word had been forgotten. Norah had said it in her mind a thousand times, and what made it flow so easily was that she believed it. There was only one right decision, and it was Alexander. She dipped her fingers into the bowl of oil held by the priest. Slowly, she drew her fingertips along his palms. "May your hands be my hands."

She ran her thumb across his lips. "May your words be my words."

Then she reached and scribed a line on his breastplate with her fingers, just above the winterhawk. "May your heart be my heart."

Norah smiled down at him. "Rise, Lord Justice."

Alexander stood with emotion thick in his eyes. Then he took his place by her side, and cheers of approval deafened the hall.

Alexander was already in the great hall by the time Norah arrived. He watched as she stepped into the celebration, and cheers erupted. Several lords and their wives stopped by to offer their well-wishes to him, and he forced himself to peel his eyes from her long enough to extend his thanks. Then he turned his attention back to her.

She was beautiful. She captured the room the way she always did, filling the air with her light. He couldn't help but smile. He heard a faint call to his right, but it wasn't enough to pull him away.

"Alexander," the voice came again, more sharply now.

*Catherine.* Although not required now that she was no longer queen regent, he bowed his head. "You look stunning today," he greeted her.

She stood beside him with her eyes across the hall on Norah. "Flattery won't win my support."

Her words surprised him. Alexander looked at her. "Do you not support me as lord justice?"

She didn't answer, and it wounded him.

He pushed out a breath. "Did you not name me so yourself?"

"It's not that you won't make a fine lord justice, Alexander. The gods know you already do. But Norah wasn't here to cloud your mind before."

His pulse beat heavily in his ears. He looked out across the hall. "Do you question my commitment to my duty?"

Catherine put her hand on his arm, drawing him to look back at her. "Of course not. But it will only make the path harder. For both of you."

"My place is by her side. She's my queen."

"But she's not yours."

He knew this, but her words cut him. Still, he showed nothing. He admitted nothing.

Catherine sighed, looking back out across the hall. "But regardless of my worry and my attempts to keep you from it, you were always destined for this. I wish your father were here. He'd be so very proud of you."

He drew in a breath as he fought back a wave of emotion. "Are you?"

Catherine squeezed his arm as tears brimmed her eyes. "Of course I am." Then she stepped up on her toes and pulled him down, kissing him gently on his cheek. "Congratulations, my dear boy. There's no one more worthy. I only fear for you both." Then she squeezed his arm once again before leaving him to the celebration.

Her words hung heavy, reeling him into a mist of disquiet, that he almost didn't notice Norah approaching.

"Congratulations, Lord Justice," she said.

A smile crept back to his lips, and his worry was forgotten, as all worries were when she was near. "Congratulations, Queen Norah," he said with a bow.

"Please don't call me that," she said in a hushed voice. "I'm barely keeping it together between yesterday and today."

"Oh, I'm sorry. Your *Regal High.*"

She laughed, and for that moment, he'd never been happier. He wanted to help take the burden away and make her forget—even if for only a moment—that the world hung on her shoulders.

"I feel like since the priest said it, it's proper now," she said.

"It *is* proper."

She shook her head, amazed. "How did you even manage that?"

"With my charm," he joked, and she laughed again.

To have her back, to have her laughing again... He hadn't dreamed it was possible. The deep pools of her eyes drew him in and held him. She was beautiful. And she was home.

He forced himself to break away and look back out across the hall, just as a familiar face approached.

His smile faded, and his chest tightened. He knew this was something he'd have to manage eventually, but he had hoped it wouldn't be tonight. Norah followed his gaze to the fair-haired woman. It was Ismene, the woman Catherine had been working so diligently to see him wed. He stood quietly as she approached.

As she drew close, Alexander forced a welcoming nod. "Queen Norah, may I present Ismene Dartan," he said.

Ismene gave a polite smile and curtsied.

"Ismene," Norah said. "A pleasure to meet you."

"The pleasure is mine, Queen Norah. Welcome home, and congratulations!"

Norah's eyes turned to Alexander, searching him for additional clues as to who this woman was.

Ismene looked at him for her introduction as well. Excitement danced across her face.

"Ismene is a friend," he said, avoiding eye contact with her. This wouldn't be the introduction she was hoping for.

Norah smiled at Ismene. Alexander knew her well enough to know it was forced.

"Well then," Norah said, "we shall be friends too."

"You're too kind, Your Elegance."

"Regal High," Alexander said. He knew Ismene wouldn't be the only one he'd correct. He only wished it didn't have to be here, like this, tonight. Ismene was a kind soul, and she had the best of intentions.

"Of course," Ismene said quickly, and curtsied to Norah. "Your Regal High." Then she turned to Alexander. "And congratulations as well, Lord Justice."

"Thank you, Ismene," he said, trying to keep the discomfort from his voice.

There was an awkward silence, and Ismene let out a breath. "I'll let you enjoy the evening. Congratulations again, Your Regal High," she said, giving another curtsy. "Lord Justice," she added.

Alexander gave a small bow as Ismene disappeared back into the crowd. He waited anxiously for Norah's reaction.

"She seems very nice," Norah said finally.

An easy compliment to agree with. "Yes, she is."

"And beautiful," she added.

Many men thought so, but Ismene's beauty held nothing for him. He shifted and then gave a stiff nod. He didn't want to talk about Ismene with Norah.

Norah's lips moved, as if to say something else, when James found them. Alexander let out a silent breath of relief.

"Queen Norah," the councilman said, taking her hand. "Congratulations. May the gods smile down on you."

Her smile widened, bright and warm. "Thank you, James," she said. She squeezed his hand. "I mean it. Thank you."

James patted the top of their clasped hands. "Of course, my dear. It's my duty and my joy." Then he turned to Alexander and grasped his shoulder. "Your destiny, my boy. Congratulations."

Alexander nodded as pride swelled within him. James had always believed in him, and it brought him joy that James was here to see him named lord justice. "Thank you, James."

The councilman smiled and gave a nod and a warm cuff on his shoulder, then left them to continue on.

When they were alone again, Norah turned back to Alexander. "Are you courting? You and Ismene?"

Alexander couldn't help the chuckle that escaped him at the forwardness he knew so well. He should have known she wouldn't let the conversation go that easily. But he had no secrets. "If your grandmother has her way."

"She's arranged you?" she asked, wide-eyed. "Are you to be wed?"

Another lord stepped forward with well-wishes for them both, and Alexander took the moment to collect his calm. While he'd answer anything Norah asked, it wasn't a comfortable topic.

The visiting lord bowed and departed, and they came together again.

"I'm sorry," she said. "That was rude of me, and intrusive."

"You're no intrusion," he said quickly. "And"—he brought his eyes to meet hers again—"I have no intention of marrying. It doesn't mean your grandmother won't try."

She gave a smile. "No, I suppose it doesn't."

At the mention of her grandmother, he glanced around the room and found Catherine looking back at him. He wondered how long she'd been watching, and how much she'd seen. His shoulders tightened.

Music picked up through the air. If he stayed, he'd ask her to dance. If he asked her to dance, he'd hold her hand in his, and if her skin touched his, he'd lose himself. So he couldn't stay.

"I'll say good night, though," he told her, "and not monopolize your time, as there are many who'd like to talk to you." Although there was no one who could want to talk to her more than he did.

A ripple of objection flashed in her eyes, but she didn't voice it. It was better that way. He gave a small bow. "Good evening, Regal High."

And she smiled a smile that he'd think about the rest of the night.

# Chapter Seventeen

"You're upset with me," Norah said.

Catherine sat in the side chair, petting a gray, long-haired cat in her lap as she watched Rebecca hold up dresses against Norah for approval.

"Disappointed," she replied. She flicked her hand, and Rebecca dropped the purple dress she was holding on to the bed and picked up a yellow one.

Norah bit the inside of her cheek. Catherine hadn't said but a few words to her since the coronation the day before, when Norah had named Alexander as her lord justice. "I know you didn't want me to choose him—"

"No, I didn't," she said sharply. "But it's not about that, Norah. We agreed we would meet with the council and decide."

Norah huffed a short breath, her frustration rising. "I didn't agree. I was told. But *I* am the one to choose my lord justice, and *I* chose Alexander. He was good enough when you chose him. He's clearly done a fine job, and he's the only one with James's support."

"The selection for lord justice doesn't require James's support."

"You say that now only because he didn't agree with you about Lord Branton."

Catherine's mouth fell open, but she didn't come back with another retort.

They sat in silence.

Finally, Catherine said, "I wish you would have told me that was your decision, instead of catching me by surprise."

Norah sighed, the fire inside her snuffed with guilt. "I do too," she admitted, her voice coming softer now. "I was just... afraid that you'd talk me out of it, and I didn't want to be talked out of it. I'd made up my mind. I know Alexander. I trust him. James trusts him."

"James doesn't know the implications."

"And what are the implications?" Norah asked, the heat returning. All this cryptic talk, she couldn't stand it anymore.

"Oh, Norah. Are you really so naive?"

And she certainly couldn't stand people continuing to talk to her like she was foolish. Even her grandmother. Her skin burned.

A knock on the door interrupted them, but Catherine's eyes didn't move from Norah. "Finish dressing. It's time to meet the council."

While Norah hadn't forgotten about the state, one benefit of being overwhelmed by the world was that it desensitized her to the crushing weight of other things sometimes. But her mind turned back to the meeting with the council, and her stomach twisted. It had been delayed to move up the coronation, but she had to face it now.

Catherine lowered the cat gently to the floor and stood. Then she moved for the door but paused and eyed the dresses. "Wear the blue. I'll see you in the judisaept."

Norah pushed out another breath, brimming with frustration as the door closed behind Catherine. She wanted to scream. Did Catherine think she could decide everything?

Rebecca reached for the blue gown.

"No," Norah told her. "I'll wear the green."

The council was already in the judisaept when Norah arrived, as were her grandmother and Alexander. She had thought her nerves had calmed as she had walked through the morning air, but the anxiousness came flooding back as soon as she saw them. The iron gaze of her grandmother didn't help. Perhaps she should have worn the blue dress. She felt childish now, which did nothing for her confidence.

While Catherine hadn't spoken to her much since the night before, she had worked to prepare her as much as possible for this meeting. Norah had her planned responses—her very vague and very short responses. They'd focus on the alliance with Aleon and *the marriage*. Norah would rather talk about anything else, but she reminded herself of the circumstances: the state of Mercia, the plight of their people, the threat of the Shadow King. She knew what she had accepted by taking the crown. It didn't make it easier, though.

The councilmen were so deep in a heated conversation that they barely noticed her entrance.

"Councilmen," Alexander called their attention when he saw her.

Edward turned. "Ah! Queen Norah." He bowed. "Forgive us. We were caught up in some disappointing news. But let's get started. I'd like to welcome you to your first state."

"What news?" she asked.

He paused in surprise but quickly recovered. "Nothing for you to worry about. These matters are why you have a council." His tone held an air of condescension that brought a heat to her cheeks. "Now, as Lady Catherine reminded me, you've not spent much time with the council, even before your... leaving. And it would be good to get reacquainted."

A small whisper of relief filled her lungs. That was very smart and very much appreciated. She glanced at Catherine, her earlier morning frustration forgotten, and her grandmother gave her the faintest of nods. But the mention of disappointing news still needled the back of her mind.

Edward motioned to each council member around the room. "Councilman Alastair, Henricus, Elias, Charles, and of course you know James."

Each councilman gave a respectful bow of his head as his name was said, and James smiled reassuringly. Catherine had walked through their descriptions with her before, and Norah felt solid on them now.

"We know you're stepping into a role that can be overwhelming for any person," Edward said. "And we'll guide you through each challenge."

They looked to her for a response. She had to say something, something that didn't sound like a woman completely in over her head. She clenched her hands together as she nodded. "Thank you, Councilman Edward." Her eyes rounded the table. She could feel her pulse in her palms. "Thanks to all of you. I only want to serve Mercia the best I can. I trust that, true to your titles, you'll counsel me in these matters of state to do what's right for our people."

The councilmen nodded, with smiles on their lips. They were pleased. *Good*. This was a good start. Her confidence grew... slightly.

Edward motioned to the chair at the head of the table. "Please, Queen Norah."

She took her chair, and the councilmen followed in seating themselves.

Edward nodded. "So, we'll start with—"

"The news," she said, now that they were past formalities. "Let's start with the news that came."

The room fell silent. It felt like the wrong thing to say, but why would it be wrong? News had come. She was queen. She should know.

"Ah," Edward said finally, clearly surprised again. "Very well." He wet his lips. "Word has come that a usurper has overthrown King Orrid, the king of Rael."

She wasn't familiar with the king of Rael, or his kingdom. Not that she was quick to assume this wasn't bad news, but she couldn't help but feel thankful it wasn't directly related to Mercia. Or was it? "Is the king of Rael a friend of Mercia?"

Edward puffed a small breath, seemingly amused at her inexperience, and her cheeks grew hotter.

"He's a godly man. It's a tragedy."

That was a yes, then? But before she could ask more questions, he pivoted the conversation.

"But let me once again convey how happy we are that you're with us. Now, to more pressing matters."

He was moving her on, and she didn't have the boldness yet to stop him. Not that she was keen to. She had enough to focus on in Mercia without worrying about another king in another kingdom.

"We're most eager to hear about your time away from us," he said.

All thoughts of the king of Rael fell from her mind, and she forced a dry swallow. She knew the planned response—she'd been with an undisclosed ally who wished to remain that way, and her father had committed her to secrecy. It was such an underwhelming answer. No one would buy it. She wouldn't, in their place. And if they didn't believe her, what would be her standing with them then? She needed their favor, and she was already off to a mediocre start at best.

Norah glanced at James. He nodded. She knew his position—there was little benefit to continuing to keep her condition from the council now that she was queen. They could do nothing against her. Perhaps they could actually help her, guide her. And she was desperate for just one weight off her shoulders. With everything she was facing, she couldn't waste energy holding a charade as well.

"Queen Norah?" Edward said.

She realized she'd just been sitting there. "I... um..." She glanced around the table at all the eyes looking back at her. "I, uh, actually don't know. I've lost my memories."

The councilmen shifted in their chairs and looked at one another.

As she said the words, she realized it sounded almost as unbelievable as a secret ally. At least it was the truth, and she could speak it confidently. She avoided her grandmother's eyes. It was another disappointment, she was sure. Add it to the list.

"Lost your memories?" Edward sputtered. "And you didn't think it important to inform this council before the coronation?"

The knot in her stomach grew. She had... but she didn't answer that.

Edward turned his lit eyes on Catherine. "You knew. You knew, and you didn't tell us."

"I made decisions for the good of Mercia," Catherine said flatly.

"The good of Mercia!" Edward exclaimed in a shrill voice.

Alastair spoke now, narrowing his eyes on Norah. "And how are we to know you're Queen Norah?"

NICOLA TYCHE

"Oh, come now," James said angrily. "Don't be absurd. There's no doubt she's Queen Norah. There's no mistaking her. She's been gone for three years, not three decades."

Edward gaped at him. "You knew about this beforehand? And you said nothing?"

James flicked his hand through the air. "Because I knew you'd say ridiculous things like this."

Norah swallowed. She'd expected this conversation to go very differently. She had needed it to go differently. Could she get it back on track? Could she quiet them? She was queen.

But she found herself not needing to quiet them, as the room naturally fell silent.

Edward spoke first—of course he'd speak first. "Well, this adds a complicated element, especially considering the letter this morning."

What letter? A weight grew in her stomach. More news? Different news? She was trying to lessen the burdens on her shoulders, not add more.

"What letter?" she asked. Her eyes found Alexander's, where she hoped to find calm, but it wasn't calm she saw. Behind his stoic gaze, something bothered him. Her heart beat faster, and she swallowed the rising lump in her throat.

Edward's thin lips curved into a frustrated smile. "A letter from King Phillip of Aleon."

Heat rushed through her. Catherine had just been in her chamber. How could she not have said anything? She shot a glance at her grandmother but found only an equal look of surprise. She hadn't known either.

172

"He sends his elations at your return," Edward continued, "and he hopes he's not too forward in proposing that you suggest a date for the marriage."

That was too forward.

Edward gave a judgmental gaze. "He, of course, assumes the alliance between Mercia and Aleon still stands."

Did this condescending man always speak for the council? She stole a glance at Catherine, whose eyes told her to keep herself composed.

"Where's the letter?" she asked, hoping to buy herself time to pull her thoughts together.

Edward's lip twitched. "It was short, Your Elegance. But I would propose—"

"Regal High," Alexander interrupted, creating an awkward silence in the room. "And she asked for the letter."

"Edward," James said, lending his own voice.

Edward paused and swept his eyes around the room. "Of course," he said finally, and pulled a small envelope from his pocket. He rose and brought it to Norah, presenting it with a small bow of his head. "Your Regal High."

She took it, unfolding it and running her eyes down the parchment, but she made it no further than the first line—*Dearest Norah*—before the words blurred together. She had known this was the next step, what was expected of her, but... naming a date... It hadn't felt so real before.

Her eyes welled, simply from the weight of it all, and a wave of panic washed over her. The only thing worse than her council seeing her struggle with this conversation would be if they saw her become emotional.

"As I know Lady Catherine has explained," Edward continued as she pretended to read, "our provisions are nearing dangerously low levels and will be depleted well before winter's end."

"How much is there?" she managed to get out. "How long do we have?" How long did she have?

"Not long. But don't worry yourself about the numbers. We'll see to that. We need your attentions on Aleon, for King Phillip can provide what Mercia needs." He wanted her to focus on the marriage, not the issue. Anger sprouted in the depths of her mind and spread through her veins.

"Time is of the essence," he pressed. "You must think of our people." Of course she needed to think of the people. But was a marriage the only solution? She needed to think—and it was impossible under his guilting stare, under the pressure.

Her anger thickened, and her words came before she could stop them. "I won't be hasty to make a permanent solution for a temporary problem."

The councilmen shifted in their chairs, clearly unsettled by her response.

"Hasty?" Edward scoffed. "This is perhaps the longest anticipated marriage in the history of mankind. And it's not merely for today's problems. With this alliance comes the great army of Aleon, which we'll need to stand against the Shadow King."

She'd not forgotten. All eyes were on her, but no words would come. She had no rebuttal for these points, no defense. And it was impossible to think under Edward's smug gaze.

"Queen Norah knows what's necessary," James said, breaking the silence. "She'll fulfill her duty. We'll leave it to her and Lady Catherine to decide on a date."

James's response was certainly more diplomatic than the words forming in her head.

"That's enough for today, councilmen," James added.

But Norah stopped them. "There is one more thing," she said, glancing around the table. Her anger fueled her; her fear was gone. "From now on, any letters addressed to me will come directly to me."

Edward's eyes darkened, but he bowed. "Of course, Regal High."

The councilmen all bowed before shuffling out of the judisaept. James lingered as the room emptied.

"Thank you, James," she said when they'd gone.

He nodded. "I know this was a difficult meeting for you. But, Norah"—he paused until her eyes met his—"you will choose a date, and you'll seal our alliance with Aleon."

Her stomach twisted. Whatever hope she had of a different solution was quickly fading. James gave her a stiff nod before following the rest of the council out. Norah turned her gaze to Catherine, whose green eyes were aflame. Norah knew Catherine was angry about revealing her memory loss, but she couldn't deal with it. Not right now.

"I don't want to hear it," she said shortly.

Catherine's face was cold as stone. "Then I won't burden you." She strode from the judisaept, leaving Norah alone in the emptiness of the room.

She put her hands on the edge of the table and rested her weight forward. Her legs didn't feel like they'd hold her, but she couldn't sit down again. She couldn't argue with the situation, or even with the resolution. A marriage—it was very logical. It was just... sudden. And suffocating. The air in the room was heavy. She drew in a breath but couldn't breathe.

Norah turned and left the judisaept in a haze. Everything was getting away from her. She had no control, no choice. She felt like a... girl... a child. Her guard picked up behind her as she walked. She glanced back. It was Titus. She couldn't think with the sound of his steps in her ears. "Hammel's hell! Can you just stop following me for a moment!" she snapped.

He frowned. "I can't leave you, Regal High."

"Stop calling me that!"

"Titus," Alexander's voice called from behind them. "I'll see her back."

The guard gave a nod and left them in the empty hall.

Norah stood for a moment with Alexander. His presence brought a calm she so desperately needed, dissipating her anger, but the anger had been the only thing holding her emotion back. She bit into her bottom lip, trying to keep the tears at bay.

Alexander ambled forward, prompting her into a walk beside him. He didn't speak, only walked, and the silence was settling.

"They don't really see me as a queen, do they?" she asked finally. "Alastair challenged who I am, but it hardly seems to matter at all, so long as I wear the crown and marry. That's all they care about. I could be anyone, as long as I look the part and do what they say."

"But you aren't just anyone," he replied. His voice came softer. "Norah, this has been the plan for the past ten years. Mercia needs the alliance with Aleon. Of course they would be eager for it, now that you've returned."

Norah frowned. "So I should just marry?"

"That's not what I said."

She stopped, looking up at him. "What are you saying, then?"

His lips parted, but no words came.

"Would you have me do this?" she asked. "Would you have me wed King Phillip?"

The line of his jaw tightened. "There's been a lot said today. Put it from your mind for a while. When the emotion is gone, you'll be able to think more clearly."

"There's nothing I can do to put this from my mind."

Alexander's brow twitched, as though he'd had a thought.

"What is it?" she asked.

"I have an idea. Come on."

Her eyes narrowed.

"I promise it's not a tomb."

# CHAPTER EIGHTEEN

Norah raised a doubtful brow. "We're going in *there*?"

Alexander stood at the mouth of a cave that trailed deep into the darkness from the icy mountainside. She had followed him outside the castle, pulling her cloak over her face and tucking her hair inside to slip by undetected. He'd led her to the cliffs and to a small cleft large enough for them to step down into one at a time. Along the narrow walk they went, looking out over the sea of ice, and then carefully sidled along a ledge to where they stood now.

"A cave?" she asked.

"I'd normally allow a lady first as a gentlemanly courtesy, but you should follow me."

"Gladly," she said, waving him ahead. She followed him into the cave, and the light faded as they made their way deeper. A small rush of excitement ran through her.

Alexander paused, turning to her and holding out his hand. "It's going to get dark. Very dark. Just hold on to me, and I'll lead you. You needn't be afraid."

She had a number of feelings at the moment, but fear was not one of them. She smiled as she took his hand. They made their way farther into the cave, and it wasn't long before Norah couldn't see anything at all. "I didn't expect this today," she told him.

"I admit it's highly unconventional and certainly not endorsed by your grandmother. In fact, I'd appreciate if you would overlook it when next speaking to her."

She grinned into the darkness. "My lips are sealed."

They walked slowly, with Alexander giving her hand small reassuring squeezes as they went.

"How much farther?" she asked.

"Still a ways yet."

Her curiosity grew. "What's back here?"

"A magical place," he told her.

The cave grew colder, and darkness hung around them like a thick shroud. Norah found herself moving closer to him and taking his arm with her other hand.

She was about to ask another question when the darkness abated and she could make out Alexander's form and the walls of the cave around them. They kept to the left and curved through another tunnel that, suddenly, opened into a vast cavern with a large pool of turquoise water. Light poured in from somewhere ahead, past an island rock formation in the water.

Norah let out a breath in awe. "It's beautiful."

"Isn't it?"

"How did you find it?"

"*We* found it," he said. "You and I. When we were younger." He had stopped, but their hands were still together, and his eyes met hers. "This is where you liked to come when the weight of the world was too heavy. Just to get out from underneath it, if only for a moment."

Her chest tightened. The world was heavy now.

He stood close, so close, facing her with their fingers entwined, and suddenly the world felt very far away. The warmth from his hand spread up her arm and over her skin, pooling in her stomach. His gaze traveled over her face and down to her lips; they stayed on her lips. His mouth parted slightly as he leaned even closer. Her breath came faster. She wanted him closer still.

But he inhaled and stepped back, pulling his hand from hers and putting some space between them. Her mind tumbled, but she caught herself and straightened.

"The water is warm," he told her, looking out across the cavern. "The pool is fed from the hot springs in the rock."

"Is it really?" she asked, overly feigning interest. She was desperate for something—anything—to steer the conversation from where they'd been. She crouched down at the edge of the pool and dropped her hand to the water, but as her fingers touched its warmth, she stopped. Visions seemed to ripple in the pool. Not that she could see, but that she could feel. Something was here.

She scooped the water up and let it fall between her fingers. There was a yearning in her spirit, a freedom in the pool that called to her. And there was something... familiar. She knew this place, but the memory was just beyond her grasp. Yet it was close. So close. She scooped up another handful, listening as she closed her eyes. The sound of the drops as they hit the pool and echoed off the walls. The feel of the warmth between her fingers... The water called to her mind, called her back. There was a memory here.

"I want to go for a swim," she said breathlessly as she stood.

Alexander drew up a hand with a shake of his head. "I don't think that's a good idea."

But she didn't care. She reached back and pulled the ties loose on her dress.

"Queen Norah," he said uneasily, "you can't seriously take off all your clothes right now."

"I've got on at least three layers. I'll be decent enough."

Alexander shifted but quickly saw he didn't have a choice, and he turned his back as she pulled down her dress and wriggled out of it. She paused at her underskirts, looking up to make sure she remained unseen. He waited with his back to her, and she pulled them off, adding them to the pile of clothing. Then she slowly stepped into the water in her chemise and silk underwear.

The water felt incredible, and she leisurely sunk down to her chin. The tension seemed to flow out of her. She already knew she loved this place, even if she couldn't remember it.

"Are you coming?" she called to him. She'd feel silly if she were the only one. She'd make him share the awkwardness, at least.

He stood at the edge of the pool, seeming to wrestle with his proprieties.

"Come on," she called. "It's amazing!"

"I know it is," he called back with a chuckle. Finally, he relented, giving a small shake of his head as he shrugged off his cloak and jacket and pulled his shirt over his head. He kicked off his boots and tossed them next to his cloak.

She turned away as he pulled off his breeches, stripping down to his braies, but she turned back when she heard him splash in. The clear turquoise water did little to protect her modesty, but her undergarments covered her enough, and she wasn't feeling modest at the moment, anyway. She waited as Alexander waded deeper and moved toward her. For a moment, she forgot about the pull of the water on her mind.

They lingered in the beautiful silence, facing one another, circling. A warmth eddied in her stomach, a current that carried her to him. He moved closer, and her pulse quickened. Closer still, he came. She could reach out and touch him if she wanted.

And she wanted.

Her eyes were on his lips, the lips that had kissed the back of her hand, the lips she somehow knew. She could so easily imagine them against her own. Was she only imagining? Or was she remembering?

Norah pushed herself back, putting it from her mind. She dared not let her thoughts wander there for fear she might follow them.

With the hold between them broken, he pushed back as well, letting out an echoing breath. He swam toward the stone formation jutting from the center of the pool, and she followed. Norah reached the rock and gripped the damp surface. She softened her kick so as not to hit her knees against the jagged edges hidden underneath.

"Watch your knees," he warned.

*She knew.*

She looked up at the top of the rock formation reaching toward the ceiling of the cave, close to a ledge that protruded out over the pool. "Looks like that would be fun to jump from," she said.

"It is," he replied.

She gaped at him in surprise. "You've done it?"

"I have."

"No you haven't!"

Alexander grinned. "I'll do it now." He gripped the edge of the rock and hoisted himself from the pool.

She drew in a breath as his braies clung to his skin and the water rolled off his back. Perhaps she shouldn't watch him, but she wasn't caught up anymore in what she should or shouldn't do. Not here.

He reached high and climbed up the mass of rock, faster than she thought he might. Perhaps he *had* done this before. Still, it was high. He reached the top and stretched his leg to the ledge on the cave wall.

She cringed at the thought of him falling. "Be careful," she called.

But he moved to it easily. Then he flashed her a grin and jumped. She let out a squeal as he hit the water and a large splash rained over her. He broke the surface, laughing as he wiped the water from his face. "Did I get you?"

Of course he had tried. She splashed him back, and he laughed again.

"I don't know whether that was brave or foolish," she said.

"I've done many brave and foolish things here," he replied, serious now.

She stilled. She wanted to ask him. The question was on her lips, but her fear kept it inside. Had they both done brave and foolish things here? *Together?*

They quieted as they drew closer to each other. Was the water growing warmer? It felt warmer. Still, her skin prickled.

But he broke the silence as he pushed back. "This way," he said. "There's more to see."

The moment to ask had passed. She cursed her bashfulness.

He made his way around the rock formation. On the back side, the pool widened and curved to the left. They swam on, and around the corner, the cavern opened to the sky. Light hit the rippling water, and it sparkled in the sun.

She gasped in amazement. "It's incredible."

They waded for a long time, marveling at the natural beauty. Alexander's face held a rare grin, and it brought her a deep happiness with it. If only they could stay here, away from the weight of the world.

He moved to the side and took hold of the rock as he looked up at the sky. "It's beautiful in the moonlight," he told her. "With the stars above. You used to try to count them."

They used to swim here at night? She gripped the rock, edging beside him so she could still herself in the water.

"How many are there?" she asked.

He shook his head with an amused grin. "You'd come up with a different number each time."

*Each time.* As in, they'd been here under the stars more than once.

Their eyes found each other again, and they fell silent. He drifted closer to her, close enough again to touch. This time, she did. She reached out her hand, slowly, and pressed her palm flat against his chest. The racing of his heart matched her own.

He drifted even closer.

His eyes matched the sunlit pool, and water droplets glistened in the gold of his hair. He was beautiful. She moved her hand up his chest, over his shoulder, and behind the nape of his neck, pulling him ever so softly to her.

And he followed.

She leaned in, tipping her head slightly and bringing her cheek to his. They were so close. Not touching, but so close.

His breath dusted heat over her ear. She dropped her lips to his neck, not with a kiss—just the feather of a touch. The muscle across his shoulders tightened under her hand, and his breaths came faster now. So did hers. She trailed her lips up, still not kissing him, although she desperately wanted to. She traveled along his jaw and over his chin and paused a whisper away from his mouth.

They shouldn't be here, like this. Yet they lingered. He smelled like he was hers, and she breathed him in.

He ran his hand up the back of her neck and into her hair, and he parted his lips. His body pressed closer, and her breasts brushed against his chest through her chemise. She wanted him closer, still. His fingers gripped her tighter.

They couldn't be here.

He closed his eyes. An eternity passed in the quiet of their breaths. He swallowed. "We should go," he said, before opening his eyes again.

His words found the sanity of her mind, and she pushed back from him.

His face sobered. "I'm sorry," he said. "I shouldn't have brought you here." There was a sadness to his tone, a disappointment in himself. "We should go," he said again. He pulled back and away.

But it was as much her fault as it was his. "Alexander," she said.

He floated back the way they'd come, moving slowly to keep from splashing.

She sighed and followed.

They reached the point at which they'd started, and Norah found her footing in the shallows. Alexander had already exited the pool. He picked up his breeches and pulled them on.

Norah stepped out of the water and found her dress. And as if putting on undergarments with damp skin wasn't enough of a struggle, she found the back lacing was just beyond her grasp. Heat flushed across her cheeks. She hadn't thought things through when she'd stripped it off.

She glanced back to where he stood waiting for her. "Will you?" she called to him, and turned her back for him to help with the ties.

Her ask was met with silence, and she thought he might refuse. Then he stepped behind her. He was still for a moment before he reached out and pulled the lacing tight, closing the back of her dress and skillfully looping each fix.

Alexander shifted closer, and the warmth of his breath tickled her shoulder. A wave of familiarity rippled through her. *The dream.* It hadn't been just a dream.

She risked pushing him further away, but she couldn't help herself. "You've done this before," she said. "For me."

He didn't answer. But she knew. He was quick to put up walls, quick to put distance between them, but he seemed to forget sometimes, lapsing into a life that still called to her, a life she desperately wanted back.

"Are you ready?" he asked when he finished, stepping them back into the coldness of normalcy.

She gave a nod.

Alexander offered his hand, with his fingers politely together, for the walk back through the cave. She took it. He moved to start, but she pulled him to pause.

"Alexander. Thank you for giving this back to me. It did take my mind off things for a while."

His eyes gave a sad smile, and he nodded. Then he led her into the darkness, toward the castle and the pressures that waited.

# CHAPTER NINETEEN

The skirts were heavy but still allowed ease of movement. Norah pulled them on quickly, wondering what was in store for her. Alexander had knocked on her door early, instructing her maid to have her dress for the cold. She didn't like the cold much. Regardless, she was looking forward to whatever he had planned. Her mind drifted back to the day before, back to the cave, and a warmth pooled in her stomach. But she pushed it down. She couldn't allow herself those feelings. Not when she knew her future.

She stepped out into the hall, where Titus was waiting.

"The lord justice is just down the stairs," he told her.

"I'm sorry I snapped at you yesterday," she said back over her shoulder as she walked.

"You don't need to apologize."

That was what he was obliged to say.

"But I want to. I was having a bad day." She reached the stairs and started down.

"I know. I heard."

She frowned. "Do you hear everything?"

"Most everything."

Of course. What did she expect? She reached the bottom stair, where Alexander was waiting, and he gave her a low bow. She tried to ignore the stir in her stomach.

"Regal High," he greeted.

His tone and formality sat strangely with her, but she pushed the feeling down and gave him a small smile. "Lord Justice. You've captured my curiosity. Where are we headed?"

He turned and led her down the hall and outside into the courtyard. "It's not so much where we're headed as what we're doing," he said, piquing her curiosity further. He waved back to Titus, who fell farther behind. His voice dropped lower. "But first, I want to apologize. I shouldn't have taken you to the cave yesterday. Please, forgive me. I'd... like to forget it even happened."

While not intentional, his words stung. "I don't want to forget," she said, shaking her head. She'd forgotten enough.

"Norah," he said softly. "Please." His eyes were filled with an emotion she couldn't read. Sadness? Regret? It unsettled her, but she couldn't look away. He shifted his gaze, releasing her.

"Where are we going?" she asked, changing the subject.

He let out a sigh but seemed to accept her rejection of his completely foolish idea to forget the cave. She couldn't have it again, but she wouldn't forget.

"Where are we going?" she asked again.

The corner of his mouth curved up, but only for a moment. "You'll see," he said.

She followed him past the stables and around to the sparring field, where a boy was leaning weapons against the fence in preparation for the day's use. Alexander made several gestures with his hands, and the boy gestured back before bowing to Norah.

"What are you doing?" she asked him, puzzled.

"This is Cade. He works with the smith and sees after the sparring field. He's deaf and speaks with his hands."

She looked at the boy, amazed. He could speak with his hands? Then she realized she was staring and shifted. "Oh, um... how do I say hi?" she asked curiously.

Alexander chuckled and simply held up his hand. The boy smiled.

"I suppose that one's easy," she said sheepishly.

Cade drew a sword from the weapons' hold and held it out for her. She raised a brow at Alexander, and he nodded.

"Thank you," she said as she took it awkwardly. "How do I say thank you?"

Alexander cupped his fist and then extended his fingers. Norah copied it, and the boy gave her a large grin and then bowed. Alexander nodded to the boy, who bowed again and left them to the quiet of the morning. She watched him go, still impressed by his ability to adapt.

Alexander pulled his own sword from its scabbard.

"So... a lesson?" she asked with an uncertain smile.

His face grew serious, but there was excitement in his eyes. "Not exactly. You remembered the poem. And the dance." He paused, leaving out the cave. "And perhaps you've had glimpses of other things. I want to see if you remember the sword. If I'm right in my suspicion, you won't need a lesson."

Norah gave a skeptical smile as she took the sword, but once it was in her hand, she felt a comfort she hadn't expected. She rolled her wrist, getting familiar with its weight. She looked back at Alexander in surprise, and he gave her another nod.

Not giving her much time, he stepped forward with a swing, but she brought her blade up, countering and stepping to the side. She gripped the hilt tighter. The sword brought her power, confidence. Excitement swelled within her. She launched her own attack, cutting forward and driving him to step back. He spun to give himself more space to escape her. Their blades sang through the air, ringing into the morning.

Her ferocity grew with each strike, and she found the fight growing within her. But on a defensive turn, her boot slipped, and she stumbled. She tried to regain herself for a counter, but the tip of Alexander's blade met her chest.

She stilled, and he stepped back, letting her catch her breath. Norah let out a quiet laugh in surprise. "That was... unexpected," she finally managed to get out. "It seems I'm not terrible."

"Certainly not terrible," he said, out of breath himself. "A little out of practice, but even so, the better of many men."

"Out of practice?" she feigned offense. "You only got me because I slipped."

He grinned and took a ready stance again. She attacked this time with an arcing side swing, and he used his blade to deflect it. She pursed her lips. *Smooth.* Very smooth. He countered with a swing of his own. She tried to mirror him, but she didn't have his strength. He crossed his sword against hers and used it to push her backward and up against the fence near the weapons' hold.

He smiled, his face close to hers. Their blades were still crossed between them as he pinned her.

"Did you slip again?" he asked.

Her eyes narrowed. Was he really teasing her? She pushed against him, but he didn't let her free.

He winked. "Or did you forget how to defend yourself?"

He *was* teasing her. With her free hand, she whipped her knife from its sheath just inside her jacket and brought the tip to his chin. "Did you forget you gave this to me?"

His smile grew, and he gave a light chuckle. "No, but I did forget how good you are with it," he admitted, "and how quick you are to use it."

Norah grinned. "Does this mean I win?"

Their stares locked as they stilled.

"I think so," he said. Then, quieter, "Although I have to confess, I don't feel as though I've lost."

Warmth coursed through her, despite the cold. He only needed to lean a little closer, and she could meet his lips with hers.

*No*—they couldn't let themselves go there again.

As if he had the same thought, he pulled back, releasing her.

She drew in a breath, trying to regain her senses. "I've trained?" she asked, finding her words.

He shrugged. "Something like that." He held out his hand for her sword, and she gave it to him. He took it and pushed it back into the weapons' hold. "Sword training is not part of a princess's curriculum, but you wouldn't have that. So, growing up, every day you'd ask me to teach you what I had learned. We'd spend the evenings practicing in the back paddocks." He gave her a smirk. "I'd say I'm an excellent teacher."

She couldn't help a laugh. His eyes burned bright, and he smiled back at her.

Then his face sobered. "I have to go," he said.

"Oh." She bit the inside of her cheek to hide her disappointment. *Another wall.* It was for the best.

"Your grandmother has committed my presence," he explained.

A smile crept back to her face, and she nodded. That was better than a wall. "I understand. I should get back as well."

He delayed a moment, and she hoped he might find a reason to stay.

"Good day, Queen Norah," he said finally.

"Good day, Lord Justice."

He gave a small bow and took his leave.

Norah walked back to her chamber, surprised by the morning. She could fight—somewhat. That was good to know. She suddenly became aware of Titus behind her again. Had he seen her? Of course he had. "Did you know I could do that?" she asked.

He motioned to the break in his brow. "How do you think I got this scar?"

She stopped, and her mouth dropped open. "Are you serious?"

He chuckled and shook his head. "No," he said, and she scowled.

Back at her chamber, Norah opened the door to see Catherine waiting for her. "Grandmother," she said. They had spoken a little since the meeting with the council, enough to settle things between them. Mostly.

"Where were you?" Catherine asked.

"Just... out for a walk." She expected Catherine to press her more or find something else to chastise, like seeing Norah in her outerwear, but the woman had something else on her mind. Norah noticed she held a box in her hand.

"A gift has come for you. From Phillip."

Norah's stomach turned sour. She was afraid to ask. "What kind of gift?"

Catherine pulled the top from the box to reveal a stunning sapphire necklace. Smaller jewels plated the sides, and there was a large stone pendant in the center. "Isn't it beautiful?"

"It is," Norah replied. It was beautiful, but she didn't want jewelry. She wished King Phillip knew her better. Perhaps then he would have sent her a knife. She chuckled.

"What's so funny?" Catherine asked.

Norah pursed her lips and shook her head. "Nothing."

"Here, he sent this as well." Her grandmother handed her a small painted portraiture of the king.

She reluctantly took it. He wasn't much older than she was, and he had a strong, square jaw and bronzed-brown hair. His nose was straight, refined, but not feminine. His eyes were as blue as Alexander's. Well, not quite as blue. He was very handsome, she hated to admit, although she didn't like the mustache. "Do you think he really looks like this? Or maybe they just paint him favorably. He *is* king."

"I've laid eyes on him myself, as have you. He really does look this way."

She bit the side of her cheek. "Do you think he'd shave his face if I asked him to?"

"By the gods, Norah."

She shrugged with a frown.

"You should wear the necklace today."

Norah shifted, drawing her brows together. "I... don't think it will match." She looked at the small portraiture again and put her finger over his mustache. He had kind eyes. But she wouldn't wear his necklace.

"Norah, you haven't even chosen a dress yet."

"I have, in my mind. It doesn't match."

Catherine snapped closed the necklace box. "You are impossible sometimes." She sighed. "Get ready. I want you to attend worship with me today at the temple. It will be good for the people to see a pious queen. And it will do you some good to get out."

Norah felt quite the opposite, but she knew her grandmother was trying to give her something else to think about, and she smiled appreciatively as she went to decide on a dress.

Norah smiled as she and Catherine arrived at the temple and were heartily greeted by those walking in. She wasn't particularly interested in attending, but Catherine was right—it felt good to be out.

The temple was larger than Norah had expected, and as they entered, she noticed the rows of cushions on the floor, for kneeling. Her eyes caught the priest at the front, who motioned her forward, and she made her way toward him.

"Yes, yes, all the way forward," Catherine whispered behind her.

The priest smiled with a nod, motioning to the first row on the left, but as Norah looked around, she stopped. To her right, across the walkway, was Alexander, looking back at her. She was about to smile at him, but just as quickly, she saw Ismene, who had taken her place on the cushion beside him. Ismene gave a bow of her head, and Norah returned the nod, swallowing back her sudden swell of jealousy.

"Kneel on the cushion," her grandmother whispered from behind.

Norah turned her attention forward and found the cushion, dropping to her knees and sitting back on her heels. Catherine lowered herself beside her with a hand from the priest.

With everyone in attendance, the priest raised his arms, beginning the prayer. Norah couldn't rid herself of the fire building inside her. Alexander had said her grandmother committed his attendance.

She set this up.

Norah's cheeks burned with anger: at her grandmother's manipulation, at Ismene. She couldn't help herself and swept her eyes to where Alexander sat. A jolt ran through her as their stares locked. She tried to pull away, having been caught, but his gaze held her. It cupped her breath in her chest and seeded warmth across her skin. Her anger dissipated.

"Norah." Catherine's harsh whisper filled her ears, bringing her eyes forward again.

The morning wasn't as long as she had expected, and she found herself fueled by the silent exchanges with Alexander during the priest's prayer. As the worship ended, an older woman called Catherine's attention, and Norah rose with a start, seeing her chance.

Alexander was one step ahead of her, meeting her with a slight curve of his lips. "Queen Norah," he said.

"Lord Justice. I didn't know you were going to be here."

"Nor I, you, but—"

"Queen Norah," Ismene greeted as she approached them.

A flash of fire ran through her, but Norah forced a smile. "Lady Ismene, so good to see you again." The words were stiff on her lips, but she hoped they hadn't sounded so.

"And you, Regal High," the young woman said with a curtsy.

"I should be off," Norah said, looking for an opportunity to escape.

Her eyes locked with Alexander's again. His face was solemn, almost apologetic. Was he apologetic?

Alexander bowed, and she gave a nod in return before leaving them and making her way outside. She shouldn't have come.

She became all too aware of Catherine beside her as she walked. Norah glared at her grandmother. "Must you be so obvious?" she snapped, not bothering to disguise her irritation.

Catherine looked straight ahead, unbothered. "I don't know what you're talking about. And you've no concept of obvious."

Norah gave her a scowl and walked faster, stalking back toward the castle.

# CHAPTER TWENTY

Norah sat on a branch of the white oak tree as the sun set and the air turned colder with the fading light. It was an old tree with low boughs, one of the few trees on the rocky isle, and it sat thick and sprawling like a giant hand rising from the earth.

She fought the jealousy she knew she had no right to feel. Alexander was not hers, but she couldn't help the possessiveness clawing inside her. She bit her lip in broken concentration as she threaded the thin strands of leather through several tiny shells she'd found among the rocks. Her morning guard, Liaman, had shown her where to find them. He had told her that in summer the water came higher and teemed with life around the castle, then left the shells as it receded. Now they could be found in the crags underneath the snow. She tested the length around her wrist and added a few more.

Norah glanced up to see Alexander approaching. He waved off her guard, who left them and headed back toward the castle.

Alexander leaned against the tree, watching quietly as she finished the bracelet. She waited until she tied her knot before she looked up and forced a smile.

"Are you unhappy with me?" he asked.

She took in a breath and let it out slowly, then shook her head. "No," she said. Not with him.

"But you *are* unhappy?"

She looked out across the reach of the isle to the setting sun. She was unhappy, but she didn't have the right to be, at least not where Alexander was concerned. And she certainly couldn't share that with him.

"Here, let me see your hand," she said, changing the subject.

He held out his wrist for her. His skin was warm against her fingers as she tied the bracelet in place.

"There. Now you'll see it and think of me." As soon as she spoke the words, she regretted them. They sounded too possessive.

His eyes met hers. "I don't need a reminder for that," he said softly.

Norah's heart wavered in her chest. She might not have the memories, but there was no mistaking that there had been something between them. Something forgotten, but still there. Something buried far beneath the surface.

The words came out before she could stop herself. "Were we lovers?"

Her question sobered him, and he stepped back. She feared his answer but was desperate for it all the same.

Burden hung from his brow as the words sat silent on his tongue. "Our fathers never would have allowed us to be together," he said finally.

"That's not what I asked." She wondered if his heart was beating as heavily as hers.

"I would never dishonor you, Norah."

Her question remained unanswered, and it hung in the air.

"We should get back," he said, a formality returning. "Your grandmother will be wondering where you are."

But she didn't want to leave.

He offered his hand, and she took it, but as she slipped down from the tree, she stumbled, falling back against the trunk and pulling Alexander with her. He caught his balance on the bough and hooked his arm around her, steadying her. The closeness stilled them. A tremor ran through her, and Norah gasped as an image flashed in her mind. It was an old image, a memory.

"Are you all right?" he asked.

"We were here before," she breathed.

He froze, and his eyes burned. "You remember?"

"Yes. No." She shook her head but didn't take her eyes off him. "But I remember you. Here, like this." She reached her hand up and threaded her fingers through his golden locks. A wave of warmth washed through her despite the winter air. "Your hair was slightly longer," she whispered.

Norah drew her fingertips to his cheek, feeling the smoothness of his shaven face. The heat in her stomach grew, but the flash of the image was fading. Alexander's face. His golden locks. His eyes, young and mischievous. They were just moments, but she needed them. She needed to hold on to them.

She pulled him closer. "I know they're here."

His brow creased. "What's here?"

She searched his eyes, and the image reached out once more. Younger Alexander. The Alexander that smiled. She drew in a ragged breath, feeling a stitch in the canvas of her being.

"Norah?" His voice brought her back.

She shook her head. "No, no. They're here."

"What's here?" he asked.

"Stop talking."

She looked into his eyes again—the depths of their blue were drowning. It was Alexander. He was stirring her memories. Her breath quickened.

*Summer lazed around them, and they lay on their backs under the tree, laughing. Alexander rolled to his side and caught a lock of her hair.*

*She smiled at him. "Where will we go?"*

*"Wherever your heart desires."*

*"By the sea," she said. "Where the water is warm, and we can lie in the light of the sun."*

*He leaned over, stroking her cheek with the back of his fingers. "You are the sun," he said, and kissed her tenderly.*

The vision faded. She gripped him tighter, trying to draw more of the memory.

"What did you see?" he asked.

Familiarity flowed from where her skin touched his. Norah brought her other hand to his face and pulled him even closer. Her sight clouded. Before she could think of her actions, she lifted her chin and brought her lips to his. He stiffened but let her pull him in.

There was a sudden shattering, and the memory was as clear as the present.

*Darkness sat around her as she waited at the tree for Alexander. Her heart raced, and she smiled to herself, pulling her bag closer. She'd brought only the things most important to her; this was all she was taking. There would be no more castles, no more life of privilege, but they would be together, and that was all that mattered.*

*A silhouette in the darkness made her jump, and she laughed as she recognized him, feeling silly. "You startled me," she said, reaching out and taking his hand. She could see his face in the moonlight.*

He wasn't smiling back at her.

"Is everything all right?" She looked around him, noticing he wasn't holding anything: no supplies, no belongings. "Where's your pack?"

"There is no pack," he said, and she felt a strange pit in her stomach. "Norah, I can't take you from here. We can't go."

"What?" She shook her head. "What are you saying?"

"We can't go. You can't go."

Confusion flooded her. "I don't understand. We planned, we—"

"You're going to be queen, and if you leave now, you'd be abandoning your people."

"I don't want to be queen! I want to be with you! I love you, and this is the only way we can be together."

He pulled his hand from hers and stepped backward.

"Alexander," she pleaded, stepping forward to bridge the gap. "We love each other. We're going to be together."

"No," he said. "We can't."

A surge of desperation ran through her. "We can! We can go right now. You don't even need your pack. Let's just go!"

"Norah, we're not going," he said more firmly.

The heat of emotion sprang across her cheeks.

"We can't," he whispered.

"I don't accept that!" she cried.

His face hardened. "I don't love you!" he said sharply.

Her breath caught in her throat at the harshness of his words. "That's not true," she breathed. "That's not true."

"You're going to marry King Phillip. Everything you want, he can give it to you."

"I want you!"

*Alexander shifted in the quiet. "That will pass. Go back to the castle, Norah." Then he pulled back, fading into the darkness.*

*She was alone.*

*Norah sank to the base of the tree as a sob escaped her.*

She broke away from Alexander and stumbled back against the tree, touching her cheek, wet with tears. It was just one memory, but every emotion she had ever felt came flooding back: the love, the deep affliction of the heart, the agony of it breaking.

"You left me." Her voice didn't sound like her own.

"Norah—"

"Like I meant nothing to you." She shook her head as she bit back the bitterness of shame. How foolish she felt to have developed those affections for him all over again.

"Your grandmother discovered us," he told her. "She reminded me of my duty and told me what I should have told myself."

"Then why do you play with me now?" she cried.

He shook his head. "No. Norah, I—"

"I want to go back." She slipped past him and headed for the castle. She didn't want to hear what he had to say. It would hurt.

"Norah," he called after her.

But she didn't stop. She couldn't.

Norah lay in the bath, drawing in the heat from the water and desperately trying to focus on anything to take her mind away from the ache in her chest. She closed her eyes and leaned against the back of the tub, cursing her emotion. Catherine hadn't wanted her to name Alexander as her lord justice. Now she knew why. Perhaps she had always known but didn't want to see.

Regardless, as much as she hated to admit it, she wouldn't have chosen differently for her lord justice. Mercia needed Alexander. She still needed him.

The chamber door of the bedroom opened and closed, but she didn't sit up. She didn't open her eyes. There was only one who disregarded the social graces of her privacy.

"Norah," Catherine called.

She stayed, unmoving, not answering.

"Norah!" Her grandmother's voice came more urgently now.

Under the warmth of the water, a chill ran over her skin. Did Catherine know she had been with Alexander? Had he said something? Is that why she was here?

Catherine burst into the bath chamber. "By the gods, child! Did you not hear me calling you?" She didn't give Norah time to reply. "Samuel sends for us. A vision's come—of you! The first one since you left!" She disappeared into the side cabinet chamber.

Norah sat up in the tub, and her stomach knotted. "Of me?" Her mind drifted to the memory that had returned at the tree. Surely it wasn't a coincidence.

Catherine bustled back into the bath chamber with a gown and undergarments. "Why are you still in there? Get out! Quickly!"

Norah stood and stumbled out of the water. She wrapped a towel around her as her grandmother shoved the undergarments into her arms.

"Do you know what the vision is?" Norah asked.

"Not yet. Samuel only said to come. Gods, child." Catherine frowned. "Have you not a single thing on yet?"

Norah struggled with the clothing as it stuck to her damp skin, but she managed to wriggle into most of the items thrown at her. Catherine pulled tight the lacing on her corset before she had fully situated it, and it choked off her breath. The gown came over her head, and Norah thought she might fall over.

"Your hair is soaking wet," Catherine chided as she pushed the locks aside and fastened the gown up her back.

Norah frowned. "Well, I was... in the bath."

Dressed, Norah pushed her feet into her silk slippers. Catherine took a towel roughly to her head and then dragged a brush through her mane. Norah didn't mind the rush. It was better than primping, actually, but an anxiousness swelled inside her at what the vision showed. She wasn't sure she wanted to be in such a hurry to see it.

Norah looked in the mirror of the vanity. She looked normal enough.

"You look fine, my dear," the woman said, and herded her out of the chamber.

They hurried down the cobbled walkway outside, to Samuel's gallery. It wasn't far, but it would have been nice to have remembered her cloak. Her hair was still damp, and she shivered in the evening winter air.

"Would you like me to get a cover, Regal High?" Caspian asked from behind her.

She hadn't noticed the captain had joined her evening guard. She smiled back at him. "It's not much farther, but thank you."

They reached the seer's door, and Norah followed Catherine inside.

"Samuel!" Catherine called as they weaved through the paintings toward the back room.

"Queen Norah," Samuel greeted when he saw them. "Come, come." He waved them back. "It is not finished, but it is clear enough to see."

They stepped around the easel to discover a large and complex scene across the canvas. A battlefield. Norah's eyes were drawn to herself riding atop a black horse. Her hair was wild in the wind around her.

Bodies littered the ground, and the dirt was stained with blood. She recognized her own Northmen—fighting, dying. There were others battling beside Mercia, with colors of royal blue. Her gaze shifted to a man mounted on a destrier, charging the battle beside her. He wore a leafed crown on his full-faced helm and held his sword in the air. She almost touched the image, but remembered it was still wet. "Who is that?" she asked.

"That, my dear, is King Phillip," Catherine said proudly.

Norah leaned closer. His armor was a polished silver, and on his shield was the sigil of a lion encircled by four stars. She wished she could see his face and frowned in irritation as her eyes drifted across the rest of the image. Black figures saturated the left side of the painting.

"Shadowmen," her grandmother said.

A different army, of black and rusted red, caught her eye. "Who are they?"

Catherine shook her head. "I don't know."

It was impossible to tell who fought whom through the sea of death. Norah's stomach turned. How many kingdoms were in this battle?

"War is coming," Catherine said. "And not just any war, another Great War."

"Queen Norah," Samuel interrupted. "There's another."

Her head snapped up, and her eyes widened. "Another vision?"

He nodded.

Her stomach tightened as they followed him to a second easel where another painting sat. This one was smaller but just as haunting. It was an extension of the first. The battle raged on, and in the center of the painting fought a man clad in armor. But he wore no helm and his golden locks shined bright against the backdrop of war. *Alexander*. He wielded a sword above his head, with his teeth bared. His body twisted in attack on a man that had been knocked to the ground, a man with his arm outstretched against his fate. Norah's breath caught in her throat at the fated man, for on his head was a horned helm.

Catherine gasped. "By the gods!"

*The Shadow King*—the man her father had warred against, the man who sought to destroy her. He would fall in this war. Alexander would kill him.

Catherine clutched Norah's arm, almost pulling her over. "Norah! With Phillip by your side, we'll defeat the Shadow King!"

Well, Alexander would defeat him. But Mercia was joined with Aleon on the battlefield. Norah swallowed back the knot in her throat as she moved back to the first painting. She looked closely at Phillip on his chestnut stallion. This was the man she was expected to marry, the man that would feed her people and help win this war.

"Norah, you can't deny this," pressed Catherine from behind her. "Think about your people. You must do what is best for them. This winter rages on, and they look to you. And more than that, these visions are what await you. You need this marriage to Phillip, and soon."

*Marriage*. There it was again.

"Phillip is a good king," Catherine stressed further, seeming to read her mind. "You could come to love him in time."

Norah clenched her teeth. That wasn't how love worked. Perhaps she wished it did. She backed away from the easel. How helpless it felt to have no control, no choice. The images suffocated her. She stumbled numbly back through the sea of paintings and toward the door.

"Norah," Catherine called after her.

Norah pushed out into the winter, sucking in the icy air. It stung her lungs but felt good. It cleared her mind, helped her think. This wasn't about love. This was about helping Mercia and her people. They wouldn't survive the winter. And if this war was to come, she would need Phillip by her side, like in the painting. She would need his army.

Her grandmother was right, and she hated it. Catherine stepped out of the gallery, and they stood on the cobblestone walk. For once, her grandmother was silent.

"Will you help me write a letter?" Norah asked finally. "To this King Phillip of Aleon?"

Catherine let out a breath as she put her hand on Norah's arm. "Of course, my dear."

# CHAPTER TWENTY-ONE

Despite the eternity of night, the morning sun came too soon. Norah lay awake in bed, looking at the ceiling. Perhaps she'd acted too hastily, but it was too late now. She rose sluggishly as Rebecca opened the draperies and brought in her dress. The cold water woke her fully as she washed her face.

Catherine entered her room as Rebecca fastened the last of the clasps on the back of her dress, and Norah looked up at her in the reflection of the mirror.

Her grandmother gave her a sympathetic smile. "I won't pretend today will be an easy day for you."

Norah didn't respond. By now, the council was already aware of the new vision. She would go to them this morning and announce her acceptance of marriage to Phillip. In a week's time, she would travel to Aleon, where they would be wed. That would be her life.

Norah stepped out of her chamber and into the hall leading to the stair. She noticed the captain, Caspian, on guard with Titus, as he had been the evening before. *Odd.*

When they reached the judisaept, the council was waiting.

So was Alexander.

She tried to avoid him, but his gaze caught hers. She couldn't escape. There was a desperation in the storms of his eyes. And something else. But she couldn't think about that right now. She took her place at the head of the table, but she didn't sit. This wouldn't take long, and she couldn't bear to be there any longer than she needed to.

Norah swallowed, forcing an even tone. "As you're all aware, a new vision has come."

The council cast approving eyes on Alexander, clearly already feeling victorious over the Shadow King. Norah didn't. She wasn't sure if she could get the rest of the words out. "As queen, I can't see a clearer path than the one with Aleon. I've written to King Phillip, accepting his proposal of marriage, to continue the strong alliance between Mercia and Aleon."

The councilmen grinned and clapped, nodding in agreement and triumph. All except for Alexander.

"I'll leave in a week's time." She had more to add, but she couldn't speak it through the tears that threatened. She couldn't let them see her cry. "If you'll excuse me, councilmen," she said shakily. She turned and left before they could answer, stepping out into the hall and trying to catch her breath.

"Norah," her grandmother called from behind her.

But she couldn't face her. She couldn't face anyone. She hurried down the pillared walk and through the great hall, with only the sound of the captain's steps behind her. Of course he would follow.

When she reached the stairs leading up to her chamber, she paused, looking back. Catherine hadn't come after her. She glanced at Caspian, frustrated. There would be no getting rid of him. She turned and took a separate small hall toward a side drawing room. She wanted to be alone, as alone as she could be, and perhaps no one would look for her there.

The chill of the room would have normally pushed her from staying long, but she welcomed it now. It helped her stave off the tears that threatened. She'd do whatever was needed to help her kingdom and her people, but that didn't mean she'd resolved her emotion.

Norah stood by the window, looking out over the reach of the isle. The room had a view of the small sparring field on the west side, where she had tested swords with Alexander. Her mind moved to him. As if on cue, she heard footsteps behind her and turned to see him.

His presence forced more feelings that she was trying so hard to keep back. She turned to the window again, focusing on the sparring field outside and the men practicing on it.

Alexander drew close beside her. "Norah," he said softly. He waited until she looked at him. His face was etched in sadness, and it unleashed her own.

She closed her eyes against the overwhelming wave of emotion. Eternity spun around them in the silence.

"Norah," he said again, and she opened her eyes to him. "That night at the tree... it was the night before your father took you. It was the last time I saw you, and it's haunted me since. Had I known..."

He stopped himself and pushed out a long breath between his teeth.

Her eyes searched his. "What would you have done differently had you known?"

But he didn't answer.

She nodded. *Nothing.* She needed to accept this was what they were. She moved to leave, but he caught her hand.

"Norah."

His touch pulsed a warmth through her, and she stopped. Her eyes dropped to where his hand wrapped around her wrist. He loosened his hold but didn't let her go.

They stood as if they each feared the reaction of the other.

Alexander stepped closer. His fingers relaxed around her wrist, and ever so softly he grazed her palm as he ran his hand down over hers. His caress prickled her skin as he entwined his fingers between hers.

"Did you lie to me?" she whispered.

His breath clipped.

She lifted her eyes to his. "Did you lie when you said you didn't love me?"

His lips parted, but there were no words. She wanted to beg him to tell her he lied.

He leaned even closer as he lowered his head, with only a breath between them. If she raised her chin, their lips would meet. Her body betrayed her, rolling her upward.

"Norah," he breathed. "I—"

A tap on the doorframe by the captain broke the moment. She had forgotten he was there, and a flush came to her cheeks. But she didn't have time to mull over it. Someone was coming.

Alexander's jaw tightened as he pushed out a long breath. They couldn't be found like this. He pulled his hand from hers and stepped back, but their eyes stayed on each other's.

Catherine reached the room, drawing Norah's gaze as she entered. The woman stopped when she saw them. "Norah," she said. Her tone was stiff, a warning.

Norah glanced back up at Alexander. The words that she desperately needed to hear from him, they wouldn't come now. Perhaps it was better

212

they were left unsaid. They would either further break her or make it that much harder to do what she must. Either way, no good would come of them. She swallowed back her need and moved around him to leave. She couldn't look at her grandmother as she stepped past her and out into the hall.

"Norah," Catherine said, but she didn't stop.

Caspian stood, waiting. He'd been the one to alert them. Had he seen them? She averted her eyes, heat creeping back to her cheeks, and quickened her pace toward her chamber as he fell in step behind her.

"Norah," Catherine called from behind.

She didn't want to hear whatever her grandmother had to say. She didn't want the judgment, the chastisement. She couldn't bear it on top of everything else.

"Norah," Catherine called again.

She paused.

Catherine caught up to her. Her eyes were shadowed in a cloud of sorrow that tempered her icy fire. "Norah, you mustn't make it harder than it already is. You're so close, child. Don't let yourself be distracted."

Norah let out a breath of disbelief. "Distracted?" The bitterness lay thick on her tongue. She couldn't hold herself back any longer. "No! I have agreed to everything that's been asked of me, everything thrust upon me. I wear a crown I don't want, I'll marry a man I don't know, and I'll go to war with an enemy for a cause I don't fully understand. And now you tell me to feel nothing?" She shook her head. "I won't pretend I don't. I can't."

"Norah! You'll watch your words in these halls!" Catherine shushed her as she glanced around them.

"Or what?" she snapped. With a glance of finality, Norah turned and strode back to her chamber.

Alexander looked out from the window of his chamber at the torchlit square down below. The alcohol stung his throat as he took another drink from his chalice. He could still feel the warmth of her hand in his, the way their wrists had touched, the brush of their arms as he had stepped closer. The nearness of her lingered on his skin, and her breath on his lips. She was so close, and yet beyond his reach, as she had always been.

She had asked him if he had lied. He'd hoped himself wiser and stronger now, solid in his decision that what he'd done was best for Mercia, best for Norah. The truth was, if faced with that decision now, he wasn't sure he was strong enough to make the same choice. The heartbreak in her eyes when he had left her at the tree—it had haunted him the last three years. Now to see it all over again, and to lose her again, he didn't think he could bear it. The pain twisted inside him—not the dull ache of wanting, but the kind of pain that makes a man fade to nothing.

A knock from the hall interrupted him. He set his glass on the small table by the side chair. When he pulled open the door, he wasn't surprised. *Catherine*. He opened the door wider, and she swept inside.

Alexander stood, waiting for the admonishment he knew he deserved. But it didn't come.

Raising his eyes, he didn't find the anger he had expected, or the disappointment. There was no offense or rebuke. Only sadness hung between them, and it further opened his wound. He wanted her wrath, something that would take his mind from the pain. He needed it. Her sympathy would be the breaking point.

Catherine closed the gap between them, and her worry-worn eyes found his. "You've always known this would come."

His throat seized. He couldn't speak.

"You knew you couldn't love her," she said.

He knew. He'd always known. Yet he couldn't not. He drew in a breath and pushed it out, choking back the loss that threatened to break him.

Catherine sighed as she reached up and brought her hand to his cheek. "My dear boy," she said softly, "I feared this for you. For both of you. I've done everything in my power, but"—she ran her hand down to his chest and gave him a gentle pat—"you both have such stubborn hearts." She smiled sadly.

He feared his words wouldn't come without emotion, so he said nothing.

"I haven't come to chastise you," she said, smoothing the center trim of his doublet. "But I want to be sure you haven't forgotten yourself. You are the lord justice of Mercia."

*Lord justice.* A position he had aspired to his entire life, now a position that meant nothing when compared to losing Norah. However, his conditioned courtesies answered for him, and he felt himself nod.

Catherine gave him another pat and then stepped toward the door. As she opened it, she paused, turning back. "Alexander, when she leaves for Aleon, you won't go with her."

His head jerked up, and his eyes caught hers. "What?" he breathed, finally finding his voice. "She can't travel alone."

"You say that as though she's traveling half the world away. She'll be well within the safety of Mercian lands until she reaches Aleon. And she won't be alone. She'll have the captain and an army to escort her to the border, where King Phillip will meet her. In her absence, you're needed in Mercia with the rest of the council. That's your duty, Alexander."

*Duty.* He had given his life to duty. And it had ripped out his heart.

With a final gaze, Catherine stepped out, closing the door behind her.

Norah woke on the side chair where she'd fallen asleep, with her eyes still puffy from tears. It was dark outside. She stood as she reached up to push her hair back from her face. She opened her chamber door slowly to find Caspian and Liaman on watch.

"Queen Norah," Caspian greeted her.

"How long until morning?" she asked.

"Quite some time yet. Should I send for your maid?"

She shook her head. "No. Could I just get some water? And maybe something small to eat?"

"Of course." He nodded to Liaman, who left quickly for her requests.

Norah left the door open and sat down at the vanity, looking at herself in the mirror, but not seeing. Caspian stood in the doorway, facing outward. How awkward it felt with him now. "What you saw yesterday," she started, "what you heard—"

"I saw and heard nothing, Regal High."

"You would be a poor captain of the guard if that were true."

Liaman returned with some water, wine, and an assortment of food on a small plate. Caspian took it and excused him, leaving them to talk privately. He put the plate on the vanity in front of her and poured some water into a chalice. Norah eyed the wine, but she had spurred enough judgment for the moment, so she kept herself from reaching for it.

He gave her a sympathetic smile, as if reading her mind, and filled another cup with wine. "He wouldn't want you to hurt like this," he said softly.

Hurt was a good word. It did hurt. *And Caspian knew.* She shifted uncomfortably in her chair as she looked up at him. "What do you know of how he feels?"

His face sobered. "Forgive me," he said quickly. "It's not my place. I shouldn't have spoken."

"I don't want decorum. I want you to answer."

Caspian let out an uneasy breath. "I've known Alexander his entire life, and you've always been the center of it."

She swallowed. "He hasn't shared this with me."

"You mean he hasn't spoken the words that betray his duty? Because that's what he'd be doing." He paused. "It's not my place, but I urge you caution. He gets closer and closer to a danger I'm not sure you understand. If the council were to know, they would remove him."

"He's *my* lord justice," she argued. "*I* named him. *I* am queen."

Caspian frowned. "If the council thinks Alexander stands in the way of an alliance with Aleon, even you won't be able to save him."

Norah's heart beat heavy in her chest as a fear seeded itself within. What did *that* mean? She looked back at her chalice. "Is that why you've taken to guard work? Am I so obvious now it requires a captain's attention?"

"It requires a friend's attention," he said. "Discreet attention."

Her cheeks flushed with embarrassment.

"You must take care to not show your feelings in front of anyone else," he told her. "And trust your grandmother. She loves you both, and she works to protect you *and* the lord justice."

# CHAPTER TWENTY-TWO

Preparing to depart Mercia felt surreal. Norah had only known it as home for a short time, but it was strange to leave. She knew nothing else. Her grandmother would continue in the role of regent in Norah's absence, with the council's support. Perhaps it was better. Norah hadn't exactly mastered being queen.

Packing everything had been time-consuming. It would take a week to travel southeast through Mercia to the border of Praetoria, the first kingdom of the Aleon empire, where Phillip would meet her. Weather permitting, they'd reach the imperial capital of Valour in another week. The army gathered across the bridge on the mainland, readying the horses.

In the castle, Norah said goodbye to her grandmother. "Are you sure you'll be all right?" she asked. While Catherine would travel to attend the wedding, policies prevented them from traveling together, so her grandmother would follow separately.

Catherine clasped Norah's hands. "Child, don't worry about me. I'll join you in Aleon in time for the wedding."

*The wedding.* The mention of it made her stomach turn, but she forced a smile and kissed her grandmother's cheek. She turned as

Alexander entered. He paused when he saw her, then seeming to remember himself, he said, "The army is ready."

Norah glanced back at Catherine and then followed him out into the courtyard.

Caspian held her horse for her, and she mounted as gracefully as she could manage, knowing all eyes were on her, although the only eyes that mattered were Alexander's.

And his stare nearly broke her.

He reached out and gripped Caspian's breastplate, clutching him in a silent plea.

"With my life," the captain assured him.

Alexander's gaze met hers again, the storms in his eyes haunting her. Would she see him again? He looked back to Caspian and clasped the captain's shoulder tightly. "With the gods' speed, brother."

Caspian nodded and mounted his own horse, and Alexander's eyes locked back on Norah.

"I know Mercia's safe in your hands," she told him.

"Do you still have the blade I gave you?" he asked.

She did—strapped to her calf inside her boot. She nodded.

"Keep yourself well, Norah."

"Goodbye, Alexander," she whispered, and gave herself one last look of his face before she turned and urged her mount across the bridge.

Travel was slow with a large army; the first week felt like a year. Normally they'd have reached the border by now, but Alexander had increased the guard from one hundred to five hundred men, slowing their pace. It was hardly necessary, as Mercia bordered Aleon, and Norah wouldn't be leaving the safety of the kingdoms, but the council hadn't argued, so neither had she.

Inside her tent, she pulled off her dusty riding skirts as Rebecca laid a fresh riding dress out for her. Today had been especially long, and Norah's muscles ached from the ride. She thought about opting for the carriage in the morning, but the boredom of sitting in a cramped box for hours didn't appeal to her.

Thoughts of Alexander had filled her mind through the long hours of the day and well into the night. She wondered if he was thinking about her. She hoped he was, but then again, she hoped he wasn't. The longing was a curse she didn't wish for anyone.

Norah sighed. Two more days until they reached the first Aleon kingdom of Praetoria. And Phillip. She shifted uncomfortably in her saddle at the thought of seeing him. Or meeting him, rather, since she didn't have any memory of him at all. She'd decided to tell him of her memory loss right away. Her heart picked up a little. Perhaps he'd reconsider the wedding. But she pushed the hope away as quickly as it came. No. If he'd waited three years for her to return, it was because he was committed to the alliance with Mercia, memory loss or no.

She turned her attention back to the journey. She should enjoy the quiet while she could. Her life would be very different once she was wed to Phillip. She already missed the castle. She even missed Titus, but he'd arrive with her grandmother a week after Norah reached Aleon.

Rebecca ducked outside and returned with a basin and a pitcher of warm water.

"Would you like me to bring you some stew, Regal High? There's fresh venison tonight. It's delicious."

Norah smiled as her stomach grumbled at the thought. "That does sound good, but I think I'll get it myself. I'd like to sit by the fire for a little while, anyway."

"Of course, Regal High," her maid replied, and then ducked out of the tent.

Norah poured some water into the basin and washed her hands. They were so dry from the ride, and the water felt good. She longed for a hot bath. That would be the first thing she did when she reached Aleon, she promised herself. She dampened a cloth and cleaned her face and neck, letting the warmth refresh her. After re-braiding her hair and pulling on the clean, pale-blue riding dress, she felt almost a new woman, and she went to find the venison stew.

Caspian stood by the main fire, laughing at a story a soldier was recounting. Seeing her approach, he straightened and motioned to the men nearby for a bowl of stew. One was quickly delivered, and he handed it to her. "Be careful, it's hot."

She smiled, taking it from him. "Thank you." Rebecca was right—it was delicious. "Compliments to the chef," she said.

Caspian stretched out his hand toward the soldier he'd been talking to. "That would be Anderson."

Anderson bowed his head with a wide grin, and she raised her bowl to him in salute. Then she made her way closer to the fire to soak in the warmth. The air was crisp, but the heat from the flame danced across her face. Tiredness seeped into her body and pervaded her mind, but her spirit smiled. Despite the circumstance, there was freedom away from Mercia, away from the castle and eyes of judgment and expectation.

"It's a clear night," Caspian said, coming up behind her. She looked up at the stars. Surely there were millions. She ran her hand over her face, feeling the transfer of heat from her cheeks to her palms.

"I've sent a bird to the lord justice," he added, "to let him know we're in good health and two days from Praetoria."

The mention of Alexander drew her mind back to the hopelessness of her situation, but she forced a nod. "Good."

A fire went up in the distance, a perimeter check. It was quickly extinguished, and another continued the pattern. Each post took its turn, signaling all was well.

"How long has it been since you've stepped on unfrozen earth?" she asked him, dragging her boot through the dirt.

"I spent last summer on the isle, so it would have been the summer before," he answered.

She felt born of the winter, not able to recall anything else.

"They say Aleon has winters like our summers," he said. "I should very much like to see that."

Summer. Norah liked the thought. "Me too," she said. She drank the last of the savory liquid from the bowl. A wind rustled through the camp, and she shuddered. "Thank you for the company. I think I'll retire now," she said. "I'll see you in the morning."

But he didn't answer. His attention was to the south.

"Captain?"

"Wait." His voice came low, making her skin prickle.

She followed the direction of his gaze but saw only darkness. "What is it?"

"No signal."

She looked back into the night, straining her eyes to see. "What does that mean?"

"Something's not right," Caspian mumbled. He turned back to Norah. "I think returning to your tent is a good idea."

Norah's pulse quickened. It was probably nothing, she told herself, but she couldn't shake the unease.

The captain turned to the soldier closest to them. "I want to know why there's no signal. Go!"

But as the soldier turned, a wisp of an arrow cut through the dark and hit him in the chest, dropping him to the ground. Then a flurry of whistling darts came, and chaos filled the night.

It took Norah a moment to understand what was happening. Hands pulled her back, and she looked to see Liaman beside her. Soldiers scrambled for their shields and raised them overhead, coming together and forming a defensive circle around her. Her army was spread through the darkness; she couldn't see them all. A scream sounded in the distance, then it was brutally cut short. Her stomach turned.

They were under attack. Her heart raced.

An agonizing pause came, and she forced herself to push the panic down. She looked to Caspian as he and Liaman stood together with more of her soldiers in front of her. They'd keep her safe.

A second onslaught of arrows came, with the groans of dying men, and then there was another pause. Her men fell on either side of her. Another wave of her soldiers tried to join in her defense but were downed as quickly as they came. Those remaining kicked back the bodies of the dead and circled closer, their shields up and swords ready, and the panic she was trying desperately to keep at bay surged through her.

Shadows moved around them, but the enemy was invisible, and her men fell one by one. All she could see was darkness. It was enough to set fear into the bravest of hearts, but her men stood fiercely.

"Hold!" Caspian ordered.

She heard the *sip* of an arrow into flesh, and Liaman stumbled back, bumping against her. In the firelight, an arrow protruded from his chest.

"Liaman!" she screamed.

He waved her back as he forced himself to stand and pull his shield back up. But she knew it wouldn't be enough. And her panic turned to anger.

Another onslaught of arrows came, and two more men fell. Anger erupted into fury. She had to do something. Her men were dying all around her. How many remained? She couldn't lose another.

"Enough!" she raged. She ducked out from behind her men, screaming into the night. "Show yourselves, cowards!"

"Norah! Get behind me!" Caspian bellowed.

A haunting call reverberated through the night, and an eerie silence settled around them. Her remaining soldiers pulled tight around her with their arrows fixed on the darkness as Caspian pulled her back again.

A shadow loomed into view—a mounted fiend, larger than any man. His destrier, the color of night against night and plated in dark metal, snorted and screamed like a hell horse of Hammel as it pulled at the bit. The rider sat cloaked in darkness, broad shouldered and armored in shadows and chain. His horned helm was silhouetted against the moonlight.

She recognized the helm—the helm from Nemus's vision, the helm from Samuel's paintings.

"The Shadow King," Caspian said.

"I know who he is," she seethed. The tension of bowstrings sung around her as her remaining soldiers aimed at the king. But she called out, "Hold!"

His army was there; she could feel them. Ever so slowly, she made out the dark, shadowed shapes. Then Norah's breath caught as she realized they were surrounded by them. Hundreds, or more, of them, barely visible from behind the black of their shields.

"Demons," Liaman whispered beside her. He'd somehow managed to stay on his feet.

"If they were demons, they wouldn't be carrying shields," she said between her teeth. She looked back at the mounted man, forcing as much strength as she could into her voice. "You're who they call the Shadow King?"

Even in the night, she felt the Shadow King's eyes upon her, and the hair on the back of her neck stood on end.

"North Queen," he responded, his voice thick and haunting.

She stepped forward again. She wouldn't let him see her fear. "You attack the Mercian queen on Mercian lands. Do you mean to provoke a war?"

"We've been at war for a long time."

She squirmed under his unseen stare, but she didn't dare turn away. Her fury built. "Stop hiding and fight like honorable men!"

A low rumble came from him. A laugh. "I am not an honorable man," the Shadow King said.

The whir of another arrow came, and the soldier to her right fell. Two of her archers loosed arrows into the darkness, and a counterstrike of arrows hit them in return, killing both. Another arrow hit Liaman, and he sank to the ground. This time, he didn't get up.

"No!" she cried, but Caspian clutched her tightly behind him.

It was only Caspian with her now. A dark shape rushed toward him, and her captain swung to meet their attacker. The clash of their weapons echoed in the night, and Caspian kicked him back. Another Shadowman came from the side, and Caspian turned to defend, but he was hit from behind by a third.

Caspian tried to counter but was met by a fourth who swung and cut into his sword arm, making him drop his blade to the ground. He stumbled back, stunned.

"Caspian!" she screamed.

The Shadowman attacked again, and, without a sword, Caspian was easily overpowered and knocked to his knees. The Shadowman grabbed a fistful of his hair and held him before the king.

"Go," the king growled to Caspian from atop his beast. "Go tell the Bear I have your queen."

The Bear? She didn't know who that was, but she didn't have time to mull over it.

In one final effort, Caspian whipped a blade from its sheath at his side and delivered a quick stab to his captor's leg, who fell back, releasing him. Caspian let out a cry as he then hurled the blade toward the king, but he'd thrown it with his left hand, and the dagger missed its mark, burying itself into a tree.

Norah jumped forward and grabbed Caspian's sword from the ground and moved in front of him to meet her enemies. She let her fury drive out the fear. If they didn't expect a fight, they were mistaken.

"Take her," the Shadow King growled.

"Norah!" Caspian yelled.

A soldier rushed her with a sword, but she met the attack fiercely, driving him aside and ripping her blade through the soldier's leathers. Another jumped at her, trying to knock her to the ground, but she sidestepped him and sank her blade into a third attacker. The Shadow King dismounted, drawing his own sword. She inhaled deeply, calculating and focusing her anger. Committing, she attacked with every ounce of strength she had.

But the force of his strike knocked the sword from her hands, dislocated her shoulder, and made her cry out. She gritted her teeth against the nauseating pain and looked desperately for another weapon.

He caught her from behind and picked her up by the waist. She flailed back with her good arm, catching the chin of his helm with her elbow and flinging it from his head. She couldn't see his face, but her fingers met his flesh, and she clawed at him with her nails. He caught her hand and twisted it down, pinning it beside her. She struggled, but the pain in her shoulder took the breath from her, and she felt her consciousness fading.

"No!" Caspian's bellow came from behind her.

This was it, she thought. She wasn't afraid. No one escaped death. She just hadn't expected it so soon.

Hands gripped her, and she drew in a ragged breath. Pain shot through her chest and down her arm, but she wouldn't cry out again. She was pulled upward, and it was too much. The pain crept into her mind, and everything grew dark.

The army marched silently through the night as the king carried his prize—a snow-haired queen cloaked in pale blue under the light of the moon.

# CHAPTER TWENTY-THREE

Norah woke in a tent, on her side, lying across a bedroll with a thick fur that had been dropped over her. The bedroll gave little cushion to the hard ground, and her joints protested as she stirred. Clinking metal and voices outside swirled in the fog in her mind. It took a moment for her senses to come, and then she bolted upright, remembering. An ache shot across her chest and down her arm.

Her shoulder.

She moved it gingerly. It had been reset, but it was still sore. At least she could move it.

She still wore her riding dress, and even her boots were on. Remembering her knife, she fumbled desperately under the bottom of her skirt and swore under her breath. They'd taken it; only the empty sheath remained strapped around her calf. A tremor ran up her spine as she thought of the Shadowmen searching her, touching her. She bit back the emotion threatening to surface—she couldn't be emotional now.

She had to focus on the positive—anything that could give her strength.

She was alive and seemingly unmolested. That should bring some relief, but there was little relief to be had. So many of her men were dead.

How many had been captured? How many might have escaped? Liaman had fallen.

*Caspian.* A crushing weight fell on her. He couldn't have survived either. She covered her face in her hands, emotion shuddering through her.

Norah tried to swallow back her sorrow. She needed to assess her situation and figure out what to do. She looked around. The tent was bare save for her bedroll and the fur. She was alone. Daylight spilled in through the heavy canvas, and the continued sound of men outside drew her attention. She rose and crept toward the front flap of the tent, listening closely. Her heart beat wildly in her chest. She'd been captured, but she wasn't restrained.

She gathered her nerves and stepped out to face her fate.

A guard standing outside stepped back from her in surprise, clearly not expecting her to so boldly emerge. A head wrap covered his head and face—all but his eyes. He wore fitted, black breeches, armored at the knee and tucked into a high boot. Looking closer, she realized that what she'd thought was a shirt under his cloak wasn't clothing at all, but inked markings covering his bare skin.

He gripped his spear tighter, and she stiffened, anticipating a fight, but he made no move to keep her inside the tent. She took a step forward and garnered some confidence as he took another step back. Perhaps he wasn't permitted to engage her, and her courage grew.

Norah looked around. Shadow soldiers were busy at work, sharpening weapons and tending horses, but when they noticed her, a quiet fell over the camp. She shifted uneasily. The army was massive, with men as far as she could see. Her eyes widened in surprise. There were men *and* women. They all wore wraps over their faces and were clothed in black and covered in ink markings. However, the women wore breasted plating that was feminine, but threatening all the same. She'd never seen a woman soldier in Mercia.

Although their faces were covered, Norah could see they were darker-skinned people, the color of bronzed sand. All eyes were on her, but no one moved to challenge her. She grew bolder still.

Norah let her gaze roll over the masses, taking everything in, when she saw him.

The Shadow King.

He stood beside a tent nearby, fully armored and crowned with his horned helm, just as she had remembered. Another man stepped into view, and Norah's breath caught in her throat. She recognized the monster from Nemus's vision of the future her father had stopped, the one of a fallen Mercia. This was the brute who had killed Edward and the councilmen in the vision—the demon commander, *the Destroyer*. She had almost snickered at the title when she'd first heard it, but she wasn't snickering now. He was even larger than the king, which didn't seem possible, and looked very much like he enjoyed destroying anything he could touch.

She swallowed. Don't show fear, she told herself. As if that were possible.

Norah stepped toward them. A tension rippled through the air, but no one moved. She continued toward the Shadow King. As she drew closer, the sound of blades drawn from their scabbards cut the air.

The king held up his hand to steady his army and let her come nearer still. She couldn't see his face, but she imagined something wicked underneath. The chest plating of his armor was dark and battled, but polished. His arms were covered in a light armor of small overlapping scales for fluid range of motion. She made mental notes to think on later. He waited, letting her inspect him. *Arrogant.*

"Where are my men?" she demanded.

His voice came as it had before, dark and haunting. "What men?"

Her pulse raced. He had to have taken some of them captive. "I had an army."

Another deep chuckle vibrated in his chest. "*Had*," he replied. "And five hundred men do not make an army."

Her chest tightened. Were they all dead? "What happened to them?" she asked between her teeth.

"Dead. All except one to deliver a message. I only hope he doesn't die before he reaches the North. Perhaps I should send birds after just in case." His eyes smiled from under his helm. "I regret you missed it. I lined them up on their knees and slit their throats, one at a time. You can be proud, though. No one begged me for their life, like so many do."

Her body shook. Caspian. Liaman. Aaron. Daniel. Tears threatened. "What about my maid?" she seethed, her voice quaking.

"She took her own life," he replied. "That wasn't my doing."

Her lip trembled. *Rebecca.* "Everything is your doing!"

He chuckled again. "I suppose it is."

"Every soldier of Mercia will come for me," she spat.

The Shadow King gave another dark, rumbling chuckle. "Good. I'm counting on it."

Alexander stood in the watchtower, looking blankly out over the horizon. It had been five days since the last message had arrived, two days longer than expected. A deep worry grew in his core. Caspian wouldn't have carelessly forgotten, knowing Alexander would be waiting on the messages. *Every* message.

Footsteps came behind him, but he didn't turn around. He knew who it was.

"Still no word?" Catherine asked.

He gave a small shake of his head. "Something's wrong."

She stood beside him, looking out across the bridge to the mainland. "We don't know that yet. Sometimes birds are lost or delayed. Let's wait to see if another will come."

"That's another day," he snapped, sharper than he had intended. He pushed out a breath. "If something's happened, I can't wait another day to discover it. I can travel quickly with only a few men."

Catherine frowned. "And do what? She has an army of five hundred with her. What will you accomplish with only a few more?"

Alexander wiped his face with his hand, pushing back the desperation mounting inside him.

Catherine put her hand on his arm. "My dear, I'm as sick with worry as you are, but you must think about this rationally. Another bird's due tomorrow. Let's see what comes."

Just then, a flurry on the horizon caught his attention, and he narrowed his eyes.

"What on earth is that?" Catherine asked, seeing it as well.

But Alexander didn't answer. His pulse quickened as he drew in a ragged breath. Messenger birds. *An entire flock.* He spun and raced down the spiral staircase of the watchtower.

"Wait!" she called after him.

He couldn't.

Alexander reached the bottom of the stair and broke into a run across the courtyard to the library with a crushing weight in his chest. He tore through the front doors to the staircase of the avian tower.

"Rector!" he shouted as he bounded up the stairs, three at a time, and threw open the door at the top. Rector Tusten stood by the window, holding a bird in his arm that had just landed. He looked up at Alexander in confusion and held out his hand. Alexander, out of breath, took the small piece of parchment. His body shuddered. It held no message, only a dark earthen stain.

"What is it?" the rector asked.

He ran his finger over the rippled parchment. "Blood," he breathed.

The rector's hands trembled as he released the bird onto the table. "What does it mean?" he asked.

Alexander looked to see a pile of similarly stained parchments on the corner of the rector's desk. More birds were still landing. Whoever had sent them, had sent them *all*, and their message would all be the same.

The capital bells sounded, and Alexander pushed by the rector to look out the window. A rider on horseback crossed the bridge, into the courtyard. Alexander clenched the parchment in his hand as he spun around and made his way quickly back down the stairs.

Catherine had just reached the library by the time he was coming out. "What's going on?" she demanded.

Alexander paid her no mind. Panic rose in his chest as he saw the rider, slouching over and clinging to his horse. Guards pulled the blood-covered man down, and Alexander's breath caught in his throat as he recognized Caspian. The captain's right arm hung limply.

*"Where is she?"* he roared, grabbing him by the breastplate.

"Gone," Caspian said hoarsely. "He took her."

Alexander's voice shook. "Who?"

"The Shadow King."

A deep and aching horror rippled through him, followed by a rush of rage. He turned and bared his teeth with a roar. "Ready the army!" he thundered. "We march tonight!"

"Wait!" Catherine cried. "Wait! This is obviously a trap. You can't blindly rush in! We need a plan."

Alexander ignored her.

"The council will override you," she said, breathless.

He whirled toward her with a fire under his skin. "That would take the *collective* council. Henricus and James are in Damask. They cannot assemble in time to stop me."

"Alexander," Catherine cried as she grabbed him by the arm. "Think about what you're doing!"

He ripped his arm from her hold and strode out to meet his army.

# Chapter Twenty-Four

The Shadowmen were silent travelers. Norah didn't find herself particularly keen on conversation, but she wanted information. However, the day passed without words, and at night she slept again in the quiet cold of darkness. She took comfort in the thought that Alexander would come for her with the full force of the Mercian army. She wondered where the Shadow King planned to meet them. They weren't headed northwest, toward Mercia, but instead they rode south along the rocky hills of the midlands.

They stopped midafternoon and watered their horses at a small stream. Norah wished it were larger so that she might throw herself in it and float away. She crouched down and scooped the water to her lips. It was cold as ice and stung her fingers, but she drank her fill.

She felt the king's dark presence behind her, and she looked back over her shoulder.

"Eat," he ordered as he tossed a small pouch of bread and dried meat on the ground beside her.

She glanced at it but didn't move to pick it up. She wanted to eat. Her stomach begged for it, but she had no intention of taking food from the Shadowmen. She rose, leaving it, and said nothing.

His eyes narrowed underneath his helm. "Starve then."

But Norah didn't plan to be in his hold long enough for it to matter.

The next day passed much like the one before. Despite the move south, the winter was merciless. The wind stung her cheeks, and she couldn't help the shivers that ran through her. She buried her hands in her horse's mane, trying to warm them.

As the afternoon waned, energy picked up through the army. Something was coming—something that excited them. As they made their way through the hills, she caught sight of mountain peaks and knew immediately where they were going.

*Bahoul.*

It's where the unit of her Northmen had been heading—the unit whose heads the Shadow King had sent back to Mercia. She shuddered at the memory.

Catherine had told her about Bahoul—a walled stronghold across the rocky mountains separating the Shadowlands from Mercia's southern reaches. It had once belonged to the Shadowmen, but her father had driven the Shadow King back and took it. Mercian forces occupied the stronghold now. The Shadowmen had tried to reclaim Bahoul several times, but Alexander led defenses that had held the mountains. The fortress was near impenetrable, and even a small resident army could defend against a much larger foe, so long as they stayed within the stronghold.

Her pulse quickened. Was he going to try to retake it now?

They made their way through the rocky hills and along a small ridge, but as they started down the other side, Norah's breath caught in her throat.

Another massive army of Shadowmen waited between the hills, just out of sight from the stronghold. Her heart beat faster. The Shadow King reined up his horse and looked back at her. "Are you ready, North Queen?" he asked with a haunting snarl. "Tomorrow, I take back what's mine. Then the Bear will bring your army, and I'll take them too."

*The Bear.* He'd said that name before. Beurnat the Bear—Alexander's father? He'd died in the war. But she said nothing.

The king's eyes were still on her. "I'll kill them all," he said. "This time I'll make sure you watch." He was trying to get a reaction from her, but she kept her gaze forward and remained silent. She wouldn't give him the satisfaction.

Norah lay awake in the darkness. It was morning. She had been given no tent that night, only a thin bedroll and a fur, and she was surrounded by Shadowmen. But that wasn't why she hadn't slept.

Her stomach turned. The Shadow King would use her to get her Northmen to hand over the stronghold, and then bait Alexander and her army into battle. If the Shadowmen succeeded in taking the stronghold now, the Mercian army would be at a severe disadvantage when they arrived.

As the faintest light of morning chased back the darkness, she pushed herself up to sit. A blanket of mist lay around them. A low chuckle reverberated through the fog. Her skin prickled.

"A perfect morning for battle," the king's voice came.

She couldn't tell from which direction, and she shuddered. Her heart beat faster. It was a terrible morning for battle. The mist would cover the

Shadow army. Mercia had the best archers in the world, but they could do nothing if they couldn't see.

Then, through the mist, she saw him as he stepped in front of her.

"Are you ready, North Queen?"

The king's demon appeared to her right, and she jumped. He grabbed her.

"What are you doing? Let me go!" She twisted against him, but he squeezed his arms around her until she couldn't breathe, then bound her wrists with the long rope.

He dragged her to where his destrier stood, and mounted. Then he pulled up a spear, as if he needed another weapon in addition to the sword on his back and the massive battle-axe resting across his thighs. He urged his mount forward, jerking the rope—and her—toward what she surmised was the base of the mountain stronghold.

Norah's mind raced. The commander had touched her and held her tight as he bound her hands. She'd felt not the body of a demon, but a body of flesh and bone. He was a man, a brute of a man, but a man nonetheless. *And men bleed.*

Her skin flushed with the heat of fight.

She tried to work loose the rope around her wrist as he pulled her along, but it was hopeless without a blade. A *crack* under her heel caught her attention, and she glanced down to see a partially buried skull in the ground. She jumped sideways in surprise. Her eyes widened as she realized they were the scattered remains and timeworn fragments of weapons from battles past. They covered the ground. Were these Northmen she walked across, or Shadowmen? She shuddered. The commander pulled her along, and she stumbled forward.

They stopped at the base of the mountain stronghold, but the mist still covered them.

"Northmen!" the brute boomed in a deep, resounding thunder. "I have your queen! Come and claim her!"

He was trying to draw them out.

"They aren't fools!" she spat at him.

He gave a low chuckle. "Your screams will make them come." Then he jerked the rope, pulling her toward him. Her anger surged. She fought back, but she was no match for his strength and only stumbled forward.

But Norah had no intention of allowing herself to be used against her army. In a split decision, she lunged toward him, running and sliding under his horse. She gave the animal a sharp blow to the underbelly as she skirted out and then reeled back, pulling the slack of the rope tight against its hind legs. The animal reared, and she threw her weight against the rope, making the beast lose its balance and crash to the ground atop the brute. She pulled the rope free, twisting clear of the animal's kicks as it tried to right itself.

The destrier rolled off the commander, who stirred and gasped for breath. As the animal staggered back to its feet, she jumped up and struggled onto it. Her window of opportunity would be short, and the Shadow army was near. Her bound hands made movement difficult, but she spurred the beast forward. Under her thigh, a short sword had been stowed in the saddle. She thanked the gods and slipped the hilt up, sliding her bound wrists up the blade and freeing herself.

Norah stretched forward to give the destrier his head to run. She'd lost her direction in the mist, and she prayed she was headed toward the stronghold.

And then she was falling.

She hit the ground with a force that knocked the wind from her. Rolling to her side and struggling for breath, she looked back in horror to see the horse had been downed with a spear. The beast struggled to rise, and thrashed for a moment, but then gave up and lay in silent agony. Behind, she could only make out the commander's form in the mist, on his knees, still not fully recovered. But he had recovered enough to spear the horse—he could have hit her.

Norah gasped as her lungs gave her air again, and she stumbled up to her feet.

The commander rose, pulling up his axe and moving toward her.

She raced back to the horse and pulled the short sword from the saddle and stood to meet her enemy. The king's brute lumbered closer, and she backed away. He reached the animal, swinging his axe and plunging it into its neck to give it peace.

And then she heard them—all around her in the mist.

She couldn't see them, but she knew they were there. *The Shadow army*. The king appeared on her left and swung down from his horse, pulling his own sword. A soldier beside him tossed him a spear as well.

Norah clutched her sword firmly in her hand, widening her stance for more control and settling her breath. She praised her younger self that she had learned how to fight, and cursed her current self that she hadn't practiced more in Mercia, but she knew she was dangerous with a blade. Her shoulder still ached, but she pushed it off and braced for the king's rage.

He took long strides toward her, with his sword in one hand and spear in the other. She was no match for his strikes; she'd have to be quicker. Her stomach twisted. She hadn't been quick enough when he'd taken her before—it had been like she wasn't even fighting, like she was nothing.

Fear coursed through her, but she couldn't let that take over. Still, her body shook at the thought of countering the thunderous blow of his strikes with her own.

The king swept the body of the spear at her, attempting to knock her off her feet, but she darted back. He swung again, harder this time, his patience waning, and she twisted sideways, dodging the blow. He wasn't trying to kill her, but the strength of his swings could seriously hurt her. Not that he cared.

He swung again, and she jumped back but collided with the fortress wall behind her. Her head struck the stone, and a pain cracked through her skull, darkening her vision.

And then he was on her.

He grabbed her by the throat, pressing her hard against the wall. Norah dropped her sword and clawed at his hand, but it held.

"Do not test me, North Queen," he snarled.

But Norah wasn't testing him; this wasn't facetious rebellion. She needed to get away, she needed to be free. Her life depended on it. Mercia depended on it. So she fought. With everything she had, she fought.

Her fingers grazed the hilt of a dagger at his waist, and she snatched it, ripping it across the unarmored forearm of his spear hand. He snarled again as he dropped the spear and tried to catch the knife, but in a final effort, she drove it between the break in his armor on the side of his breastplate. Her angle was off, and the hit wasn't true, but he roared in pain. Then she threw up an elbow and caught him at the base of his throat, just under his helm. She just needed to get him off...

He crushed her against the wall, leveraging his weight to overpower her. She couldn't breathe. As he recovered, he pulled her to him, tight. She was no match for his strength, and, with no more weapons, no more energy, she stilled.

Norah panted between her teeth as she waited for his wrath. He had warned her, and no doubt she'd suffer his anger now. But it wasn't anger that she saw in his eyes underneath his helm. Surprise, perhaps? Disbelief?

"Hold her," he growled. His brute commander stepped forward and seized her arms, not gently.

The king gathered himself for a moment and then pulled the blade from his side with a grunt. Then he stepped toward her with the blood-covered blade in his hand. Terror rippled up her spine. What was he going to do?

A horn sounded from the mist behind them, and he stopped and turned. From behind her, the brute let out a low whistle.

Just then, a soldier on horseback stepped through the mist. He called to the king in the Shadow tongue. The king straightened and looked at his brute.

*News.*

He growled something unintelligible back to the messenger, who only gave a nod. Then he looked at her with eyes of night under his horned helm and shifted.

News that bothered him.

The king snapped an order to a soldier, who brought him a leather cord. He stepped forward and caught her wrists, clenching them tightly and tying her hands. Then he jerked her from the commander and pushed her toward the army. She didn't fight. There was no chance for her now, but seeing the brute commander limp back to another horse brought her a wave of satisfaction.

The king pushed her in front of him as they walked. His presence behind her made her skin crawl, but she focused her eyes ahead and kept walking. She stumbled over a sliver of a spear protruding from the frozen ground but caught herself—she'd almost forgotten the field of death they were walking across. She kept her eyes on the ground to watch her step. Just then, she spotted a sheath belt, half-covered in frozen mud, with what appeared to be a knife inside it. Or maybe it wasn't a knife at all. But if it was...

She faked another stumble and dropped to her knee over it, quickly grabbing at the hilt. Her heart leapt. It was a knife—a rusted knife, but a knife nonetheless. The king grabbed her arm and pulled her back to her feet, and she tucked the blade up her jacket sleeve the best she could manage with her hands tied.

A soldier brought a horse, a smaller palfrey—no doubt a less energetic mount, and the king dragged her toward it. She struggled against him. "I can manage myself," she hissed.

He shoved her forward. "Get on."

She grabbed the pommel, careful to keep her knife hidden in her sleeve, and mounted the palfrey. The binding cut into her wrists, but she gritted through it. She glared back at the king as he mounted his destrier beside her.

*Wait*. Was that it? Were they leaving?

"What about the mountains?"

"Change of plans," he said shortly. "The Bear comes for you."

She swallowed. Did he mean *Alexander*? Had he confused him with his father?

"He brings your entire army. Just as I expected."

"Well, if it's a change of plans, it's not *exactly* as you expected," she cut back.

His eyes burned into her. "Your army will meet their fate all the same. And you can watch, before you join them."

He was trying to scare her. It was working.

Taking one last look at the stronghold, he gave a frustrated snarl and led them away.

She shifted uncomfortably as they rode. She knew he wanted the stronghold of Bahoul. What had been the news? What had changed? He had expected her army, and they were coming. What was different?

"Where are we going?" she asked.

The king ignored her, and hot anger flushed her cheeks.

They rode all day, until the darkness of night came. She had managed to slide her stolen knife undetected into the empty sheath in her boot. At least now she had a weapon.

The ache in her shoulder crept up her neck and made her head throb. The fight, the fear, the struggle—it had drained her. When they finally stopped, she thought she might fall from her horse in exhaustion.

The king dismounted. "We'll camp here."

The army started their work, tethering their horses and erecting their tents. The king grasped her arm, pulling her from her horse and dragging her through the tasked soldiers.

"Let me go!" She struggled against him. "I can walk myself."

He gripped her arm tightly as a warning but finally released her and kept walking. She followed. She struggled to keep up. The army had no fires burning, and she wasn't used to maneuvering through the darkness.

"Where are we going?" she asked him again, and again he didn't answer. Anger flashed through her. "If you think you can best my army, you're mistaken. They've beaten you back before, and they'll do it again."

He whirled around and grabbed her, pulling her close. "They had Aleon." There was a deep irritation in his voice. "But now they come with nothing. And your men are archers and peace wishers. My army is skilled in true battle, and we do it often. The Northmen march to their end."

He released her and kept walking.

He was right. Phillip wouldn't yet know of her capture to send forces to join them, and without Aleon, they weren't strong enough to defeat the Shadow army. This nightmare was only just beginning.

They came to a large tent in the darkness. He pushed her inside and stepped in after her. It was dimly lit by a small candle. Dread rippled under her skin with him so close.

He reached to pull off his helm, and she looked away, afraid to see what it would reveal, but she couldn't help herself, and her eyes found their way back to him. A wave of surprise hit her. He was younger than she'd thought, aged by battle, but perhaps only a few years older than she was. His shoulder-length hair was tied back and was black as his cloak. The bruises and scrapes from her fight during her capture were bold on his face. *Good*—he deserved it. An old scar ran from his brow to his cheek. Apparently, she wasn't the only one who disliked him.

But this wasn't the man she'd thought he was. "You're not the Shadow King," she said coldly.

"You were expecting something else?" he asked. "A monster, perhaps?"

She scoffed. "Stories, meant to scare people."

He ambled toward her, the darks of his eyes almost drowning her, but she stood firm.

"You're flesh and blood," she said coldly. "Like your brute. You're men. And I'm not afraid of men."

"You should be," he said hauntingly.

Her eyes narrowed at him. "My father battled the Shadow King. You're not him. Where is he?"

His face darkened, and he shifted uneasily. She had struck something within him.

"You'll sleep here," he growled. Without another word, he ducked out of the tent and nodded to the soldier outside.

Was that it? Was that all he would tell her? She snorted in frustration and jerked the tent flap closed, but she did take a small comfort in being alone. A *small* comfort.

She blew out the candle and struggled for clearer vision in the darkness, then felt for the stolen dagger against her calf inside her boot. They still didn't know she had it. It brought a calmness to her. She wanted to run, but they would be expecting her to, and she didn't want to think about what would happen if she was caught trying to escape again. She struggled against the binding. She could cut it off, but then they would know she had the knife. No, she needed to wait.

Norah curled up on the bedroll. Her mind was filled with thought after thought, thoughts that sowed fear deep inside her, but she tried to push them out. She needed sleep.

She shuffled awkwardly to reach her bound hands down to her boot and curled her fingers around the knife. It wasn't Alexander's knife, but it would do. She held it as if it were his hand. And finally, sleep came.

# CHAPTER TWENTY-FIVE

The tent provided little warmth, and Norah shivered in the early morning chill. She lay long after waking, wishing for a fire. The Shadow army built no fires. She clenched her hands together; they ached with stiffness. Hearing voices outside her tent, she recognized one as the king's and quickly stumbled up from the bedroll.

He ducked into her tent but paused when their eyes met. "We leave now," he said.

She stood and eyed him coldly. She knew she'd dealt him a painful injury with the dagger, but it didn't show. He stepped closer to her, but she stood her ground. He reached out and grabbed her wrists, inspecting the binding.

She twisted away. "As you left me," she said sharply.

He towered over her, but she narrowed her eyes and faced him squarely. His face hardened, and he turned, leaving her alone once again.

Norah paused but then followed him out to find the palfrey from the day before saddled for her. She mounted as gracefully as one could manage with bound hands. The king mounted his destrier and reined up beside her. He held out a wrap of salted meat. She only shot him a daggered gaze in response.

"Eat," he said irritably.

She didn't want to accept food from him, but she was incredibly hungry. She needed to keep her strength, she told herself. Reluctantly, she took the meat.

He eyed her with a bitter smile. "Tell me, why come out now? Why come out freely after hiding for so long, where it was so easy for me to take you?"

Norah refused to answer him. She looked out across the hills as she bit the inside of her cheek, silently cursing. She'd been foolish for thinking the journey to Aleon would be an easy one, even if it was through Mercian lands. She'd been foolish for leaving the safety of the castle when the Shadow King wanted her dead, and for thinking he hadn't yet known of her return. Now he had her.

They rode most of the day in silence. The sun was out, but it did little to provide warmth from the winter air.

The king's voice pulled her from her thoughts.

"Who taught you to fight?" he asked.

She looked at him, her eyes narrowing. "Do you have some tips for me?"

He seemed surprised but surprised her back when he moved his horse closer to answer. "You let me get too close to you," he told her. "Your advantage is speed. You need to protect it with distance."

She scoffed. "Since you're free with your advice right now, how might I get this distance?"

"You won't," he said darkly. "You won't escape me, North Queen."

"Who are you?" she asked.

"You don't believe I'm salar of Kharav?"

*Salar of Kharav*? "I don't believe you fought my father in the Battle of Bahoul."

"I did not. Kings die. You should know this."

Norah paused as the realization hit her. "You're his son?"

He looked forward, ignoring her question. "Where have you been all these years?"

In turn, she didn't answer.

"Why did you wait so long to wed the Aleon king?" he asked.

"I wasn't sure if I liked him," she said flippantly. "Where did your brute commander come from?"

He shifted in agitation.

"Are you the Shadow King's son?" she asked again, not willing to give him information without receiving any in return.

"I am the Shadow King," he snapped.

There was a long silence between them. Finally, he spoke. "I am Mikael Ratha Shal, salar of Kharav, or the Shadowlands, as you call it."

"Salar?"

"Yes. *King*. I'm the son of Rhalstad Ratha Shal, who's the man your father fought in the Battle of Bahoul. Now, tell me where you've been."

It was no longer a question.

"My lord justice taught me to fight," she said, not willing to answer any of his other questions.

He didn't press her for more, which was good, because he wouldn't get more.

In her tent that evening, Norah's mind raced with the events of the day. If Alexander came for her, he'd be walking into a trap. She had to get away before they took her farther.

She strained to hear any sounds around her, but it was eerily quiet. How was an army of that size so quiet? She reached down and slid her dagger from her calf strap and worked quickly to cut off the binding from around her wrists. Except, the blade was rusted and dull, and her movements weren't *that* quick. Finally, with her hands free, she reached out to touch the back of the tent. *Cloth*. She worked patiently, cutting upward. She'd give anything to have Alexander's knife again. She could chew an opening faster, she mused. Once an opening was big enough to look through, she peered out to check for guards. She'd hoped there would be no soldiers behind the tent, and she breathed a sigh of relief to find none. Norah continued cutting, creating an opening large enough to fit through. She pushed the fearful sickness down as she gathered her courage. Once again looking out, she snuck through the opening and crept away, crouching close to the ground and not daring to breathe. There was nothing to hide her, and she cursed her light-colored clothing as she hurried through the darkness.

Norah made out the shape of a large tree in front of her, and she sidled up behind it to catch her breath, her hands shaking. Where was she? She needed to head north, back to Bahoul where her Northmen were, back to safety.

She darted from her brief cover to continue on, but a hand snaked out in the darkness and grabbed her from behind. She stifled a scream and sliced at her captor with her dagger. The blade hit something, but she wasn't sure what—his arm, his side? Had she gotten him at all? Maybe it had only grazed his leathers. She lashed out again, but he gripped her tight, thwarting her attack. Struggling desperately, she dropped her head to the hand on her shoulder and sank her teeth into the flesh, but he didn't release her. She tried to catch him with a butt back from her head, but he was a large man, and she hit only his chest. He clutched her tighter.

With her free left arm, she clawed back, reaching for his eyes. He twisted his head, and she caught only the flesh of his cheek and his lip through the wrap on his face. Norah ripped her arm upward and caught him on the brow with the heel of her palm. It sent a jolt of pain to the core of her bone, but it would be worse for him.

A blow to her stomach knocked the wind from her, and he pulled her close from behind. The warmth of blood dripped from his face and onto her shoulder as he wrestled her hands down. He squeezed her so tightly she could hardly breathe, and bile rose in her throat. *The brute.* She wrenched her body against him, only incenting his arms tighter. She feared her ribs might crack. Unable to breathe and with her energy depleted, she stopped struggling, and he pulled her back toward the tent.

"Let go of me!" she snapped at him.

When they reached the tent, the king was waiting for her. Norah tried to sheath the dagger in the sleeve of her jacket. She hoped the brute hadn't noticed it since she wasn't entirely sure whether she'd actually cut him in the darkness. Her wrist throbbed, and she prayed she hadn't broken it.

The commander released her in front of the king and called out in the Shadow tongue. She looked back at him in irritation, cursing him under her breath. The king stepped forward, grabbing her arm, and pulled the dagger from her sleeve. Not letting her go, he dragged her into his tent.

"You have more weapons?" he growled.

"No," she said stiffly. Like she'd have told him...

"Show me."

"I don't have anything else," she insisted.

"Undress," he commanded.

*The audacity.* The heat of anger rushed to her cheeks. "I will not!"

He grabbed her hand and pulled her to him. It was her injured wrist, and a pain shot through her. She tried to jerk away, but his grip was tight, and she cried out. He snaked a hand around her waist, feeling for another dagger. She twisted, throwing the elbow of her free arm up and catching him in the cheekbone. The strike hit hard, and he stumbled slightly. She used the momentum and twisted again, driving her shoulder into him, and they fell onto the bedroll.

Norah tried to roll away, but he still had hold of her wrist and jerked her back, scooping her underneath him. Using his body weight, he held her down. She fought to keep her arms at her chest as he tried to pull them above her head. She struggled with all the strength she had, but she couldn't move. In a final effort, she cracked her head forward, butting his face. It briefly stunned him, and his body weight crushed the breath from her.

Recovering, he forced her arms above her head and crossed them, scooping a fistful of her hair and completely immobilizing her. Repositioning his weight, he straddled her, holding himself above her and allowing her to breathe again.

"Stop making this harder!" he snapped.

"You mean stop fighting you?" she hissed. "Does it make you feel strong? Is this what you meant when you told me I should fear men?"

"You should fear a king!"

*"Kings die,"* she seethed, quoting him.

His face sobered. A gash spanned across the bridge of his nose where she'd hit him, and blood ran down his face. His lip was split, and she couldn't remember if it was an old wound from their previous tussle or a new one. He ignored both. Slowly, he moved his free hand down her stomach, feeling around her waist. She tensed but couldn't move.

She struggled again as he unbuttoned her jacket, but he continued to hold her. Her breath quickened as he ran his hands up her hips and sides. She looked away, shaking with rage, and waited. He used the back of his hand to touch her, a move that felt strangely considerate, but it only fueled her frustration.

Moving down, he ran his hand over her outer thighs and pulled her knee up to reach around her calves through her boots. He finished but didn't let her go. They lay in silence, the king above her. The dark pools of his eyes didn't hold the bitter hostility they once had. While he certainly wasn't gentle, he wasn't trying to hurt her, and despite his hold, her anger started to dissipate.

The king released her, standing up and straightening his clothing. He wiped the blood from the bridge of his nose and flicked his tongue over his lip.

She sprang to her feet, her heart pounding as he watched her. He swallowed and shifted. Her fury dampened slightly as she tried to make sense of him. He seemed at war in his mind, but then he pulled another leather cord from his packs and approached her again.

"Must I do this forcefully as well?" he asked.

She stewed in her anger but held out her hands to be bound. The skin was raw, and she grimaced as he pulled the cord tight around her wrists. His eyes locked with hers as he finished—they were almost apologetic, but only for a moment.

He called for another bedroll, and her stomach turned at the realization she'd be sleeping in the same tent as him. A bedroll was brought quickly, and she eyed it irritably before settling onto it.

Norah turned her back to the Shadow King and tried to imagine herself alone. She didn't hear him behind her, and it made her uneasy, but she didn't dare look back at him. Tears threatened. She bit her lip sharply, forcing an even breath. She couldn't allow herself to cry.

Despite the circumstance, and the binding, she did sleep. In her dreams, she saw Caspian's face. She saw her men falling, one after another, and all she could do was watch.

# CHAPTER TWENTY-SIX

Norah woke to an empty tent. The king was gone. She combed her fingers through her hair, re-braiding the locks and tucking wayward strands behind her ear as best as her bound hands could manage. What had they done with her things when they captured her? She found a basin of water, which she hoped was fresh, and washed her face and hands. Then she stepped outside. The sun hadn't yet come up, but light seeped over the hills. Crisp air chilled the dampness that remained on her skin. She shivered.

The massive Shadow army had started assembling, but there was no sign of the king. She turned and, almost colliding with a soldier, jumped. It wasn't a soldier, she quickly realized, but the king's brute. She couldn't see his face with the wrap on his head, only his eyes, which were like the king's—dark pools of night. There was something unnatural about him, and she swallowed back her fear. He wasn't really a demon, she told herself. She had hurt him.

He held a horse for her, remaining silent.

"Where's the king?" she asked, taking the reins and being careful not to touch his hand.

He didn't respond as he turned and mounted his own horse.

"I know you can speak," she muttered, and settled onto her own mount.

"Don't try to escape," he warned.

"I'll take your request into consideration."

The brute looked back over his shoulder, his impatience with her obvious. "Don't try to escape, or I'll walk you naked behind me with a rope around your neck like a dog."

Norah swallowed back her horror at the thought. She suspected he was just trying to frighten her, but she decided it was better not to test him. She'd made a spectacle of him the day prior, and he seemed like he would enjoy humiliating her if he could.

"Well, lead on," she mumbled.

They headed west, breaking away and leaving the army behind. Frost covered the ground, and the wind stung her cheeks. They'd hit snow before the day's end. She wished she had her belongings—the thicker gloves, the warmer clothing.

They rode in silence. She resisted the urge to ask questions. She knew he wouldn't answer. The army fell farther behind them as they rode. She wanted to turn back. It wasn't that she wanted to be back with the army but rather that she didn't want to be alone with the brute.

Time passed, and she grew more uneasy. Where were they going? Where was the king? Was the commander planning to kill her? Why else would they have left the army? Why else would they be alone?

The smell of smoke interrupted her thoughts. As they reached the top of the hill, she gasped at the sight. A small walled city lay in ruin before them. They drew closer, and the magnitude of destruction hit her.

Impaled heads lined the front gates, a grotesque message for anyone who passed. Her stomach turned, and she looked away, but there was nowhere to look that didn't show the horrors that had happened. Charred bodies littered the ground, and buildings smoldered. Her horse snorted nervously. A child's shoe lay in the mud, and Norah's breath quivered. What had happened here?

The king met them at the collapsing town center, waiting atop his horse of night, and she looked at him in horror.

"How could you..." Norah couldn't finish.

"This isn't my hand," he said.

"Then who?"

"That's a question for you, North Queen."

Confusion needled her. "What?"

"These are lands protected by Mercia, and this isn't a normal attack."

Norah swallowed back the bile in her throat. "That doesn't mean this was an attack against Mercia."

"Perhaps not." He paused. "Or perhaps it does."

Norah looked at the city, overwhelmed by the death around her—the death of all these innocent people. Anger rose inside her.

"Do you really not know who might have done this?" he asked.

"Mercia has only one enemy," she said bitterly. And she was staring right at him.

"No one has just one enemy." His eyes, dark and strangling, locked with hers. "And there are men worse than I, North Queen. You'll do well to remember that."

Who could be worse than the Shadow King? The thought struck Norah hard, and she swallowed the sickness rising in her throat.

He turned to the two soldiers that accompanied him. "We're done here."

Her brow furrowed. "That's it? We're going back?"

The king urged his mount forward. "Would you rather stay here?" he called over his shoulder.

She would rather not have come here at all. Norah bit her trembling lip. She couldn't bear it anymore; she was sick in her mind and her heart. But what could she do? Nothing. She could do nothing but follow behind.

The ride returning to the army was as silent as it had been with the brute. Norah tried to push the images from the village out of her mind. How could someone cause such devastation? And why?

The winter days were short, and darkness set in on them early. Norah trusted her horse to follow when she lost sight of the king in front of her. She nodded off as they rode, wishing she were back in the tent, warm in her bedroll.

Suddenly, she woke to being pulled off her horse. A hand covered her mouth before she could scream.

"Quiet," the Shadow King whispered in her ear.

Norah struggled against him.

"Quiet!" he hissed.

Her heart pounded, coursing alarm through her veins.

He pulled her through the darkness to a cover of brush, and they peered through to see a group of men sitting round a fire. There were eight, maybe nine—more than the number of soldiers with the king. They spoke in a language she didn't recognize.

"Drifters," he said quietly.

Norah's stomach turned, remembering her encounter in the Wild.

"Stay here, and stay down," he whispered, then disappeared.

Norah crouched low, listening and trying not to breathe. She struggled against the binding around her wrists, wishing for her dagger again, as she watched the men around the campfire.

Suddenly, one man straightened and looked out into the darkness, opposite her direction. He called to the others, who quieted and drew their swords. They left their fire to investigate, and Norah strained to see them as they disappeared into the night.

The darkness was quiet around her. Where had the horses gone? Where was the Shadow King and his brute? Where were the drifters now? Her heart beat in her throat. She was alone. She crouched lower.

Suddenly, the sound of a fight rang out. Weapons sang together in the night. She couldn't see them, but she could hear them from a distance away.

Her heart skipped. She was alone...

Was this the moment? Could she escape?

Before she could talk herself out of it, she turned and stumbled down the hill behind her. The binding around her hands made it difficult to run. Bushes tore at her clothing. A thin branch from an unseen tree caught her in the face and cut into her cheek, but she didn't slow. She didn't stop. Her legs burned, and her lungs felt like they were going to explode. She tripped on something and fell to the ground, stifling a cry as a jolt of pain ran up her arm, but she gritted her teeth and pulled herself back up. She had to keep going.

Norah knew she needed distance, and she fled farther into the night. She came upon a steep bank and thought she might not reach the top, but she pushed herself up and stumbled down the other side. Through the trees, then through the open, she ran. At some point, she stumbled through a stream, breaking the thin layer of ice on top and soaking the bottom of her riding dress. Still, she ran. When she couldn't go any farther, she let her legs slow. They shook with fatigue, and she steadied herself against a tree. Her breath echoed through the darkness, and she tried to calm it so she could listen.

Quiet. There was quiet all around her. Her wrists were raw. She needed to get the binding off. The moon provided little light, just enough to show the trees around her.

Which way?

Norah took a deep breath and decided to keep in the direction she was headed, but a shadow loomed in front of her and grabbed her. She screamed, and a sharp blow caught her across the face. She fell backward onto the hardness of the cold ground, knocking the wind from her lungs. A cackle escaped from another man to her right. He called something to her attacker she didn't understand. She struggled for a breath, but the man was suddenly on top of her, pinning her down. He yelled at her with a clipped accent, and there was no wrap around his face. These weren't Shadowmen.

He forced her bound arms above her head and held them there. The rope ate into her wrists as she desperately fought to pull them free. She screamed, but another blow to her face stunned her.

More men called out, encouraging him on. Another set of hands grabbed her, helping her captor hold her. She fought harder. The man on top of her pulled at her breeches underneath her riding dress, but he couldn't get them loose.

"No!" she screamed, struggling against them. The cold blade of a knife cut up the leg of her breeches under her riding dress.

Norah bucked frantically, panic setting in. The man on top of her forced his hips between her legs and reached down to release himself. The curve of his shoulder hit her chin and she bit into it. Hard. He grunted and delivered another blow to her face.

This couldn't be happening. She kicked, but she was no match for him. He gripped her thigh to hold her.

Just then, another shadow swept over her, and a fountain of warmth sprayed across her face. *Blood.* Her attacker's weight came off her, and his hands released her. She was free. She scrambled backward, but her arms were still bound.

The sound of steel meeting flesh hissed through the night, and the silhouettes of bodies dropped to the ground as they were cut down. She stood shakily. Her legs didn't feel like they could carry her. She pushed herself away from the sound of death, stumbling through the trees. She stifled her cries, her fear helping her focus on one thing: escaping.

But hands grabbed her again, and she screamed.

"Let me go!" she cried, trying to wrench away.

"Stop," a voice rumbled.

But she wouldn't. She couldn't. She needed to be free.

"North Queen," he said, holding her as she lashed out at him with her bound fists. She couldn't help the sobs as desperation closed in around her. He pulled her close, holding her tightly—not the hold of capture.

"North Queen," he said again.

*The Shadow King.*

Her fight weakened as the realization came, and a wave of relief washed over her, but still, she couldn't hold her emotion.

"Calm yourself," he said quietly.

A blade slipped between her wrists, cutting loose the binding, and he peeled it away. It was sticky with her blood, and stung as he pulled it from her skin. She stood shaking as he knelt and cut her tattered breeches from her leg. The warmth of his cloak came around her, and she didn't fight as he scooped her up in his arms.

The sound of horses drew near, but he didn't put her down. Surprisingly, he swung up on his destrier while holding her. She was relieved; she didn't think she could stand.

They rode slowly. She tried to fight the helplessness that wrecked her, but she couldn't. There was no fight left in her. His arms tightened around her as he carried her, and she turned her face into his chest as the tears came.

# CHAPTER TWENTY-SEVEN

Norah and the king reached the Shadow army camp and arrived at his tent. He slipped off his horse and set her down. She was a little unsteady on her feet, but she caught herself. Feeling the chill against her bare legs, she drew the cloak tighter around herself and ducked inside.

A few moments later, the king entered. Without his helm and armor, he didn't seem like such a monster now. He put a clean cloth and small washbasin by her bedroll. "I'll be outside," he told her.

He turned to go, then stopped. He pulled his shirt over his head and draped it by the basin. "You can wear this until we find you something else."

With that, he left her in the dim candlelight. Her hands shook as she slowly pulled off the cloak. Her jacket was dirty but still serviceable, and she peeled it off her arms. The riding dress, on the other hand, was torn up the side. She wouldn't be able to salvage it. She pulled off her chemise. It was only torn at the bottom. If a shirt and breeches could be found, she might be able to pull herself back together somewhat.

Norah trembled as she soaked the cloth in the water and scrubbed her skin. Her eyes welled, and she blinked the tears away. The feeling of helplessness, of violation, returned. A sob escaped her. She scrubbed her stomach, her legs, everywhere she had been touched. Her skin stung under the cold-water scouring. She'd never feel clean again. She put her chemise back on and pulled the king's shirt over her head. It was large on her and covered her past mid-thigh.

She reached up to re-braid her hair and felt the swelling from the blows she had received. There was still blood on her face. She needed clean water, but she couldn't bring herself to ask. She rolled her torn clothes into a ball and dropped them beside the bed. As she crawled under the blanket, her body shook uncontrollably. She reached out and pulled the cloak over her as well, rolling to her side and drawing her knees up, defeated.

After a time, the king cautiously entered the tent, eyeing the blood-tinted water and Norah, curled up and watching him from underneath his cloak. He took the basin out and returned with fresh water and another cloth. He lowered himself to the ground beside her and submersed the cloth. "Your face," he said as he wrung the water out.

Slowly, she sat up, but she couldn't look him in the eye. She reached for the cloth, but he pulled back, meaning to tend to her himself. She didn't have the will to fight him.

Norah looked away as he brought the cloth to her brow just below the temple. It was where the first strike had caught her. She flinched at the memory. He drew the cloth over her skin with unexpected gentleness, sponging away the dried blood. She tensed as he touched her chin, turning her face toward him. He surveyed her right cheek and the split on her lip, then cleaned around them as well.

"I suppose we look the same now," he said.

"Why are you being kind to me?" she snapped. She couldn't bear his pity on top of it all.

"I respect my enemies."

Anger flashed through her. "Really? Respect?" she hissed, meeting his eyes. "The North Queen—captured, humiliated, beaten..." She couldn't help the shaking in her voice.

His nostrils flared, and he looked away. Turning back to her, he said, "I take no pleasure in seeing you this way."

It surprised her that she believed him.

He dropped the cloth into the water and stood up. She watched him, still wary, but felt herself start to calm. Her eye trailed down to his thigh, where blood seeped through his breeches. Had he been wounded? She bit back the words that almost came out; she refused to show concern for this man. This was his fault. He was the cause of all of this.

Norah curled back on the bedroll, pulling the blanket and cloak over her again, and waited for sleep that wouldn't come.

Mikael was angry. More than angry. He looked over the North Queen as she lay curled on the bedroll underneath his cloak. She'd run. If she'd stayed hidden, she wouldn't have been caught and this wouldn't have happened. He'd told her to stay put. She didn't listen.

He stooped to pick up the washbasin and ducked out of the tent.

"Salar," a soldier called to him, and offered to take the basin, but Mikael shook his head.

"I'll take care of it," he replied.

He tossed the water out and walked down to the nearby stream to get more. His leg ached, but he welcomed the pain. It distracted him from the embarrassment of his failure. She was fast. Even with her hands bound, it had taken quite some time to catch up with her. He remembered how he'd heard her scream and how it had cut off suddenly. He'd raced toward the sound, his heart pounding.

Her attackers were Horsemen. He'd seen them in the darkness; he'd seen the man on top of her. Mikael remembered the rage he'd felt when he ripped the man's head back and dragged his blade across his neck. It was too kind a death.

When he'd pulled the body from her and killed the second man holding her, she'd struggled to get away. She was like a wounded animal, trying to flee, to fight, to stay alive. He and his commander killed the rest of the Horsemen, but not before one caught him in the thigh with a blade.

He shook his head, remembering her ferocity at the base of the stronghold. She was good in a fight. *Too good*. She may have actually defended herself if she hadn't been tied. Why had he tied her? He'd been angry that she'd tried to escape again, but it was something he would have done in her place.

This queen surprised him. He rolled his shoulder and winced at the stretch of the stitches under his arm where she'd stabbed him with his dagger. She was strong. Bold. Not at all what he'd imagined her to be. He almost regretted what he would do to her. He would try to make it painless.

When he returned to the tent, she lay as he'd left her, under the blanket and his cloak. Her eyes were closed, but he doubted she was asleep. His men had found a small shirt and some extra breeches from an accompanying weapons boy, and he laid them beside her.

Mikael stood over his own bedroll and pulled off his leathers, boots, and breeches. He eyed the gash in his thigh. It was deeper than he'd thought, and he grimaced as he bound it with linen strips. He hoped the blade hadn't been poisoned, but knowing the Horsemen, with their mixes and tonics, he wasn't confident. No matter. He was a large man, and strong. It wouldn't be the first time he'd taken a poison blade. It might make the next few days particularly painful, but he could manage pain.

Blowing out the candle, he settled onto the mat, looking up into the darkness. It took a long time for the tiredness to set in as he replayed the events over and over in his mind. When sleep did come, it came lightly, and he found himself drifting awake again. In the quiet of the night, he listened to the sound of her breathing. Her breaths were clipped and irregular—silent cries. His chest tightened. It stung him more than the Horseman's blade.

# Chapter Twenty-Eight

Mikael rose before dawn. He quietly gathered his leathers and boots. The queen was still asleep and wearing his shirt; he'd have to get another.

His body moved stiffly. The wound to his thigh made it difficult to walk, but as he stepped out into the morning, the cold air seemed to bring back his strength. Fresh clothing was waiting for him outside, and he pulled it on.

One of his captains approached and looked at him with a raised brow. Mikael supposed it did seem odd that he'd be dressing outside his tent.

"Salar," the captain greeted.

"Katya," he replied as he pulled on his boots. "What did you find out about the city?"

Katya shook her head. "We've found nothing."

Mikael paused. "Nothing?"

"No, Salar."

The king shook his head. "That was a walled city with armored, fighting men. It would have taken an army to destroy it."

"Well, it's as though they've disappeared," she told him.

"The same is said of us. Find them. And what of the drifters we caught last night?" They'd had some spoils. Obviously, they looted the city after it had been destroyed. "Find out if they saw anything."

Katya shook her head. "They're all dead, Salar."

Mikael's brow furrowed. His men had brought four of them back to the camp alive. "What?"

She motioned to the bodies nearby. "It appears one killed the others, then himself."

"Why?"

She shook her head again. "Maybe they feared the death you might choose for them. Or maybe they knew something they didn't want us to find out."

"Now what could that be?" Mikael asked under his breath. He'd have to think on it later.

"Are you well, Salar?" the captain asked, a slight concern across her brow.

"I'm well enough," he said. "Have two horses readied."

"What should we do with the bodies?"

Mikael glanced back at the drifters. "Leave them for the birds."

Katya gave a nod. "Yes, Salar."

"North Queen."

Norah woke to the king calling her, and she turned to see him standing by the front flap of the tent. She sat up, briefly confused, but then the memory of the night before came back to her. His cloak still lay over top of her, and she clutched it in her fists.

"I want to show you something. Get dressed. Come with me." He ducked out, giving her privacy.

She was still in his shirt, but she spied the fresh clothing by the bedroll and rose quickly to pull it on, along with her jacket and boots. Her mind swirled with the events of the night before and the king's strange kindness. Then she pushed it away. She wasn't sure what had happened, but nothing had changed. She was still a prisoner, and her army was marching to wage a war she knew they couldn't win.

Norah emerged from the tent. While she'd salvaged her jacket, she still shivered in the morning chill. She was surprised to see the king standing with two horses saddled.

"Where are we going?" she asked.

He didn't answer, and she felt a flash of annoyance. Could no one answer a question?

He held out a cloak for her. Her irritation faded, but only slightly. She slipped the cloak around her shoulders, thankful for its warmth. Her horse pawed the frozen ground as she mounted, sensing its rider's anxiousness.

Norah paused when she saw the bodies of the drifters. She knew they were dead, but she felt a pang of fear twist through her as she thought back to the night before.

Beside her, the king mounted his destrier.

"Are they the men who..." she couldn't finish.

"No. Your attackers were Horsemen. These are some of the drifters from around the fire we saw on our way back from the village."

Horsemen? Were they close to the Tribelands? That would put them well south of Mercia.

She looked back at the drifters. Their skin was a waxy blue, and the eyes of one man were still open. Norah swallowed back her nausea. There was a strange marking centered on one's forehead. It was dark. Dried blood, perhaps. She pulled her gaze away and turned back to the king, who was waiting.

"Are we leaving the army again?" she asked. That couldn't be good.

"We'll catch up to them."

He urged his horse forward, and she followed. They parted from the army and rode up a hill to a wooded area. The bitter wind brought tears to her eyes and froze them on her cheeks. She urged her horse to keep up with the king's destrier as they rode through the trees. Bramble crept out onto the trail, but she could tell it once had been a well-worn path. An uneasiness sat in her stomach as she wondered where he was taking her. She didn't think she could handle the sight of another destroyed city.

She watched him as they rode. He wore his armor but not his helm. Without it, he seemed less of a monster. The events of the night prior confused her. Apparently, she was a responsibility of his, but why had he tried to comfort her? Why did he care? She didn't understand, but she couldn't mistake his brief kindness for the safety of trusting him. He wanted the North. He wanted her dead.

Her mind turned to Mercia. She envied who she'd been a week ago, before she knew the horrors of this war, before she knew her helplessness. The lingering winter was the least of her concerns now. She knew Alexander would bring the whole of the Mercian army for her, and if they were decimated, there would be nothing left to protect Mercia. The Shadow King would destroy them all. She needed to escape and get her army back to Mercia to protect her people.

They came to the edge of the wood, and rolling hills opened in front of them. She saw an abandoned country manor in the distance and sighed in relief. There were no torches or impaled heads—that was a good sign.

The king reined up for a moment. He looked down at the house and then scouted the tree line. She watched him, noticing something was off. He was pale. Sweat beaded on his brow despite the cold. She opened her mouth to say something, but the mountains in the far distance to the north caught her eye. *Bahoul*. Her pulse quickened. Alone with the king, she felt her freedom close.

The king scanned the land with a careful eye. Seemingly satisfied that there was no immediate threat, he spurred his destrier forward, and she followed behind. As they got closer, she looked over the manor. It was close to collapsing.

The king slowed his horse, taking in the scene around him. "I haven't been here for a long time," he said.

"What is this place?" she asked.

He didn't answer, and she pursed her lips in frustration.

He looked around a little longer. "His name is Soren," he said finally.

Norah's brows drew together. "Who?"

"My lord commander. My *brute*, as you say. You asked where he came from. This was his family's home. My father charged him with this land. It stretches over the mountains to the north."

"To Bahoul? The mountains that Mercia holds?"

"The mountains you stole from us," he said with an edge of anger in his voice.

"After you attacked us," she threw back defensively.

"Because you'll take my throne."

"I don't want your throne!"

He stilled, and quieted.

Norah looked back over the failing manor. A calm returned. "What happened to them—his family?" she asked.

"Murdered. By the North." His words were like steel, and they cut her.

She swallowed the sickness in her mouth. She couldn't bring herself to ask how, but she didn't have to.

He took an unusually strained breath and continued. "We had set a camp here for our wounded. When my father's armies retreated back to Kharav, the North followed but not just to the border. They flanked them all the way back to the mountains and beyond, destroying villages, farms... farmers."

Norah bit her chapped lips, watching him.

He continued. "We were here, and they came upon us. They murdered everyone: Soren's mother, his brother, his sister. Everyone."

Norah forced herself to breathe.

"We fought," the king said, "but it wasn't enough. My father fell. I was injured. Severely." His eyes glazed as he stared at the manor. He straightened, and his voice came only slightly stronger. "Soren's father had been captain of the Crest, a great warrior, before he became lord of Bahoul. He told Soren to get me back to Kharav, to protect me. And then he took his sword and ran to hold off the Northmen while we fled. That's the last we saw of him."

Norah couldn't speak. She'd only heard of the triumphs of the Great War, not the tragedies.

"We traveled for days, until we came to Aviron, a small kingdom along the borderlands. We thought they would help us, but they knew who I was the moment they saw me. They captured me, they..." His voice trailed off. "Soren found a way to free us, and we fled again. We finally reached the canyons and were able to make it to Kharav. He was going to return to his home, but I told him, 'There's nothing left for you anymore. We're brothers now, and you'll stay with me.'"

Norah looked back over the farm in horror, swallowing the emotion in her throat. "That's why he hates me so much," she said softly.

The Shadow King gave a weak snort. "And you killed his horse," he added.

"*He* killed his horse," she corrected.

"Letting you escape wasn't an option," he snapped back defensively, then paused. "There's nothing he wouldn't sacrifice for me, for my cause." His voice came softer. "Even that which he holds most dear."

Norah wasn't sure she believed the brute capable of holding something dear. She looked back at the falling manor. She didn't want to believe her father would cause such devastation either.

The king gave a thick cough, and she glanced back at him. He was looking down at his hand. His lips were tinged with blood. He swayed in his saddle and started to slump forward.

"Are you all right?" she called to him.

He didn't respond.

She urged her horse beside him, warily leaning closer. "King Mikael, are you all right?"

Something was wrong. His breaths came short and shallow, and his movement was lethargic.

"Are you unwell?" she asked.

"I'm well enough," he struggled. "We should get back." He shifted his weight to rein his horse around but started to fall.

She reached out and caught him, gripping him tightly. "What's happening?"

He blinked and grabbed her arm. "I'm fine, just help me to my horse."

"You're on your horse! What's wrong with you?"

His senses seemed to return somewhat. "The blade," he said. "It's the poison."

She shook her head as confusion hit her. "The blade? What blade?" Then she remembered the night before. "Are you talking about the wound on your leg? Were you stabbed? That was yesterday! By now..." Her words fell. By now, it would have spread through his body.

She stopped. She had a horse. Her eyes found the mountains in the distance, and they called to her. The mountains where she'd find her Northmen. They could take her back to Mercia. *Back to Alexander.*

She turned back to the king. Surely his commander didn't know they were here. She looked back at the mountains. Even if she wanted to save him, it was unlikely. She couldn't stop poison.

He wavered, and she gripped him tighter to keep him upright, struggling as the horses moved.

"Hammel's hell," she cursed, deciding. She really hated herself right now.

Norah urged her mount closer and awkwardly climbed onto the king's destrier behind him. She put her arms around him and reined the horse back toward the tree line.

"If you fall off, there's no way I'll get you back on," she told him. "I'll leave you here!"

He gave a weak snort.

Where were the soldiers when she needed them?

Norah urged the destrier forward. She cursed again as anger welled inside her—anger at herself, at the situation, at the king. "How did you even get stabbed with all this armor?" she snapped. "And why didn't you get help earlier? Are all men so daft?"

Her flurry of scolding fell on unconscious ears, and she clenched her teeth in frustration. She eyed the tree line for the path to return, but it seemed to have disappeared. Norah struggled with the weight of the king as she swept the base of the trees. Her search yielded nothing. She pulled the horse up, feeling she had gone too far, then turned the destrier around. The king's weight shifted to her left, and she clung to him to keep him from falling. She cursed again under her breath, with fear that she might not be able to get him back seeding inside her. Just then, she spotted the path between two oversize trees, and she breathed words of thanks to whichever gods were listening.

The ride from the army to the manor hadn't seemed far, but the way back along the path felt like a year. Her arms burned as she struggled to keep the king upright. She breathed a sigh of relief when they broke through the trees, and she saw the army marching in the distance.

"Soren!" she cried at the top of her lungs.

Movement rippled through the ranks as they looked to see what was happening.

"Soren!" she cried out again.

A large man mounted on a horse broke away from the army, galloping toward them, and she knew it was him. When he reached them, he reined up beside her, his horse rearing and exciting the king's destrier, almost making her lose her grip on the Shadow King.

"What happened?" the commander thundered.

"He said something about a poison."

The commander barked out an order to the men who were running toward them, and others broke from the ranks as well. Despite the cover on his face, she could see the alarm in his eyes. He snarled out another blast of commands and then spurred his horse away.

Soldiers surrounded the king's mount, and Norah slid off as they pulled him down and carried him to a tent being erected close by. They looked at her warily but left her alone, and she followed them inside as they laid the king down on the bedroll. She watched as they stripped him of his armor, feeling lost to help. Did they have the means to save him?

"Where's your healer?" she asked.

As if on cue, another man ducked inside with a small pack. He flung a sharp gaze at her as she edged closer to see better, but quickly turned his attention back to the Shadow King. Blood soaked the king's breeches, and the man used a dagger to cut the fabric. Then he peeled the dripping bandages from around the king's leg to inspect the wound.

Norah swallowed nervously. By now, it should have scabbed over. It hadn't. "It's not clotting," she mumbled, and looked at the soldier. "Is it because of the poison?"

He gave her a sharp glance but didn't answer.

"Do you people not speak?" She wiped the hair from her face with her forearm in frustration.

The soldier pulled a needle from his pack and threaded a thin strand through it. Horsehair, perhaps? She didn't bother asking. He set to work on the wound, pouring a cleansing mixture over it and then bringing the skin together, carefully closing the flesh. Blood seeped out while he worked. When he finished, he pulled out strips of bandages and wrapped them tightly around the king's thigh. It was too tight, she thought, but she stayed quiet. He pinned it closed.

"What now?" she asked as he covered the king with a blanket.

The soldier eyed her darkly. He didn't answer.

"We wait," a feminine voice said.

Norah looked up with a start and saw a woman standing in the corner of the tent. She hadn't noticed her there before.

The woman clipped out commands in the Shadow tongue, and the other men ducked out of the tent until only she remained with Norah and the king.

Norah watched her, fascinated. Not only was this woman a soldier, but clearly, she held a position of power. She wore a wrap over her head and face, like the men, showing only her eyes. What revealed her sex, aside from her smaller frame, was her breastplate, which was sculpted of a woman's body, in every detail. Its brazenness almost made Norah flush.

She caught Norah's gaze on her armor, and the woman's dark eyes hinted at a sinister smile. "Do you like it?" she asked, her voice provocative and taunting.

Norah knew the woman was enjoying her discomfort, and a flash of irritation rose in her cheeks. "Does the Shadow King make all women wear such things?" she asked shortly.

The woman raised a brow. "Make us?" She laughed. "I designed it," she sneered. "We want our enemies to know who they fight in battle. We want them to know our women can gut them."

Norah swallowed back a patronizing reply. The woman's statement was a powerful one, and it struck her deep within. Her irritation faded. Mercia could learn a thing or two from these people. "Fair," she mumbled.

The woman shifted, clearly surprised at how the conversation had turned.

Norah drew her gaze around the tent, unsure of what to do. Then she looked down at her hands, which were stained with the king's blood. She wrung them together.

The woman called out again in the Shadow tongue, and within a few moments, a soldier entered with a basin of fresh water.

Norah glanced at her, appreciating the small kindness. She wasn't sure how to respond in these situations, still being held against her will and with war on the horizon, and she bit back the thanks on her tongue. She submerged her hands into the basin, and the water turned pink as she washed the blood from her skin. "What's your name?" she asked.

The woman's eyes narrowed, and Norah bit the inside of her cheek, feeling foolish. Of course, she wouldn't answer.

"Katya," the woman replied, surprising her. "Captain Katya Sator."

Norah's eyes widened. *Captain.* She pursed back her smile, trying to keep it to herself. Yes, there was much Mercia could learn.

Her eyes moved to the king again, and worry rippled through her. Blood dripped from his left nostril.

"Oh no," she breathed as she scrambled beside him. She turned his head toward her, and a small trail of blood trickled from his ear. She looked at Katya in alarm, and the woman called out to the others.

The soldier who had stitched the wound ducked back into the tent, and Norah backed up as he checked the king by moving his head and eyeing the trail of blood.

"What does it mean?" Norah asked him, her fear growing. "What's happening?"

The soldier looked back at Katya and spoke to her in words Norah didn't understand. But the captain's eyes revealed her own dismay.

The sound of horses outside caught their attention, and suddenly, the brute commander pushed through the front of the tent, leading a man behind him: a Horseman. It had been Horsemen who had attacked her. Bile rose in her throat, and Norah shuddered bitterly.

The commander motioned the man closer, and Norah backed up quickly to give space. The Horseman tipped the king's head to the side and saw the blood run from his ear, then quickly searched a small pack strapped to his waist. He pulled out a vial of liquid and poured it into the king's mouth, holding his head for the antidote to run down. More blood ran from the king's nose and ear.

The Horseman looked at the commander nervously. Norah's heart beat heavy in her chest; she understood that look. The outcome was bleak.

The commander growled out orders in the Shadow tongue, and everyone cleared out, including Katya and the Horseman. He eyed Norah darkly but let her be. Then he sat on a trunk not far from the king and waited.

He pulled the wrap from his head, and she realized it was the first time she'd seen him without it. Mikael had told her they were the same age, which had been hard to believe with his face covered, but she saw it now. The sharp line of his jaw tapered squarely to his chin, and his nose fell straight and symmetrical under his dark brow. He held a similar look as the king. It was a handsome face, she loathed to admit. Everything else about him was as she had imagined, though. His thick, black hair was tied back, and the hair on his face was cut short, almost to the skin.

She spotted the marks down his cheek, from where she had caught him with her nails, and the bruising around the stitched split in his brow. She held back the smile of pride in her work.

He looked up to see her watching him. His eyes were black. Murderous.

Norah pulled her gaze away. The sun was setting, and her body ached. "What if it's too late?" she asked, putting her own hatred aside. "How long before we know if the antidote is working?"

"What do you care?" he snarled.

"I brought him back, didn't I?" she snapped.

There was a silent rage about him. He wore his hatred on his skin. Norah let out a long breath. She didn't have the energy to fight with him. She pushed herself back to a bedroll on the other side of the tent.

"You won't stay here with him," he said shortly.

"By all means, appoint me another keeper," she challenged.

Anger flashed across his face. She knew he wouldn't risk trusting another to watch her. "If you try anything—"

"Obviously," she said, cutting him off.

His nostrils flared in anger, but he didn't say anything else.

Norah lay down on her back. She needed sleep. She pulled the furs over her, trying to get comfortable, and closed her eyes.

# CHAPTER TWENTY-NINE

She woke to the cold. It was still night, but dim candlelight kept the tent from total darkness. Norah didn't stir, trying to keep the warmth trapped under the furs, but she opened her eyes to see the commander sitting beside the king. She watched him.

His hand was on the king's chest and his head hung with emotion. His brow sat heavy with worry. Despite his callousness, his pain touched her. And something more caught her attention.

He whispered to the king in the Shadow tongue as he gently pushed the hair back from his brow. He let his thumb graze the sleeping king's cheek and brush over his lips. His eyes held a longing sorrow she'd seen before—in Alexander's eyes. She didn't have to understand the words to understand the meaning. *He loved him.*

Mikael had told her the commander was like a brother. Soren had saved him during the war, brought him home. Of course they cared for each other. But this care seemed beyond the love of a brother.

Norah pinched her eyes closed tight again and steadied her breath. She saw nothing, she told herself. She wouldn't give the brute another reason to want her dead.

When she opened her eyes again, it was morning. Surprisingly, she'd slept. The tent was empty, except for the king, who was still asleep. Where was the commander?

Her mind turned to Mikael. Slowly, she pushed off the blankets and moved to his side. His breaths were deep and steady. Gently, she took his head in her hands and turned it to the side. No blood came from his ear—a good sign. His color seemed to be returning—also a good sign.

She pushed the blanket back from his leg to check the dressing. No blood had soaked through. "That's good too," she found herself whispering. What was wrong with her? She scolded herself. She should have left him; she should have escaped. But a stinging disappointment needled her—she knew if given the choice again, she'd choose the same.

Norah reached to pull the blanket back over him but paused, letting her eyes trail up the exposed skin of his side. His body was well muscled. Even in his state, he had a strength about him. She ran her fingertips over the ripple at his hip, but then caught herself and quickly pulled the blanket back over him, tucking it under his side.

She noticed a scar that ran half the length of his collarbone and then curved sharply over his chest. The price of his pact with evil, her grandmother had said, was *his heart*. She reached out and drew her fingers across it. Then she spread her hand wide, feeling the rise and fall of his breath. Under her palm, his heart beat slow and rhythmic. She smiled to herself. How funny the human mind could be, what it could imagine and what it could believe. Her eyes traveled over the inked markings across his chest and torso: bold lines in intricate patterns. She traced her fingertips over them. His skin was smooth. And warm.

A scabbed wound on the inside of his arm, just above his wrist, caught her eye. It was where she'd cut him in their fight at the base of Bahoul.

She brushed over it; it was healing quickly. His hand turned upward on its own, offering more of his forearm and startling her. She drew her gaze up, and it locked with his.

His eyes pierced her, and her heart rose in her throat. How long had he been watching her? The intensity of his stare was paralyzing.

"Is there water?" he asked.

She let out a breath of relief as his words broke his hold on her, and she could pull her eyes away. She nodded and retrieved a cup by the front of the tent. Kneeling beside him, she held it to his mouth, and he drank deeply. "Careful," she told him.

He lay back when he was finished, looking up at her. "You're still here," he said weakly.

"I'm trying to remedy that," she mumbled.

He stirred, trying to get up, but Norah put her hand firmly on his chest, pushing him back down. "No. You need to rest."

The corner of his lips turned up ever so slightly, and she cursed herself. She didn't care if he needed rest. She didn't... she didn't care.

"What happened?" he asked.

"It was the poison. It almost took you."

His brow dipped as the memory came back to him. "We were at the manor."

Norah nodded.

"And you brought me back?" he asked.

"I don't really want to talk about it."

He gave a small snort. "You could have run, escaped."

Heat rushed to her cheeks. "I said I don't want to talk about it," she snapped. She was frustrated, at him, at herself.

He paused for a moment, then asked softly, "Tell me, why didn't you let me die?"

"Because I don't want you dead!" she replied angrily. "Why is everyone so intent on killing one another? All everyone talks about is war. What about peace?" She pushed out a breath as she shook her head, exasperated.

The king's brows drew together in an expression that was hard for her to read.

Just then, the commander returned. He looked at the king, surprised to see him awake. Relief flashed across his face. Then he looked at Norah, and his eyes darkened. He spoke low and in the Shadow tongue. Mikael responded, and she could feel the commander's anger. Whatever the king had told him displeased him. He cast Norah another dark look and then ducked back out of the tent.

"Get ready to travel," Mikael told her. "We can't stay here."

"Where are we going?" she asked.

"To friends."

"What friends?"

He gave a labored chuckle. "You won't like them."

Her stomach felt heavy.

Outside, Norah found the commander readying his horse. It wasn't as large as the previous destrier, but she watched him as he tightened the cinch of the saddle and then patted the beast's shoulder. He paused when he heard her approach, but he didn't turn to look at her. He was still without his head wrap, seeming even more like a man.

"I'm sure you're relieved," she said. "He's going to be all right."

He looped the horse's reins back over its neck.

"Soren," she started, "Mikael told me about your family. I didn't realize—"

He spun and caught her by the neck, almost pulling her off her feet. "He is *Salar*," he snarled, "and I am *Lord Commander*. Don't make the mistake of thinking you know me—I am not a friend. I'll use you to draw the Bear, then I'll till our fields with the burnt bodies of your armies and savor a harvest grown in Mercia's destruction. It's this alone that keeps me from choking the life from you right now."

Norah struggled for air, frightened by his sudden aggression. "I'm under the king's protection," she gasped.

He gave her a wicked smile. "He told you our story, yes? Then believe me when I say there is nothing I can do that Salar would not forgive."

He pulled her closer, bringing his lips to her ear. "*Nothing.*"

Norah's eyes widened, and she struggled against him. He released her, and she sank forward, gasping for breath.

His nostrils flared, and he gave her a merciless scowl. "Good day, North Queen," he said stiffly, and left her in the cold of fear.

Norah sat on her horse, watching as the Shadowmen carefully laid their king into a makeshift haul. She knew exactly where they were going. A group of Horsemen waited as the army prepared to move. More than anything now, she needed to make her escape. But under the watchful eye of the commander, that would be impossible. Her hands weren't bound anymore, but he'd tied the lead of her horse to his saddle. As the army moved out, they fell in behind the haul, where the king's brute could keep his eye on the king and on her.

It was a long ride, and one that probably would force another change of plans, she expected. Her anxiousness grew at the thought of Alexander gaining ground on them. While meeting the Shadow army with the king down was the optimal time, she couldn't say she hoped for it.

When they arrived at the Horsemen tribe, it was larger than Norah thought it would be. Adobe houses sat in large groupings around a central town square. They brought the king to a center house of mudstone and thatch, where they laid him on a large bed. Norah was quiet, watching all the activity as he was made comfortable—blankets were rolled out, food was brought in. Weakness slowed his movements, along with weariness from the travel. But his tired eyes found her.

"Eat," he said.

"Why are we here?" she demanded. "Are these not the people who assaulted me and tried to kill you?"

"They didn't know who they were attacking. The Horsemen tribes are friends of Kharav." He paused, taking another labored breath. "And it wasn't safe to camp where we were. Abilash will keep us until I can travel. Now eat."

"I'm not hungry." It was a total lie. She was near starved.

"You'll need your strength."

Norah scowled at him. Fine. She'd eat, but she'd be angry about it. She took a loaf of bread and a small cut of meat. "Who's Abilash?"

He gave her a mischievous look. "A Horseman king. I think he'll take a liking to you." He smiled, and she could tell he was teasing her. "He's looking for a wife."

Norah gave a repulsed laugh. "I'm not to be had."

"Because you're betrothed to the Aleon king?"

His reminder of her marriage needled her. "Because I'll marry who I deem worthy," she snapped.

He shrugged. "Abilash is a king."

"Then he should find a woman who thinks that's good enough."

She saw the corners of his mouth turn up in amusement. He watched her, thoughtful. "What makes the Aleon king worthy?" he asked.

Norah didn't answer. She wasn't sure he was. What made any man worthy? His kingdom? His wealth? None of that mattered to her, especially now. Her chances of escaping lessened each day. There was fight still inside her, but she knew she would likely never make it to Aleon, or back to Mercia.

The day passed slowly, with the king drifting in and out of sleep. Norah watched him as he moved about restlessly in his sleep. What haunted his dreams? She knew what haunted hers. She was still lost, failing to simply remember. She was failing as queen. Failing her kingdom and her people. Failing Alexander. All she could picture was Alexander walking into a trap. If anything happened to him...

As night fell, she looked out across the village, seeing the houses filled with firelight. How wonderful it must be, she thought, to be with loved ones in the comfort of a simple home. Where there was no pressure of the crown, no vengeful enemies. How wonderful it must be to choose a life of the heart—these were the things she longed for.

"You didn't answer my question," the king's voice came from behind her. She turned to see him sitting up in the bed.

She raised a brow. "There are many questions you haven't answered for me."

"Ask one, then. I'll answer."

She eyed him suspiciously.

"Truthfully," he added. "I'll answer truthfully." His breathing was uneven. His strength was returning, but it still took energy for him to hold himself up.

"All right, then," she said, biting. "What have you planned for me? Is it to kill me?"

He cast his eyes around the room, molding his response, then his gaze locked back on hers. "I have planned for you to die, yes."

Norah let out a long breath. She'd thought she'd fear the answer, but it wasn't fear that ran through her now, just sadness. A sadness she'd let down her kingdom, her grandmother. Alexander.

"Now my answer," he commanded.

Norah's mind was a blur. What did he want from her? "What is your question?"

"Why is the Aleon king worthy?"

Confusion flooded her. "Of all the questions you could ask me, that's the one you choose?"

His eyes bore into hers. "Tell me why."

Norah felt a heat come to her cheeks. This question felt most personal to her, most invasive. "You only have one," she warned, a bitterness rising in her.

"What is it about him?" he asked again.

There was nothing about him. Norah remembered nothing, so she knew absolutely *nothing* about him.

"Why do you want to marry him?" he pressed.

"I don't!" she snapped. She let out an emotional breath. She shouldn't have said that.

"Then why are you?" he asked.

"Because he has what I need," she said, relenting.

He gave a wry smile. "An army? To fight against me?"

"You're out of questions."

He snorted. "No matter. I already know the answer. I know what you need."

"You don't know anything about me," she cut back. No one did. Not even her. A cold calm returned. She turned back to the window to take her peace in the dream of village firelight.

# CHAPTER THIRTY

A noise stirred Norah from her dreams. It was light outside, early morning. She lifted her head to see the king. He was still asleep. She heard faint cries from a distance and rose quietly to the window. At the edge of the houses in the Horsemen's village, she spotted a high-walled corral with a group of men trying to settle a frenzied horse. She glanced back at the king, who lay silent in his slumber.

Quietly, Norah slipped outside the house, looking curiously toward the corral. Shouts echoed from the men; there was alarm in their voices. She briefly forgot about the Shadow King and hurriedly walked over to see the commotion. A guard by the door made no move to stop her, but he followed close behind.

As she reached the corral, she slowed, her eyes wide. Men held ropes around a horse's neck, and they fought to bring it under control. The animal lashed her head about, and a series of screams pierced through the air. Norah quickened her pace. She reached the enclosure and leaned against the thick beams, fascinated.

The mare pulled back against her restraints, and the men quickly drew together in front to hold her. A man approached her from the side, with a halter in his hand. When the horse spotted it, she tried to rear again. The man looked back at his teammates with a grin.

Norah became aware of a presence beside her. She didn't need to look to know it was the commander, and she kept her sight on the men in the corral, ignoring him.

The mare tossed her head again and pulled back against the ropes. Norah felt the beast's will to fight. Freedom was precious. Suddenly, the mare charged. She tore through the small group of men, knocking two of them to the ground and beating them with her front legs. Hooves met flesh with a sickening thud. The other men scrambled back, each pulling his rope, but they didn't have the power to control her. The mare reared, whipping herself free from them, and set her sights on another man to her right. She rushed at him, shouldering him into the wall of the paddock, and whirled to find her next victim.

Norah gasped, stepping back. Her worry shifted to the men in the corral. Two of the men staggered to the edge and slipped through the railing, but one still lay in the center. Men yelled at the mare to draw her attention as others tried to approach the man, but the mare charged them again, pushing them back.

The man on the ground in the middle of the paddock stirred, reaching up an arm and calling out to his companions. His pleas angered the mare, and she attacked again, beating him viciously with her hooves.

"Why aren't they helping him?" Norah said, gasping, to the commander, putting her contention aside. "Will they do nothing?"

He snorted. "And what would they do? That mare is more valuable than all their lives together."

His words confused her. How could a horse be more important than men?

The mare let out an angry scream and pummeled the man again. He cried out once more and then fell silent.

"Help him!" she pleaded.

He chuckled. "There's no helping him."

Norah felt sick. If no one would help him, the man would die. She couldn't just stand there and do nothing. Before she could talk herself out of it, she slipped between the railings of the high-walled corral. Shouts rang out, and the mare reared, screaming into the air. Men yelled what she surmised to be warnings at her, but she ignored them.

"Get out of there!" the commander boomed behind her.

She ignored him too.

"Get out of there!" he roared again as he started to climb the railing. He was too large to fit in between.

Norah looked at the mare across the paddock. The horse had backed away from her victim, intrigued by Norah's presence, but stomped her hooves agitatedly.

The commander barked out an order to the Horsemen and, although the language was foreign, she could hear the vexation in his voice. Men climbed the railing of the paddock, standing tall with ropes in their hands.

"No!" Norah called to them. She looked back over her shoulder at the commander. "Tell them to stand down. They're only making it worse."

"Back up slowly and get out of there," he told her.

"I have to help him!" she insisted. She stepped toward the man on the ground, and the mare snorted but warily stayed.

"North Queen!" the commander growled. The mare reared again as the commander swung himself over the top of the corral.

"Wait!" Norah cried, making him pause. "Just wait." Slowly, she inched toward the man and knelt beside him, keeping her eyes on the mare. He lay crumpled on his side. She touched his face, but he didn't respond. Blood ran from a deep gash on the side of his head. Slowly, she rolled him onto his back. He was alive, but his breath was faint. He needed help. Norah rose slowly, looking at the horse. The mare shook her head, tossing her mane. This was no ordinary horse. The beast called to her.

The mare was snowy silver with a dark face and matching legs. As Norah drew closer, she could make out the dapple in her coat. Her beauty was intoxicating, but what caught Norah's attention was the brilliant fire in her eyes. She'd seen eyes like these before. And it dawned on her—they were the same as the fox in the Wild, where Alexander had first found her. They had to be connected somehow.

"Don't!" the commander called to her, but she ignored him.

The animal's wild eyes looked at Norah through her thick mane, and her nostrils flared nervously. Norah clicked her tongue, drawing the mare's ears forward. She stepped closer and reached out her hand. "It's all right," she said softly.

The animal tossed her head again but finally stretched out her neck to nose Norah's hand. Norah waited patiently.

"You're all right," she whispered. Slowly, she moved to scratch the mare's chin, and then ran her hand up the animal's jaw. The horse threw her head up, but Norah paused, and the animal calmed.

"Easy, you're all right," she soothed. Slowly, Norah reached out again. She ran her hand down the horse's neck and chest, patting her. She loosened the ropes and pulled them away.

"That's better, yes?" she said to the animal. "Will you let him go? Death's not the answer."

The mare snorted, but Norah felt her yield.

"Collect your man," she called back to the Horsemen. The commander echoed her in a foreign tongue, with a few additional words she was sure, and they hurried warily to gather their man.

The mare flicked her ears and pawed the ground but stayed. Norah drew her hand along the animal's neck and shoulder, still working to calm her.

"North Queen!" the Shadow King's voice boomed from behind, and she looked to see him making his way toward the enclosure. The commander straddled the top of the corral with a spear in hand, and a man she assumed to be King Abilash stood below. Her stomach turned at being the center of their attention.

"I'll get you out of here," she whispered to the mare and then turned to face the ire of her own captors.

She strode to the edge of the corral and slipped out between the railing. The commander dropped to the ground from the top and stood beside the King Abilash. Both looked astonished.

"What is this power you have over the Wild?" Abilash asked. "How do you do this?"

But there was a fury inside her heart. "She doesn't belong to you. Why do you have her?" she demanded.

Her offense caught Abilash by surprise. Then he noticed the Shadow King approaching and gave a bow. "Salar, I'm glad to see you're recovering, my friend," he said, in an effort to change the subject.

Anger rose within her at being dismissed. "No thanks to your men," she said shortly. "Is that how you treat your *friends*? Attacking those under their protection and then poisoning them?"

Abilash, his face heavy with dishonor, looked at Mikael. "My men didn't know who they were attacking, and we suffer great shame. We offer you our deepest apology and whatever you require to mend the bond between Kharav and our people."

Mikael didn't appear to be in a forgiving state. "The North Queen's attackers. I want their families. Ten years' servitude in Kharav as restitution for their crimes."

Abilash nodded reluctantly.

Norah gasped. "Their families?" Mikael's eyes found hers, and they held a warning, but she couldn't help herself. "Sins of the father are not sins of the son," she said, objecting. "You punish innocents."

His face gave away nothing, but she knew she was pushing him for clemency he wasn't accustomed to.

"There must be recompense," he said.

"One fitting of the crime!"

His eyes blazed. "And what do you think is fitting of assaulting a queen?"

It wasn't lost on her that he called for restitution only for her grievance, not his own. Norah felt like the men guilty had already paid the ultimate penalty, but he wouldn't leave with nothing. "What about the mare?" Norah asked, and Abilash's eyes widened. She knew the horse was valuable if they would let men die over it. "We'll take the mare instead."

A tension rippled through the air, one that Norah didn't understand. The commander's face darkened—he was perhaps offended by her audacity to bargain as a prisoner.

Mikael looked at her with reluctance in his eyes, but then he turned to Abilash and surprised them all. "I'll have the mare," he said.

Abilash's face hardened, but he gave a stiff nod. "Our friendship with Kharav is very dear to us. If the North Queen can ride the beast, it's hers."

Norah sensed Abilash doubted she could ride the mare. She doubted it herself. Mikael shifted uncomfortably, and she feared he would interfere.

"I accept," she blurted, and turned back to the enclosure before he could stop her.

Norah approached the mare again, and the horse shook her head. "Easy," she whispered, reaching out her hand. The mare allowed her touch, but Norah wasn't sure about riding her. "I told you I'd get you out of here, but you have to trust me. Can you do that?"

The mare snorted.

"I'm going to trust you too," she said. "I'm going to trust that you won't maim me or make a fool of me. We can help each other."

Ever so carefully, she stepped to the side of the mare, who snorted again and turned to watch her. Norah reached over her back and slowly put weight on the animal. The mare waited. Summoning her courage, Norah gathered a fist of mane in her hand and jumped up, rocking her weight forward over the horse's back. Mounting a horse with no saddle wasn't the most elegant of actions—it was certainly not how she pictured herself doing it in her mind, and she struggled a bit before she swung her leg awkwardly over. Her heart pounded in her chest as she waited for either acceptance or a quick throw. But fortune was with her, and the mare moved quietly underneath her. Norah urged her forward and toward the gate. "Open it," she called.

The men looked at each other in astonishment and swung the gate open wide, watching in awe as Norah rode through.

The commander gave a beat to the ground with his spear as she passed. "Don't get any ideas," he threatened.

She frowned. He'd already struck a horse from underneath her, and she knew he'd do it again. Away from the enclosure, she slid off the horse, sure the mare would immediately bolt, but she didn't. Norah reached out and ran her hand under the thick mane, reveling in the warmth. "You'd be crazy to stay," she said, "but I could really use a friend right now."

The mare gave a snort and shook her head but seemed even-tempered and calm. Norah gave her a pat, leaving her there and making the short distance back to Mikael and King Abilash.

Mikael's eyes had a look that she didn't understand, but he turned to Abilash with a nod. "I forgive the transgressions of your people. Restitution has been paid."

"We look forward to your return," Abilash told him. Then he gave another stiff nod and turned back to his waiting Horsemen.

"I'll ready the men," the commander told Mikael as they walked toward the center house.

"What?" She didn't understand. "Are we leaving?"

"We are."

So soon? "We can't leave. You can barely walk. You're not fit to travel." She followed Mikael into the house.

He paused, gripping the back of a chair and leaning against it to rest a moment.

"Why the hurry?" she asked.

"We need to get back to the army before Abilash changes his mind and thinks about the fact that his men outnumber the few of us here."

Norah shook her head, still in a cloud of confusion. "Why would he change his mind? You showed mercy on all those innocent families."

"You required his most prized possession," he snapped.

"Are his people not what he cares for most?"

"No," he growled with a fury that shook her. "That is a horse of the Wild, and his mastery over it can make him a very powerful man among the tribes. I shouldn't have taken it from him."

"If you're so angry about it, then why did you?" she cut back.

"Because you asked it of me!"

Norah's breath faltered. He looked just as surprised by his words as she was to hear them.

Mikael pulled his eyes away and picked up his cloak. "Get what you need," he said, pulling it over his shoulder. "We leave now."

# Chapter Thirty-One

The dark was fading; it was almost morning. They'd traveled in haste the day before. She'd ridden a small packhorse, not being trusted with an energetic mount, but the mare had followed along behind her. Tension still hung around her, with the commander's hatred for her seeming to grow with each passing hour.

Her whole body was sore, but she readied quickly after waking. Outside came the sounds of metal and leather packs: men preparing to leave. She pulled her hair back from her face and tied it behind and then slipped into her boots and jacket. Snow fell from the sky as she ducked out of the tent. There wasn't enough to coat the ground but it was enough to warn of the coming storm. The sound of the Shadow King and his commander in a heated conversation made her pause.

They stopped when they saw her emerge, and the king broke away toward her. "A storm is coming," he said as he neared. "You'll go with the lord commander."

She didn't like the idea of that at all. "Where are you going?"

Mikael paused with hesitation on his face. Then he said, "Gregor brings the Japheth army to join me against your army. I'm going to meet him."

The fact he'd answered her question surprised her, but the mention of his allied forces more than surprised her—it filled her with a sickening horror. Mercia wouldn't have Aleon with them, not yet. She didn't even know if Phillip was aware she'd been taken. The Shadowlands and Japheth against Mercia alone—her army would be decimated.

His eyes burned into hers. "This is my one opportunity. Did you think I wouldn't come with everything I had?"

There was nothing she could do, and the weight of the threatening devastation crushed her. "So, you've planned a slaughter? There's no honor in that."

"I told you, I'm not an honorable man."

No, he certainly wasn't.

"You'll go with the lord commander," he told her. "And I'll meet you in three days' time." He looked at the horse of the Wild. "He has orders to spear the mare should you try to ride her."

Norah wasn't sure why riding the mare would be such a concern, but his threat only fueled more fire inside her. "After you've risked so much to give her to me?" she asked angrily.

"Don't make that risk be in vain," he warned.

Norah's cheeks burned with fury. She pursed her lips and looked out into the frost of the morning. There was nothing she could do to help her army—nothing she could do to even warn them. And she didn't want to go with the commander. Her chances of escaping him were slim, and he'd surely see her dead.

"North Queen," the king said, seeming to read her mind. "You'll be safe with the lord commander. You have my word."

"What good is your word if you're not an honorable man?" she asked coldly.

Norah and the commander rode in silence as snow continued to fall. The mare followed behind without a lead. It was so peculiar. It was as if the animal knew her.

She watched the large, fluffy flakes as they landed on her arms and melted into her jacket. Wet snow was dangerous, and she pulled her cloak tighter around her. "How much farther?" she called.

He didn't respond. Naturally.

"Did you not hear me?" she pressed.

"Before nightfall," he clipped shortly.

Norah pursed her lips in agitation. His answer brought little comfort. Nightfall was still a far way off. Despite her cloak, the wetness had begun working its way into her layers, and she started to shiver. As they rode on, the wind picked up and the air felt colder. The snow began to layer on her arms and legs. The winter wind burned her face, and she buried her chin into the fur collar of her jacket. Time passed slowly, and Norah found just breathing to be difficult.

She couldn't bear it any longer. "We need to stop," she called to the commander. "We should build a fire."

"We can't stop."

They continued into the late afternoon. Norah couldn't control her shaking. The cold stabbed the inside of her chest, and she couldn't draw a breath.

They trudged on, with their horses starting to struggle in the snow. The reins slipped from her frozen fingers. She couldn't make her hands work to get them, but her horse followed his. Her teeth chattered, and she bit her tongue but didn't feel the pain. Sleep called to her.

The commander looked back at her and mumbled what she assumed to be a slew of curses. He reined back beside her and pulled her from her horse, sitting her in front of him. She would have rather frozen to death, but she didn't have the strength to fight him. He wrapped his cloak around them both and urged his destrier forward again.

The temperature dropped quickly as nightfall drew near. The commander held her close as they rode, trying to build warmth between them. Norah could barely hold her head up. Her body was so cold that it no longer shivered.

"Stay awake," he said, but she couldn't keep her eyes from closing. "North Queen," he snarled, "you need to stay awake."

But she couldn't help but let the darkness consume her.

Norah's eyes fluttered open, and she found herself tangled in Alexander as they lay in a wheaten field under the summer sun.

"Alexander?"

He smiled down at her, his blue eyes shining.

She'd missed him. "Am I dreaming?" She put her hand on his chest and spread her fingers against his skin.

"North Queen," he said.

"Why do you call me that?" she whispered. His body felt good close to hers, and she burrowed into him. "I'm cold, Alexander. I'm so cold."

He wrapped his arms around her and held her close. His warmth was inebriating, and she smiled as she nestled deeper. Norah let her lips graze his chest and felt a surge of heat inside her. She kissed the smooth warmth of his skin and let herself rest blissfully in his arms.

She opened her eyes again, and confusion rained over her as dark markings sprung from his skin. Ink bled into ominous patterns, patterns she'd seen before. The summerscape fell away, and she was inside a stone room. The darkness of night was held at bay by candlelight and a crackling fire behind her.

But her eyes were on the markings.

Panic flooded her. She sat up quickly and gasped as she saw the commander lying on the bed, looking back at her. The covers fell away, revealing her near nakedness underneath, and she grasped desperately at the blankets, pulling them to cover her chemise.

He chuckled in amusement as he rose from the bed, and her breath shook in horror at seeing his nakedness as well.

"Now you're not dreaming," he jeered with an evil smile. He walked around the bed and crouched in front of the flame, putting another log on the fire and stirring the embers with his sword.

"Don't worry yourself," he said, although he seemed to relish her panic. "I wasn't improper with you."

Heat radiated from her face. "What do you consider improper if not forcing a woman naked into bed?"

"You cannot imagine," he said in a low, disturbing voice. "But you're not entirely naked. And I didn't force you. You were merely an unwitting participant."

"Of which I'm sure you enjoyed," she snapped.

"Quite the opposite. I like a good fight," he said wickedly. "Actually, I would have preferred to leave you to die in the storm, although it would have been too kind a death."

She found his words as chilling as the winter air. What was to be her death then? She couldn't think of that right now.

"Why are we both without clothes?" she demanded.

"They were wet, and you needed to be warmed skin to skin. Do you not know how to survive a north storm, *North* Queen?" he taunted her.

Norah snorted, astounded at his brazenness.

The commander stood, again not bothering to cover himself. She averted her eyes, pulling the blanket up higher. He walked over to her shirt on the floor, picking it up and dropping it on the bed.

She grabbed it and pulled it quickly over her head, trying to keep herself covered with the blanket. Her underwear was still on, she noted, appreciative of the small assurance that he hadn't been entirely free with her.

"I want my breeches," she said.

He nodded to them lying across a chair by the fire, along with his own clothes. "They're not dry. You'll have to wait."

The commander sat on the edge of the bed, and she pulled her feet away from him, tucking her knees up to her chest and wrapping her arms around her legs. He gazed at her hands and then reached out and grabbed one. Norah tried to jerk it back, but he held it firmly. She struck him in his face with her other hand and he let out a growl. She tried to strike him again, but he caught her wrist and pulled her closer. Redness rose on his cheek from her blow.

"Let go of me!" she spat.

He ignored her and pulled her hands up, looking closely at her fingertips.

"What are you doing?" she hissed.

He grasped her face as she tried to bat him away, but he pulled her closer, looking carefully over her.

"The winter didn't eat your skin," he said. "You're lucky."

"That's the opposite of what I would consider myself right now," she said shortly, finally beating him back.

He released her. "You should be thanking me you're alive."

She snorted in disbelief. "I should be thanking you for saving me from a situation you put me in to begin with? And only to kill me later?"

Irritation flashed across his face, and he turned away from her. "Who is Alexander?" he asked.

Her eyes darted up to him, and her pulse quickened. "Why do you ask this?"

"Because it's what you called me... before you kissed me." He gave a cruel grin in satisfaction at the horror on her face.

"I did not!" she hissed.

He chuckled. "You were on your way to marry the Aleon king, but you love another. A secret love?" he taunted.

"Like your love for the king?" she spat back.

The commander jerked his head up in surprise. His smile faded. "Of course, I love Salar," he said. "As any warrior should."

"Except your love is different," she challenged.

His jaw tensed, and he shot her a look she hadn't expected—fear. It confirmed what she had only suspected. He was in love with the king. A love he hid, a twin to her own tragedy. She felt a pang of sympathy for him, but that sympathy was short-lived.

"Does he know?" she needled, still angry at his impudence. "I imagine that might change things between you two."

He lunged forward, pinning her to the bed with a fiery rage. His skin burned with the heat of fight, and his hand clenched her at the base of her neck with a force that made her struggle to breathe.

"Is this where you remind me how you can kill me?" she said through her teeth.

He ran his hand higher around her neck.

"Do it," she seethed. What did it matter anymore? If death was to come, better not to wait in fear.

The commander's lip quivered in fury as he bared his teeth. Then, suddenly, he released her and pushed himself off and away from the bed. "You won't speak of this again," he snarled.

"And you won't speak of Alexander," she countered.

A pact sealed in animosity. Surprisingly, he seemed to settle. He pulled out a flask and some wrapped meat and dropped it on the bed beside her.

Just then, Norah heard a shuffle outside the room. "What was that?" she asked.

"The horses."

"Inside?"

He shrugged. "No one to care."

She wasn't sure what he meant by that, but she found herself looking around the room. They weren't in a simple house.

She picked up the flask and brought it to her lips, surprised to find whiskey instead of water. She suppressed a cough as she swallowed, then drank again. Her stomach grumbled as she bit into the meat. She hadn't realized how hungry she was.

The commander stood watching her as she took another drink.

"When will the king be here?" she asked.

"Two days."

"What about the storm?"

"The army will keep him well."

Norah finished the meat and took another drink. The warmth of the alcohol spread under her skin, and her shivering calmed.

The commander rose to put another log on the fire. He still walked with a slight limp from when his horse had fallen on top of him at the stronghold. *Good.* She hoped it still hurt. Her eyes stopped on a freshly healing cut on his side, and a smirk pulled at her lips that she *had* managed to get him with her knife when he'd caught her trying to escape. Served him right. She hoped that still hurt too.

Norah let herself look at him. His body was thick and muscled from fighting. Ink patterned his chest and shoulders, running down his arms. His skin was smooth and hairless, and she followed the lines of his form lower. Unlike the king, the commander bore the markings over his thighs as well.

He looked at her, and she quickly turned away.

"Are you just going to stand naked by the fire until your clothes dry?" she asked irritably.

"Would you rather me come to bed with you?"

"Don't be ridiculous," she hissed.

He chuckled, entertained by her anger.

They sat in silence for a while. The commander sat by the fireplace and leaned back against the wall. She turned her back to him and pulled the blankets tighter around her. She needed rest; escaping took a lot from the body. She listened for the steady rhythm of the commander's breath to tell her he was asleep, but it never came.

Norah woke to the commander still sitting by the fire. It was morning. "Do you ever sleep?" she asked shortly.

He gave her an annoyed look but didn't respond.

She rolled her eyes. "They say no sleep will make a man go mad."

"Perhaps I'm not a man."

"Or perhaps you're already mad." She found herself thinking of the king, wondering how he was faring through the storm. "If the king dies, will you kill me?" she asked him.

"He won't."

"What if he does?"

"I said he won't," he said sharply. "But yes, I'll kill you."

His words no longer scared her. "How?"

He smiled. "I'll let you choose, so long as it's slow."

She lay back on the bed and looked up at the ceiling of stone. Perhaps this was to be her death: a death of despair with an intolerable brute.

The hours passed. Waiting was tiresome, and the time passed painfully slow. The commander stepped out often, leaving her alone, which she was thankful for. His nearness made her skin prickle.

A shuffle sounded outside the door of the room. It was the horses, she told herself, but her curiosity grew. Norah opened the door to what she thought was a hallway, but she found a great hall instead. They were in a castle. It hadn't seen people for some time. Had it been abandoned?

Their horses stood in the center of the hall, and Norah clicked her tongue as she approached. The mare nickered. Norah looked around as she patted her, running her hands up the animal's neck and under the warmth of her mane. Bales of hay sat in a corner with a large tub of water. As she moved her fingers under the mare's long, draping hair, she noticed it had been brushed, as had the other horses'. It surprised her that the commander had cared. What surprised her even more was that the mare had let him.

The hall was cold. Most of the windows were broken, letting the winter wind blow through the walls. Something outside caught her eye. She made her way to the large wooden doors and pushed them open, stepping out into the winter.

Norah gasped as she looked around. The old ruins of a city lay around her. It was a large city, and the quiet of long-abandoned lives made her uneasy. She heard the commander behind her and turned. "What happened here? Where are all the people?" she asked.

"Dead," he said, with a faint curve at the corner of his mouth.

"What happened to them?"

He gave a rumbling chuckle. "Me."

Norah gaped at him in horror. "You did this?" she breathed. "Why?"

His eyes, thick pools of black that choked out her breath, turned on her. "Why not?" he sneered.

# CHAPTER THIRTY-TWO

When Norah woke the next morning, she found herself alone. The fire burned with fresh wood. The commander wouldn't be far. But she couldn't spend another day in this room; she had to do something. She opened the door to the great hall. It was empty. There was no sign of the brute, or the horses. He must have taken them out. She made her way across the hall and started up the staircase, her curiosity getting the better of her.

Norah passed from room to room, exploring what remained of the battle-torn castle. Heavily dusted and broken furniture lay strewn across the floors, with shattered busts in various corners and torn tapestries on the walls—remnants of those who had lived here. She passed a room that made her pause and pushed the door open wider before stepping inside. It was a girl's room, with pastel palettes and floral side panels. Someone had put thought and care into this room, someone who had loved its occupant—a mother, perhaps, or a grandmother. She imagined it in its former glory and smiled sadly. The ripped bedding matched what was left of the draperies. Her heart hurt. Was this all she would find now? The ruins of happiness past? Everything destroyed by darkness and death? A hopelessness washed over her. Glancing around, she caught her reflection in a three-paneled vanity mirror.

Norah walked slowly toward it. She hardly recognized herself. Her left cheek was bruised just under her eye, and the cut on her lip marred the softness of her mouth. Her eyes welled. The feeling of hopelessness turned to anger, and she cried out in rage as she slammed the side panel closed, shattering the mirror and dropping shards of glass all around her.

She broke down, sinking into the chair with a sob. All felt lost. Alexander was marching toward a force that would decimate the armies of Mercia, and she had no way to stop it. She should have never allowed herself to be brought here, never allowed herself to be taken. She should have never left the castle isle.

A large piece of glass on the floor caught her eye, and a calmness returned as she slowly picked it up. She would die soon. She wondered how they would kill her. Her hand curled around the glass; she shouldn't give them the satisfaction.

Norah rose and walked to the double doors leading out to a balcony, pushing them open and stepping outside. Looking down to the ground far below, she didn't remember climbing so many stairs. She wondered if it would hurt—death from falling—and she looked back at the shard of glass she clenched in her hand. Perhaps it was a better way to depart than cutting herself.

If she were to die, would it end it all? She'd no longer be a threat to the Shadow King. He'd have no reason to pursue the attack against Mercia. She would no longer be used as bait for her army.

Norah leaned forward against the railing.

She *was* going to die, she told herself; the Shadow King had told her. It was better for it to be by her own hand, on her own terms. She wished she could have seen Alexander again. She closed her eyes, imagining him, imagining his smile.

She leaned farther, inhaling deeply.

Suddenly, a hand grabbed her arm, pulling her backward and spinning her around.

Norah gasped.

The Shadow King. His gaze pierced her, seeming to see everything of her. Did he see her anger, her disappointment at her failure? The shame of her defeat?

There was a sadness in his eyes, remorse in his triumph. And something more. She felt a wave of confusion. She expected him to be angry, but he wasn't angry. He was *afraid*.

"North Queen," he breathed.

He let go of her arm, but still clasped her wrist. She could feel the stickiness of blood as she clutched the shard of glass in her fist.

"Do you find me unbearable?" he asked.

"I find this entire situation unbearable," she said coldly.

He brushed her closed fingers gently, and she found herself opening her hand, yielding her weapon. He carefully pulled the blood-covered glass from her palm and tossed it away from them.

"Perhaps you regret not leaving me to the Horseman's poison."

Frustration coursed through her. "Why would you say something like that? Why can't you believe I don't want you dead?"

"Because all my enemies want me dead, especially the North."

"I'm not your enemy!"

His nostrils flared. "You were on your way to build an alliance with Aleon. For power, for their army—"

"For food!" she cried. "You want to know what makes Aleon worthy? What I need? It's food! My people will starve without provisions for the winter!"

Mikael shifted in surprise, and then his face softened. She turned away to hide her emotion.

"And yes," she continued, "Aleon brings the strength of unity—arms, soldiers, protection against a threatening kingdom, specifically *you*. I won't pretend I don't want that strength, because I do. I know the stories. I've seen the destruction you've caused. I want Mercia to stand tall against any foe." She paused, and her voice came softer now. "But that doesn't mean I want a foe to stand against. I want to protect my people. That's why I accepted the marriage."

The air settled between them.

"But you don't want to marry the Aleon king," he said.

She gave a defeated shrug. "What does it matter?"

"It matters if you would want to take my throne."

Norah let out an exasperated breath. "I don't want your throne!"

"As *my* queen," he added.

Her head jerked up, and her eyes widened. "What?" she breathed.

"You want to save your people. You want to avoid war between our kingdoms."

Norah shook her head. "I don't understand."

"What don't you understand? You're betrothed to the Aleon king. I offer my own hand instead."

"Why would you do that?"

He shrugged. "I break your alliance with Aleon. There is no war; I change fate."

*Change fate.* How much did he know of his fate?

"Not only do I double my army," he added, "but I gain the best archers in the world, access to Mercian steel, and a renowned fleet of ships. Kharav becomes a force even Aleon won't challenge. And"—his voice came softer—"I wed a queen worthy in her own right. You'd be my salara."

Norah felt light-headed. She wasn't sure if she was hearing him correctly. "Why would I marry you?"

"So long as you align yourself with an enemy of Kharav, you'll also be an enemy. You want to avoid a war? Only *I* can give that to you. And..." he paused, waiting for her to look up at him, "you'll still have whatever you require for the North—food, provisions, horses. My army, should you need it."

"All this just so I won't wed King Phillip? Why not just kill me to save yourself the trouble?"

He stepped closer. "Because I don't want you dead either, North Queen."

Her breaths came shallower now. "But I thought that was your plan."

He pulled out a handkerchief and wrapped it around the cut on her palm, closing her fist inside his and holding it tightly. "That plan expired well before I even told you of it."

She didn't know why his saying that affected her so. She swallowed. "Is that all? We just marry, and all's well with the world?"

"Yes. And..." He paused as her eyes found his. "The Bear is mine."

Norah shifted uneasily as a weight grew in her stomach. "Beurnat the Bear has been dead a long time now."

The king shook his head. "No. I saw the Bear just a year ago when I tried to retake Bahoul." His eyes darkened. "And I saw him again, recently, in the vision of my fall."

Norah's heart beat faster. It was Alexander that defended Bahoul. And it was Alexander in the vision, striking down the Shadow King.

And the king had seen it. It's why he wanted Alexander. Not just to change fate but to change *his* fate.

Then she froze. He'd said *seen*.

He had a traveler seer, someone who could show him the visions. How powerful was this seer?

"So, we'll be wed," the king said, "and the Bear will be mine."

She forgot about the seer as a flash of anger ran through her, and she pulled away from him. "Alexander will never be yours."

"Alexander," he said thickly, letting the name roll over his tongue. "Is that his name? *Alexander*." Then he snorted, frustrated by her answer. "He's but one man."

"Then he should mean nothing to you," she cut back.

"I will have the Bear," he said, his anger rising. "Think of it as the price of peace."

"Then you'll have nothing!"

His face hardened. "So will you," he snarled.

In a single movement of fury, she wrenched away from his loose hold and grasped the hilt of his sword, pulling it free from its scabbard. He moved after her, but she brought the blade up, halting him. "So be it," she said as she backed against the railing of the balcony. She already had nothing else to lose. She stepped back toward the rail.

He held up his hand. "No!"

She stopped.

"No," he said, his breath coming quicker. "Don't."

Neither of them moved. His eyes held an intensity that unsettled her, but she stood firm. Then his face softened slightly. Still, she didn't move.

"Those are your terms?" he asked finally.

Norah's breath caught in her chest. Was she setting terms? Was she seriously considering marrying the Shadow King? She lowered the sword but took another step back. She didn't feel herself standing before him. Perhaps it was all another dream, a terrifying dream. Suddenly, the image of her on the Shadow throne came crashing back. She swallowed. Was this what she had seen? Perhaps the vision hadn't meant that she'd take the Shadowlands by force. Perhaps this had been her fate all along.

She took a deep breath and looked around. Fate or no, she couldn't live like this, with death and destruction. She couldn't marry a man who did these things for pleasure.

"Before I answer that—what is this place?" she asked him. "What happened here?"

The king paused, letting his eyes wander. He grimaced, as if there was pain for him here. "This is what's left of Aviron."

"Where you were captured when you fled Bahoul?"

He nodded. "They sympathized with Aleon. They were enamored by the charm of the empire and Aleon's riches. Their king, Jaiah, planned to send his daughter with the offer of marriage, along with the gift of my heart cut from my body."

Her skin prickled.

"They cut open my chest..." His words drifted as he looked out across the hills from the balcony. "But they underestimated Soren." He paused. "I don't remember how we made it out. I don't remember fleeing to the canyons. Only that he got us out and brought me home."

Her breaths came unsteadily.

"After my coronation," he continued, "I appointed Soren as my lord commander, and he gave me my first gift as salar—the kingdom of those who'd sought my death."

Norah remembered the story her grandmother had told her about the destruction of Aviron. If only Mercia knew what had really happened. She turned away, trying to gather her thoughts. Vengeance was never a defense of one's actions, but things weren't always as they seemed. These stories she'd been told, the stories that drove fear into so many, they weren't the truth. At least, not entirely. And she had the power to change everything.

But regardless of the circumstance, she couldn't condone this devastation. "If we're to wed, I'll defend only," she heard herself say, looking back at him. "Mercia won't invade another kingdom for you. I won't have this... all this destruction."

He gave a slight nod.

"My people will have food and horses and weapons," she added.

He stepped closer to her. "All that is mine will be yours. Everything and everyone." There was a weight to his tone, one of assurance. He was committing to her. "And all that is yours will be mine," he added.

"Except Alexander," she said firmly.

He sighed, yielding. "I accept these terms."

Norah's heart beat in her throat.

"Are we betrothed then?" he asked.

The circumstances were suddenly very real.

"I suppose we are," she replied, as the weight of sadness shrouded her heart.

# CHAPTER THIRTY-THREE

The journey toward Kharav seemed endless. Mikael let her ride the mare of the Wild freely, to her surprise. She followed the king as they made their way through the rocky hills. The commander was quiet, somber. No doubt the news of their marriage weighed on his mind. Norah almost felt sympathy for him.

As the sun climbed higher in the sky, something felt off. "We're heading west?" she asked.

"Your army draws closer," he told her. "We go to meet them."

"They're not behind us?"

"No. They didn't march for Bahoul. They will come directly through the Tribelands."

The realization hit her. He had relented too easily in trying to take back Bahoul. Now she understood. He had discovered her army wasn't headed there. That had been his change in plans.

Her heart raced in her chest. Alexander was close. She wasn't sure she believed the king's promise not to take him, not to harm him. There was nothing at all that prevented a battle, only the words spoken between them.

"What will happen when we meet them?" she asked nervously.

He looked at her calmly. "Announce our marriage and send them home."

"Right," she breathed, feeling the slightest of reassurance. But her mind wandered to Alexander again, and her anxiousness returned. She didn't know how she'd tell him she was marrying the Shadow King. Would he understand? Would her people understand?

"How is it you can ride her?" the king asked, bringing her mind back to him. "How can you ride a horse of the Wild?" His question caught the commander's attention as well.

Norah looked down at the animal and shook her head. "I don't know. I think she understands me somehow." It was a mystery to her as well, but there was something different about the mare—they had a connection... like she'd had with the fox when she was lost in the forest.

He raised a brow and looked at the commander, and they rode on. Norah still didn't understand the significance of the mare. Her mind had been so consumed with Alexander and her army that she hadn't given it enough reflection. This was a special animal. Perhaps if she had her memories, she'd know why.

The journey was quiet, and Norah found the time blurred as she lost herself in her thoughts. They were tormenting thoughts—Alexander's face when she'd tell him she was to wed the Shadow King, how she'd leave him to return to the Shadowlands. Each hour weakened her resolve.

She shivered against the winter air and pulled the hood of her cloak forward, trying to find some warmth. Just then, in the distance, Norah spotted movement. She squinted her eyes against the wind.

Horses.

Riders.

Moving quickly toward them.

They drew closer, and her pulse raced. A sword gleamed in the air, held high by the lead rider. They were attacking.

"Mikael!" she called, pulling the mare back.

Norah's chest tightened. She didn't even have a weapon. The Shadow King sat quietly on his horse in front of her. He raised his fingers slightly to calm her, but she couldn't take her eyes off the advancing Horsemen, feeling panic well within her. But Mikael seemed indifferent, and Norah forced herself calm. While she considered herself to be ill fated in marrying him, she did trust he'd keep her safe.

The commander slid off his mount and pulled out his axe. She looked at the other soldiers and noted that they hadn't taken up their arms. But the commander stood, wielding his axe, and waited.

A shrill scream sounded from the lead Horseman, and Norah realized it was a woman. The woman's horse bore down on the commander with a thunder. Just before she reached him, she leapt from her mount and met his blade with her own. The clash rang through the air as she hit the ground and tucked into a roll, leaping up and turning to meet him again. The rest of the Horsemen fanned out to either side, surrounding them.

The woman fought him back with a fury, and Norah was mesmerized. She was clothed in soft leather and furs, fitted to her form. Her dark auburn hair was pulled back in braids, and black markings lined her eyes. She bared her teeth as she exchanged blows with the commander, but there was a hint of a devilish smile—she was enjoying the fight.

She swung high, and he met her blade with his axe, striking it down with a force and pushing her backward. The woman pulled her sword back quickly, slicing into the flesh of his arm and drawing blood. She moved to attack again, but he spun and delivered a blow to her side. She countered with an elbow and caught him on the brow. The commander reached out and grabbed her, sweeping his leg under her and taking her to the ground. She loosed another elbow to his shoulder, and he winced. Pinning her with his weight, he looked at her to yield. Instead, she ripped down the wrap from his face and drew him down into a deep kiss.

Norah gasped, not fully understanding what was happening. The commander broke away in surprise and disgust, releasing the woman. She flashed a fiendish smile and rose, pulling her sword from the ground. "You're losing your edge, Soren," she goaded him, eyeing his arm. She stepped forward, looking closer at him. "Or perhaps you're still recovering from whoever gave you that look." She grinned, nodding at the bruising on his face.

The commander shot Norah a glance, and the woman followed his gaze. It was as if she hadn't realized they were there.

"Tahla," Mikael greeted her.

"Salar," she replied with a nod, a formality coming to her. Then her eyes widened as they found Norah. "Savantahla?" she gasped. Tahla drew closer to them as though she were looking at a ghost.

Norah didn't understand, but she remained still, keeping the hood of her cloak pulled down low. It took her a moment to realize the woman was looking at the mare, not her.

Tahla glanced at the commander and then back to the horse, stepping even closer. The commander's axe came up, halting the woman. She scowled at him but then turned her attention back to Norah.

"How is this possible?" she asked. "How do you ride with Savantahla?"

Norah still didn't understand.

And Mikael didn't answer her question. "We seek accommodations for the night, as my armies pass through. We go to meet the Northmen at the far Canyonlands."

"The Northmen?" she said with surprise, lifting her brow. Then her face hardened slightly. "You go to battle the North Queen?" she asked, glancing at him for a moment but then looking back at the mare. "You call us to go with you?"

"No." Looking at Norah with a slight curve in his lip, he opened his hand and gave a nod. She pushed the hood of her cloak back, showing herself. "This is the North Queen," he said.

The woman drew in a bewildered breath, speechless. "The North Queen commands Savantahla?" she asked finally. "And rides with you?"

"We go to announce our marriage," Mikael said. "The union of Kharav and the North."

"Sol!" Tahla exclaimed, which Norah assumed to be an expression of disbelief. "Marriage?" the woman asked, looking at the commander, not seeming to believe the king. "Kharav and the North?"

A smile came across Tahla's face, and her brows raised in astonishment. "That's unexpected. I don't know what to say." She paused, shaking her head. "But the Uru would be honored to host you this evening. And to host Savantahla." She swung onto her horse with a big grin and waved them to follow.

Norah urged her mare close to Mikael as they rode after the Horsemen toward their village.

"I don't understand. Who's that?" she asked Mikael quietly.

"Tahla Otay of the Uru. Her father is chief." He paused. "When Soren and I escaped Aviron, I was near death. Tahla and her father helped me, healed me, and saw us through the canyons and back home."

It was all coming together for her now. Bahoul. Aviron.

"The Uru are the largest of the Horsemen tribes," he told her. "And they're friends. They're keepers of the western Canyonlands, one of the only two entryways into Kharav."

Norah had heard of the Canyonlands but didn't fully appreciate their magnificence until they came into view. Massive cliffs of black rock rose from the ground, as if split by the gods, creating thin passages in their crevices with an eerie darkness at their base. As they wove deeper into the dark labyrinth, she urged her mare closer to Mikael's mount.

The ground beneath them held patches of ice, but as they rode farther, she noticed small trails of running water. Deeper into the canyons, the water ran faster. They moved to the banks, and at the end of the canyons, the water poured into a large river.

They followed it around until the earth broke and Norah heard the sound of waterfalls. A path emerged and narrowed, and the descent became steeper. She fell back, behind Mikael, as they rode single file. The trail turned sharply and then climbed back up. They rounded another corner, and a massive village sprawled out in front of them. Small structures were carved into the hillside, revealing hundreds, perhaps thousands, of families and stone homes.

The sight took Norah's breath away. "It's beautiful," she said.

Tahla glanced back at her and smiled.

As they approached the village, people gathered at the edge. There were many, but as they drew near, Norah spotted a man with a regal stature. He wore a wrap beautifully twisted around his head and adorned with beaded overlays, and in his right hand was an intricately carved wooden staff.

Tahla called to him in Urun tongue, and he looked wide-eyed at Norah and her mare. He replied and bowed his head low. Norah shifted uncomfortably as the Uru people dropped to their knees, bowing as well.

"My father says it's a great honor to host Savantahla," Tahla said. "We give thanks to Savan for this blessing."

Norah glanced at Mikael. He gave her a small smirk, amused by her confusion, and slid off his horse. She watched as he made his way to the chief and bowed low to the old man, his reverence unmistakable. The chief reached out and put his hand on Mikael's shoulder and then pulled him into an embrace. Norah was surprised at the emotion that touched her, and she swallowed it back with a smile.

The army set camp outside the city. Norah left the mare with other horses by the river and followed Mikael to a large fire with people gathered in a circle around it.

"Why is Abilash a king and... this man... a chief?" she asked him.

"Coca Otay is his name. The Uru are one tribe, and Coca Otay leads them. Abilash has taken many tribes. He is a chief of other chiefs."

"Is Abilash chief of Coca Otay?"

"I would never allow that," he told her.

Strange, Norah thought, that Mikael had such influence on the Horsemen tribes. She watched as the Uru welcomed him, bowing, smiling, and giving him small gifts. They respected him here, loved him even.

A hefty Urun woman offered Norah a hot drink and motioned for her to sit. She took a seat on a large stone and watched the celebration around her. They were happier about her marriage than she was, but Norah had to admit she wasn't *unhappy*. Everything was so different from what she had expected. Even Mikael. Especially Mikael. Nothing was as it seemed, nothing was as she'd imagined. What else was hiding in this strange, special world?

# Chapter Thirty-Four

The fire blazed brightly in the late afternoon's dying sun, and the sound of celebration rang through the Urun city. Norah sat quietly, soaking up the warmth and enjoying the first feeling of ease since her capture. She watched the flames of the fire reach into the night as dancing Horsemen celebrated around it. Pulsing, twisting, turning, they moved their bodies to the sound of the drums—like spirits not bound to the earth.

She sensed eyes on her and looked over to see Tahla watching her.

The chief's daughter moved to the large rock beside her and gave her a friendly smile. "I'm sorry, I don't mean to stare," Tahla told her. "I just didn't believe the stories. But now you're here."

"What stories?" Norah asked, puzzled.

"The North Queen with winter hair. I couldn't even picture you. Can I touch it?"

Norah smiled awkwardly. "My hair?"

Tahla grinned with a nod.

*Strange.* Norah shrugged. "Sure."

Tahla reached out and combed her fingers through the blonde locks. "I don't know what I was expecting. I imagined ice in some form." She smiled sheepishly. "It feels like normal hair."

"It is normal hair," Norah said, and both women laughed.

"Do all people in the North have light hair?"

Norah nodded. "Most of them, although not as light as mine. Many are more golden haired."

Tahla's mouth opened in surprise. "Even the men?"

"Yes."

"That sounds beautiful," the chief's daughter said with a smile.

Norah thought of Alexander. "It is," she said, and they laughed again.

Tahla quieted, but still radiated a burning curiosity. "How do you command Savantahla?"

Norah didn't know how to answer. "I'm not even sure what that is. Do you mean the horse?"

"Savantahla means the spirit of the Wild," she explained. "Animals from the land of the Wild, they're all Savantahla. Horses, birds, wolves, foxes. Savan is in all of them."

"Foxes?" Norah asked in surprise. Her mind drifted back to the fox in the Wild. Now she was certain they were connected. But how were they connected to *her*?

"Any animal of the Wild. You know them by their compulsive beauty, and their eyes."

Norah thought about the mare. She was beautiful. Her mane was thick and long, and even without the sun, her dappled coat shined. Norah knew that compulsive beauty, and she knew the eyes: a hypnotizing gold. "I don't command her," Norah told her. "I only ask of her."

Tahla paused. "They say only witches can speak to Savantahla."

Norah raised a brow and rocked her head to the side. "I'm not a witch, although I have been accused of being one."

"How did you capture her?"

"I didn't. King Mikael took her from a man named Abilash as recompense... for a transgression."

Tahla's eyes widened. "King Abilash? Salar took Savantahla from King Abilash?"

"The king didn't seem very happy about it, but Abilash gave the horse willingly. We parted on good terms."

"I can assure you that you didn't part on as good of terms as you think. But he dares not defy Salar. Not alone anyway, unless he wants his tribes to starve. And he was probably scared of you and your witchery." She smiled. "Horsemen are extremely superstitious people."

Norah realized that the Shadow King must help the Horsemen with provisions through the winter, too, and she smiled at the witchery jest. "The king said the mare was quite valuable to them."

Tahla nodded. "Tribes of the Horsemen compete for land and power. If Abilash had Savantahla, he could rally more tribes to follow him."

"Over a horse?"

"The animals of Savantahla are not ordinary animals. You cannot track them. They speak to the earth, and the earth speaks back. You can't tame them unless they want to be tamed. They have great power, and anyone who controls Savantahla has great power too."

Norah looked back at the horse, which was grazing by the others along the river. She wasn't sure what this great power could be.

Tahla smiled. "I was named after Savantahla. *Tahla*."

"Ah," Norah said, "I hear it."

"My mother died in childbirth. I should have died too. But I didn't. My father said I was so wild out of the womb that the spirit must be within me. It's a strong name." She looked at the horse with a smile. "Few have seen Savantahla. Your visit is a great honor."

The warmth of gratitude filled her. "Do you want to see her?" she asked. "Touch her?"

Tahla let out a gasp. "Surely she wouldn't let me."

Norah shrugged. "We can see."

The chief's daughter jumped up eagerly, making Norah laugh, and the women made their way toward the river. The other grazing horses took little notice of them as they approached, but the mare tossed her head and snorted.

"Easy," Norah called to her. "I bring a friend who wants to meet you."

The mare shook her head again but let them draw near. Norah scratched her neck under the thick mane and gave her a gentle pat. Turning back to Tahla, she held out her hand. "Come here."

Speechless, Tahla stepped closer, and Norah brought their hands together to the creature's silver coat. Tahla let out an emotional breath, running her hand down the mare's neck. Norah smiled at the love and respect the chief's daughter had for the animal. This horse was special. Norah just wished she knew what her connection was to it.

Norah grabbed a fistful of mane and pulled herself onto the mare's back. "I think she likes you," Norah said, reaching down. "Do you want to try a ride?"

"What?" Tahla breathed in disbelief.

"Come on."

Tahla patted the mare gently, unsure, but she grasped Norah's hand. Norah pulled her up and behind her. The mare danced anxiously but seemed amenable.

"Good?" Norah asked.

"Beyond!" Tahla exclaimed. "I've only dreamed of such things!"

"Let's go!" Norah whispered to the mare, and the beast kicked into a gallop along the river. The rippling water caught the last rays of sun, and the curve of the earth rose to meet them. Tahla let out a squeal of joy, spreading her arms wide, as if in flight, and Norah laughed. Norah urged the mare faster, and they flew over the banks of the river. The wind whipped through their hair, and tears stung Norah's eyes. Finally, she slowed the mare to a walk, breathless.

"I can't believe this is happening!" Tahla squealed.

Norah smiled back at her.

"It feels like we've left the earth behind." The chief's daughter laughed, looking into the purple sunset. "And now we ride among the heavens."

It was heavenly. Beauty lay all around them, but the weight of her circumstance pulled her spirit back. "I suppose we should return." Norah sighed. "The king will have noticed my absence and fear my escape."

"Your escape?" Tahla asked. Then she paused as the realization came to her. "You don't want to marry him?"

Norah's silence answered for her.

"Look," Tahla told her, pointing behind them. Norah slowed the mare to a stop and looked behind them. There were no tracks along the muddy bank of the river, no trail of their ride. Norah's breath caught in her throat.

"See?" the chief's daughter said. "The power of Savantahla."

Norah let out a shaky breath, realizing her chance.

"You could go," Tahla said softly. "If this isn't what you want, if you don't want to marry him."

Norah wanted to run. She closed her eyes and breathed in the pull of freedom. "Why would you help me?" she asked Tahla. "Is Kharav not your ally? Your friend?"

Tahla paused for a moment, and then let out a breath. "Six years ago, my father forced me to marry. And on my wedding night, when I didn't want to give myself to him, my husband beat me, then took me anyway."

"Oh, Tahla. I'm so sorry."

"Don't be. I got my revenge."

Norah's stomach turned. Was that her future?

"Salar's a good man," Tahla said, seeming to read her mind. "And he'll be a good husband. But I'll not be idle for a woman marrying against her will. Ride two days west, past the ruins of Choan, and then turn north. You'll find yourself deep into the Tribelands, but with Savantahla, any tribe will give you shelter, safety, provisions."

Norah's heart beat wildly in her chest. The mare pranced underneath them, feeling her energy. Norah reached a hand down to calm her. She turned back toward Tahla, smiling sadly. "You don't know how much your kindness means to me. And it's true I don't want to marry him. But this marriage will end ten years of war. My Northmen are marching as we speak. Battle is imminent; thousands will die. And Mercia needs help. The winter drags on, and my people are desperate. We have no food. This marriage seems to solve everything. I have to do it."

"You're a strong queen for your people."

"I want to be."

Tahla smiled and put a warm hand on her arm. "Then we'll return. But always remember it's your choice."

Norah smiled and urged the mare back the way they had come. The sun had set, and the sky grew darker. "You spoke of the ruins of Choan," she prompted. "The border kingdom the Shadowlands destroyed?"

Tahla snorted. "That sounds like a Northern way to describe it, but yes, I suppose."

"How would you describe it?"

"It was a kingdom that almost wiped out the Uru. They wanted our land along the river. They attacked our villages, took our horses, slaughtered our people."

A wave of horror washed through her. "What happened?"

"Salar came. He drove Choan back. But after the battle, after Salar returned to Kharav, they attacked again despite his warning not to. So, he did what he had to."

He'd protected them. Norah swallowed. "He told me the Uru helped him after he fled Aviron, that you saved him."

"Death was coming for him. We gave our best crops and furs to the spirits, and we prayed for six days. On the sixth day, his fever broke. Then we showed them through the canyons and home."

Relief filled her. The king hadn't destroyed Choan for fun. He'd been protecting them. He'd been protecting the people who'd helped him in his time of need—people who'd sacrificed for him, who cared for him.

How different everything was than what she'd thought she'd known. But still... all this death.

"Is your husband dead?" she asked. Then she chided herself. It was too personal a question, too prying.

"Publicly—who knows? Privately, in the most beautifully horrible way."

Norah's stomach twisted, but she couldn't muster sympathy for such a man. "What happened?"

"Soren."

Tahla didn't need to say more. Norah could imagine. She noted that Tahla called the commander by his name. "You two are close?"

"I've known Soren since he was a boy. Now he's all grown up and thinks he's a fancy lord, but I never let him forget I can always get him with a blade."

Norah smiled. Tahla was a beautiful spirit.

When Norah and Tahla arrived back at the village, a crowd of children surrounded them, cheering at Tahla, who grinned back at them. The woman slid down, and Norah returned the mare to the other horses beside the river.

The chief was waiting. "You rode Savantahla?" he asked Tahla incredulously.

"By Savan's grace, and Salara's," she said, smiling back at Norah.

Tahla's use of the Shadow title surprised Norah, but it felt... nice. She pushed the feeling down. She didn't want to like it. She didn't want to be salara, *the Shadow Queen.*

Norah's eyes found Mikael's. He looked shaken—he'd feared she'd left. She gave him a small reassuring smile before Tahla pulled her attention back.

"Come!" the chief's daughter said. "I have something for you I think you'll like."

Norah glanced back at the king and then let Tahla pull her away again. She followed the Urun woman up a path, through the rock, and down a trail that curved around, revealing a large waterfall with a pool at the bottom. Torches circled the pool, chasing back the night.

"This place is amazing," Norah said.

"Come on!" Tahla said excitedly as she pulled off her clothes.

Norah laughed in surprise, and she looked around shyly.

"Don't worry. It's private for us," Tahla assured her.

Getting naked and jumping in a waterfall in the middle of winter after getting betrothed to the Shadow King was not what she'd expected herself to be doing right now. But Tahla's spirit made her happy, so she pulled off her boots and wriggled out of her clothes.

Tahla dove into the pool, disappearing underneath and then rising back to the surface. She grinned at Norah, waiting.

"What are you waiting for?" she asked.

Norah took a deep breath and jumped, prepared for the sting of the cold. But to her surprise, the water was warm, and she let it carry away her burdens in its current. She came to the surface and breathed, finding Tahla. "It's warm!" she exclaimed.

"It's fed from a hot spring in the falls," Tahla told her.

*Like the cave.* Norah paused, reliving the memory. She thought of Alexander. He was marching on Kharav right now, ready for war. He was coming for her.

"Are you all right?" Tahla asked.

"It just... reminds me... of a place back home. I was thinking of it."

"Do you miss the North?"

Norah nodded. "Parts of it. Mainly the people."

"You'll see it again, though. Right?"

Norah forced a smile. *Maybe.*

"Come on," Tahla called to her, swimming toward the falls. "Come over here."

Norah followed and found herself under a shower of hot water. After the long days of riding, it felt incredible.

Tahla reached into a basket that had been placed by the falls. "Here," she called, holding something out in her hand.

"What is it?"

"Corian. It's a soap root. Smell it."

Norah brought it to her nose and breathed in its sweet fragrance. "Smells incredible."

"Wash your hair with it. You'll breathe its scent all night."

Norah grinned as she lathered the paste into her hair and rinsed it in the falls. She took a deep breath. She finally felt clean. Clean from the journey. From the fear. From the pressure. Clean from the sorrow and the heartbreak. She knew it was temporary, but for now, she would relish it.

A stack of folded garments lay by the pool as they made their way out of the water.

"Here," Tahla said to Norah, handing the clothes to her. "Put these on."

Norah shrugged into a long-sleeved dress, and Tahla tied it behind her. They laughed as they combed out their hair, and for a short while, the weight of the world felt a little lighter.

"Thank you for this," Norah told her. "Your kindness—"

"Don't." Tahla smiled, grabbing her hands. "We're sisters now."

Norah smiled and then nodded, feeling a little emotional. In this moment, everything was perfect.

Tahla and Norah made their way back to the celebration and sat by the fire, enjoying cups of warm, sweet wine.

"He has his eye on you," Tahla told her, "and I don't think it's for worry of your escape."

Norah looked across the fire to see the Shadow King gazing back at her.

"Do you not like handsome, powerful men who change the fate of kingdoms for you?" Tahla asked.

Norah smiled but then grew serious. "He changed it for himself. And there are many incentives in this marriage for him. I'd be foolish to believe he had feelings for me or to let myself have feelings for him."

"I don't know about that." Tahla smiled back toward the king. "That look doesn't say, 'Hooray! I'm getting archers and steel and rocks!' or whatever you have in the North."

Norah smiled at her. "I appreciate your effort to scheme a love affair into my situation, but I don't want to hope for that. It's better I accept this for what it is—an arrangement that will help both our kingdoms. I believe he and I could be friends, allies. That's what I hope for."

"Fine, I understand," Tahla whispered with a mischievous smile.

The evening wore on, and Norah mingled freely through the warm acceptance of the Uru. It surprised her how much she enjoyed herself. She'd been desperate for the freedom to be out and to breathe and to be herself, even in Mercia. Why was she able to feel this freedom only now, after being captured by her enemy?

She saw the king on the other side of the fire, still gazing back at her, and she gave a small smile. She hadn't spoken to him since they'd arrived, having been spirited away by Tahla. Norah gathered her courage and made her way around the fire to him.

His eyes shifted over the dress Tahla had given her as she approached. She raised a brow. "Do you like it?"

He stared at her a moment, and she thought he might not answer. Then he said, "I do." His voice was thick, a different tone than the light jest she'd expected. Alexander would have politely complimented her, but the king's gaze held more than a compliment.

He stood and stepped closer. Too close. Norah pulled the outer wrap tighter around her shoulders; he still unsettled her. He grasped a lock of her hair and brought it near his face, smelling the corian. Her skin prickled, and she pulled away.

The king's brow furrowed, and his lip twitched. "Do you not want me to like it, North Queen?" he asked.

She didn't know how to answer. Did she?

He stepped closer again, his voice low. "Will you come to me tonight?"

She puffed a small breath of surprise with a sting of offense. To his *bed*? "Why would I?" she asked, taken aback.

Confusion flashed across his face. "Because you're to be my wife."

"But I'm not yet your wife," she snapped.

His words came choppy. "Then why do you fashion yourself... with scent in your hair?"

"Because I like to be clean and feel beautiful and smell... not like I've been battling and riding for weeks. Not everything is about pleasing a man, you know. Women like to do things for themselves!"

Mikael took a step back, clearly not expecting her response. He'd mistaken her self-attention, and she could tell she'd hurt his pride.

He gave a stiff nod. "Of course," he said. "I'll leave you, then."

A wave of regret ran through her, but she wasn't sure of the reason. She had no intention of being intimate with the king, yet she found herself not wanting him to go. But she pushed it down. She felt nothing for him.

He paused, turning back to her. "North Queen," he said, his eyes piercing into her. "You do... look beautiful."

She felt nothing for him, she reminded herself.

# CHAPTER THIRTY-FIVE

The morning sun spilled over the horizon as the Shadowmen prepared to leave. Tahla approached with a smile as Norah readied her mare.

"I brought you something to take back with you," Tahla said, holding a satchel out.

Norah took it and peeked under the flap. Inside were small jars and wraps of oils, balms, and soaps. She'd already felt a deep appreciation for the extra clothes that Tahla had provided. She smiled. "I know I've only been here a short while, but I want to thank you. Not only for your hospitality, but for your friendship. It was very much needed and so appreciated."

"I'm glad we're not going to war, Salara. Riding Savantahla is a moment I'll never forget. Remember, we're sisters now. Whatever you need, say the word." Tahla cocked her head and looked over Norah's shoulder at the horse. "Take care of her, yes?" she called out.

The mare snorted, and both women laughed. Norah turned and swung up into the saddle, then looked down. "Goodbye, Tahla," she said.

"Goodbye, Salara," the chief's daughter replied.

The king sat on his destrier, waiting patiently. When she was ready, they started out into the morning. He brought his horse up along hers, glancing at her.

"What?" she asked without turning.

"You said something yesterday that made me question."

She finally looked at him, waiting.

"Have you lain with a man before?" he asked.

Norah snorted in surprise, offended. "Do you question my honor?"

His brow creased. "What does virginity have to do with honor?" he asked.

Norah didn't know what to say. "If it doesn't matter, then why are you asking?"

"It's good I know," he said. "For our wedding night."

A pit grew in Norah's stomach as she tried to swallow the tightness in her throat. "Well, if we make it to our wedding night, we'll talk about it then." She urged her mare ahead, leaving the king and the conversation, and tried to push the subject from her mind.

The Shadowmen camped at the top of the canyons for two days before the Mercian army arrived. War horns sounded, and Norah wondered what Alexander must be feeling as he readied for war, coming for her. She was desperate to see him, but she wasn't sure she could face him.

She stood quietly, looking down from the cliffs at the legions organizing in the distance. The Mercian horns sounded again in anticipation of battle. And she was suddenly aware of the Shadow King beside her.

"They're preparing for an attack," she said.

"Then how happy they'll be when they learn they won't die today," he replied.

"What of the Bear?" the commander called, coming up behind them.

Norah's pulse quickened. "What of him?" she said shortly, looking at Mikael. "Do you forget our agreement?"

The commander's eyes were on Mikael, ignoring her. He waited for his king's response.

Mikael looked back at him with a ruthless calm. "The Bear's not to be harmed."

The commander snorted in anger. "He will engage."

"I said he's not to be harmed. Make sure every warrior is aware. I'll have the head of any man who raises a hand to him."

The corners of the commander's eyes tightened, but he turned back toward the army. Despite Mikael's words, Norah's concern for Alexander rose. She glanced at him warily.

His nostrils flared, and he slipped his helm back on. "Why is this man so important to you?"

Norah's heart threatened to beat itself out of her chest. She was certain he could hear it. "Is your lord commander not important to you?" she challenged. "Would you so freely give me his head if I asked for it?"

Mikael looked out at the Mercian army in the distance, but he didn't press her further. "As I've said, he's safe. But he's to return with your army to the North."

Norah nodded. That's what she wanted—her army back in Mercia and Alexander safe. She hoped it would be that simple.

The commander returned, followed by a small group of soldiers with covered carts. She looked at Mikael, puzzled, and he pulled back a tarp, showing bags of rice and dried goods underneath.

"For your army," he said. "Our scouts have reported they're low on provisions. When you return to me, I'll send more." He stepped closer to her. "I'm sincere in my commitment, and I trust you are as well."

She hadn't expected offerings from him in good faith. The gesture left her speechless as she stared at the wagons.

"North Queen," Mikael said, drawing her to look back at him. "You'll send the Bear—this Alexander—back to the North."

The commander's head jerked up in surprise. He recognized the name. Her stomach dropped as the fiery rage of his eyes burned into her, and she clenched her hands to keep from shaking. To her astonishment, he said nothing, but she knew it wouldn't be a detail he would dismiss.

She forced a nod to Mikael.

"You'll have until tomorrow with your army, then you'll come back to me," he told her.

Norah nodded again. "Tomorrow."

She mounted her horse, and the mare stirred anxiously underneath her. The commander mounted beside her, and she snapped her head toward Mikael in surprise. "He's not necessary," she said.

"He's most necessary," Mikael replied stiffly, and he clapped a hand on the neck of the commander's horse. "He's yours to command, but he'll not leave your side."

Norah severely doubted that Soren—no, not Soren, *the lord commander*—would follow anything she commanded of him. She shot him a steely gaze. With one last look at the king, she urged her mare forward, down the narrow path leading to the trenches of the canyon.

"Your Alexander is the Bear," he snarled when they were out of earshot.

"We agreed not to speak of it again," she said over her shoulder.

"That was before I knew who he was." The path widened, and he brought his horse alongside hers. His eyes burned into her, but she refused to look at him.

"The Bear is your lover," he pressed.

"No." She shook her head. "Whatever was between us, it was a long time ago." A time she couldn't even remember.

They rode down farther, passing into the shadows of the canyons.

"Will you weep when I kill him?" he asked.

The question sent a tremor down her spine and caught her breath in her chest. A rage rippled through her. She snapped her head to catch his stare, her teeth bared and eyes blazing. "If he dies, so does this marriage, and my alliance with Aleon will be certain. Will your king forgive you for that?"

He grabbed her arm, jerking her close as he pulled them to a stop. "I don't give a fuck about Aleon. It's the Bear that brings Salar's fate, and I'll take his head no matter the consequence." His eyes smiled cruelly. "Perhaps it won't be today." He paused. "Or perhaps it will. But make no mistake, I am going to kill him."

"Take your hands off me," she said between her teeth.

The commander snarled, but for the first time did as she'd told him and released his hold. He pushed his mount forward again, continuing through the dark labyrinth of the canyon walls.

She had no choice but to follow. Panic swelled inside her. He'd come to kill Alexander, and there was nothing she could do. The Shadow army watched from the top of the canyon, and Japheth waited just to the east.

If her men killed the commander, the Shadowmen and Japheth would attack the Mercian army and easily overwhelm them. If the commander killed Alexander, her army would counter, leading to the same end. She needed to keep the peace, keep the commander from Alexander, and send her Northmen back home.

Light returned as they neared the end of the canyon's break, and the commander paused and looked back at her. His eyes brimmed with dark fire through the split in his head wrap. He sat larger than a fully armored man, yet he wore no armor, save the pauldron on the shoulder of his sword arm and the black poleyns above his boots. He'd forgone his winter tunic, showing off the inked markings across his chest and arms, and carried his massive battle-axe. His horse wore crested armor, and red war paint ran down the beast's chest like blood. She rolled her eyes at the display. No doubt her army would be uneasy, though.

They emerged from the depths of the canyon, toward her army waiting beyond.

A cry rang out: "The Queen!"

They drew closer to the Mercian army, and she knew Alexander would have recognized her by now. While she wore Horsemen clothes from Tahla, there was no mistaking her hair, especially in contrast to the darkness of the commander beside her. She combed the ranks for him, and then she stopped.

A large mounted man waited at the front of the army, with the crown head of a white Northern bear as a pauldron on his shoulder. *The Bear*. His helm gleamed under the sun, and his horse pawed the earth at his rider's impatience. *Alexander*.

She cast the commander a stern look. "Will you really be the cause of a war your king works to avoid?"

He gave a malicious chuckle. "Are you sure *I* will be the cause?"

She glanced back to see Alexander break from the Mercian army, racing toward her with a cavalry behind him. Her heart leapt to her throat. He wasn't coming simply to meet them—he was coming to free her.

He was attacking.

Surely his eyes deceived him. Alexander stared with his heart racing, watching as two riders emerged from the canyons and rode toward the Mercian army.

He knew them instantly.

*Norah.* His hand tightened around the hilt of his sword. *And the Destroyer.*

His enemy was taunting him. He didn't know what nefarious plan was at work, but he had come for Norah, to save her. And that is what he'd do, no matter the consequence. No matter the sacrifice.

His archers along the front line drew back their bows. They were the best in the world, and right now, they had one target. At this range, they wouldn't miss the Destroyer, but Norah was too close.

"Hold!" he called. He scanned the top of the canyons where the Shadow army looked down at them. What was this trickery? No doubt the Shadow King was using her to draw the Mercian army closer, to draw Alexander closer.

But it didn't matter if it was a trap. He'd come.

He looked at Titus to his right. "We go fast and hard. I'll take the Destroyer. You get the queen and ride for Aleon. Do not stop. After this, there will be no Mercian army. Only King Phillip will be able to protect her. Get her to him. At all costs."

The giant of a soldier nodded. "Yes, my lord."

Alexander swept his gaze across his cavalry and tightened his grip on his sword. His destrier pawed the earth and trembled underneath him, feeling the charge building. "With me!" he roared. He hit the face cover of his helm into place with his blade and spurred his destrier forward. His eyes locked on Norah and the Destroyer. He pushed everything else out. Nothing else mattered except getting her to safety.

A battle horn sounded from the Shadowmen at the top of the canyons, and Alexander pushed his mount faster. The Shadowmen would sweep down and overwhelm his army quickly, but not before he reached Norah, not before Titus got her away.

The Destroyer pulled up his massive battle-axe—a weapon Alexander had fought before, held by a monster he'd fought before.

Ten years of war. And this was the beginning of the end.

But just before Alexander reached them, Norah spun her horse in front of the Destroyer, putting herself between them. "Stop!" she cried out.

Alexander's destrier came to a grinding halt, and the rest of the mounted soldiers swept around them in a circle. What was she doing? Confusion flooded him. "Norah! What's the meaning of this?"

"Put down your sword!"

Alexander raised it higher, and his horse reared.

"Put down your sword!" she demanded again.

He pulled his destrier back in bewilderment, looking at Norah and then back to the Destroyer. He gave a quick glance at Titus, who sat ready to snatch her but paused in his own bewilderment.

"The lord commander comes under treaty," she said, loud enough for everyone to hear. "He's with me." She shot the Destroyer a warning look, and he lowered his axe.

*With* her? "How?" Alexander seethed. He glanced back at the Shadow army on the ridge, then back to Norah.

"It's not for us to discuss here."

What did that mean? He looked at the carts behind her and pointed his sword at them. "What's that?"

"Provisions," she said, "for our soldiers. Let's return to the army, and I'll explain."

"You negotiate with the Destroyer?" he asked icily. He pointed his sword at the monster. "Get off your horse," he ordered him.

"He'll do no such thing," Norah snapped, taking him aback. "I'm queen, and I said put down your weapons. I won't be made to explain myself as I suffer to avoid war. Draw back, Lord Justice, and let him pass!"

Her ferocity stunned him, and Alexander pulled his destrier back. Norah urged her horse toward the Mercian army with the Destroyer beside her. Alexander gave another look to Titus, who stared back at him wide-eyed, and he pressed his destrier to follow.

The Mercian archers still had their bows drawn. The Destroyer's horse reared and let out a ghostly scream, but Norah called out to the army to stand down.

The Northmen looked at each other, as equally confused as Alexander, but they obeyed and parted for the carts and the Shadowmen delivering them. The Shadowmen pulled the carts to a stop and stood, waiting for their next command. Did Norah really command them?

"We'll take them from here," she said. "You can return." The Shadowmen left to rejoin their army as the Northmen, including Alexander, watched in shock.

"What about him?" Alexander called, pointing his sword at the Destroyer.

She glanced at the monster, who sat silently, but he didn't fool Alexander. There was still an evil within.

"He stays with me," she said.

Alexander could only gape at her and grip his sword tighter.

They rode to the back of the army, up a small hill where a tent already stood, and dismounted. Alexander's eyes searched Norah for answers. What was going on?

"There will be no battle," she said abruptly. "Tell the men to rest and make camp."

*No battle? Rest?* "It's early still," Alexander argued. "And what do you mean, there will be no battle?"

"I'll stay here with you until tomorrow," she replied. "And then you'll return to Mercia."

*Return to Mercia?* What?

She ducked into the tent, where the Northmen soldiers scrambled to arrange things for their queen. The Destroyer followed her in and stood to the side. Alexander stepped in behind them, glaring. He still couldn't believe it—the commander of their greatest enemy stood mere steps away, and Norah acted as though he were a friend.

Alexander dropped his voice low. "Norah, are you going to tell me what's going on?"

"Leave us," she said to the other soldiers inside, and they emptied the tent.

He glared at the Destroyer. "She said *leave us*."

Norah shook her head. "He won't go."

"I'll make him go." Alexander stepped toward him.

She reached out and clasped his arm, stopping him. "No. He's been ordered to stay."

*Ordered*? "By whom?"

She swallowed. "By the Shadow King... to whom I am betrothed."

Her words cut his heart from his chest. He couldn't breathe. *Betrothed*. "Betrothed?" His shallow breaths came faster but still starved his lungs for air. "But you're to marry the king of Aleon."

"I've changed my mind." Her voice cracked as she spoke.

Alexander stepped backward. No. *No*. "You were to unite our kingdoms." His eyes cut back to the Destroyer. "He's the monster we're fighting. You betray Mercia!"

"I am saving Mercia! Now there will be no war. No more death. The winter carries on, but our people will have food."

"Aleon will give us the provisions we need."

"But the Shadowlands will give us peace! Yes, Aleon can help us, but Phillip will bring another Great War with him." She shook her head. "I have to do what is best for Mercia."

"They will destroy us!" he seethed, with tears of rage in his eyes.

"They don't want war."

Alexander shook as he stepped in front of the Destroyer. "No? This one lusts for it," he said between his teeth.

The monster eyed him from underneath the wrap around his face. Alexander bared his teeth. This was a beast of a man, but he wasn't afraid. Only a coward would cover his face.

Norah stepped between them. "I need to write a letter to my grandmother," she said. "And it will take me some time. Distribute the food to the army. There will be more tomorrow."

"The army won't eat food from the Shadowlands."

"They will if you tell them to. Prepare for the journey back to Mercia." Her voice broke again, and it threatened to break him as well. She didn't want this. He had to find a way to stop it.

"Go," she said.

But he couldn't leave her. Not with this monster.

"Go!"

His face tightened in overwhelming bitterness, and it crushed him, but he obeyed and stormed out of the tent. He stopped just outside, pausing to suck in a deep breath and swallow back the bile rising in his throat.

Norah was to marry the Shadow King? *No.* That wasn't going to happen.

He wouldn't let it.

A low chuckle vibrated from the commander as he pulled the wrap down from his face and lowered the head of his battle-axe to rest on the ground.

Norah glared at him. "I'm sure you find this all very amusing."

"Some of it," he answered with a smirk.

"Ah, you found your tongue."

She turned from him, but he caught her arm. "Return to Salar today."

"What?" She pulled her arm away. "Why would I do that?"

"I know a desperate man when I see one."

"Alexander's not desperate," she cut back. "He's thinking about what this means for Mercia."

"He's thinking about you in his enemy's bed."

She slapped him sharply across the face.

He bared his teeth against the sting, but his eyes blazed back at her. "He's making stupid mistakes. He should have marched through Bahoul. That would have been the smart choice."

Norah swallowed. That's why the Shadow King had taken her to Bahoul. They had expected Alexander to go there. It had been *the smart choice*.

"But instead, he marched straight through the Tribelands," he told her. "And he drove your army much faster than he should have. Look at your men. They're tired, spent." He paused, with a slight curve of his lips. "His emotion controls him. And that makes him easily beaten."

He leaned closer to her. "Would you like to make a wager, North Queen? If you stay here tonight, there will be war. You give him time—time to think, to plot, to plan, for the madness to take hold—and he won't let you go." He smiled. "And I'll kill him."

Norah's pulse quickened again. She wasn't confident Alexander could stand against the king's brute. If she went back now, the commander would go with her, keeping Alexander safe.

"And if I return today?" she asked. "You won't harm him?"

His eyes burned with an unsatisfied fire, but finally, he gave a single nod.

Tears stung her eyes, threatening to fall. "Let me write my letter, then. And I'll go."

Norah folded her penned letter, pouring the wax and stamping it slowly. This wasn't a letter of good news, but her grandmother would be relieved at her safety, and Norah was sure she would understand. This marriage changed everything, for everyone.

Alexander stepped into the tent and eyed the commander, finding him as he had left him, with the head of his axe resting at his feet and his hand on the handle. Then his gaze found Norah. She stood and stepped close to him. He was silent, hesitant to speak in front of the commander, but his eyes bore into hers, and she could see the sadness inside him.

"So this is why they call you the Bear," she whispered, touching the crown head of the beast on his shoulder.

His voice came in barely a breath. "I was so afraid I wouldn't see you again."

Her lip trembled, and he stepped closer. She couldn't stop herself—she swept forward and threw her arms around him. He wrapped his arms around her and held her tightly. Tears fell as she breathed him in. If this was the last she'd see of him, she wanted to remember everything about him—how he felt, how he smelled. She only wished she could kiss him. She wished she could tell him she loved him. But that wouldn't help either of them now. Especially not with the commander so near.

*The commander.*

Remembering his presence, she pulled back, wiping her cheeks and inhaling deeply. "I'm going back today," she told Alexander.

His breath quickened, and he shook his head. "No, stay. You said you would stay until tomorrow."

She swallowed the lump in her throat and held the letter out to him. "For my grandmother."

He reached out and took the letter. "Norah, you can't."

"Will you tell her I'm well?"

Alexander reached up and gently brushed the bruise that still marred her cheek. His eyes were thick with emotion. She'd forgotten about her face. It had healed mostly, but there was still evidence of a fight. How difficult it must be for him to see her this way.

"What have they done to you?" he breathed. His gaze shifted back to the commander.

"This isn't their doing."

"All of this is their doing." He shook his head and dropped his voice. "Norah. You can't do this. You can't go." His words broke. "I can't let you go this time."

"Don't you see? It's the only way."

"What about Aleon?"

"If I wed Phillip, there will still be war," she argued. "Yes, Aleon gives us the means to fight, but we still have to. You saw the vision. With Phillip by my side, this war carries on. Thousands will die."

His brow dipped. "You think Phillip won't bring a war if you marry the Shadow King?"

"With what? He can't fight Japheth and the Shadowlands and Mercia. He won't be happy, but there's nothing he can do. Alexander, an alliance with the Shadowlands is the only alliance that can bring peace."

"Norah, please," he begged.

Norah put her hand on his cheek and shook her head softly. "It's too late," she whispered through her own tears. "I made a promise, and I can't break it now. Look around us. These men, they'll all die. You'll die. I have to do what's best for Mercia." And what was best for *him*.

"This isn't it," he said hoarsely. "You can't marry him."

Norah's heart broke. "I'm sorry."

She stood up on her toes and brought her lips to his cheek, kissing him a longing goodbye. Then she pulled away and stepped out of the tent and into the winter.

# CHAPTER THIRTY-SIX

Norah and the commander rode in silence back up the pass to the Shadow army camp where the king met them with surprise. Mikael called out in the Shadow tongue and the commander responded in kind.

The king reached out to help her as she slid down from the mare. She could tell he was at a loss for words over their early return. "You said you would send more provisions," she reminded him, forcing her voice steady.

"That I will," he assured her.

She gave a small nod and walked past him, toward the large tent. She was starting to fall apart and needed a place to be alone. The king let her go. Tears streamed down her face by the time she ducked inside, and she fell onto the bed and wept.

It was daylight when she woke to the sound of the king's voice outside the tent. She wiped her eyes and sat up, surprised she had fallen asleep, and even more surprised it was morning. A thick fur had been draped over her. She heard the king enter and looked up to see him holding a bowl of steaming soup and a wineskin.

He held the bowl out for her. Norah took it and drank down the savory broth. Her stomach grumbled. She'd eaten nothing the day prior, and she was famished. She finished the bowl quickly.

He held out his hand for the bowl, and she slowly gave it back to him.

"Do you want another?" he asked.

*Yes.* "No."

The corners of his mouth turned up. He moved to the flap of the tent and extended the bowl to a soldier outside. "Another," he said.

He held out the wineskin, and she took it, eyeing him.

"Why did you return?" he asked.

She took a drink of the wine. A deep one. It was good, and she hated it. "Because I said I would. Did you not expect me to?"

He didn't answer.

The realization came to her. "That's why you sent the commander with me, wasn't it? To kill me if I tried to leave?"

"He was to kill the Bear."

Her heart quickened. "We agreed—"

"It was only if you would have broken our agreement," he interrupted her.

Anger pulsed inside her. "But I didn't."

"And the Bear is still alive."

"Stop calling him that," she snapped. "He's my lord justice."

She pushed a breath out to slow her heart. The name didn't even bother her. She just needed to be angry at something—at him. She needed the anger. It was the only thing holding her together. A soldier returned with another bowl of soup, and Mikael held it out to her.

Her eyes welled, and she took it.

"Do you want some bread?" he asked.

A tear rolled down her cheek, and she shook her head.

He gave a gentle smile and sat down beside her. Then he held out a bread roll.

Another tear fell as she took it, but there was a warmth about him that surprised her, and settled her.

He sat in silence with her as she ate the bread and drained the second helping of soup. She could have downed a third, but she didn't dare say it. When she'd finished, he said, "My kingdom has good food." The corner of his mouth turned up. "That's important to you, yes?"

She wiped her lips and held her empty bowl. "What?"

He shrugged. "You eat a lot."

"What's that supposed to mean?"

He shrugged again. "That you eat a lot."

She stared at him. Was that a bad thing? She ate like a perfectly normal person. Yes, Alexander may have occasionally teased her...

She jerked. *Alexander.* They'd be heading back to Mercia. She set the bowl down. "Have they departed?"

"They're preparing now. Go to the cliff. You'll see them."

Norah rose quickly from the bed. As she pulled on her cloak, the fastening caught in her hair. She tried to pull it free, but it held in the braid. Heat rushed to her cheeks as she fumbled with it in front of him. He rose and stepped forward, stopping her. Gently, he untangled the locks from the clasp and straightened the cloak over her shoulders.

She wavered for a moment. "Thank you," she breathed. Their gazes caught each other, and they stilled. The darks of his eyes held her, quieted her.

*Alexander,* she remembered.

She peeled herself away, and then she ducked out of the tent, hurrying toward the cliff and freeing her tresses from the disheveled braid as she went. She reached the edge, out of breath. The wind blew her hair wildly around her as she looked down at her army. She saw the horses and the wagons of food the Shadow army had delivered.

And she saw Alexander.

He was already mounted on his horse, conferring with his soldiers. One pointed up at her and he spun to see her.

The army started their march. The cold of the wind burned her skin, but she stayed and watched them leave. Alexander waited for the last soldier to depart, still looking up at her. He raised his sword to her—a silent vow. With a last longing look, he turned to join the army back to Mercia.

Norah made her way to her tent. She expected another rush of emotion to come. But it didn't. Perhaps the weight of everything had taken all the emotion. Maybe she had nothing left. She reached the tent where the king still waited inside.

"We'll depart shortly," he told her.

"I'd like to change, if that's all right." Tahla had given her a leather-and-linen layered dress to meet her army, and like Mercian dresses, it wasn't made with comfort in mind. She'd rather wear the riding dress for the journey to the Shadowlands.

"Of course," he said with a small nod, and stepped out to tend his army.

She stripped off the heavy dress and stood for a moment, naked, letting the chill of the air clear her mind and quiet her soul. Then she put on her breeches and boots and pulled the riding dress over her head. She cursed under her breath as she found she could only tie it loosely behind.

Why must all dresses have fastenings in the back? She reached behind awkwardly, trying to pull the leather lacing tighter, tempted to don the weapon boy's clothing once more instead.

Mikael entered, startling her, and she quickly turned her back to him, flushing.

"I'm sorry. I thought I'd allowed enough time," he said.

Norah turned her head, looking at him out of the corner of her eye. She paused for a moment, gathering her courage, then asked, "Can you help me?"

He stepped toward her slowly.

She reached up and pulled her hair away, waiting.

"Would you like it tighter?" he asked.

"Please."

He pulled the hastily tied bow undone and paused, letting his fingers skim the skin between the edging. Her skin prickled.

"I want to see you," he said, his voice low and thick. "Would that imperil your honor?"

She looked back over her shoulder. His brazenness astonished her. "No, but it doesn't mean I'll let you."

He chuckled and fixed the lacing tighter. Then he stepped closer, and she felt his breath in her ear. "Are you unmoved by a man's suffering? You'd make a decent torturer."

A flush crept up her skin. She knew it was a jest, but there was an underlying message of desire. What bothered her more was that she liked it. She turned around, eyeing him boldly. "You'd make a decent lady-in-waiting," she said, then ducked out of the tent to prepare for their departure.

The Shadowlands were well suited to their name. They rode between the canyon cliffs that towered over them and held back the light—they were dark and foreboding, like the men they homed. It took a full day to reach the end of the labyrinth, where the trail opened and the rocky darkness fell away to reveal the beauty of terraced mountains, even in their winter slumber.

Norah's eyes widened. It was like stepping into another world.

Mikael nodded out over the terraces. "In the spring and summer, this will all be lush and green. It will be beautiful."

"It's already beautiful," she said. She hadn't imagined a place of such dark renown could be so lovely. She noticed the paddy fields. "The Shadowlands grow rice? Is that your trade?"

"Our main one, yes."

"Is that what you trade with the Horsemen?" That must be how he'd become so close to the tribes.

"It's what we trade *through* the Horsemen, with everyone," he told her. "Including the North."

Norah's brows creased. "Mercia doesn't get their rice from the Shadowlands."

He chuckled. "The whole world gets their rice from us. They just don't know it."

Norah shook her head, amazed. "The Horsemen take it to market for you?" she asked. She thought longer. "Do you feed them as well? Is that what Tahla meant when she said Abilash dare not defy you, unless they want to starve?"

He didn't answer, but his smirk told her it was.

"Do you control all the Horsemen tribes?" she asked, her curiosity growing.

"Most. Not all."

She thought about their departure from King Abilash and what Tahla had told her. "Do you think there will be consequences with Abilash now?"

"If so, I'll deal with them, but they're of no matter." He looked at her. "I have what I want."

A wave rolled through her stomach, stirring feelings that confused her. Despite their history and start, he had been kind to her, protected her, this Shadow King with his destroyer of men. "Tahla told me what happened at Choan, how you saved the Uru."

He shifted uncomfortably in his saddle. "You believe her?"

"I have no reason not to."

He pulled up his horse and looked at her with a steely gaze. "Don't."

Her brow creased in confusion. "Don't believe her?"

"Don't mistake me for a good man, North Queen," he warned. "You'll be sorely disappointed."

Norah's chest tightened, surprised at his sharpness, and they continued on in silence. The terraced mountains gave way again to the black rock of the Shadowlands. Her pulse quickened as an enormous castle loomed in the distance against the skyline. It was like nothing she'd ever seen. "Even your castle is black," she said, more to herself than to him.

"It's made from the black mortite under our earth," he told her. "It's also why the canyons are so dark. It would have been a greater feat to build a castle any color other than black."

As they neared the castle, it was even larger than she'd originally thought, larger than Mercia's castle and with an even larger city sprawling out from its walls. The gates, adorned with gold scripts, were as ornate as they were strong, and she marveled at them as they passed through. The expansive courtyard was packed with people craning to see the king and the strange woman he'd brought back with him. They brought their horses to a stop, and Mikael dismounted.

She slid off her mare, and murmurs rumbled through the crowds as they recognized her. She immediately became self-conscious remembering the beating to her face and pulled the hood of her cloak over her. The throngs of people parted as Mikael led the way, and they cheered their king as he passed.

They reached the polished stairs and intricately sculpted doors, and Mikael led the procession inside. As the great doors closed behind him, he turned and called back to her, "Come."

Then he and the commander started through the castle. Did he think she was a dog? Norah rolled her eyes but reluctantly followed. They turned down a large hall, larger than the great hall in Mercia but just as beautiful. Dark, polished tile patterned the floor and sprang up the walls to the arched ceilings overhead. Symmetrical geometries created intricate designs, weaving complex patterns that drew the eye to every corner of the room.

At the end of the hall, a woman stood, regal and majestic. Silver kissed the long hair that had once been a brilliant black. She looked at Mikael with warmth and affection as he walked toward her.

"Mother," he greeted her, kissing her cheek and bringing her hands to his lips.

Norah immediately felt a wave of anxiousness in anticipation of being presented to the king's mother. It would have been nice to have cleaned up first.

The woman's brow dipped as she grazed his beard with her fingertips. "What happened to your face, and your hand?" she asked as she reached out and touched his arm in horror. She turned to the commander with a scowl, clearly annoyed at his poor keeping of the king, but her eyes widened in seeing his wounds and accompanying limp. "From the Northmen?" she asked.

"Not the Northmen," Mikael said, stepping back and turning to Norah. "The North Queen."

It was not the introduction Norah had been hoping for.

The king's mother looked at her incredulously, her eyes darting from Norah to the lord commander and then back to Mikael again. She drew closer and looked over Norah in astonishment.

"Your Majesty," she said to Norah, with a cold steel in her voice. While her eyes were rimmed in loathing, she held her etiquette, much as Norah expected Catherine might do. The woman looked at her son, searching for direction, but he gave none.

Apparently, Norah's arrival was as unexpected to his mother as it was to her.

The king's mother turned back to Norah. "We'll see you comfortable during your stay here," she said stiffly. "I'll take you to your chamber." She looked back at Mikael with displeasure and then turned toward a side hall. "Come," she called to Norah.

Norah pursed her lips. She was beginning to see the resemblance.

The woman led her down the hall to a large staircase. At the top of the stairs and at the end of another hall, they came to an open chamber.

"You're surprised I'm here," Norah said, breaking the silence.

"I'm surprised you're alive," the king's mother said bluntly. "And yes, that you're here." The woman turned and looked at Norah more closely, disappointment brimming in her eyes. "But I am sorry for your condition. It doesn't please me you've been handled in this manner. It's not right for a queen."

Norah realized she was referring to the bruising and cut on her face. "This wasn't your son's fault." The woman seemed as surprised at Norah's defense of him as she was herself. "I mean, most things are," she added, "but not my appearance."

The king's mother was quiet. Her lips parted slightly, but no words came out.

Maids filled a tub with steaming water and draped a linen gown over a side chair.

"We'll find you an appropriate gown for the evening," the woman said stiffly. She gave Norah a small nod. "Your Majesty," she said, and left her to the bath.

Norah waited as they all made their way out and closed the doors behind them. She looked around the room. It was ornately decorated with dark, heavy furnishings and tapestries of black and gold. The windows in the room were tall tri-sets of thin glass panels, separated by iron staves like a beautiful cage. Even if she was no longer a prisoner, she still felt like one.

Norah sighed and peeled off her soiled clothing. She welcomed the chance to feel clean again. The water burned her skin as she stepped into the bath, but she didn't care. She wanted to burn off everything that had happened since she'd left Mercia. If only she could wash away this situation. She closed her eyes and sank underneath the surface, relishing the sting of the water over her body and face. When she could hold her breath no longer, she pushed herself up, gasping for air.

Norah worked the soap into a rich lather and rubbed it into her skin. It smelled like springtime. She hated that she liked it. The water changed color as the soil came off, and she was surprised at how dirty she'd been.

She wanted to stay in the bath, soaking in its warmth, but she didn't want the king's mother to return with her unready. Quickly, she finished washing and climbed out, drying off and slipping into the linen gown. She shivered. Castles were cold. Especially enemy castles.

# CHAPTER THIRTY-SEVEN

The sun set on her first day in the Shadowlands, and Norah fought to keep control of her emotions. Her duty had been to free Mercia from the darkness of the Shadow King, but here she was, marrying him and joining their kingdoms together. Her stomach turned at the thought of her grandmother receiving her letter. She'd understand. She'd see this was what was best for Mercia and her people. Wouldn't she?

But Norah couldn't escape the nagging fear that wasn't how her marriage would be seen, and she would be doing all this for nothing. The thought threatened to break her. She forced her mind to focus on one task at a time. Bathe. Dress. Breathe.

There was a knock on her chamber door and the king's mother swept into the room before she could answer, with a maid close behind. Very Catherinesque. A pang of homesickness struck her. What she wouldn't give to see her grandmother right now.

"I've brought several dresses," the woman told her. "We should find at least one that fits for this evening."

Without a word, the maid shuffled Norah in front of the mirror and lifted a yellow dress against her form.

The king's mother looked at it in the mirror's reflection. "No," she said, and the maid laid it aside on the bed.

The maid held a green dress, and the woman again shook her head. Norah swallowed. She would have been fine with either of the dresses.

The maid held up a third dress—burgundy with heavy embroidery down the center.

"That will do," she said.

Despite the woman's coldness, the marked reminder of Catherine brought emotion to Norah's eyes. She forced it back.

The maid helped her into the dress. "It fits well," she said as she moved to Norah's back and tied the straps. "Your being the same size as the princess makes it easier."

Norah glanced up at the king's mother. "You have a daughter?" Her heart leapt at the thought of another young woman in the castle—perhaps someone like her.

The woman glared at the maid, who continued working in silence. "I did," she said shortly.

Norah's heart broke for her. The woman had lost a daughter. She didn't know what to say, or whether to offer her condolences. "I'm sorry," she said softly.

The room was silent. That made it worse.

"What should I call you?" Norah asked her, changing the subject. "Do you have a title here in the Shadowlands?"

The woman looked at her with eyes of black sapphire. For a moment, Norah thought she wouldn't answer.

"My name is Analil. In Kharavian tongue, as this is Kharav, not *the Shadowlands*, I am called Salara-Mae, if you wish."

It wasn't her intent to so quickly offend her future mother-in-law. She gave a small nod. "Forgive me, Salara-Mae. And thank you for your counsel. Kharav it is."

After dressing, Norah followed Salara-Mae down the stairs, through the great hall, and into a large dining room, and her eyes widened at the expansive table. The king sat at the end, with the commander seated to his left. The king looked up as she entered, pausing in his conversation, and straightened. Their eyes locked. He'd washed too. His hair was tied back, and his beard trimmed short, almost to the skin. Without his armor, he wore a sleeveless tunic, prominently displaying the ink markings down his arms and just below his neck. Heat flushed across her cheeks. He looked... very nice.

She realized the commander looked different as well. He'd forgone his wrap and was openly showing his head and face. His hair was tied back like the king's. He wore a tunic similar to Mikael's, which was better than his normal form of none at all. At first glance, he looked very much like the king, although he was certainly *not* like the king. And he looked... *not* nice.

A chilling snarl came from her right, and Norah gasped as two beasts crouched low, ready to attack. Their heads and frames were like enormous wolves, but they weren't wolves. Their necks and chests were thick and maned in dark fur, but their backs sloped to a smaller, thick-muscled hind, like they were built for fighting.

Salara-Mae glared at Mikael. "Control your dogs," she snapped angrily.

The king's eyes drifted to his lord commander, who called over his shoulder, "Cusco. Cavaatsa." The beasts settled back to lie on the floor.

"Forgive us," Salara-Mae said to Norah, eyeing the commander sharply. "We've had very few guests for some of us to hone our manners. But as you *are* our guest, please," and she waved Norah to the end of the table, opposite Mikael.

Norah glanced at him, uncomfortable with his mother's unawareness of their betrothal, but she gave a nod and sat gracefully. When would he tell her?

A young woman pulled fruit and meat from the platters and filled her plate. Norah watched her, noting her soft brown hair. She was different from the people in Kharav. Catherine had told her Kharav took people as slaves. Was this woman a slave?

"Must he drink that filth in front of me?" Salara-Mae's voice cut through the air.

Norah glanced around the table to see what had upset her. The king's brute held a chalice in his hand and was cheekily taking another drink before setting it on the table. She wondered what was inside it. He seemed to hold Salara-Mae's contempt. She wouldn't even speak directly to him, which was surprising. And somewhat entertaining.

"Well, we didn't know you'd be joining us for dinner this evening, Mother," Mikael answered in his commander's defense.

Salara-Mae scowled at her son, who took a bite of food and chewed it slowly, unfazed. Then she straightened her shoulders and turned to Norah. "I take my dinner in my chamber, as I prefer an early meal. I'm sure you'll prefer to do the same during your visit."

*Visit.*

Norah held a grape in her fingers. It was the largest grape she'd ever seen, and she popped it in her mouth. Salara-Mae looked at her as though she expected her to respond. *Nope*. Norah pushed in two more grapes. Then her eyes found Mikael, who was looking back at her.

She stopped mid-chew.

"It's more than a visit, Mother. The North Queen and I are to be married," he announced, rather abruptly.

Norah forced herself to swallow her mouthful of half-chewed grapes and frowned. Perhaps he could have waited for just a little better timing and maybe had a softer approach or a bit of a buildup? But there it was—out.

A coldness swept through the room. Norah's heart raced in her chest.

Salara-Mae carefully put down her glass and smoothed out the cloth on the table in front of her. "If this is your attempt at humor, it's ill spun."

Norah shoved another set of grapes into her mouth. She wouldn't be available to speak for this engagement.

"This isn't a humorous matter," he replied. "I will wed the North Queen."

"You'll do no such thing!"

Norah pushed in another two grapes without having chewed the others.

"You speak to your salar," he reminded his mother.

"What would your father say?" she hissed.

His voice was as sharp as steel. "My father's dead."

Norah swallowed her grapes and took a deep drink from her chalice. It wasn't exactly how she'd hoped this conversation would go. She wondered if it would have been different in Mercia. Probably not. She was starting to appreciate that she'd only had to write a letter to Catherine and the council.

"I would speak with you alone," Salara-Mae said to her son.

Norah would be perfectly fine with them speaking alone.

"No need," he said stiffly. "My decision's final."

Norah thought the lump in her throat might choke her. She focused on controlling the shake in her breath.

Salara-Mae moved her icy gaze to Norah and then to the commander. Surely a fire burned inside him in violent agreement with the king's mother, regardless of the bitterness that sat between them, but he gave no support to her protest.

The room was ghostly quiet. Mikael took a drink from his chalice. Norah took a bite of the marinated meat. Mikael was right. The food was good here. And it was the only thing helping her get through this conversation.

"I think I'll retire," Salara-Mae said, pushing back her chair and rising.

"You haven't eaten," Mikael said.

"I'm not feeling well. I'll take something later, in my room, if my appetite returns."

"I trust you'll be better tomorrow after you've rested."

She looked at him coldly. "I seriously doubt it." Despite her abhorrence to the idea of their marriage, she wasn't without etiquette, and she gave a small bow to Norah. "Your Majesty."

Norah struggled to swallow the meat and gave a nod back. "Salara-Mae."

The woman turned and left with two guards at her flank.

The king's brute took another drink from his chalice, and Norah saw the color on his lips: a dark iron red. *Blood.* Blood filled his chalice. His eyes locked with hers, and the hair on the back of her neck stood on end as her stomach twisted in revulsion.

"We'll announce our marriage tomorrow and celebrate," Mikael told her, as if everything were perfectly normal. Was drinking blood normal? "Then we'll begin preparations for a wedding that will happen in a few weeks' time."

*Wedding?* Right. She peeled her eyes from the commander. Another topic that threatened to empty her stomach: she was to be married.

Norah drew her bottom lip between her teeth. "When will I be able to return to Mercia?" If she could just get home, she could... pretend, perhaps, that this was not as terrible as it seemed.

The king paused in lifting his chalice, stilling for a moment as he looked at her. "You won't."

What? Her pulse quickened. "Not even to visit?"

"You'll be salara," he said, and then took a drink of wine. "Your place is in Kharav."

Norah's chest tightened. She couldn't breathe. She hadn't expected to return right away to Mercia, but she'd hoped at some point she would. Even in going to Aleon, she would have traveled back and forth between the two kingdoms.

His words made everything real for the first time. This was her home now. She might never see Mercia again. Or her grandmother. Or Alexander. The weight of everything threatened to crush her. She needed out. She rose abruptly, gripping the edge of the table for support.

"Excuse me," she managed to utter before she made her escape from the room. She didn't wait for acknowledgment. Her mind was a haze as she wound through the maze of halls, toward her room. Her panic grew with each step, and she was desperate to find her chamber before she fell apart. But each hall, each door, looked the same. The sound of a guard so close behind, following her disoriented course, further overwhelmed her. She couldn't hold herself together anymore. She stopped, backing against a wall to catch her breath, and covered her face with her hands. Her cheeks burned with embarrassment, which only fueled her emotion.

A soft touch on her elbow startled her, and she looked up to see one of her guardsmen. He moved his hand, motioning her back the way they had come. She wiped her cheeks and stepped forward slowly, allowing him to lead. They wound back through the halls, and she tried to regain her composure. Relief filled her when he stopped at the door of her chamber.

"Thank you," she whispered through her shaking breaths, and then slipped inside.

# CHAPTER THIRTY-EIGHT

Norah sat at the small table in her chamber in the fading darkness of morning, a heavy weight in her chest. The king had issued an announcement of their marriage, and tonight there would be a celebration, but she didn't feel like celebrating. She should, she told herself. She was avoiding war. Her kingdom was safe. Alexander was safe.

A small knock rattled her door, and a servant entered, carrying a gown over her arm and a small tray of bread and fruit. The young woman was the same one from the dining hall—fair skinned with soft hazel eyes and brown hair. Norah wanted to ask if she was a free woman, but that seemed rude. So she didn't. The maid avoided Norah's eyes as she set the tray on the table and then draped the gown over the side chair. She gave a small bow and left the chamber without a word.

Norah stared at the tray, then picked up a strawberry half the size of her palm. She closed her eyes as she bit into it, letting its sweetness fill her senses, and imagined herself somewhere very far from the kingdom of Shadows.

But she only gave herself a moment. She needed to dress. Gods only knew what was in store for her today. Quickly, she rose and shucked off her nightgown before pulling on the dress that lay over the side chair.

She breathed a few words of thanks that it had front lacing. Salara-Mae hadn't offered her a maid, and she wasn't going to ask for one. She'd manage herself. She pulled her hair back into a braid and washed her face in the basin. The cold water made her shiver.

Dressed, she waited. She wasn't sure what for. Was she expected to stay in her chamber, or—

A hard knock on the door startled her. She wasn't expecting anyone so soon. In fact, she wasn't expecting anyone at all. She opened the door slowly to find the lord commander looking back at her.

"I would speak with you in the hall," he said shortly.

"No, thank you," she replied and moved to close the door, but he caught it with his hand. "Please," he said between his teeth, with more bite than request.

Norah sighed. He wouldn't leave until he accomplished whatever he was burdened to do. Reluctantly, she stepped into the hall and was surprised to find a group of soldiers with him.

The commander turned his gaze on the closest man. "This is Captain Artem. He leads the Crest, the protectors of the royal family, and now apparently you."

*Apparently.* The ring of distaste in his words wasn't lost on her. She drew her eyes over the captain, who didn't bow at his presentation and didn't speak. His mouth was a hard line as he stared back at her.

He was different from the other Kharavian soldiers, and different from the lord commander. He wore armor, something she hadn't seen much of in the Shadowlands, aside from the king. Older than the commander, in his fifties perhaps, he wore no wrap on his head. Gray touched the temples of his black hair above his angular face that held a peppered shadow of a short beard. But it was his eyes—his eyes told her of an evil within. She shuddered.

"You'll have at least two men with you at all times, four if you step outside the castle walls," the commander said.

"That's really unnecessary," she said.

"It's not negotiable," he growled back, and her face flushed with the heat of anger. "You'll always have at least one guardsman who speaks the Northern tongue." He held his hand out, and four of the dozen men stepped forward. With their faces covered, they all looked the same, except she thought she recognized one's eyes as the soldier who'd helped her find her chamber the day before. She gave a nod back, with a small sense of comfort that at least one of her guardsmen could be kind.

"You'll never be without your guard," he said. "Am I clear?"

Norah pursed her lips together. "Perfectly." Just like at home.

But this wasn't home.

The morning passed slowly, and Norah felt awkwardly confined to her room. Not that it mattered, she told herself. She didn't have an appetite to see the castle right now. So she waited and tried to pretend, if only for a moment, she wasn't trapped in the darkness of the Shadowlands. *Kharav*, she reminded herself.

She lay across the bed, looking up at the great beams along the ceiling. Then she let her eyes close as she thought of Alexander—his face, his eyes, the warmth of his hands. She could almost feel them around hers. A tear fell from the corner of her eye to her soft locks underneath.

A knock on the door pulled her from her thoughts, and she sat up as she wiped her face. Would this be how she spent her time—constantly answering her door? She opened it to see her guard. Not the nice one.

"We will escort you down to the celebration."

Her brows drew together in confusion. "So soon? It's barely midday."

"Yes, but it's already started."

"Oh." She felt a wave of anxiousness. She wasn't one for social celebrations, especially ones celebrating her, especially ones celebrating her unfortunate marriage. "Will it last all day?" she asked.

"Of course."

"Wonderful," she mumbled to herself. "Give me a moment."

She closed her door and leaned back against it, inhaling deep breaths. Celebrations were better than war, she told herself. That's why she was doing this. This was best for Mercia.

Not for her.

But she couldn't think about herself. Not just because she couldn't be selfish, but she had to control her emotion. Maybe she could pretend it was someone else's marriage. Yes, *someone else's*. She went to the vanity, wiping her face and tucking a few wayward locks behind her ear.

"Someone else's marriage," she said to her reflection. "I'm very happy for them. May they have a long life, much happiness, many children"—wait, no—"*No children.*"

Then she let out a breath and opened the door, waving the guard to lead her.

People filled the hall from end to end, and her eyes widened as she entered. The magnitude of it all was overwhelming. Everyone grew quiet with her arrival, and all eyes fell on her. *Someone else's marriage.* She forced herself forward.

Her wandering gaze found the king seated at the large center table at the front of the hall, and he stood when he saw her. He picked up his chalice and held it high, and the room erupted in clapping as the crowd parted for her. She made her way toward him.

His eyes smiled. "Please," he said, motioning to the chair beside him. A servant pulled out the chair as she took her seat.

He sat down beside her. "I'm happy to see you, North Queen."

"Good," she said smartly, but gave him a small smile.

His eyes lingered on her. "I thought you might be angry with me for how we left our conversation last evening."

She looked down at her hands. The thought of not being able to return to Mercia still tore her heart from her. "More... sad."

He shifted in his chair, and his mouth opened to speak, but he said nothing. He looked out across the celebrating hall, then back to her. His brows drew together. "You're sad?" He leaned back in his chair. "But you'll be salara."

As if the two weren't the same.

He let out an unsettled breath. "You'll return to the North again. I promise you this."

She straightened in her chair. *When?*

"But tonight, I want you to enjoy yourself," he told her, looking out across the great hall. "Celebrate. We're to be married."

Did he have to remind her? Norah noticed the king's mother was absent from the festivities. She wondered how long she'd have to endure before she could excuse herself. Could she excuse herself from her own wedding celebration? She glanced around—was there at least some food?

Three women approached. They lined up before the king and gave a low bow. They were beautiful, with dark honeyed skin, hair like black silk, and large brown eyes. Sisters, maybe? Her gaze moved over the ornate embroidery of their dresses, the gold around their wrists, and the adornments in their hair. Women of status.

"Salara," Mikael told them, introducing her.

The women smiled politely at her, giving another low bow.

"Myral, Rasha, and Heta," he said to Norah. "They'll be with you in the villa, where you'll stay once we're wed."

Royals maintaining separate spaces wasn't surprising; it was customary in Mercia as well. Forced friends—odd—but Norah liked the idea of not being entirely alone. "We'll be good friends, then," she told them, giving a polite smile.

The women bowed again and then left as gracefully as they had come.

A string of music caught her ear, and she glanced up to see a dancer in the center of the hall. Norah took in a breath of astonishment at her clothing, or rather, her lack of clothing. The woman wore only braided weaves of richly patterned cloth around her hips and small bells that jingled with each movement. Beaded bracelets wrapped her wrists, and she shook them in unison to the rhythm of the music. Heavily beaded adornments covered her neck, with intricately woven strands cascading over her chest. The nipples of her bare breasts were pierced with small golden rings.

Norah's eyes widened as the woman moved her hips to the fluted song. She'd never seen anything so brazen. Such entertainment in Mercia would be the ruin of a good name. Her cheeks flushed with embarrassment, but she couldn't look away. The dancer had lighter hair, blonde, like her Northmen. Norah wondered where she was from.

"She's beautiful, yes?" Mikael said as he watched the dancer.

"Um..." She swallowed, unsure how to answer. Despite her discomfort, she was mesmerized. The dancer flowed with the music, her body rolling like the waves of the sea. She was light on her feet, as if she weren't held by the pull of the earth. Her eyes locked with Norah's. She was close enough for Norah to see their emerald depths. The woman smiled.

The dancer spun, and Norah finally broke from her hold. She glanced at Mikael, only to find him watching her.

"You like her?" he asked. His eyes flashed with amusement.

Norah's cheeks flushed, like she'd been caught. She swallowed back her embarrassment. "I've just never seen anything like her."

"She's all the way from Elam, given as a gift to Japheth's King Gregor, but I won her from him in a bet." He smiled, smugly pleased with himself.

Disgust knotted in her stomach. She found nothing pleasing about gifting or betting human beings. Bitterness rippled across her tongue. "Do people's lives mean nothing to you?" she said before she could stop herself.

His smile faded. "She's a slave."

"She's a person," Norah snapped.

Anger flashed across his face at her rebuke; he was clearly unaccustomed to being chastised, but he didn't respond. He only sat for a moment, then gave a small wave of his hand. The music died. He called out in the Shadow tongue, and the dancer stopped. She looked at Norah with a troubled face.

"What are you doing?" Norah asked him.

The dancer bowed low and quickly left the hall.

"What's going to happen to her?" she asked, her alarm growing.

"Whatever you decide. She's yours now."

She sat back in her chair. "What?" Was he serious? *No*—he couldn't be. Was he? "I don't want her."

"Then you'll have to figure out what to do with her."

*Gods*, he was serious. Norah scoffed in frustration as she looked back out across the hall. She knew she'd offended him, but she didn't really care. He was offensive. The Shadowlands were offensive, with their slaves and their bloodlust. This was a mistake; she couldn't marry this man. She had to get out of here. She had to... escape... somehow. Get back to Mercia...

And prepare for war. Because that's what she would cause: *war*.

Norah sighed. She couldn't leave. She had to make this work. But she vowed to herself that she would change things.

The celebration wore on through an endless evening. Mikael settled. She felt his eyes on her, often, but didn't look at him. Finally, she bid her parting and, thankfully, slipped away. As she walked to her chamber, her mind spun around her. She had to find a way to live here, despite her abhorrence of the idea. She had to learn how to live as queen of the Shadowlands.

Norah opened her chamber door and jumped at the figure inside. "Hammel's hell," she breathed as she recognized the woman—the green-eyed dancer.

The woman bowed low. "I'm sorry, Your Majesty. I didn't mean to startle you."

She gripped the side chair close by, her heart still racing. "What are you doing here?"

"I'm yours now," she said quickly.

Norah drew in a sharp breath and clipped it out again. "No, you're not mine. That's not... *no*."

Panic flashed across the woman's face. "Do you not find me pleasing?"

"I don't," Norah said shortly. "You have to go. No one can see you here."

The woman fell on her knees in front of Norah. "Your Majesty! I'm sorry I displease you. But I beg of you, please don't send me away! Let me try again."

Norah shook her head as she swallowed back the awkwardness of the situation. "There's nothing to try again, I don't want"—she waved her hand—"whatever it is you do."

"I'm most discreet. And trained in pleasure for both men and women."

Norah's cheeks flushed hotter. "That's exactly what I don't want," she insisted. "Please, go."

"Do you have a need for a maid?" she pleaded.

"No, I—" Norah paused. She did need a maid. She thought she'd be given one, but that seemed unlikely now. She eyed the woman doubtfully. "Are you trained as such?"

"I've been in Kharavian court for three years. I know the ways of Kharav, and I know what proper maids don't." Her deep-emerald eyes sparkled, begging. "I can help you."

But Norah pushed the idea from her mind. "No," she said. "I can't have you as my maid."

The dancer bowed low on her knees. "Please, Your Majesty! I can't stay at court if you won't have me."

Why would she want to? "You don't need to stay at court. Go. I free you."

"But I can't live freely in Kharav as an outsider. They won't allow it. I'll be killed."

Norah let out an exasperated breath. "Why don't you go home?"

"I can't return home. I was a gift to King Gregor. Nor can I return to Japheth. If I can't stay at court, I have nowhere. Please, Your Majesty."

Norah felt a twinge of guilt. What was she to do with this woman?

The dancer's emerald eyes found hers. "Your Majesty, I know what it's like to be a stranger in a strange land, to not trust anyone or anything around you. Please, let me serve you in whatever capacity you see fit."

Norah pushed out a long sigh. She did need a maid, and this woman might be able to help her in other ways she hadn't anticipated. "What's your name?"

"Vitalia, Your Majesty."

"Do you have clothes, Vitalia? Appropriate clothes?"

The woman gave a breathless smile. "Yes. Yes, Your Majesty."

"Very well," Norah relented. "We'll try it out. Fetch your things. Take the side room, and I'll see you in the morning."

Vitalia jumped up, smiling and bowing. "Yes, Your Majesty. Thank you! Thank you!" She bowed again and fluttered from the room.

# CHAPTER THIRTY-NINE

Norah made her way down to the dining room for breakfast with her new maid close behind. She hoped no one would recognize the dancer in a more conservative dress.

Mikael's gaze locked on her as she entered. He straightened, and his mouth opened slightly, but he didn't speak. He only stared at her, and a flush came to her cheeks.

Salara-Mae rose from her seat and stood, as proper courtesy dictated, then gave her a stiff nod and sat after Norah did, returning quietly to her breakfast.

Norah wondered if breakfast in the dining hall was a routine for Salara-Mae. She also noted the commander's absence.

"I trust you slept well?" Mikael asked. His tone seemed unsure, if the Shadow King could be such.

"I did."

Just then, his eye caught the sight of her maid standing in the wing, and he looked back at Norah in surprise.

"Is everything all right?" she asked him, feigning ignorance to what pulled his attention.

He looked at his mother, who took a bite of her biscuit, clearly unaware and indifferent to their conversation. "Perfectly," he said with some amusement.

"Does the lord commander not take breakfast here?" Not that she missed him.

The question was enough to catch Salara-Mae's ear. "No, he does not," she said sharply. "Breakfast is my time."

Norah smiled to herself. She felt a kinship with this woman who disliked the commander as much as she did.

After they finished eating, Salara-Mae excused herself, and the king rose from the table. Norah turned to leave.

"North Queen," Mikael called, stopping her. "Will you walk with me?"

Walk where? But his voice had come gently, and she gave a small nod.

He offered his arm, and she paused. It was the first time he'd extended a public physical connection toward her. A courtesy, she told herself. She swallowed, but then looped her hand under, accepting. His skin was warm, and he covered her hand with his own.

*Damn the gods.* She didn't hate it.

He led her through the halls. "I see you found yourself a maid."

"I needed one," she said. "So, I've put her to use. But"—she met his eye—"she's no longer a slave."

"Will you be freeing all my slaves around the castle?" he asked, a slight irritation in his voice.

She didn't care. "Probably."

His nostrils flared, but he didn't reply. His skin warmed, perhaps from his anger returning. She stiffened. Let it. Slavery wasn't something she'd pretend to be okay with. He glanced down at her, his eyes ablaze, but she only returned his glare.

Unexpectedly, he seemed to calm again. And so did she.

He was an interesting man, crafted of fire and war, quick to anger, quick to fight. But as he looked at her, she noticed that he was also quick to yield.

She felt it too. She didn't want to fight him either. "Where are we going?" she asked, changing the subject.

They walked a little longer, and then he paused in front of a hall with a single door. "As I said before, after we're wed, you'll stay in the villa, but this will be your sanctuary away from everything. It's for you alone."

He led her down the hall and opened the door to reveal a sprawling suite. A bed sat centered against the wall with abundant pillows and furs, and there was a plush settee by two windowed doors that opened out onto a balcony.

She walked to the balcony.

"It faces north," he said, his voice softer, "so you can look to your home sky."

The notion brought a wave of emotion she wasn't expecting, and she bit her cheek to hold it back. She looked over the rest of the room. There was a small bath chamber off the side, and a vanity against the far wall.

"No one will visit or disturb you here," he said. "Your guard will stop at the end of the hall, not outside your door. No one will enter without your invitation. Not your guard, not your maid,"—he paused—"not even me. It's here you may come when you want to be alone and be left alone."

Warmth rolled through her. "I don't know what to say."

"Say nothing. You'll be salara and above all others." His eyes were dark, but kind. "This is your home now. This castle is yours, and you can do in it what you'd like."

"Thank you," she said with a faint smile.

"Good day, North Queen." He gave her a small nod and left her to her sanctuary.

Norah let out a breath and looked around again. A sanctuary. Unlike her room, it was whitewashed and bright. She opened the doors to the balcony and breathed in the winter. It didn't seem quite so cold.

She made her way out of the chamber and back down the hall to where her guard and new maid waited. It was the kind guard—*Kiran*, she'd learned from Vitalia. Another guard stood with him; one she didn't recognize. She decided to take the king up on his statement. She could do what she liked, and she'd like to look around. "I want to see the castle," she told Vitalia. "Can you show me around?"

"Of course, Your Majesty," the maid said with a nod. "You'll love it. And just wait until you see Ashan."

"Ashan?"

"The city. Right outside the castle."

There *was* a city, Norah remembered. She wondered when she'd be able to explore it. The commander had told her she needed four guards to leave the castle, but she didn't take that as open permission. That she felt she needed permission irked her, but she decided she'd take one thing at a time.

Norah made her way around, with Vitalia quietly answering her questions as they went. The maid's knowledge surprised her, and she listened closely. The castle was beautiful, with its arched halls and intricately designed tilework, and she found herself admiring everything around her.

A large hanging portrait in the hall caught her eye and drew her closer in curiosity. Right away, she recognized Salara-Mae, and although it looked like Mikael beside her, it wasn't.

"Salar's father," Vitalia told her. "Rhalstad Ratha Shal."

Norah looked carefully at the intricate painting. The detail was so incredibly fine that it almost seemed real. Mikael's resemblance to his father was undeniable, but the senior king wore his hair cropped short and his beard longer. On the side of his head ran a large scar, starting at his temple and stretching backward.

Norah let her eyes move to Salara-Mae, except she was Salara then, who looked quite young but still had an elegant sharpness to her face. She was beautiful, Norah mused. "Do you think they were happy together?" she asked.

"Who wouldn't be happy serving their king?" a voice boomed from behind, and Norah spun to see the lord commander. He wasn't wearing his wrap, and she wasn't sure if she preferred to see his face or not. Well, she'd prefer not to see him at all. His two dogs followed obediently at his heel, their heads low, as though prowling on a hunt. They looked menacing. Like their master.

"What are you doing here?" he asked stiffly.

"I'm looking around the castle, as I was invited to," she cut back. "If you have a problem with that, go talk to your king."

His eyes darkened, then he said, "I have no problems with that. In fact, I'll join you."

Norah fumed. Of course, he knew exactly how to control her. "No need," she said sharply. "I was just finishing."

The corners of his lips turned up in a satisfied smirk, and Norah raged even more inside. She turned toward the hall to her left, not knowing where she was going, but she'd sort it out once she got away from him.

"Do you seek my bedchamber?" he asked cheekily, halting her step. "Because that's all you'll find that way."

Norah's face flushed with heat, and she glared at him as she turned and headed back the way she had come. Her steps quickened as her irritation grew to anger. She hated how he could get to her.

"Is he always so maddening?" she hissed at her guard when they were out of earshot.

"No, Your Majesty," Kiran answered.

Norah puffed a breath in frustration. "That's what you're compelled to say, I suppose. And does he always have those wretched creatures?"

"Cusco and Cavaatsa? Yes, Your Majesty. He's raised them from pups."

Norah found it hard to imagine the lord commander raising and caring for anything. "What are they? Hunting dogs?" she asked.

"Hunters of men," Vitalia mumbled.

Norah didn't doubt it. She slowed as the hall turned to the left and brightened into a glass ambulatory. Her irritation dissipated as she marveled at the large white flowers lining the outside of the glass and casting whimsical shadows from the sun onto the stone floor. She knelt by the glass, amazed. "Flowers in the winter?" she breathed.

"Rhines," Kiran told her. "Aren't they beautiful?"

"I've never seen anything like them, let alone in the winter."

"You've never seen flowers?" Vitalia asked.

She stilled. She'd seen flowers before. Small blooms of purple and yellow speckled across the Mercian mountains flashed in her mind. They weren't something she remembered seeing, yet they were something she still knew. If she saw them again, would they bring more memories? An ache grew in her stomach. If she couldn't return to Mercia, she wouldn't be able to find out. And how could she hope to gain her memories in the Shadowlands, a place so foreign to her, with nothing of her old life, nothing of who she once was?

"Do you like them?" Kiran asked, bringing her attention back.

She drew in a breath to clear her mind and smiled. "Very much."

His eyes smiled. "I know a place you'd love to see, then."

Norah followed him through the castle and outside. They curved around to the south side, and she grinned when she saw where he was taking her. Beautiful greens patterned the ground in a large garden. They made their way down the small pebble walk as she marveled at its beauty. "It all grows in the winter?" she asked, amazed.

"Some of it. These are all evergreens. They stay green like this all year. Some flowers you'll see on the winter plants..."

Kiran's words continued, but she didn't hear them. The sound of a horse had caught her attention, and she looked over her shoulder toward a grand building offset from the castle. Behind it were circled paddocks, some with horses.

"Is that the stable?" she asked.

Kiran paused in his flower tour. "Yes, Your Majesty."

"Is my horse there?" She desperately wanted to see the mare again. She had a connection to the animal. Maybe it was a connection to her old self. And she was fond of the mare—a friend in a place where she had very few.

"I would assume so," he answered. "But we should get back, Your Majesty. The lord commander will check that you've returned to your chamber, and Captain Artem, too, no doubt. And forgive me, I've led you outside the castle with only two guardsmen."

"I don't answer to the lord commander," she answered shortly. "Or the captain."

"Please, Your Majesty," he said softly. "I do."

Norah sighed. She didn't want any trouble for those who were kind to her. She gave a relenting nod, casting one last glance toward the stable, and they headed back the way they'd come.

# CHAPTER FORTY

Each day passed slowly. Norah struggled to find her place in it all. She was a queen, but she still felt more prisoner than queen in the kingdom of Shadows. Would that change when she became salara?

She pulled back the draperies on the windows, letting the morning light pour in. Vitalia had gone early to the dressmaker, but Norah spotted the tray of breakfast she'd left on the table. She smiled. Biscuits and honey. She loved honey, although she couldn't remember the last time she'd had it.

Norah dropped down and curled into the cushioned chair at the table, crossing her legs up under her and into the warmth of her nightgown, then scooted the tray closer. Perhaps she was letting this honey draw too much excitement, but she was alone, and she'd let herself have this small joy.

She broke the biscuit in half to pour the honey across but then pushed it back; she really didn't care about the biscuit, and instead scooped her fingertip into the small jar of gold. She gave barely enough time for the drip to break before she brought it to her mouth.

And it was the most amazing thing she'd ever tasted. There were hints of lavender mixed in the sweetness; it was rich and thick on her tongue.

She wanted to drink it from the jar. There was no spoon to spread it, no knife. It was meant to be poured on the biscuit. She didn't care, and she dipped in her finger again.

Norah heard movement in the hall—Vitalia, back with her dresses. She grinned and moved to the door. She was going to tell her she was the best maid ever and beg her for more honey. But when she opened the door, it wasn't Vitalia.

It was Mikael, poised to knock.

Norah stood, her nightgown loose over her shoulder, holding her jar of gold with a honey-coated fingertip. Not exactly how she wanted anyone to see her. Not how she wanted *him* to see her.

His gaze traveled down her length and back up. "North Queen," he said.

"Um..." She shifted. "Hello." She winced. The right way to address him still escaped her.

They stared at each other for a moment. "I'm"—his brow dipped as he glanced at her honey-coated finger—"sorry to disturb you."

She felt she might die a little.

His gaze rose to her face again. "I just... wanted you to know that I have to tend some things in the south. But I'll return tomorrow. Late."

She nodded, trying to act normal. "I'll... be here." She cursed herself. Where else would she be?

He nodded back. That seemed the end of his message, but he didn't move to leave. His eyes shifted down to her hands again.

"Do you... want some honey?" She cursed herself again. *Stupid*. Of course he didn't want honey. She bit her lip to keep from cringing. Gods help her.

He didn't answer, and it only made it worse. But then he stepped closer. His eyes said he wanted *something*. She swallowed but didn't move.

Slowly, he reached out and took her hand with the honey-dipped finger. She froze. Her breath stopped, and her pulse thrummed heavily in her ears. His eyes melded into hers as he brought her finger up and wrapped his lips around it.

His mouth was cool against the flame of her skin. The flick of his tongue, the graze of his teeth, sent prickles rippling across her body. Every hair stood on end. It was so brazen of him. And of her to let him. It was shameful, even though it wasn't shame she felt.

She should stop him.

But she didn't want to. So she didn't.

Finally, he drew her finger from his mouth—slow, tortuous—and lowered her hand, releasing it.

Norah stood breathless.

The corner of his mouth turned up ever so slightly. "I'll see you tomorrow, North Queen."

She could only nod.

He turned and left, and she closed the door behind him, leaning back against it. Her heart still thundered. She could still feel his mouth, his tongue. The thoughts sent heat pooling to her stomach. This man. She didn't know what to do about him, didn't know what to think.

He knew no boundaries, no restraint. Alexander would never—

*Alexander*—she pushed him from her mind. She couldn't think about Alexander right now.

She needed air. A walk. Something. She couldn't wait for Vitalia to get back with the dresses. She pulled a green front-laced gown from the side dressing room and shuffled it on. Grabbing her cloak, she slipped on her shoes and then swept out of the chamber and down the hall.

Her guard picked up behind her, and she fastened her cloak around her shoulders as she walked.

"Do you plan to go outside, North Queen?" a guard asked from behind. *Sonal.* With Vitalia's help, she was learning to tell the guards apart. She didn't like Sonal. He wasn't accommodating like Kiran, and she didn't like the way he called her North Queen.

She kept walking.

"You've only two guards," came his voice again.

"Then you'd better find two more before I reach the door." She walked quickly, hoping to avoid anyone who might stop her, like the lord commander, or the captain. As she reached the entry hall, two more guards fell instep behind her.

That wasn't as difficult as she'd expected.

"Where are you going?" Sonal asked.

She didn't answer, giving the guard a taste of their own medicine. But the corners of her mouth drew up. She knew exactly where she was going. The mare.

Outside, the air was chilly, and she pulled the hood of her cloak up but inhaled deeply. It felt good to get out of the castle—to set her mind on something other than Mikael and the morning's happening. The brief thought again brought a heat to her lower stomach, and she pushed it away.

The castle grounds were expansive, easily double the size of her castle in Mercia, and beautiful. The main courtyard had three fountains and a wide cobblestone path for daily markets and activities. Meticulously kept hedges surrounded the outer edges, and the long side garden that

Kiran showed her before held even more topiaries. She lengthened her stride toward the stable.

The inside of the stable was almost as grand as the inside of the castle, with stacked stone lifting the ceiling high to let in the light and beautiful dark-wood stalls lining both sides. Most of the stalls were empty and large enough to fit at least three horses. Then she reached one that was occupied and realized perhaps they weren't—she'd forgotten how massive the destriers were.

A knicker sounded from an end stall, and she immediately knew it was the mare. She smiled and hurried toward it. When she reached it, she looked through the top bars, and her smile widened. The mare tossed her head and let out a squeal, as if just as happy to see her.

The stall doors were split in half, with most top doors open for the horses to hang their heads out, but the mare's was closed. Norah reached for the latch.

A gravelly voice, foreign and angry, called out from her right.

She turned as what appeared to be a stable hand approached. He didn't wear a head wrap. That practice seemed reserved for soldiers.

"He says this one will take a piece out of you," Sonal said from behind her. "This mare won't let anyone touch her."

Norah glanced back at the mare, who wore a stable blanket and had clearly been brushed. Obviously, someone was able to touch her. She looked well cared for, and Norah was appreciative of that.

The stable hand spoke again. "You'd do well to let her alone," Sonal translated.

She pulled back the hood of her cloak, and the man stilled. His eyes traveled to the guard behind her, and he took a wary step back. He hadn't realized who he was speaking to.

Norah pulled back the latch of the top door and swung it open, and the mare knickered again and stretched her head out to her. She smiled and gave the animal a hearty scratch on the cheek. The mare snorted. Norah scratched her forehead before running her hand to the soft flesh of her nose. The horse nuzzled her fingers. Her smile widened, and she looked up at the stable hand. "Tell him to leave her top door open, so she can see out."

Sonal translated. The man's eyes told her he didn't approve, but he gave a stiff nod. Then he glanced once more at her guard and left them alone.

Norah turned her attention back to the mare, giving her another round of affectionate scratches, to which the mare arched her neck and leaned out farther against the bottom door. She wished she could go for a ride, but she felt she was already pushing her luck with the visit.

"I just came to say hello, friend, to see how you're doing. And you look well." She pulled the mare's head closer and gave her a peck on the face. "I'll come back later and see if we can get out of here for a little while. Maybe a ride sometime." The mare snorted again, and Norah patted her neck. "Don't hurt anyone, at least not the ones that care for you." She lowered her voice to a whisper. "All others are fair game."

The animal shook her head, and Norah gave a small laugh.

She should get back, she knew. "All right, goodbye, friend. I'll be back." She gave the mare one last scratch and reluctantly headed out of the stable and back toward the castle.

As she made her way back, she let herself admire the gardens. Norah loved gardens. Mercia's felt so quaint when compared to those of the Shadowlands, but still they were beautiful. She missed them.

She noticed a man on his knees digging a line of small holes. He was an older man; his dark hair was streaked with gray, and his skin had been weathered by the seasons.

"What are you doing?" she asked him.

He looked up with a start and rose to his feet when he recognized her. "Salara," he said, bowing low. His voice held the warmth of welcome, and his eyes smiled like summertime. "How can I be of service?"

That he spoke the Northern tongue surprised her. "What are you doing?" she asked again.

"I am planting isarium, Salara. While they're dormant."

"North Queen," Sonal said, "we should return to the castle and leave this man to do his work."

She ignored him. "What's your name?" she asked the man. One of her soldiers broke away and headed toward the castle. If only the rest would leave her too.

"My name is Bremhad, Salara."

He was such a gentle soul. He reminded her of Kiran.

"Bremhad," she repeated. "Can I plant one?"

His eyes widened in surprise—he looked a little worried even. "This isn't work for Salara."

"I'll decide that," she said, picking up a root ball waiting to be planted and looking closely at it. "Do I just put it in the ground?"

"Here," he said, crouching down, "I'll show you." Bremhad scooped some loose soil and put it at the bottom of the hole he'd already dug. Then he waved her to set it inside. She placed the root into the center, and he filled in the sides with the soil, leveling it off with a layer on top.

She smiled, looking at the row of holes. "I want to do another." She moved to the next, scooping the loose soil to the bottom as Bremhad had done, and then setting the root ball on top. She filled in the sides and added a top layer. The dirt felt good between her fingers, and the smell of earth was familiar somehow. She smiled, feeling pleased with herself.

"So, you speak the Northern tongue?" she asked.

"Common tongue? Yes, of course."

Sonal interrupted the man with sharp words in the Shadow tongue. The man's smile fell, and Norah knew he'd been warned. She shot a look at Sonal, giving him a warning of her own.

"Does everyone speak the Northern tongue?" she asked.

The old man was silent, and his eyes darted to her guard. Footfalls came behind her, and she looked back to see the lord commander approaching, followed by Captain Artem and more soldiers. Had the commander not gone with the king? She groaned inside.

"What are you doing?" he demanded.

It was none of his business. She pursed her lips. "I'm planting flowers."

"North Queen, you can't be out here digging in the dirt."

"Bremhad has already done the digging," she said flippantly. "I'm planting the flowers."

Agitation rolled off his brow. "You can't be out here *planting flowers*."

"Why not? What am I to do? Sit in my room all day?"

"Something more proper for a queen."

"You should let the queen decide what's proper for queens," Norah said shortly. "I'll go back inside once I'm finished here." She could feel the heat from his anger, but she focused on her next root ball.

The lord commander gave an order in the Shadow tongue, and each soldier quickly picked up a root bundle and dropped them into the holes lining the walkway, covering the roots with dirt.

"You're finished now," he told her.

Norah gritted her teeth, anger swelling inside her. She stood, glaring at the lord commander. His eyes returned her stare like pools of hell. But what could she do?

She turned to the old man. "Thank you, Bremhad. Perhaps I might come again? I'd like to see how things are coming along."

"Of course, Salara. I'm here every day and would be honored."

She gave the lord commander and the captain another scowl and then turned back toward the castle.

*Four guards.* Four guards now stood on duty as she stepped out into the hall from her chamber—no doubt a punitive response to the day prior. But she wouldn't give the lord commander the upper hand.

She smiled at them. "Oh, perfect. I was headed outside for another walk, so we're all ready." And she started down the hall. They fell in step behind her. Close. Too close. Suffocating. She tried to brush it off as she passed the dining hall—where she'd originally intended to go. Petty rebellion was much more important than breakfast.

Her stomach grumbled in protest. She ignored it. She'd eaten a hefty dinner the night before, taken in her chamber. Nine hells before she'd eat alone with the lord commander. And being out for a walk wasn't for naught. She hadn't properly explored the castle grounds. She wished she'd thought to bring Vitalia.

The beauty of the Shadowlands was hard to deny. In every recess of the castle sat a garden area, meticulously kept. The walls and stonework were well maintained, and even the cobblestone walks appeared to have been scrubbed clean. Tall iron posts lined common walkways, holding oil lanterns for the night.

She turned the corner of the castle, and the walk opened to a broad green space. Within a short distance were structured activity fields, each filled with training soldiers. The fields were much larger than in Mercia, and on first observation, the training was much more aggressive. Where her Northmen practiced in an organized fashion, the Shadow fields could easily be mistaken for battlefields.

Norah stopped and watched, wide-eyed. With no reservation and no restraint, the Shadow warriors fought—lethal strikes with real weapons and devastating consequences. How were they not killing one another? Her pulse quickened. Even if they were Shadowmen, she didn't want anyone hurt...

Suddenly, her eyes found Captain Artem. *Except him*. He could hurt himself all day. And so could the lord commander—wherever he was. The captain stood in the center of the far-right field as he scanned the soldiers, calling out commands of gods only knew what. And then, as if he sensed her gaze, he turned. The hair stood on the back of her neck, and she broke away to keep walking.

He'd seen her. But she didn't dare look back to see if he would come after her. She focused her eyes ahead. And then she slowed.

The king was walking toward her. A surprise—he'd said he wouldn't be back until late. It wasn't an unwelcome surprise, though. Beside him strode the lord commander. *He* was unwelcome.

Thankfully, the commander forked away and headed toward the training fields, though not before casting her a dark eye. *Good riddance.* She turned her attention back to the king. The corners of her mouth turned up, and she pursed it back. But she certainly wasn't unhappy to see him.

His own mouth held the hint of a smile, and her eyes moved to his lips. She hadn't forgotten how they felt. She swallowed and tried to shake the path from where her mind was beginning to wander.

"North Queen," he greeted her.

"Salar Mikael," she greeted back, trying out the Kharavian title. It felt very... unnatural. She wasn't sure why.

He tilted his head. "It's not customary to use both names."

She didn't want to call him Salar—a name so... distant. "All right. Mikael." That felt natural. She wasn't sure if he'd be fine with her calling him by his name, but she caught the hint of a smile, and she smiled back. "You're back sooner than I'd expected."

"I had something to get back to."

"Battle planning?" she jested. Something else dark and nefarious, no doubt.

"You."

She paused. Why did she like that? She bit her lip. "Worried I might make my escape?" It was a jest. Mostly.

But he shook his head. "No. I wanted to see you again."

She liked that even more. Had their last interaction stayed in his mind, as it had in hers?

"I heard you had the Crest working in the gardens yesterday," he said as they started toward the castle.

She glanced out at the practice fields to where the commander had picked up inspection of the soldiers. "No, that was the lord commander's doing," she said irritably. "I was planting flowers."

"A queen shouldn't be laboring in the dirt."

"It wasn't laboring," she argued. "I actually quite enjoyed it." She needed to be out of the castle and doing something. "And even if I was, I'll do what pleases me. The lord commander oversteps, and it's unacceptable."

He slowed. "I know he's not a man of gentle nature, but the lord commander looks out for my interests, and now yours."

She scoffed. "Not *my* interests."

"You judge him too harshly." His tone held an edge of defense, and she quieted. He put his absolute trust in his brute, loved him as a brother, and would defend him fiercely, even to her. The commander could divide them, and that's the last thing she wanted. She had to be careful.

Silence hung between them as they walked, then he said, "Labor in the dirt if it makes you happy. I just ask you to refrain when your people arrive for the marriage. I don't want them to think I took their queen for slave labor."

It was a jest to bridge them back to a good place. He was trying. And it was an acceptable compromise. Norah couldn't help her smile. "Yes, I can see my grandmother having heart palpitations."

Mikael's brow creased. "Surely your grandmother won't come."

His assumption surprised her. "She'd planned to travel to Aleon. Of course she'll come. Why wouldn't she?"

Mikael raised an eyebrow but didn't answer.

"This alliance is important, and I'm her granddaughter," she insisted. "I'm getting married, and I need her. She'll come."

"Of course," he replied, but doubt lingered on his face.

There would be tension between their kingdoms, understandably, and it would take time to adjust, but her grandmother wouldn't deny her. Mikael didn't know Catherine. He'd see.

"I'm sure you've already eaten," he said, "but will you join me for some breakfast?"

Her smile returned. "I'd love to."

Norah strode outside into the daylight with a spring in her step. Breakfast with Mikael had left her in high spirits. He was... different... than she'd expected. She liked it.

She decided to visit the mare again and stop by the garden and say hello to Bremhad along the way. Vitalia followed close behind, as did Norah's guard. She was disappointed to have Sonal in her service again today, but she wouldn't let him dampen her spirits.

Norah made her way along the manicured topiaries and combed the gardens for the greenskeeper, but he was nowhere to be found. Norah spotted another man by the laurels, and she approached. He bowed low when he saw her.

"Is Bremhad here?" she asked.

The man said nothing and remained bowing.

"A man named Bremhad," she said again. "Is he here?"

Still, the man said nothing.

Vitalia spoke to him in the Shadow tongue. He answered, and she looked back to Norah. "He says there's no man that works in the gardens by that name."

Norah shook her head, her brows drawing together. "That's not right. He was here yesterday. He said he's here every day."

Vitalia spoke to the man again, and then she looked at Norah with her lips pursed and shook her head.

Something wasn't right. Norah turned to Sonal. "Where's the man who was here yesterday?"

Sonal gave a frown and then shook his head. "I don't remember what he looked like."

Her eyes narrowed. *Liar.* "You know exactly what he looked like," she countered, a weight growing in her stomach. "His name was Bremhad. Has something happened to him?"

Sonal shrugged. "I don't remember him."

Anger crept across her skin. But what could she do here? She turned and strode back toward the castle. She needed to find him.

Behind closed doors and away from her guard, Norah paced the room.

"Do you think they did something?" she asked her maid. "Do you think something's happened to him?"

"Don't you see?" Vitalia whispered. "The lord commander sends you a message."

A lump rose in her throat. That was exactly the kind of message the lord commander would send. "Do you think Bremhad is all right?"

"I don't know, but if the lord commander was involved..." Her words trailed off.

Norah's heart raced. This was her fault. She had to help him. "Where would they take him? What would they do?"

Vitalia shook her head. "I don't know. Will you go to Salar?"

"I can't go to him on suspicion alone. He already thinks I judge the commander too hastily. And the brute would deny it." Then Bremhad might disappear forever.

"I have many friends in the castle, Your Majesty. I can try to find out what happened."

Norah prayed she could.

# CHAPTER FORTY-ONE

"Please don't be angry," Vitalia said in a hushed voice. The setting sun cast long shadows across the hall as they walked.

"Why would I be angry?" Norah followed her maid toward her sanctuary. She hadn't visited it since Mikael had given it to her. It was for when she wanted to be alone, and to be left alone, he'd told her. Aside from her suffocating guard, she hadn't felt that way.

Vitalia didn't answer.

Had she found out what had happened to Bremhad? Norah didn't dare ask within earshot of her guard, who'd likely helped in whatever devious plan the commander had.

The guard stopped at the end of the hall, as they weren't permitted within it, and Norah and her maid continued to the sanctuary. Vitalia's breath came faster now, nervously. It made Norah's quicken as well. What news did she have?

They stepped inside, and Vitalia closed the door behind them.

Norah couldn't wait any longer. "Did you find out what happened to Bremhad?"

Vitalia clenched her hands, wringing them nervously. Then her eyes darted over Norah's shoulder. Norah turned, and she startled at the man standing in the doorway of the side bath chamber.

"Who are you?" she demanded of the man. "What are you doing here?" No one was allowed in the sanctuary.

"It's Kiran, Your Majesty," Vitalia said quickly. "I brought him. I'm sorry. This is the only place I could think of that was private enough."

Norah hadn't recognized the guard without his head wrap; she'd only ever seen his eyes. She looked closer. Yes, she knew those eyes. They were kind eyes. But now, troubled.

He was different from how she'd imagined him. Older—perhaps a couple years older than she was. A trenched scar ran from just under the inside of his right eye and down over his cheek to his jaw. A second scar claimed the space over his left eye and channeled back into his shoulder-length black hair that was tied from behind. Perhaps they'd been from the same injury. Unlucky. Or lucky, depending on how one looked at the situation.

"Bremhad is his father," Vitalia said.

Norah let out a breath. She saw it now—the resemblance.

Kiran shifted uneasily, the muscle tightening underneath his inked skin. This was a secret—a secret he protected.

"Bremhad has been thrown in the dungeon," her maid added.

"There's a dungeon?" As it rolled off her lips, she knew it was a stupid question. Even Mercia had a dungeon.

Kindly, Vitalia only nodded. "Kiran's planning to break him out."

He shot her maid an angry glare. "You said you wouldn't tell her that."

"You can trust her," her maid pressed.

Norah gaped at him. "Break him out of the dungeon? You can't do that."

"I'm a warrior of the Crest. I can." His courtesies were gone. But she didn't fault him. Anger and fear drove him now. And he was right, he probably could get his father out, with some planning. He was an elite member of the Crest, skilled beyond any prison guard.

"No, Kiran, listen to me. This isn't the way. If you break him out, you won't be able to stay here. You'll have to leave, to flee. You'll both be hunted."

He shook his head. "It doesn't matter. I can't do nothing. And once they know he's my father, they'll know my papers are fake. I'll be thrown in there with him."

She quieted as her mind raced. He'd faked his status to be eligible for the army. She clutched her own hands. This complicated things. "Regardless, you can't break him out."

How quickly the kindness in his eyes changed to aggression. "I won't let him die down there because he made a mistake."

Confusion filled her. "What mistake?"

Kiran hesitated, then he said, "Speaking to you in the Northern tongue."

"Why would that be a mistake?" She knew the answer before she'd even finished the question. She scoffed in frustration. "Because the commander wants me to think that only a few can understand me. Better to spy on me, I see."

Kiran didn't confirm it. But he didn't deny it.

"Let me take care of this," she said. "I'll have your father released."

Kiran straightened, but he cast his gaze to the side with his lips tight and drew in a cynical breath.

"Do you not believe me?"

He looked back at her. "I believe you'll try." He didn't think she could.

"Kiran, please. Let me help you before you do something rash. Do you not love your life here?"

"I love my father more," he said.

Emotion swelled within her. Had she loved her own father this strongly? She reached out and clasped his arm. "Kiran, please. I promise you I'll get him out."

The silence was long and agonizing. But Kiran sighed, relenting. He gave a short nod.

She pursed her lips into a reassuring smile.

"Wait until we've gone," Vitalia told him. "We'll take the guard with us, and you can leave unseen."

He gave a small nod. "Thank you."

Morning couldn't come soon enough. Captain Artem had been on a task outside the city, and Norah had to wait for his return. Her stomach twisted at the thought of having to talk to him, but she didn't dare take the matter to the commander. She'd never see Bremhad again.

She strode toward the stables with her guard close behind. Kiran was among them. Her heart hurt for him. Surely it was all he could do to act unaffected, as no one knew Bremhad was his father. His nearness didn't help her own anxiousness.

She found Artem walking out just as she was approaching. He held his helm under his arm and his gloves neatly in his hand. Her brow stitched down. He didn't even appear to have traveled; his armor was still clean.

"North Queen," he greeted.

But she didn't care for his greeting, and she didn't care to offer one back. "You'll release the greenskeeper," she said firmly.

The captain of the Crest frowned. "I'm not sure what greenskeeper you speak of."

Were they all liars? "The greenskeeper that was with me when you harassed me in the gardens with the lord commander," she said shortly. "The greenskeeper that's been thrown in the dungeon. I want him released. Now."

He gave a dip of his brow, feigning concern. "I'm not familiar with the situation, but even so, only the lord commander or salar can grant pardon."

"Pardon?" she asked angrily. "He's done nothing wrong! What's his crime?"

He shook his head, frowning through the cruel smile underneath. "As I said, I'm not familiar with the situation. You should talk to the lord commander."

Yes, rely on the man who'd *caused* her grievance to *fix* her grievance. Hardly.

"I think I'll talk to the king," she replied sharply.

"As you wish."

Norah hated this man just as much as the lord commander. She cursed herself. They were probably the best of friends. She gritted her teeth and breathed deep to keep herself calm, then spun on her heel, heading back toward the castle.

The morning was still early. She'd find Mikael before breakfast—before Artem could tell the commander what she was trying to do. She cursed herself for not going straight to Mikael, but Artem was a captain, and she was queen. Even if not the queen of the Shadowlands yet, she expected his compliance. She *would* be his queen. And she fully rejected the idea he couldn't free Bremhad.

She hated the idea of going to Mikael. He already felt she was too biased against his commander, and she was bringing yet another grievance. And she was queen in her own right—it diminished her authority. But she'd do it for Bremhad. Time was of the essence. She'd sort the rest out later.

Norah found the king stepping out of his study. "North Queen," he greeted when he saw her. "This is a surprise."

"I have a pressing matter I need to discuss with you."

His brow creased, and he gave her a small nod. "Of course."

"The greenskeeper," she said.

His brow creased further. "The greenskeeper?"

"Yes, the greenskeeper, the old man I was planting flowers with in the garden. The lord commander put him in your dungeon. I want him released."

"The greenskeeper?" he asked again.

She resisted the urge to tell him to pay attention. Now she felt like Catherine.

"What's he done?" he asked.

"He talked to me in Northern tongue. Tell me, is that a crime?"

The line of his mouth thinned. "Of course it's not."

"The commander—"

"The lord commander wouldn't condemn a man for no reason."

Norah scoffed. "The lord commander would knife a man for breathing."

Mikael stopped and stiffened, and the pools of his eyes grew darker. She wasn't winning him over to her cause—she needed a different approach. As much as she hated to appeal to his mercy, she would. For Bremhad and for Kiran.

She put her hand on his arm. "Mikael, please. He's my friend."

"A greenskeeper is your friend?"

She drew in a breath as she collected herself; cheekiness and sarcasm wouldn't help her now. "I enjoy the garden here. It's a place in which I hope to spend more time. Will you not have him released? He's done nothing wrong." Norah held her breath. He'd given her a horse worth losing an alliance. Would he not give her a greenskeeper?

He sighed. "I'll see that there's no greenskeeper in my dungeon."

It wasn't exactly complete assurance, but she couldn't push him more. She gave his arm a warm squeeze. "Thank you." She glanced down the way toward the dining hall. "Are you going to breakfast?"

"No. I'm headed to Basrah, just west. I'll be back tonight."

She hated that he was leaving again, but she nodded. "I'll see you when you return."

By evening, Bremhad had still not arrived home, and Norah felt a pit growing in her stomach. Why was it taking so long to release him? Was he even going to be released? Perhaps Mikael hadn't addressed it with the commander before he'd left.

He said he'd address it, she told herself. She should trust him to do so. But the truth was, Mikael held the lord commander with a long leash, if with a leash at all. The brute had told her there was nothing he could do that the king wouldn't forgive. And she believed him.

Mikael hadn't returned by dinner, and Norah took her meal in her chamber. Her worry grew as she ate. What if she had been wrong? What if she couldn't get Bremhad out?

# CHAPTER FORTY-TWO

"Your Majesty!" Vitalia's excited voice woke Norah from her sleep. She sat up quickly, not sure if she'd slept at all. She'd been restless much of the night. "Was Bremhad released?" she asked before her awareness had even come to her.

Vitalia paused, shaking her head. "I haven't heard, Your Majesty, but you'll want to rise quickly. Northmen have arrived!"

Vitalia's words woke her instantly. "Northmen?" Her heart leapt.

"Soldiers," her maid explained. "They say they're part of the Mercian royal guard. They've come to be in your service. The man that speaks for them, his name is Titus."

Norah tried to quell her disappointment. Of course it wouldn't be Alexander, and she shouldn't want it to be Alexander, as much as her heart wished otherwise. It wasn't safe for him here. It would make sense he would send her guardsmen, or what remained of them, and it would be good to see Titus.

She slipped down off the bed. "I'm glad they've come. Where are they?"

"They're settling in the soldiers' barracks. They'll meet you in the throne room."

Norah dressed quickly. It would be nice to have her own soldiers on her guard, men she could trust. Thinking of trust, her mind wandered back to Kiran, and her stomach sank.

She opened her chamber door to Kiran and Sonal standing guard. She didn't dare ask for news with Sonal so close, but Kiran gave the faintest shake of his head, and his eyes told her his father hadn't returned home.

Her feet felt like weights as she walked. She'd promised Kiran, and she'd been so sure of herself. It hurt. She'd let him down. She let Bremhad down. And it hurt she hadn't been able to move Mikael. The lord commander had sent his message, and the king's lack of action showed his decision. What power did she have here if she couldn't free an innocent greenskeeper from the dungeon? The answer scared her.

Mikael stood in his chamber in front of a large cheval mirror while servant tailors bustled about to his mother's demands. She scrutinized every detail, requiring perfection in everything. It was late morning. He'd already missed breakfast with the North Queen, and that had put him in an unfavorable mood. But this was a hard transition for his mother. The least he could do was give her the morning.

He watched the tailors in the reflection—measuring, taping, and pinning the fabric of the garb he was to wear for the wedding ceremony. The effort was unnecessary, having three like it already in his cabinet chamber. He'd prefer his armor; that seemed to be more fitting of his salara, anyway. Mikael caught his smile in the mirror and quickly stifled it.

Just then, the door swung open with a boom as Soren pushed inside. Everyone stopped abruptly, and his mother turned to him with a scowl. "Has he no restraint?" she seethed.

Mikael looked at Soren with a disapproving eye, but he knew his commander wouldn't interrupt without reason. "Leave us," he told the tailors, which no doubt would run afoul with his mother.

"You can't be serious," she argued. "You're right in the middle of a fitting."

"I'll finish it later."

His mother cut Soren a daggered look, and then she stormed from the room, followed by the cluster of tailors.

"The Northmen have come," Soren said as the door closed behind them, completely unfazed by his mother's annoyance.

Mikael pulled off the half-pinned swath of fabric and laid it over the side chair before donning his sleeveless tunic again. "As we expected," he said, and he tucked his tunic back into his breeches. This news wasn't worth his mother's ire. He did wish for Soren to try harder to please her sometimes.

"The—"

Mikael cut him off. "Have you dealt with the old man?"

Soren stopped and gave a stiff nod.

"I don't expect that to happen again," he warned. "You've offended the queen."

Soren snorted.

"You've offended me," Mikael said angrily, and Soren stiffened.

His commander said nothing. He struggled personally with the North Queen, and Mikael sympathized, but he couldn't tolerate this behavior toward his salara.

Mikael moved to leave, but Soren caught his arm. "Salar, the Northmen—the Bear will be with them."

Mikael stopped. Now this he hadn't expected. His chest tightened. "You've seen him?"

Soren shook his head. "No, but I know he's here."

He let out a long breath with a clenched jaw. Having the Bear in Kharav would be problematic. "Where?"

"They're unloading their wagons and settling into the soldiers' quarters now. Then they go to present themselves to the queen in the throne room."

Mikael slammed his fist on the desk, spilling a bottle of ink.

"I'll take the Crest and head them off," Soren told him. "I'll bring him to you."

"No," Mikael said stiffly.

His commander let out an angry breath. "His charge was to return to the North. The agreement's been broken. Let me take him."

"Does she know he's here?" Mikael asked.

"The North Queen?" Soren shook his head. "I don't know. He's not revealed himself."

"But you're sure he's come? Because that would be very foolish of him."

Soren's eyes blazed. "I'm certain."

Mikael pulsed with the want for blood. "Then let's go to the throne room."

His sword slid smoothly out of its scabbard as he checked it. He might need it. Alexander had found it easier than expected to slip into the Shadowlands hidden among the Northmen. Perhaps he shouldn't be too surprised. Few knew what he looked like out of his signature armor. That worked in his favor. Alexander doubted he'd have made it a single step past the border had the enemy known who he was. They'd have had his head if they'd known he'd been the one to kill so many when they'd tried to retake the mountains of Bahoul the year prior. He'd left a scar on the face of their king, and he'd be the one to kill him.

He *would* kill the Shadow King.

Maybe he'd been foolish to come, but he couldn't not. Not when Norah was here, unprotected. Adrian had wanted to come, too, but it was too dangerous. With the Shadowmen, anyone Alexander loved would be a target. Especially his brother.

Alexander didn't fear his own death in the Shadowlands, at least not until he fulfilled the vision, but he still came under the guise of a regular Mercian soldier. He didn't want to be deterred or taken before he could see Norah and make sure she was all right.

He'd come as quickly as he could after returning the army to Mercia. He'd broken off from the travel company with a smaller group to go even faster. Caspian followed with more of Norah's belongings and more men—things that would hopefully bring her comfort in the hold of their enemy until he could get her out.

"Are you ready?" Titus asked him.

Alexander smiled at the seasoned guard and pulled on his helm. "Lead the way." And he followed Titus as a normal soldier would.

Norah was surprised to find the king and his brute in the throne room when she arrived. Mikael stood, armored—which seemed a little excessive. The commander's face was covered. She'd gotten used to seeing him around the castle without his wrap and had almost forgotten how monstrous he looked with only his eyes showing. He was dressed for battle in usual Shadow form—nothing covering the markings on his chest and torso except his weapons' strappings, and he wore only light armor over his breeches on his knees and the shins of his boots.

She desperately wanted to ask Mikael about Bremhad, but she didn't dare with an audience and with whatever was happening here with this display.

The ranks of the Crest guards lined the sides of the room, and the commander stood beside the king's chair, his axe in hand. It was quite a strong response to several Northmen, she mused.

The king greeted her with a small bow of his head. "North Queen," he said, holding his hand out to the throne beside his. "Please."

She hadn't expected to sit on the queen's throne before she was crowned salara, but she took her seat beside him.

He looked at her with an expression she couldn't understand. "We've not said our vows yet, but you are my salara. You still make this commitment to me, yes?"

What an odd question. He seemed to be deciding something in his mind. "Of course," she told him, and he gave her a small nod.

The doors swung open, and a small army of her Northmen entered the hall. Norah couldn't help the smile that came to her face when she recognized the bald head in the front.

"Titus!" she said, standing and stepping forward. "I'm so glad you've come."

He bowed. "Queen Norah. I'm glad to see you well."

"How was the journey?"

"It was uneventful—the best kind. And everyone is well, as I hope you are."

Her smile widened. "I am, and very glad to see a familiar face."

"Not just one familiar face, Regal High," he said as he stepped to the side. Another large soldier came forward, removing his helm.

Norah let out a gasp, and the world stood still as blue eyes smiled back at her—eyes that were never far from her mind.

*Alexander.*

But the happiness lasted only a moment, then came the fear—a crippling, sickening fear. "What are you doing here?" she breathed.

"Norah," he said softly.

She felt Mikael behind her. His voice came low and cold. "You have a guest."

She glanced back to see he'd risen from his chair and had his hand on the hilt of his sword, with the commander beside him.

"Yes," she said shakily, desperately searching her mind for how to keep the calm. "I'd like to present—"

"I know who he is," he cut her off as he stepped beside her. His eyes locked on Alexander. "My lord commander told me you'd be foolish enough to come," he snarled at Alexander. "I almost didn't believe him."

Alexander didn't answer. And he didn't bow. He only stood with an icy fire in his eyes. The Shadowmen drew closer from their position around the room. Norah's heart raced faster, and her stomach turned. Things were escalating, quickly. The commander spoke to the king in the Shadow tongue, and she heard weapons being readied. Titus stepped to Alexander's side, and the Northmen pulled their swords defensively.

Mikael gripped his own sword, moving forward, and panic surged through her. She had to stop this. She clasped Mikael's arm, stepping in front of him and looking earnestly into his eyes. "Please," she whispered softly.

He paused as his gaze shifted to her. When he stopped, everyone stopped. And they waited. His eyes moved back and forth between hers. The eternity of the quiet weakened her, but she held his arm tighter. Mikael looked at Alexander, then back to her. Finally, he growled a command, and the Shadowmen drew back.

Norah let herself breathe, but she couldn't shake the wave of nausea that twisted in her stomach. Tension still hung thick in the air.

"Lord Justice," Mikael said to Alexander, using his title for the first time, "we expected you to return to the North."

Alexander ignored the king, looking only at Norah. "I did return, but I had to see your guard back to you, or rather, what's left of them. I'm relieved to find you well."

"How else did you expect to find her?" Mikael asked, his voice edged in anger.

Alexander's eyes met the king's, and he made no attempt to hide his disdain. "Perhaps similar to how I last saw her: assaulted and ill treated."

Rage radiated from Mikael, and she squeezed his arm again—her silent plea for restraint. "As you can see, I'm quite well." She grasped at how she might redirect the conversation. "What news do you have from Mercia?" She wanted to hear of home.

Alexander eyed Mikael before answering. "All is well," Alexander said finally. "The army returned in good health. I departed after with your guard. Caspian follows shortly with additional men and more of your belongings."

"Caspian! He lives?" She almost couldn't believe it.

Alexander cast a hard glance back at Mikael. "He's still healing, but he's well and eager to lead the guard back in your service."

The backs of her eyes stung with relief. Caspian was all right.

"She already has a guard," Mikael said.

"She needs a guard she can trust," Alexander cut back.

The lord commander gave a low chuckle. "Because the North has kept her so safe?"

"Please," Norah interjected, hoping they would settle, if only for her sake. A silence returned.

The line of Alexander's jaw tightened and then relaxed again. "Your maid Serene comes as well," he said, picking back up the conversation.

She smiled. "With Grandmother?"

Alexander's lips parted, but he hesitated before he said, "No."

"No?" Her smile fell.

He glanced at the king and then back to Norah. "It's a great risk for her to come now."

"Too great a risk for the queen and regent to both be in enemy hands, he means," the lord commander said.

"We're no longer enemies," Norah said, her eyes on Alexander.

Alexander was silent for a moment. He lowered his voice. "Try to understand. It's difficult for her to accept things as they are now."

"Difficult to accept things as they are?" she said angrily. "Is that not what she's had me do from the moment I returned?" Norah swallowed back her emotion, forcing composure. The king still didn't know of her memory loss. She wasn't sure why she hadn't told him yet. She'd have to eventually, but not now. "Does she send a letter?" she asked.

He shook his head slowly.

A weight crushed her. She'd asked her grandmother to come, and Catherine had refused without even a letter. Her cheeks flushed in embarrassment at her naivete. She hadn't even doubted. The heat of tears stung the corners of her eyes as her emotion swelled. *Not here*, she told herself. She couldn't get caught up in the frivolity of feelings as she stood between Alexander and Mikael.

"You should settle the men," she told Alexander. "We'll speak more after." She needed to get him away, out of the hall and far from Mikael and the commander.

He gave a nod. "Of course." He bowed. Then, with an icy glance back at the king, he turned from the hall and reluctantly left with the Northmen behind him.

Norah pushed out a shaking breath and swallowed back the knot rising in her throat. She turned to Mikael, but where she expected eyes of storming rage, she found none. Instead, his face had softened. Worry scored his forehead.

"I'm sorry about your grandmother," he said, his voice gentle. His unexpected tenderness unleashed the emotion she had been trying so hard to keep inside, and a tear spilled down her cheek. He reached up and brushed it with his thumb. "You should take a walk through the gardens. I think it will make you feel better."

Why would that make her feel better?

Her mind tumbled as her heart quickened. Was he saying what she thought he was saying? She nodded, suddenly breathless.

With the faintest smile, he turned and strode from the throne room with the commander close behind.

Norah forgot everything else as she hurried through the halls toward the gardens. Mikael's touch still lingered on her cheek. Her being upset had bothered him—bothered him more than Alexander's being in Kharav.

By the time she reached the courtyard, she was practically running. Her guard had to move quickly to keep up with her. Her silk shoes on the pea gravel sounded like rain as she ran past the fountains and out into the gardens.

She stopped suddenly as her breath caught in her throat.

Tears sprang to her eyes when she saw the old man by the hedges. "Bremhad!" she exclaimed.

When he heard her, he turned. "Salara," he said as he bowed his head.

Norah was speechless, and it took her a moment to gather her wits. She thought of poor Kiran behind her, forced to contain himself and act detached.

"Are you all right?" she managed to get out.

"Most kind of you to ask, Salara. I'd taken ill for a few days, but I'm quite well now. I'm able to return to my work, which I am very thankful for."

No doubt his excuse was for the benefit of her guard. She nodded, blinking back the tears in her eyes. "I'm glad," she breathed. She was so very glad.

Norah tried to keep her eyes on the hall ahead of her, but they kept drifting back to Alexander as he walked beside her. She still couldn't believe he was here. If she closed her eyes for a moment, would she find it had all been a dream when she opened them? Maybe she wished it were a dream. As much as she wanted him with her, as happy as she was to see him, she couldn't think past the clawing fear that she could lose him forever to the forces that so badly wanted him dead.

Her voice came unsteadily. "Why did you come? It's not safe for you here." She needed to send him back, only she couldn't bring herself to say the words.

His eyes burned a bright blue. "I would never leave you to face hardships on your own. Wherever you go, I'll follow."

"If anything happens to you—"

"Nothing will happen to me," he assured her.

She shook her head. "You don't know that."

"Of course, I do. I have a destiny."

Norah glanced back at the Crest guards in alarm. They were far enough back and didn't seem to have heard, but by the gods, if she wasn't going to have a panic attack. She grabbed his arm and dragged him down the hall into her sanctuary, away from listening ears.

"Those are words that will get you killed!" she said in a harsh whisper as the door closed behind them.

"No, Norah. I don't die here. I do have a destiny."

"A destiny Mikael will do everything in his power to change!" A destiny she found herself wanting to change.

He didn't argue.

Norah straightened, bringing her hand to her forehead and forcing herself calm. She needed to send him home, both to see him safe and to help her manage her grandmother and the council. With Catherine refusing to come to Kharav, they'd obviously taken the news of the alliance more poorly than she'd hoped.

"What did my grandmother say?" she asked.

He sighed. "She's having a difficult time, as you can imagine."

*A difficult time?* Anger flashed inside her. What did her grandmother expect *she* was going through? "What did she say?" she asked again.

His brow dipped, and his mouth turned down. "This isn't your path, Norah. You can't marry the Shadow King."

"Does she not see this is the only way to bring our people peace?"

"You side with darkness."

"I side against war!" she argued.

"The council feels it's a righteous war."

"Is that what you think?" she asked angrily. She turned away, but he caught her hand, drawing her back.

"Norah, I don't want any more men to die. Ten years we've been at war, and I would give almost anything to bring its end." He glanced down at her hand in his. "Anything but you."

Her fingers laced through his, and the threat of tears stung her eyes. "My decision brings peace. It might not be the path any of us want, but it's what's best for our people. Does that not matter?"

He didn't answer as they stood in the painful quiet. Then he pulled her closer. He dropped his head and rested his forehead on hers, and she let his warmth settle her. His arms moved around her and pulled her even closer.

Norah reached up and brought her hand to his face, and he turned his head into her palm to brush his lips against her thumb.

"Norah," he begged her with cerulean eyes. "Let me take you away from here. We'll leave. Tonight."

"Where?" She shook her head. "Back to Mercia with nothing? To Aleon for another husband and war?"

"No," he said hoarsely. "To the sea. Where the water is warm, and we can lie in the sun."

Tears sprang from her own eyes now. The memory. Their plans. She wanted that more than anything.

But that life was gone.

"There is no sun," she whispered.

He pulled her tighter and nestled into the fold of her neck. She wished they could stay like that forever. But they couldn't. Her heart was breaking, and she couldn't bear it. "You should go."

His breath came uneven against her skin, then he stepped back and collected himself. "Yes, I'm sure the men are wondering where I am."

"I meant back to Mercia."

His brow creased, and he shook his head. "I won't leave you."

"It's not safe for you here."

"If this is the path you've chosen, it's the path I follow." He took her hand and brought it to his lips. Then he released her, leaving her broken in the center of her sanctuary.

# CHAPTER FORTY-THREE

Norah was already awake when Vitalia entered. This was the day she'd feared, the day she'd so desperately wished would never come—the day of her marriage.

Her Mercian maid, Serene, followed Vitalia in. She'd arrived with the rest of the Northern company a few days after Alexander had. Vitalia was excited at the thought of another friend, and Norah was happy to have her, although she couldn't muster feelings of happiness for long.

Her maids busied themselves around her, chatting excitedly, but Norah couldn't hear them. Her heart beat heavily in her chest. *Peace*, she thought to herself. This was what peace looked like—no impending battle; her people were fed; Mercia stood strong. She drew in a deep breath and let it out slowly. Her grandmother would come to realize this was best, as would the rest of Mercia.

Salara-Mae had overseen the making of her gown and additional details in the days before. She'd walked Norah through everything: the ceremony, the binding vow, the celebration after, and the expectations. All except the Witness. *The Witness*—the ceremony in the bedchamber that ensured the marriage was consummated, fully executed, and acknowledged by both sides. It was odd Salara-Mae said nothing of it, but Norah didn't mind. She didn't want to talk about it either. It was what she was most anxious about. To have an officiator observe such a private act between husband and wife—she didn't think she could do it. Even when Catherine had explained the ceremony in preparation for her marriage to Aleon, the thought had overwhelmed her. Now, with the Shadow King... She tried to force it from her mind. She didn't have a choice.

Norah didn't know how the morning passed so quickly. Before she realized it, she was in her dress in front of the mirror, staring at a woman she barely recognized. Her white gown boasted the color of Mercia, as she'd wanted it to, or rather, as she thought was appropriate. Strands of shimmering silver were embroidered into the fabric, starting mid-skirt and running to the ground. It looked as though she had walked through a river of crystal. Norah wasn't one for ornate adornments, but even she couldn't deny the gown's beauty. She had wanted simplicity, which she got, yet Salara-Mae had still made her look like a queen. Even Catherine would have approved. A sadness rippled through her at the thought of her grandmother, who wouldn't be here to see her married.

She forced her attention back to the mirror, fearing her emotion would get the better of her. Diamonds studded her neck. It was a common stone, but she liked how they caught the light and was insistent on them over others more expensive. Her hair fell in loose waves around her, and a silver crown sat atop her head. She wished she had her mother's crown, but she'd lost it when she was captured.

"You're ready, Your Majesty," Vitalia told her, smiling and looking at her reflection.

But she wasn't ready.

Vitalia took her hands, pulling Norah to look at her. "This is it. This is where you become queen of both Mercia and Kharav and bring peace to your people. You'll take your vows and complete the ceremony just as you rehearsed. And then you'll be salara."

Norah swallowed. Yes, just as she'd rehearsed. Then she'd be salara. She gave a nervous nod, and her maid held her hand as she led her to the great hall.

"Thank you," she whispered to Vitalia. Her maid smiled and gave her hand another reassuring squeeze, then stole away to prepare.

Norah forced one foot in front of the other. She'd had plenty of time to accept this, she told herself, yet somehow, her mind was still in denial. Her thoughts shifted to Mikael. He wasn't as she'd expected, and she wasn't entirely appalled at the idea of him being her husband. He roused feelings in her that she had struggled to ignore—feelings that might be right for a wife to have for her husband.

But those thoughts came to a halt when she rounded the corner and saw Alexander.

His eyes moved down her dress and then back up. He looked at the crown on her head, and his lips parted, but he didn't speak.

She reached up and touched the crown. "Salara-Mae had it made," she started to explain. "I..." She didn't know what to say. She what? Hoped he liked it?

Her gaze caught his, but he couldn't hold it. He glanced at the ground before he drew in a breath and raised his eyes once more. "You look like a Mercian queen."

She gave a sad smile.

Alexander looked back over his shoulder to where Caspian stood waiting. Norah had been so thankful to see the captain again when he'd arrived, and she was thankful he was with her now. Caspian nodded to her but didn't draw closer, clearly intending to give her and Alexander privacy.

Alexander turned back to her, and his eyes glistened. "Norah," he breathed.

"Don't," she said. She'd fall apart. And she couldn't fall apart. She pulled her eyes from him, unable to look at him anymore. If she did, she wouldn't go through with it.

She kept her eyes down.

"Caspian and I will be right behind you," he told her.

She nodded.

Vitalia came sweeping back, with Serene right behind. "Everything's ready," she said breathlessly as they both worked to straighten her gown. "Salar is at the front. Just walk straight to him."

She could do that, she told herself.

The doors opened, and Norah gave a small gasp at the magnitude of people. Had she really just thought she could do this?

The crowd was overwhelming, larger than her coronation in Mercia. Her eyes found Mikael at the front, with the lord commander behind him. When he saw her, the corners of his lips curved upward ever so slightly. She stepped forward, making her way through the throngs of people lining the great hall.

Norah didn't need to look back to know that Alexander was behind her. She could feel him.

She kept her gaze forward, on Mikael. It wasn't hard to do. His garb was... not what she'd expected. He wore nothing over his upper half—the Kharavian battle form—leaving visible all the markings on his skin. Around his waist he wore a dark wrap tied like loose-fitting trousers, tapered to just below the knee, showing the ink on his calves and his feet. While a seemingly simple garb, it was anything but, with its heavy embroidery and beading. His hair hung loose, a way she hadn't seen, and it was beautiful.

Still, she wavered.

When she reached him, he offered his hand. Norah moved to look back at Alexander, but then stopped. If she met his eyes...

He'd see her struggle. He'd see her on the cusp of breaking. She needed to stay strong. She forced herself to look back at Mikael and took his hand.

The prefect spoke in the Shadow tongue, but Norah knew what he said from what Salara-Mae had explained. He held a woven strip of silk in his hand, a strip of silk Mikael would loop round her waist that would signify her bond to him.

Mikael took the woven silk from the priest and looked at Norah, stepping closer to put it around her.

But she reached out and caught his arm, making him pause. "Wait," she said under his questioning eyes. She'd thought about this for a long time after she'd learned of the practice, and she pulled a silver braided ribbon from the folds of her gown. "If I'm to be bound to you, then you'll also be bound to me."

Murmurs rippled through the masses, and then all was quiet as they waited for the king's reaction.

She couldn't read his face, and her pulse quickened. What if he refused her? But she waited, not shying from the silence.

Finally, he raised his arms slightly, giving her leave to slip the ribbon around his waist. She tried to hide her relief as she reached around him.

Her hands grazed the warm skin of his torso, and she flushed but looped the ribbon into a loose knot.

The king made his own tie, pulling it tight around her waist as he looked down at her. His eyes were curious, and she gave him a small smile. She watched him during the prefect's words. There was a gentleness to him, a softness in the way he held her hand.

The people who filled the hall started clapping, and Norah turned and looked out across the crowd.

It was done. They were wed.

Her eyes met Alexander's, and she saw the glisten of his emotion. A deep, snaking pain crept around her heart, wrapping itself and squeezing tightly. She couldn't breathe.

Mikael pulled her hand over his arm, as they'd rehearsed, and he led the processional through the cheering crowd and to the dining hall for their celebration. She struggled to keep herself together. The double doors to the adjacent rooms had been opened, making the hall seem vastly larger. At the front was a table, and he led her to their places.

"An interesting addition to the ceremony," he said as they sat.

She tried to make sense of his words through the fog of her torment. "I thought it was appropriate."

He didn't answer, but the corner of his mouth turned up in amusement.

People entered, filling the tables. As expected, lords made their way to offer their well-wishes. For once, Norah welcomed the distraction, hoping it would free her of the image of Alexander's eyes still in her mind. But their congratulations reminded her that...

Mikael. He was her husband now, and she, his wife.

He clenched his jaw so tightly he thought his teeth might crack. He couldn't peel his eyes from Norah's hand in the Shadow King's during the wedding ceremony. She'd almost looked at Alexander before she took it but stopped herself. Why had she stopped herself? He knew... she tried to hide her torment, but he knew. And it gutted him.

And when the Shadow King tied the rope around her waist... like he owned her... Instinctively, Alexander's hand moved to his sword. But Caspian stepped slightly forward, bumping a shoulder in front of him and discreetly pushing him back.

Still, fight rippled under his skin. Why wait for battle? Why not kill the Shadow King now? If he waited, Norah would suffer. This man was a monster. Alexander swallowed, but the knot in his throat threatened to choke him. This king wouldn't be kind. He wouldn't be gentle. He wouldn't take care of her the way that she needed.

His pulse thrummed faster as his hand tightened around his sword. The Shadow King wouldn't hold her as Alexander would. He wouldn't kiss her softly. Alexander's breath shook. This man wouldn't love her.

Suddenly, the hall erupted in cheers, jolting him. He caught Norah's gaze for the briefest of moments. Her lips parted as she sucked in a breath. Then she pulled away, and the king led her down the center and toward the celebration feast.

Alexander followed. Caspian walked in front of him, Titus at his side. It wasn't their proper places, but it was their necessary places.

He sat at the table reserved for the Northmen—a table of honor that had been positioned close to Norah and the king. It wasn't close enough. He barely noticed Caspian waving off servants who offered wine and ale as he kept his eyes focused on Norah. She avoided meeting his gaze, but she knew he was there.

Well-wishers lined up to congratulate them, and with each conversation, Norah's forced smile staled even more. She rolled the edges of the tablecloth between her fingertips, keeping her hands busy as she often did when she was anxious... and when she was afraid and trying not to show it. Was she afraid now?

Alexander was afraid. For her. And for tonight. As of earlier that morning, the Mercian priest hadn't yet heard when the Witness would be held. But it wasn't uncommon to wait a day or two after the ceremony. He wasn't sure if it was a blessing or a curse that he didn't know when. Regardless, it consumed him.

The line of well-wishers was too long and too short. When they were finished, and the Shadow King stood and pulled Norah up with him to leave, Alexander would have given anything for more time. The hall rose to their feet, and Alexander rose with them.

Norah's eyes stared down in front of her. He silently begged her to look at him, to let him know she was all right. She'd avoided his gaze for the whole celebration. If she would just look at him...

And then she did.

Eyes, the deepest blue. Eyes, afraid.

The Shadow King pulled her hand, but she didn't move as their stares remained locked. Her lip trembled, and pain—a ripping, clawing, burning—cracked through his chest. He couldn't let her go. Alexander stepped forward, but firm hands held him.

She turned and let the Shadow King take her away.

All too soon, the celebration ended, and Norah found herself being led back to Mikael's chamber. Alexander's eyes haunted her mind, and her heart. She'd tried not to look at him. She'd made her decision, and more than anything, she hoped it was the right one, but she couldn't escape the fear seeding inside her that maybe this wasn't right at all.

Except... walking now, with her arm looped through Mikael's, it didn't feel entirely wrong.

Then her mind shifted to what was to come, and the fear came rushing back.

The room was dimly lit, and Norah forced back the nervous sickness in her stomach as she stepped inside. He followed, closing the doors behind them without taking his eyes from her. The pulsing of her heartbeat in her ears was deafening.

But the room was empty.

"Where is everyone?" she asked, her voice barely a whisper.

Mikael glanced around the room. His brows drew together. "Why would anyone be here?"

"For the Witness."

"The witness of what?"

Was he really going to make her say it? "Of our union, to ensure it's consummated. To complete the contract."

His mouth moved to speak, but no words came. He tilted his head. "But you're here. You'll know what has been done."

"It's not for us. It's so our kingdoms can be assured." She couldn't believe she was defending the Witness. Not defending, she told herself—explaining.

"Is your word not enough?" Mikael gave a small snort of amusement. "What a strange place the North is. That is normal?"

As she said it out loud, it didn't seem normal at all. "I think so? It was expected when I was to marry in Aleon. The council will require confirmation. I think."

He drew closer. "Tell your old men if they question our contract, they can come discuss it with me personally."

Norah couldn't deny the wave of relief that washed over her. Perhaps the evening might be almost bearable now, but a deep reservation still brewed in her stomach.

The darks of his eyes held a reservation of his own. The line on his jaw tightened and smoothed again. "I don't expect you to love me, Salara. In fact, I fear the opposite. But I do believe you can have a comfortable life here, and after we have an heir, I won't... require anything from you, if it's not what you want."

*An heir.* Her stomach turned again. She hadn't thought of a child, and now she felt extremely foolish. Of course he'd expect an heir, but if she dwelled on that, her courage would leave her.

She turned her attention to the room, trying to redirect her mind from the panic creeping in. It was an expansive space with few furnishings. Centered on the back wall was the largest bed she'd ever seen. Beside it sat a chair and a side table, with a standing mirror nestled in the opposite corner. Despite its size, the room seemed minimal. There were no paintings on the walls, no draperies, no personal oddities or tokens.

All right, then. The sooner they started, the sooner this could all be over. She stepped closer to the ornately carved bed and drew her hand across the black silk cascading over its edge. Must everything be made of shadows? Dark and ominous, the bed threatened to swallow her, drown her in its depths. Her heart raced. She glanced back at Mikael, and he watched her with a hesitation of his own.

He approached her slowly, stiff with restraint, but with a wanton look in his eye. Her breath quickened as she pressed back against the corner column of the bed.

"I won't take you against your will," he said.

"Well, I suppose that's a good start to any marriage," she replied dryly.

He stepped closer. "Will you allow me, Salara?"

She reminded herself why she was here. This marriage was for Mercia, for her people. She swallowed and gave a reluctant nod.

"Take off your dress," he said.

Her heart pounded in her chest. "You first," she countered. Not that there was much—he would pull off the garb around his waist and then watch her strip multiple layers of dress. Still, it made her feel slightly better.

Surprise flashed across his face. He didn't move. Their eyes locked, unblinking, each waiting for the other to break.

Finally, Mikael relaxed his shoulders, submitting. He reached down and loosened the embroidered belt from around his waist and dropped it to the floor. Slowly he untied his trousers, and she was surprised to see him pull it off as a singular wrap of cloth.

He stood only in short braies now, and she let her eyes roll over his body. Again, she noted the scar across his chest, a stark contrast against the smoothness of his skin.

She stepped closer, close enough to touch him.

He only waited.

Feeling bolder, she reached up and brushed her fingertips over the raised line of the scar. "They say you cut your heart from your chest to make a pact with Darkness."

The corners of his mouth curved up ever so slightly, watching her. "I haven't heard that story."

She raised her eyes back to his. "This pact gave you a demon commander to do your bidding. They say he collects the souls of the fallen."

"That part is probably true," he said in rare jest, and she found herself smiling. "Did you believe I was a man without a heart?" he asked. "Before I told you my story?"

"No," she whispered. She flattened her palm against the scar. "I felt your heart beat in Bahoul."

It beat now. Fast. Was he nervous? His face didn't show it. She traced her thumb down the center of his chest, and the depression underneath. His skin was smooth and warm.

"Take everything off," she told him.

He waited a moment, seeming to contemplate her authority, but then complied. She watched him with an unashamed curiosity—a curiosity he seemed to enjoy. His nakedness captivated her. She drew her hand over his shoulder as she stepped around behind him.

"Why do you mark your skin?" she asked, tracing the inked patterns that ran from his chest, over his upper arms, and to his back.

"It's my story," he said.

Behind him, she moved her hand down, her thumb along the trench of his spine. Slowly, softly, she trailed the round of his buttocks. Moving higher now, she lingered briefly at the muscled arc at his side and then drew her hand up around his other shoulder. She followed her touch, stepping back around in front of him, and ran her fingers over his body once more—feeling, testing, exploring. He stood silently for her, letting her discover him.

She let her eyes drop to his lower body, and a wave rolled in her stomach. She wanted to touch him, but a sudden shyness overcame her.

A wry smile stretched across his lips. "Am I to your satisfaction?" he asked with a slight hint of impatience.

Norah looked back down. Feeling bolder, she reached below his waist and wrapped her hand around him. A rumble escaped him, and he moved forward. She put her other hand on his chest, quietly bringing him to a stop. A vibration rumbled through him, but he stayed. Turning her attention back to his flesh, she was surprised how he could be so hard and yet so soft, and her pulse quickened at the thought of him inside her. She let her fingertips explore his anatomy underneath, and he shifted. The fire in his eyes could burn her.

His hunger sent a flash of heat across her skin, and she suddenly wanted out of her gown. She turned her back to him, pulling her hair to the side and looking over her shoulder at him.

Not needing further prompting, he reached out and pulled at the lacing on her dress.

"Gently," she insisted.

A complaining rumble came from his chest, but he slowed. Her dress fell open, revealing her corset, and he pulled loose the lacing on it too. She turned to face him and let the gown and corset drop to the floor. She stood in her chemise but then pulled it from her shoulders, letting it fall. Prickles rippled across her skin as she stood in her underwear. Summoning her courage, she hooked her thumbs in the sides and slid them to the floor before stepping out of them.

His breath quickened at the sight of her, and she flushed to see him grow even larger in his arousal. Norah stepped forward, slowly, and took his hand. She spread her fingers and measured her palm against his. His hand dwarfed her own.

Mikael moved forward, using his body to walk her backward toward the bed. She kept a firm hand on his chest to control his pace. When the backs of her thighs brushed against the edge, she paused. And so did he. Then she crept back into the sea of black.

He followed with a hunting prowl, moving between her legs and covering her body with his own. His mouth found hers, and it was hard and wanting. She clasped the base of his jaw, pushing him back to slow his storm. But she wasn't sure she still had control.

She trembled underneath him.

He pulled back. His eyes moved back and forth between hers, dark and questioning. "Are you afraid?" he whispered.

Her voice came in barely a breath. "A little."

Mikael's face softened. "You don't ever need to be afraid of me."

She believed him.

Slowly, he brought his mouth back to hers—probing, asking. He pulled back to look at her, seeking her approval before he bent to kiss her again. The kiss was soft, cautious. Something changed in him, an added tenderness, and she kissed him back. A warmth pooled inside her. Her kiss grew hungry, and he answered with a leashed hunger of his own.

Mikael drew his fingers across her shoulder and down. She trembled again, but not from fear. He swirled his touch around each breast, and she writhed, wanting more. Everything fell away—the circumstance, her worry, her mind. All that mattered was the touch of his skin against hers.

He trailed his hand lower, over her stomach and down between her thighs. She gasped, and his eyes burned darker. He slipped a finger between the lips of her sex, and she writhed against him. As he found the center of her heat, she clutched him tighter.

He made her body answer to his call. Tension built in her stomach, pulsing into her thighs and tightening every fiber in her body. Her hips rocked to her need as her breaths came faster. He took his time, watching her, waiting.

Then she shattered. Release quaked through her, making her cry out. She arched against him, but he held her tight, not letting her escape his touch.

As her body came back to her, she stilled, panting. He covered her mouth in his and captured the last of the fading release on her lips. When he pulled back, she looked up at him, and her face grew hotter. She hadn't imagined he'd be able to make her feel this way, to pull the desire from her, expose her, make her bare herself.

He moved between her thighs again, and her breath shook as he positioned himself. Their eyes met as he rolled his hips forward to meet her. He paused, waiting. She shifted slightly and opened her thighs wider for him.

"Forgive me," he whispered.

He let out a growl and pushed into her. The pain was sharp, and she sucked in a breath, balling the sheets in her fists. The second thrust put him deep within her and she couldn't help the cry that escaped. He trembled under the effort of control.

"Wait," she begged.

He buried his head into her neck, and they lay in the dark quiet of their union.

"Just wait," she whispered.

He did.

Norah brought her hand to the nape of his neck and then threaded her fingers into his hair.

Mikael drew back, pulling her eyes to him. "Are you all right?"

He made it all right, and she nodded.

Her body relaxed, and slowly, he began to move inside her. It wasn't long before the burn subsided to an ache, and the want returned. Feeling him inside her, filling her, brought a new wave of sensations. She rocked her hips, and he moved faster. His breaths quickened, and she watched him. Her fingers moved along the lines of his body—feeling him, learning him.

Intimacy with Mikael was not as she'd imagined; *he* was not as she'd imagined. She tightened her thighs to slow him and moved her hips to push him faster. Where she led him, he followed. She needed control, and he gave it to her. He gave her power. And she gave herself back to him, because what she wanted in that moment *was* him.

The muscle under his skin hardened as he reached his own release, and he buried himself deep within her. She took him; she wanted him, all of him—his body, his being. Everything else fell away.

They lay unmoving as the air quieted around them. Norah closed her eyes and waited for her body to come back. His frame engulfed her, holding her, keeping her safe, and then, ever so gently, he pulled himself from her.

She winced, and he nuzzled the side of her cheek, his breath warm against her ear. "I'm sorry," he whispered. "Are you all right?"

She couldn't answer. Was it all right that she didn't want this time with him to be over? That he'd made her forget everything else, and she didn't want to leave him? That she wanted to kiss him again? A longing stirred deep within her. Was it all right she wanted more than an alliance between them?

"Salara?"

Norah opened her eyes to find large pools of black brimmed with concern staring back at her.

"Say something," he pleaded.

"How long before you can do that again?" she whispered.

The corners of his lips turned upward. He slipped his arms underneath her and laid his head between her breasts. "What are you doing to me?"

A smile crept across her lips, and she drifted into the sweet arms of sleep.

# CHAPTER FORTY-FOUR

Norah woke with the morning sun, her eyes hazy with sleep. She stretched languidly and sat up, alone in the bed. It had been the most restful night she'd had since arriving in Kharav. The warmth of Mikael's body next to hers lulled her into dreaming; his skin brought the sweet scent of comfort.

Vitalia swept in. "You look like you had a very good night," her maid said with a grin as she piled the mix of clothes together that had been cast to the floor.

Heat flashed across her cheeks. It was strange to think of it as a good night. But it felt good between them, her and Mikael. More than good.

Vitalia poured a cup of water, set it on the side table, and laid out a new dress across the bed.

"Where is he?" Norah asked.

"He left early to go see the lord commander. He said to let you sleep a while longer."

The windows let the sun pour in, and Norah smiled under its beams. Everything felt in its place.

"How long will you stay here before you move to the wives' villa?" Vitalia asked.

Norah jerked her head up. "The what?"

"The villa, where the king's wives are."

Her heart stopped in her chest.

"What wives?" *What wives?*

Vitalia looked at her in surprise and then backed up slightly.

"What wives?" Norah asked again, her voice shaking.

Her maid swallowed. "Salar's wives."

Horror flooded her. This couldn't be true. "He has other wives?"

"Forgive me, Salara," Vitalia said quickly. "I thought you knew. You saw them at the betrothal celebration."

Then she realized. The women. What were their names again? Rasha. Myral. Heta.

They weren't sisters. They weren't meant to keep her company.

*They were his wives.*

It hadn't even occurred to her. Norah stumbled up from the bed, her mind reeling. She shook her head, unable to speak.

"It's normal for Salar to have many wives," Vitalia told her.

*Normal?* "So, I'm just one of many?" she asked, trying to hold back the flood of emotion overwhelming her.

"Only you are salara," Vitalia explained. "You assume the highest status of them all."

Norah bristled. "I don't want to be the highest. I want to be the *only*! How is this *normal*?" Her heart felt it would burst from her chest. Shame flooded her.

"Salar's father had seven wives. His father before, five."

"How many are there?" she demanded.

"Only three."

*Only three.* Norah drew in a shaky breath as an anger grew inside her. She'd foolishly believed the king felt something for her, something he hadn't felt before. But he had married before, brought a woman to his bed before. Three times before. *At least.*

Her eyes welled. What she and Mikael had wasn't special. She bit back the pain. She wouldn't let herself be another woman to him. She was a queen, and now she was salara.

"Find him," she said with bitterness thick on her tongue. "Now."

Norah sat silently on the edge of the bed, waiting. The heat of embarrassment flushed her cheeks.

She hadn't even realized. How could she not have realized?

Mikael stepped into the chamber, and she rose. When he saw her, he paused. "I don't think I've ever been summoned before," he said as he draped his cloak on the side chair by the window. While his words came in jest, there was a slight edge to them. He was offended, perhaps.

But she didn't care.

He let out a long sigh. "I'm told you're displeased about my wives."

"That's an understatement," she said icily. "Why didn't you tell me?"

His head tilted slightly, and his eyes narrowed. "I presented them to you."

"Not as your wives!"

"Who did you think they were?"

True, she could have asked who they were, but it wasn't a question she'd even considered. Just then, her stomach clenched. *We shall be good friends,* she'd told them. The embarrassment was unbearable. She wanted to crawl under the quilts of the bed and never come out. But not this bed. Not his bed, not ever again.

"And kings have many wives," he added. His tone carried an air of dismissal.

"Mercian kings don't!"

"I'm not a Mercian king."

"I'm a Mercian queen, and you're my husband!" she snapped.

He snorted, and she could see his own anger rising. He wasn't used to being challenged. "Fine," he said cheekily as he lumbered toward her. "I won't marry any more."

She let out a quaking breath. "That's not good enough."

Mikael used his size to back her against the edge of the bed, where the fire in his eyes intensified. "It'll have to be."

Anger radiated through every fiber of her being. "It's not. And you'll fix it," she demanded.

"What do you expect me to do?" His voice came edgier now. "The marriages simply are. There's no pretending they didn't happen."

"You'll annul them."

His nostrils flared. "How am I to do that?"

"You'll figure it out, or you won't be married to me."

"You can't unwed me," he scoffed. "It's done. We've consummated it." His eyes burned into her. "I know you now. Would that not bring dishonor in the North?"

He seemed to be mocking her, and it hurt.

"You don't know me," she hissed back. "And I won't recognize you as my husband unless I'm your *only* wife."

"So, this is the benefit of a Witness?" he cut back. "I'd thought it was a Northern perversion, but perhaps I'll require one now. I'll make the whole world watch."

A flash of fury swept through her, and she delivered a sharp slap across his face. He bared his teeth with a growl against the sting. She tried to strike him again, but he caught her hand.

"Is it a fight you want?" he snarled.

Norah wrenched against him, but he held her. She fought harder, making them both stagger sideways. As she flailed out, her hand knocked the water basin on a table close by. She grabbed it and swung with all her strength, hitting him squarely in the temple. The force of the blow broke the basin, and he lost his grip on her as he stumbled backward and crashed to the ground.

"Curse it, woman!" he roared as he brought his hand to the side of his face. A deep gash poured blood into his eye and down his cheek.

She gasped in concern, but only for a moment. Her fury swelled back, pushing her concern aside, and she turned and fled the chamber.

"Salara!" he bellowed.

Norah escaped out into the hall to see her Crest guard, wide-eyed and debating whether to follow her or answer the king's thunder.

"Are you not *my* guard?" she snapped, and they fell into place behind her as she hurried to her sanctuary.

His bellows echoed through the halls, and her pulse raced. Her fingers fumbled to latch the door, although there was no way it would hold him out. She sank down into the chair by her vanity, gripping the back until her knuckles turned white.

"Salara!" His roar shook her to her core. He was coming.

She forced herself to breathe, struggling for calm. He'd said she never needed to fear him, but that was before she'd hit him with a water basin and threatened to deny their marriage. Would he hurt her? Her mind raced for how to temper his anger. Perhaps if she apologized... *No.* She'd done nothing wrong. And she'd meant it when she said she'd be his only wife. If he thought he'd force her otherwise, she had another water basin waiting.

"Salara!" he bellowed, nearer now. He sounded near the end of the hall; he'd be at the door in a moment.

She gripped the chair tighter, crouching slightly, and braced herself.

"Come out, woman!"

Oddly, his voice sounded the same distance away.

"Salara!"

She swallowed. Had he stopped at the end of the hall? He'd told her that was the boundary, but surely in his anger he wouldn't confine himself to a mere verbal threshold.

"Come out!"

She most certainly would *not* be coming out.

"You can't claim sanctuary from me in the room that I gave you out of my goodwill!"

That was exactly what she intended to do.

"Come out!"

She stared at the door, not daring to move.

The hall grew silent.

She waited.

Had he gone? It remained silent.

Her breaths calmed as the moments passed, but her body still shook. He could have forced her out. Why hadn't he? She turned slowly to the vanity. Her hands trembled as she brushed back her hair from her face. What was she going to do now?

Mikael showed no intent of dissolving his other marriages. Mercia wouldn't recognize a marriage where she wasn't the only wife, and neither would she. What was worse, she'd already given herself to him. She'd naively thought she meant something to him. Tears threatened, but she clenched her teeth. She wouldn't let him reduce her to this.

# Chapter Forty-Five

Mikael sat at the table and took a long drink of wine. It had been two days since the wedding, and there was only one thing on his mind, one thing that tormented him. He looked at Salara's empty chair.

"I thought she might come this evening," he confessed. He shifted his eyes to Soren, who stabbed a chunk of meat with his knife and put it in his mouth.

Soren snorted.

Mikael rested his elbows on the edge of the table and ran his fingers over the scabbed stitching along his brow. "How long do you think she'll stay angry?"

Soren shrugged as he chewed his food. "As long as you have wives." He chuckled as he took a drink from his blood bowl. "Let her."

Mikael's anger stirred. Soren was of little help in these matters. "She said she refuses to acknowledge our marriage."

Soren snorted again. "Did she not see the thousands there to witness it?"

His irritation grew. He wasn't in the mood for Soren's sarcasm. "If she denies me, so will the North, marriage or no."

His commander gave a wry smile. "What's really lost, though? You still hold the queen within your walls. Better now—you have the Bear."

"I don't want the Bear!" Mikael snapped as he slammed his fist down onto the table, rattling the plates.

Soren's face sobered.

Mikael's words surprised even himself. They weren't entirely true. He did want the Bear. He wanted his head. He wanted to gaze into his dead eyes and spit into the face of fate. But there was something he wanted more now.

He sat back in his chair. He had to do something. "I could make her my only wife."

Soren straightened, and the line along his jaw tightened. "Careful, brother," he warned. "You'd offend three of the most powerful lords in your kingdom. That wouldn't be without consequence."

But how likely would they be to act?

Soren leaned toward him, his eyes dark and serious. "Don't do something stupid."

Mikael sighed. Soren was right. That would be stupid. "Have you heard anything from Salara?" he asked the servant who poured him more wine.

The servant bowed his head. "She said she's not hungry this evening."

Mikael swore. He knew that was a lie; that woman ate more than he did.

"She'll need to eat eventually," Soren rumbled.

Mikael ignored him. "Have meals left outside her door," he told the servant.

Soren cut him an annoyed glance. "That only aids her in hiding away."

Mikael looked at the servant. "Do as I say."

"Yes, Salar," the servant said with a bow.

Mikael crossed his arms and brought the knuckles of his fist to his lips. What was he going to do?

"She'll get over it," his commander told him. "She just needs time to learn how things are here."

Perhaps. Perhaps not.

Norah woke on the settee in her sanctuary to the sound of a knock on the door. Her book had fallen to the floor. She was surprised she'd drifted to sleep. The knock came again, stronger this time. There was a man behind it, and she shuddered. Mikael had finally come, but she still wasn't ready to face him.

The knock came louder, forceful now. "North Queen," a voice snarled.

It wasn't Mikael. Her pulse quickened. It was his brute. Mikael might have shown restraint, but the lord commander had none. She rose and walked to the door but didn't open it.

"I know you hear me," his voice rumbled.

She *did* hear him, and his hatred. And she knew he wouldn't leave simply because she didn't answer.

"You doubt I'll break down this door?"

She most certainly didn't. Norah lifted the latch and pulled the door open a small crack. His eyes met hers with smoldering animosity. "What do you want?" she asked coldly.

"I suggest you very quickly get over this foolishness. Salar has no time for these games."

"This isn't a game," she snapped.

"I caution you. It's unwise for you to press this, North Queen. You're held deep within Kharav." He paused, and then added, "As is your Bear."

Prickles rose over her skin. He was threatening her.

"It would be a shame if someone were to get hurt," he said.

"Mikael wouldn't do that."

"Wouldn't he?" he challenged. "You have no idea who he is, or what he'll do. There's only one will, and that's the will of Salar. You're a fool to think you have any power over him. And you'll be done with this nonsense, now."

With that, the commander turned and left her to the lingering warning of his words.

She didn't want to believe him, but now she wasn't so sure. She didn't know Mikael as well as she thought she had. Did he see all this as nonsense? How long would he let her avoid him? She couldn't stay in the sanctuary forever.

Her thoughts turned to Alexander. He wasn't safe in Kharav. As much as she wanted to hide away from the world, she couldn't leave him to the consequence of her fallout with the king. She had to see him and make sure he was all right. Although her stomach dipped at the thought of facing him now. She hadn't spoken to him since the wedding. Since...

Her chest tightened. It had been two days. He'd be sick with worry. She should have gone to him sooner, to let him know she was okay. Except she wasn't okay. It didn't matter; she had to see him. She unlatched the door and slipped out into the hall.

Norah paused to see a small tray of food by the door. The commander certainly hadn't left it. Vitalia must have dropped it off. And even though it called to her hungry stomach, she'd eat later. She had more important things to tend to.

Norah moved cautiously, wary of seeing the commander again, but as she neared the end of the hall, a broad smile broke across her face.

Titus and another Northman guard stood on duty. When they saw her, they gave small bows of their heads. But her smile fell as she got a closer look. Titus bore a cut on the side of his cheek and under his chin. His left eye seemed slightly swollen, with bruising over his brow. Blood stained the left shoulder of his tunic, but she wasn't sure if it was his or someone else's. The Northman beside him held similar injuries, and a glance at the Crest guards standing on the opposite side showed they weren't better off. A hallway brawl?

Wonderful. Something else to manage.

When she reached them, Vitalia jumped up from a side chair she'd been sitting in.

"Salara!"

"Hello, Vitalia," she said, pulling her eyes from the guards. She was glad to see her maid, but Vitalia knew about her ignorance of the marriages, and Norah still felt the shame of it.

"I'm so sorry I haven't come," her maid told her. "They wouldn't let me disturb you in your sanctuary, even to see if you needed anything."

Norah forced a small smile. "That's perfectly all right. I appreciate you bringing a tray by, though."

"I'm happy to take the thanks, but that wasn't me. Salar ordered food to be brought to you for every meal."

Well, that was... kind.

"Are you going to see the Northmen off?"

Norah didn't know what she meant. "For what?"

"Salar's given them provisions to take to the North. He's also arranged horses in the valley from the Tribelands. He's given your captain men to help, and they leave later today."

"Oh," Norah said. She'd never expected... Of course these allowances had been a part of their marriage arrangement—but it was an arrangement she'd threatened to not acknowledge. A seed of hope sprouted in her chest. "That's good news," she said.

"It is. Oh, and Serene has already moved to the villa. Would you like her to come here?"

Her stomach soured. If Serene was in the villa, that meant she knew about the wives. Norah wondered how long it would be before her grandmother knew. "No, she can tend to things there." One less person to bear her shame in front of. "Could you bring a few more dresses, though? There's only a couple in the sanctuary, and I'll be staying there a while."

"Yes, Salara. I'll get those right away." Vitalia started off and then stopped. "May I have your permission to wait on you there? In the sanctuary?"

"Of course," Norah told her. "I'd like that."

Vitalia gave a small smile with a bow and went to get Norah's dresses from the villa.

Then Norah set her mind on her original intention: to find Alexander. She started down the hall, and Titus moved in behind her. The slide of steel came as a warning, and she spun to look back at the guards. The Crest guard stood coiled, daggers and spears in hand with their eyes on her Northmen, and Titus had his hand on the hilt of his sword.

"Northmen with me," she said. Her Mercian guard fell instep close behind her, and although the Crest guard gave some space, she gritted her teeth as they followed behind. Yes, she'd have to do something about this. Now wasn't the time to discuss her guardsmen's assignments with Mikael or the lord commander, but she also didn't want a guard of both Northmen and the Crest with a small battle brewing behind her everywhere she went.

She pushed out a breath. One thing at a time. First, Alexander.

He paced his chamber, ready to topple this castle to the ground. It had been two days since the wedding, two days since he'd seen Norah or heard anything from her, and Alexander couldn't wait any longer. He'd tried to focus on his work—communications with the council, seeing to his men, and assigning their stations to protect her as much as he could deep in an enemy kingdom—but a dark madness kept clawing into his mind, threatening his control. What had the Shadow King done with her? What had he done *to* her? For two days...

Caspian tried to take on more and give him space to calm and sort his mind. But there would be no calm until Alexander could see her.

A knock sounded on the door, and he nearly tore it off its hinges as he swung it open. One more Shadowman who—

He froze as blue eyes stared back at him. His nostrils flared and he forced a swallow. He couldn't hold himself—he swept her into an embrace.

Norah clutched his tunic, sinking into him. He brought a hand to her head and held her to his chest. Just the scent of her settled him. She was here. In his arms. Safe. Unharmed. Or so he assumed. He quickly pulled back and cupped her face in his hands.

"Are you all right?" he asked.

"I'm fine," she replied. But she didn't sound fine.

He held her tighter. "You're not." Her lip trembled. She was wed to the Shadow King. She wasn't fine. He cursed under his breath as he pulled her back to him, forgetting all proprieties and kissing the top of her head. "I'm here," he murmured.

He'd figure out a way to get her out and back to Mercia. It didn't matter if she was wed if he could get her out before...

"The Witness?" he asked. "When will it be held?"

She didn't answer, and his blood ran cold. His heart stopped. Was it too late? A crippling nausea rolled through him. He forced himself to pull back from her; he needed her to answer him. "Norah?"

Her lips parted, and his stomach twisted. She swallowed, then said, "There will be no Witness."

Alexander let out a quaking breath. *There would be no Witness*. Had the Shadow King intended this marriage to be in name only? His eyes stung as he pulled her back to him, and he breathed his undying thanks to the gods. All he could do was hold her and breathe her in.

When he found his voice again, it came hoarse and thick with emotion. "I couldn't bear it, Norah. My mind's been filled with madness these past days." He held her tighter. Now he could breathe again, focus again. And he only needed to focus on getting her home.

"I'm all right," she whispered, but there was a strangeness to her voice, something not all right.

He pulled back again and clasped the side of her neck, brushing her cheek with his thumb and looking over her.

"I am," she said, her voice a little stronger now. "I just had to come to make sure you were too."

"I don't want you to worry about me. You have enough to deal with."

Her lip still trembled. Was there something else? Something she wasn't telling him?

"Are you returning to Mercia with Caspian?" she asked.

He narrowed his eyes. Was she really all right? Or was she changing the subject?

He shook his head. "No, but I do need to leave very soon to investigate a situation." He hesitated, not wanted to put more burden on her, but she needed to know. "Mercian villages, and others under Mercia's protection, are being attacked."

Her brow dipped. "Again?"

What did she mean *again*? "You know about this?"

She pushed out a breath. "After I was taken, we came upon a town that had been destroyed, but there was no sign of who had done it. Do you know?"

He shook his head again. "Not yet. But I don't want you to trouble yourself with it now. I'll find who it was and put a stop to it."

"How long will you be gone?"

"Not long. I'm going only to the southern reaches, so a couple weeks perhaps." He clasped her hands and brought them to his chest. "But I won't leave yet. Not right now. I need to make sure you're okay."

"I am," she assured him. "And honestly, it would make me feel better if I knew you were out of harm's way until things have settled. You should go. I'm fine. Really."

"Titus and the rest of the guard will be here with you."

She shifted. "About that—send them to help Caspian."

"And leave you alone?" *Absolutely not.*

"Alexander. Please. You can look out in that hall and see I'm most certainly not alone. I don't have command over the Crest, and until I work things out with Mikael, there will be duplicate guard and the threat of battle between them at every hall. I can't deal with that right now, I can't. Alexander, please—"

"All right," he said, yielding. As much as he hated the idea, he couldn't resolve it for her now, and it was obviously yet one more overwhelming burden.

"It will only be a couple of weeks," she said. "That's a short time."

It was an eternity away from her.

She gave a weak smile. "Go," she said. "I'll be here."

He pulled her hands to his lips. "I'll return as soon as I can." Then he'd find a way to bring her home.

# CHAPTER FORTY-SIX

Two more evenings passed and Mikael still found himself without Salara. He sat in the dining hall again, brooding over her empty chair. By now, she'd have moved into the villa. Perhaps she'd see it wasn't as she'd expected. The villa had every comfort, every luxury.

"You still let the North Queen worry you," Soren said, interrupting his thoughts.

Mikael let out a deep sigh. "She still doesn't come. She's still unhappy."

Soren shrugged. "What will she do? Leave?"

"She's not a prisoner."

Soren's face grew serious. "But you know we can't let her go."

Mikael knew this. So long as he held the North Queen, he kept her from Aleon. If he kept her from Aleon, he denied his fate. But he didn't want to hold her. He wanted her to want to stay.

"Go to the villa," he told a servant. "Tell her I... I wish for her to come. It's not required, but I wish for her to want to come. If she should find herself wanting to, wanting to eat. With me."

Soren snorted and raised a brow.

Mikael glared at him and cursed under his breath. He sounded like a rambling fool, but he worried for her.

"She's not in the villa, Salar," the servant said. "She still remains in the sanctuary."

Mikael flung his chalice across the hall, frustration coursing through him.

"Would you like me to deliver the message to her there?" the servant asked.

"No," he rasped, tempering his fire. "She's not to be disturbed there."

A banging on the door of the sanctuary made her jump, and Norah pushed her breath through her teeth. She already knew who it was: the one person for whom Mikael's rules didn't apply. She debated not opening it, but it wasn't as though he would go away.

"North Queen," he growled through the door.

Norah pursed her lips as she put her book down, and she rose to answer. She opened the door to find the commander's shadowed eyes looking back at her. Behind him prowled his dogs, as menacing as their master.

"What do you want?" she asked, not bothering to hide the iciness in her own voice.

"I came to suggest you might dine with Salar tonight. Each day only brings greater discord." It wasn't a friendly request.

Her eyes narrowed. "I didn't know you were so eager to see me again."

"I'm not," he snarled. "But his waiting for you is even more disturbing than your presence. At least pretend to settle your grievance."

"If he wants amends, then he shouldn't send his dogs!" She moved to close the door, but he jarred it with his foot and flung it back open, and she stumbled back into the room.

"I come on my own accord."

She bared her teeth. "You're not allowed here."

"There is nothing I'm not allowed!" he raged. "You'll do well to remember that."

And yet he didn't step inside.

"This is *my* sanctuary," she snapped.

"And you have it by Salar's grace! How much longer do you think that will last? It's by that grace you live here in comfort, and by that grace your Bear's still alive."

"Leave!" she seethed, her anger casting aside any fear.

Fury dripped from his skin, but she drew closer in challenge. He couldn't scare her. Alexander had left; there was nothing he could do.

Finally, he relented, storming back down the hall the way he'd come. Norah shut the door behind him and sank onto her bed, breathing deeply to calm her shaking.

She couldn't let him get to her. Despite everything that had happened between them, she didn't believe Mikael would hurt her. She didn't believe he'd let his commander hurt her. And with Alexander gone, she had time to work on a solution. But what was the solution? What could she do if nothing changed?

Outside her door, a tray rattled with a slight clattering of dishes—another meal being delivered. Her stomach reminded her she hadn't eaten.

Norah opened the door and moved to take the tray from the small table that had been set up by the wall. She stopped. On the tray sat a bowl, and inside were three small, rolled parchments.

She pulled open one of the parchments, and her heart thrummed in her chest. Then she quickly glanced over the rest. Her hands trembled.

There were three.

Three annulments.

For three wives.

And they bore the king's seal.

Her silk shoes fell silent on the stone floors as Norah hurried through the castle with Vitalia close behind her. Her heart raced as she went. The king had annulled his marriages, which she'd doubted he'd do. Despite his coarseness, he cared. And what surprised her more was that *she* cared. The commander was wrong. She *did* know him.

They reached the throne room, but the king wasn't without company. Norah paused in the wing, watching out of sight.

Mikael sat on his throne, listening to a man in an emerald-green cloak. An embroidered golden crest on the chest of the man's jacket caught the light as he moved, but she wasn't able to make it out fully. His skin was darker than that of the Kharavian people, but not black like the people of Etreus. He wore his hair cropped short but his beard long.

"An envoy from Serra," Vitalia whispered. Her breath came shallow. "Perhaps it would be better to speak to Salar later."

Vitalia was afraid. But of what?

"Who is that—Serra?"

"It's the slavers' kingdom. South. Across the Aged Sea."

Norah swallowed. The kingdom that dealt in slave trade. Her own revulsion swelled. She watched them. Norah understood the man's words as he spoke to the king. "They speak the Northern tongue?"

"The Northern tongue is the Common tongue. Almost all kingdoms use it for trade and relations."

That meant everyone spoke the Northern tongue. After what had happened with Bremhad, she'd known it was that way in Kharav, but she hadn't realized it was a common language across kingdoms. A bitter taste crept over the back of her tongue and down her throat as she thought about the lord commander. And as if thoughts made him appear, her eyes found him. He stood to the right of the king's throne, looking murderous, as always.

"King Milar disagrees," the envoy told Mikael as Norah started to listen in. "He proposes a reduction of Serra's share by one third, or an increase in provisions from Kharav."

"They talk of trade?" Norah whispered to Vitalia.

Vitalia nodded, visibly upset. "Kharav trades slaves with Serra and provides provisions to support them."

"Go back to the sanctuary," Norah told her. "I'll return after I've spoken to the king."

"Are you sure?"

"Yes," Norah whispered. "Go."

Vitalia left her standing in the wing, and Norah turned her attention back to Mikael.

"He awaits your answer," the envoy said.

"I've already given it," Mikael replied. His face didn't show the anger that Norah heard in his voice.

"King Milar says this is unacceptable."

Mikael rose from his throne. He walked down the stairs, calm and composed. Then, in a single movement, he pulled his sword from his scabbard and cut down the Serran guard beside the envoy. Norah's heart leapt to her throat, and she clasped her hand over her mouth to stifle a cry.

Mikael grabbed the envoy by his jacket and forced him to his knees as he swept the tip of the blade to the man's neck.

"No!" Norah called out, stepping forward from the shadows of the wing.

They all turned at the sound of her voice. Mikael's eyes met hers, and he stopped.

"What are you doing?" she cried.

He looked back at the envoy, and his face darkened again. "Sending my answer to King Milar."

"Don't harm him," she said. "Please."

Mikael paused for a moment, looking back at the envoy. He angled the tip of his sword against the man's throat. "Salara asks for mercy," he said finally. "Your gods smile on you today." He released the envoy, and the man scrambled backward and to his feet.

But Norah didn't feel relief. She stared at the dead guard on the floor. Blood pooled around him and veined out along the grooves where the patterned stone joined together to form its image.

"Leave us," Mikael said to the room. The Serran guards collected their dead companion and ushered their lord out and away from the loosely leashed danger. The Kharavian soldiers followed, clearing the room and leaving only Mikael and Norah.

And the lord commander, of course.

Norah peeled her eyes from the smeared blood on the stone.

"I'll have it cleaned," Mikael told her.

Is that what he thought she cared about? "Will you bring back the life you took?" The life he'd taken so easily, like it had been nothing.

Her words silenced him for a moment. "These are not good men, Salara," he said finally.

As if that justified murder.

Mikael glanced at the parchments in her hand. His eyes met hers again, and his expression shifted. "You read them?" he asked.

Norah looked down at her clenched hand. She'd forgotten she was holding the marriage annulments.

"This is what you wanted, yes?" he said, his voice softer now.

Yes, but no. None of this was what she wanted.

The lord commander stepped forward, the line between his brow creasing. "What have you done?" he asked the king.

Was he serious? This man was truly unbelievable. Norah glared at him, finally finding her voice. "You're fine with him killing a man but not absolving a marriage?"

But he did not respond to her reproach. His eyes stayed on the king. "Salar?"

"Leave us," Mikael told him.

The commander's eyes shifted to Norah, and she could see the swelling rage within. But he said nothing, only turned and left them in silence.

"Walk with me?" Mikael asked, only he didn't wait for her to answer before moving them forward and out of the throne room.

"Do you kill all your trade envoys?" she questioned as they walked.

"Not all of them."

She wasn't sure if he was being cheeky or serious. Anger touched her cheeks either way. She didn't like this Mikael—the dark Mikael. He drifted closer to her as they walked, close enough to touch her. He'd better not dare.

They reached the great hall, and he slowed. From the corner of her eye, she saw him looking at her. "I spared him."

"Because I asked you to. Not because you had mercy in your heart."

They stopped and stared at each other.

"Has it come already?" he asked. "Your loathing for me?"

Did she loathe him now? She wanted to.

"Not that I thought it would take long," he added. His voice came fainter, as if he were speaking more to himself than to her, as if he were regretful, even. "I just hadn't expected it so soon." His face fell, and his eyes softened. "What would you have me change?"

His question wasn't what she had anticipated. What would she have him change? His kingdom? Their values, their culture, their way of life? Anything she could ask for was too much or not enough. Or both. She stayed quiet.

He shifted his gaze forward again and let out a long breath. "The villa is yours alone now. Will you be moving there?"

Her mind was still on the man that had just been killed; she couldn't think about the villa, other than that she would most certainly not be moving there.

"You don't want the villa?" He paused a moment. "Have you seen it?"

No. She didn't need to see it. She didn't *want* to see it. She didn't want to stay where there had been wives before her, women he had known in such an intimate way. But she didn't want to argue about the villa right now. "I'm sure it has everything I need," she managed finally, hoping to put the subject to rest for now.

"But you don't want to stay there," he pressed.

*Fine.* "No," she admitted. "I don't want to stay there. I'm fine with the sanctuary." The sanctuary was hers. Kind of.

He stepped in front of her. His voice dropped low. "I've been with no other since I've met you, no other woman. I want you to know this. If it's important."

Her breath hitched in her throat. And her heart... "It is," she whispered. He was trying. Could she try? "Thank you for telling me."

He nodded, and they continued walking.

She swallowed. "What did you do with your wives?"

He shifted his weight back. "They returned to their homes, to their families."

So, no violent ends. That was good. "You'll see them provided for?"

He looked at her curiously. "I've allowed them to keep the Provision Promise moneys. It's a substantial amount."

She wasn't sure what that meant. Perhaps something like a dowry or a bride price. She bit the inside of her lip. That didn't seem enough.

"Is there something more you'd have me do?" he asked.

"I don't want them to be dishonored. They come from noble families?"

He shifted uncomfortably. "They do."

"You should give them more. Land, perhaps."

He nodded.

"You'll see them taken care of, then?" She wanted confirmation.

"I will."

She paused. "Do you have any children?"

He fell silent, then said, "No."

His answer surprised her and relieved her at the same time. They stood awkwardly in the silence.

"I should retire," she said. It was enough for now.

"Can I walk you back?" he asked, drawing closer.

*No.* But she found herself giving the faintest of nods. He offered her his arm. She wavered a moment, but then slipped her hand under and let him take them forward. He put his hand over hers, locking her to him. Her skin tingled under his touch, but she couldn't let herself forget so easily. He'd just killed a man, like it had been nothing. He would've killed another had she not stopped him, all while discussing the trade of people's lives as if they were bags of grain.

Could she bear this, the price of peace? She'd known who she'd married. Maybe it had been foolish of her to expect change quickly. Maybe over time...

She needed to try.

When they reached the door to her sanctuary, he stopped but didn't release her hand. Nor did she pull it away. His eyes churned like the tempest of a storm. They were dangerous—she could get lost in them. A want tugged at something within. Did she want to get lost in them? *No.* She couldn't trust this man. He moved closer, and she leaned back against the door.

"I'm glad you've come out," he said softly. "I'd like to see you out more often. If you want to return to the gardens, or even go for a ride, or if you'd like to simply come dine with me, I'd like that."

He moved his hand to brush her cheek, a brush that left her skin all too quickly. "Good night, Salara."

"Good night," she breathed, and slipped inside her sanctuary.

# Chapter Forty-Seven

Her mind swirled around her. Norah sat at her vanity in her sanctuary, reeling in a mix of emotions. She would continue to struggle in the kingdom of Shadows, this kingdom of blood and battle. And what could she do? Could she change this world?

Maybe when Mikael let her closer. She wanted him to. She wanted to be closer.

Was she letting *him* closer? She still hadn't told him of her memories; she wasn't sure why. Maybe telling Mikael meant letting her old self go, and she didn't want to let go. With Mikael... she feared she would lose herself more, in this dark world. This world wouldn't help her find herself. She had nothing of who she was before to remind her, except Alexander. And if he could, Mikael would take Alexander from her. But Alexander was hers. She needed to protect him, to protect the person she used to be.

But still she wanted to tell him. She wanted Mikael closer. The divide between them tore at her. She chastised herself for hinging her happiness on her relationship with the king, but these feelings were complicated. This marriage wasn't for love, she reminded herself. This was a marriage that would protect her people. She should be happy if she could achieve civility with a solid alliance. Why wasn't she happy? Mikael was working to mend things between them. Why wasn't it enough?

Why was her heart asking for more?

Norah decided a ride would help clear her head. She'd slipped into the stables to visit the mare a few times now, but the animal needed to go out beyond the stall and the paddocks. And Norah had been hiding away in her sanctuary too long; she needed out too. Mikael had suggested a ride, and it was a good idea, although he probably meant the two of them together. She'd overlook that. She felt bolder now that Mikael was trying to resolve the distance between them, bold enough to go by herself. To her surprise, her guard didn't object. Perhaps Mikael had leashed his commander.

Norah found the mare happy to see her, and she smiled. She saddled the horse herself before mounting and breathing deep the air of near freedom. "Let's go," she told the mare, and urged her from the back gates of the castle and into the hills. The Crest followed close behind. She was glad the Mercian guard had gone with Caspian and that she didn't have them both to contend with.

The mare didn't need encouragement and stretched out into a gallop. They took the south side out of the castle to keep out of the city and headed to open lands.

They rode well into the late morning, and Norah felt a strength returning. Despite the winter cold, the freedom warmed her. It was the first time she'd been outside the castle grounds, her first time away from the king and the commander.

At the top of a hill, Norah slowed the mare, smiling back and waiting for her guard to catch up.

"Salara, please," Kiran called to her. "Will you not keep closer to us?"

"I'm sorry." She grinned. "It just feels so good to be out."

His eyes smiled back from underneath his wrap. "I know what you mean."

Suddenly his face changed as his gaze shifted to something in the distance, and Norah followed it to see rising smoke against the sky.

"What's that?" she asked.

"Likely a camp. Outsiders. Not Kharavian."

"Who then?"

He shook his head. "I don't know. But let's get you back, and I'll send forces to investigate."

Norah had no intention of being stuffed back into the castle. "I'm not going back." She gave a cheeky smile. "This is my kingdom now. I want to know who visits me."

"Salara," he protested.

"Come on!" And she urged the mare forward.

They covered the distance quickly but slowed as they reached the last hill, making their way up with care. When they reached a view of the camp, Norah's curiosity grew.

Five young men sat around a campfire. Norah put them close to Adrian's age. She heard their laughter and smiled, appreciating their fun. Then annoyance flashed within her. Who were they, and what were they doing here? They were too young and foolish to be wary of danger approaching. She needed to send them on their way.

"Salara," Kiran cautioned.

"Come on, Kiran," she said over her shoulder. "They're only boys."

They made their way down the hill, and the young men stood quickly when they sighted them approaching. The Crest guard circled them, and the men held out their hands, showing no weapons.

"Who are you?" Norah called to them.

"Who wants to know?" one of the men cut back. His accent told her he wasn't from Kharav, as Kiran had surmised.

"Salara wants to know," Kiran snapped at them.

The man's eyes widened, and he looked at his friends.

"Who are you?" Norah asked him again.

"Ando," he replied quickly. Norah could hear the fear in his voice. He glanced at his friends again.

"Where are you from?" she asked.

"We've made a mistake, Your Majesty," another man said quickly. "Please."

"They're from Osan," Kiran told her.

Norah hadn't realized they were so close to the neighboring kingdom.

"They're forbidden to cross the border," he added.

"Please, Your Majesty," Ando said. "We mean no harm. We'll be on our way."

"Why are you here?" she asked.

They looked at each other hesitantly.

"Well?" she prodded.

"We lost a bet," Ando admitted. "We are indebted to spend a night in the Shadowlands. We didn't think anyone would be here. Please, Your Majesty."

She turned to Kiran. "Let them go."

"The lord commander would never let them live," he told her.

"Well, the lord commander isn't here." *Thank the gods.* She looked at the young men with a scowl. "This isn't a place for games. Go back home and consider yourselves lucky."

"Yes, Your Majesty. Thank you! Thank you!"

They bowed appreciatively, and Norah waited while they collected their things. They gave one last bow before they clambered onto their horses and spurred them off over the next hill. Norah smiled after them. *Boys.*

"We should return to the castle now," Kiran called.

"Let's wait a bit and then ride to the top of the next hill. I want to make sure they're off." She took a moment to drink water and rest. "I think we should make this a regular event," she told Kiran. "I like it out here."

"Thank you for the warning," he said wryly.

She chuckled. "All right, let's see if they've gone."

They rode up the hill to check on the young men, but as she reached the top and looked down, her pulse quickened. A small group of soldiers had stopped them. *Kharavian soldiers.* And in the center, she saw the commander.

"This isn't good, Salara," Kiran said. "You should go back. You don't want to be out here."

But Norah wasn't thinking about going back now. She urged the mare down the hill, with her guard following close behind her. She reached the bottom as the men were being pushed to their knees.

"Lord Commander!" she called out, breathless.

He stood by the young men and turned when he heard her. His eyes narrowed. "You shouldn't be out here," he said darkly. "Return to the castle."

"I won't! What are you doing?"

"Your Majesty!" Ando called to her. "We told him you released us."

"Ride on or watch them die," the commander snarled at her.

The threat made Norah shudder. "No, these boys are returning home. I'm salara. You'll release them!" she demanded.

A wicked smile came to his eyes. "Where the security of the kingdom is concerned, I act on behalf of Salar. You have no authority here."

"They're just boys!"

"They're men. Not that it matters."

Norah slid off her horse and stepped close to the commander so no one else could hear her. "If you're angry at me, then let's resolve that, just you and me. But I beg you, let them go."

"I would never act in anger against Salar's wife," he said in a tone that chilled her more than any winter.

"Anything you ask," she begged. "Please!"

He paused. "The Bear. Give him to me, and I'll let them go."

Bile rose in her throat. "You ask for what you know I can't give."

Before she could react, the commander ran Ando through with his sword, and the young man fell forward onto the ground.

"No!" Norah screamed as he turned and dropped another. She begged of Kiran, "Make him stop!"

The Crest guard gripped his sword handle but didn't move. "We can't do that, Salara."

The commander cut down another man—so casually, so easily. Then he stepped toward the next. Norah clasped her hand over her mouth, stifling another scream, feeling completely helpless.

"Wait!" the man cried as the commander stepped toward him. "Wait! I'm the prince! Prince Jeord. If restitution is required, it can be paid! Just let us go. We'll leave right now!"

The commander paused, and his eyes held a haunting smile. "Prince Jeord. I didn't recognize you." He leaned closer to the young man. "I have a message for your father. Restitution *is* required. Tell him to bring his army and pay in blood."

Jeord gaped in horror. "You want war?"

The commander looked at Norah. "It's been said I lust for it."

Jeord stood, shakily backing away.

"Run along," the commander said. The other two young men scrambled up with Jeord, but before they could run, the commander dropped them both with his sword.

Norah let out a short scream. This couldn't be happening.

The commander eyed the prince, who stumbled back with a cry in his throat.

"Just you," the commander said as he stooped down and wiped his sword on one of the dead men's clothes. "Go."

Jeord whimpered, backing away. Then he turned and ran, stumbling but catching himself again.

The commander watched him until he was out of sight. "Stake the bodies by the border," he told the Crest. "Bring the horses." Norah staggered back in shock, and the commander turned to her. "Let's go."

"I'm not going anywhere with you!" she seethed.

His eyes grew darker. "Get on your horse, or I'll drag you back."

She knew he meant it. Still shaking and filled with horror, she climbed back on the mare.

Mikael sat in his study, poring over the deeds of his lands. He looked for more to give his ex-wives, as Salara had asked of him. It surprised him she'd asked this, but then, she was always surprising him.

He knew it wasn't easy for her in Kharav. Could she see how much he was trying? Soren was furious with him, and understandably so. There would be consequences with the lords, he knew. But he was willing to suffer the cost.

Footsteps echoed in the halls, and the door to his study slammed open against the wall.

"I hope you're proud!" Salara seethed as she stormed in.

He rose from his desk in alarm. What was going on?

Her eyes blazed with a fire he hadn't seen before, not even when she'd been upset about his wives.

"How better to show your strength than by killing boys!" she spat at him.

Mikael darted his eyes to Soren, who had walked in behind her.

"What's the meaning of this?" Mikael asked.

"A group of boys crossed the border, and I sent them back," she told him. "But they ran into your brute along the way, and he slaughtered them!"

"They weren't boys," Soren countered. "They were nearing twenty."

"Boys!" she cried.

"Old enough to battle," Soren argued. "And from Osan."

She gave the commander an appalled look and shook her head in disgust. "What's wrong with you? And what does it matter where they're from?" She turned back to Mikael. "He does this in your name! The prince was with them, and your monster sent him back with a threat to his father—he openly invites war!"

Anger flared within him. She didn't understand the ways of Kharav, and Soren was certainly ensuring her introduction to them was most unpleasant. He'd deal with him later. "Salara," he tried to calm her. "You'll come to understand we must do necessary evils to keep Kharav safe."

She shook her head again. "No. Don't pass this off as a necessary thing! Any competent man would've seen they weren't a threat."

He looked at Soren, who waited quietly, unfazed. Mikael gritted his teeth. Heat veined under his skin at his commander's indifference to her upset. But she would need to understand that Kharav was a kingdom of war. He turned back to her. "We defend our borders most savagely. This is known to our enemies with certainty, and it's this certainty that keeps us safe."

Her face twisted. "That's your answer? Safety?" She backed away from him as she shook her head in disgust. "Well then, enjoy your safety thinking of slaughtered boys!" She turned and stormed from the study.

Mikael pushed out a breath as he slowly rolled the parchments and wrapped the leather cord around them. His fury built from deep within, and it took every ounce of strength he had to control it. He waited until she was out of earshot before he cast a sharp eye at Soren. "Have you no sense?"

Soren's brow hung darker. "You would have done the same," he argued.

"Not in front of Salara! She thinks we thirst for violence." The harming of innocents—it bothered her. Deeply. "She doesn't understand our ways. She isn't hardened to them."

Soren sighed. "I let Jeord live. His father will see it as a mercy. They dare not bring war against us, and that piss prince will think before he crosses our border again."

"You fail me."

Soren shifted back. Mikael had never uttered those words to him before. "I told her to leave. What else was I to do?"

Mikael's frustration grew. "You should have let them go. Her loathing is already upon me, and you push her further away!"

"Is it not better now than later, brother?"

Mikael slammed his fist on his desk. "I'm not your brother—I am salar!" he thundered. "And so help you if I lose her."

Soren stepped backward, clearly taken aback by Mikael's rage toward him. His eyes flashed with his own anger, but he bowed his head in submission, and Mikael pushed past him and out of the room.

Norah stood in the library. She stared at the books on the shelves, but she didn't see them. She couldn't stay here any longer; she couldn't be here. Her heart longed for Mercia—its grace, its refinement, its civility. Kharav... Kharav was a kingdom of monsters.

She drew in a deep breath. With this marriage, she kept these monsters from Mercia, she reminded herself. But how much more could she bear?

Norah squeezed her eyes shut and gritted her teeth. She would endure as much as she had to.

The doors opened behind her, and she turned to see Mikael. She cursed herself for lingering too long.

"Salara," he greeted as he neared. "I'm glad I found you here."

Norah stepped around a large table, putting it between them. She wasn't so glad. She didn't reply.

"Talk to me," he said.

*Fine.* "Would you have killed those boys?"

He paused. His hesitation answered for him. She knew he wanted to move her past it, but she couldn't. These weren't things she could turn a blind eye to.

"I would have released them," he said. "If you'd asked me to."

"And if I wasn't there to ask?"

Mikael walked slowly around the side of the table. "Will you judge the man in front of you, instead of the one in your mind?"

"Because the one in front of me is so much better?" she cut back, moving so the table stayed between them.

Mikael's brow creased, and then he sighed. "I don't want things to be like this between us. I do care for you, Salara."

The fire of her fury died down ever so slightly, but she didn't want it to die. She told herself she'd change things—she had to change things. And it would start by the lord commander being held accountable. "What will you do about him?" she asked. "What will you do about your commander?"

"I've spoken to him."

"That's not enough."

He looked down, and then nodded. "All right."

She hadn't expected him to agree. Was he agreeing? "You'll deal with him?" she asked.

"I will. These things won't happen again."

But relief didn't come. She didn't entirely believe him.

"Are you on your way out?" he asked.

She looked down at the books in her hand and then toward the door. She knew what he would ask if she said yes.

But he didn't wait for her reply. "Can I walk you?"

He moved to the end of the table where she stood, and he held his arm for her. He was trying, she told herself. She did want him to try.

And she had to try too, for Mercia.

Slowly, she slipped her arm under his. He put his hand over hers and started them toward her sanctuary. They walked in silence, but there was a calm in his touch, a warmth. It wasn't the touch of a monster. She felt his eyes on her. Her breaths quickened, but she kept her eyes forward.

When they reached the hall to her sanctuary—the boundary—he stopped, turning and looking down at her. "Will you dine with me tomorrow?" he asked.

He was trying. And she would try. Slowly, she nodded.

"Good night, Salara," he said softly. Then he released her and left her to the quiet of her sanctuary.

As evening came the following day, Norah arrived in the dining room to find Mikael alone. He stood when she entered. "Salara," he greeted.

She slowed as she approached the table, looking around. "Where is the lord commander?" He always ate his dinners with the king.

"He won't be joining us anymore," he said.

Norah paused in surprise. For the commander to be sent from the king would be a heavy blow to him, but she couldn't muster any sympathy, and she couldn't deny the relief of his absence. They both took their seats at opposite ends of the table, and servants set plates of food before them.

"And I've told him he's to obey your commands as my own," he added.

She didn't know what to say. He'd given her control over the most powerful man in his kingdom, a man he loved as a brother. He'd told her he would deal with the commander. And he had. Whether the commander obeyed her—that was a different matter. But this was a good start. "Thank you," she said finally.

They ate in silence, with their eyes catching each other occasionally. The tumbling in her stomach returned, and Norah couldn't help the small smile on her lips. When they were finished, they stood.

"Can I walk you?" he asked as he moved to her end of the table and offered his arm. She slipped hers underneath, and he covered her hand in his, leading her toward her sanctuary. She was starting to like this walk.

When they reached the hall, he stopped, but he didn't let her go. "Can I take you to your door?"

A nervous flutter hit her stomach. Why was she nervous? She *did* want to bridge this gap between them, for them to be closer... She nodded.

When they reached her sanctuary door, she moved to pull her hand from his arm, but he tightened his hold, and they both stilled. His dark eyes flickered between hers, and his lips parted slightly. Then they closed, as if he were nervous too. Was he nervous? Her stomach fluttered more.

"Can I kiss you, Salara?" he asked ever so softly. He lowered his head to hers, but paused, waiting for her answer.

Her breath hitched in her chest. She wanted him to kiss her. So why couldn't she say yes? This was a harsh kingdom, and he was a harsh king. The memory of him killing the Serran envoy's guard filled her mind. He could be ruthless, and cruel. Although he wasn't cruel to her.

But that wasn't enough.

He'd given her control over the commander, she reminded herself. He'd asked her what he needed to change. For her...

His lips were so close. Her body threatened to betray her warring mind, conspiring with the gravities of the earth to pull her closer. She only needed to lift her chin.

He drew in a breath as he gave a small nod and pulled back. She'd hesitated too long, and her stomach dropped. She could still tell him yes—

"Good night, then," he said, his voice polite.

She could still tell him... "Good night," she whispered.

He turned and walked back the way they'd come.

# CHAPTER FORTY-EIGHT

The ink dried slowly on the parchment as she wrote, and Norah blew the letters dry. It had been hard to write a letter to her grandmother. She'd started over many times and still wondered if she should start again. She folded it, stamped her seal, and watched the wax harden.

The door opened, and Vitalia entered, carrying a plate of dried fruit and bread. She smiled at Norah. "Is that a letter you're sending?"

She looked at the folded parchment in her fingers. "To my grandmother." She wondered what Catherine was doing at that moment.

"Do you miss her?"

Norah did. "Salara-Mae reminds me of her."

Vitalia frowned. "So, no?"

Norah couldn't help the laugh that escaped her. It pushed the sadness away, if only for a moment. The quiet returned. "I do miss her. I wish she understood." She inhaled, trying to breathe energy back into herself and shift her mind to lighter thoughts. "I want to do something different today." She thought for a moment. "Do you think we could go to the market?"

"I doubt the lord commander would approve of that."

Norah shrugged. "The lord commander has no say." There was a freedom to the words. "And I'll take a proper guard."

"That does sound amazing." Vitalia grinned. "I'll fetch your cloak."

Norah stepped out of the castle and breathed in the winter morning. It felt good. She decided to walk through the gardens on her way to the front gates, and she smiled when she saw Bremhad tending a tall set of shrubs.

"Salara," he greeted her with a bow as she approached.

"Good morning, Bremhad."

She gazed over at the rows of small shoots that had been planted a few weeks prior. They seemed to be coming along. "I was wondering about the planter boxes under the windows outside the great hall. In my sanctuary, there's a balcony. Could you put the same there?"

"Of course, Salara. I would be happy to."

She smiled. "Thank you."

Norah's step had a new spring of life. She grinned at Vitalia as they left the walls of the castle and wandered into the busy market of the city. *Finally.* The feeling of freedom was one she'd hungered for—one that had escaped her, even in Mercia. But not any longer. She glanced over her shoulder at her guard behind her and saw Kiran didn't share her same glee. She couldn't help but be amused. Beside him was Bhastian. She didn't see him as much as the others in the Crest. A close man of the lord commander, he took duties for the brute often, no doubt spying on her for him.

Norah strolled through the market stalls, looking over the handiworks and art. She hadn't expected to garner so much attention, but all eyes were on her. Many bowed as she passed, and some smiled. No one was unkind.

"Here, taste this," Vitalia said as she held out a small red treat.

Norah put it in her mouth and laughed at the burst of sweetness. "What *is* that?" she asked.

"They're candies made from mountain berries."

"They're delicious!"

"Here." Vitalia dumped a pile into Norah's hand.

Norah laughed as they walked on. Just then, a child ran across the cobbled street, but stopped abruptly when he saw her. He stared at her, wide-eyed. She smiled and held out one of the sweets for him, but he only stood frozen. Just when she thought he might not take it, he grabbed it from her hand and ran away. She looked at Vitalia with amusement and laughed again.

A few moments later, a cluster of children came, eager to see the North Queen who was handing out treats. Bhastian scolded them, and they scampered off, but not without leaving her empty of sweets.

"I see you're already gaining favor," Vitalia told her with a grin.

Across the way, in a larger market stall, Norah noticed a beautiful sheer fabric and wandered toward it. "What is this?" she asked the woman in the stall as she ran her fingers over it. The woman answered in Kharavian tongue.

"Butterfly silk," Vitalia told her.

"From butterflies?" Norah asked incredulously.

"From the valley."

"How do I buy some?" she asked her maid in a hushed voice. "Do I need to go get money?"

"No, Salara. They'll charge the castle. Just take what you like."

The woman smiled, folding the rolls of silk and chattering excitedly. Norah didn't even know what she'd use it for, but she'd figure something out. Perhaps as a gift for her grandmother. Suddenly, Vitalia's face fell, and Norah turned, following her gaze to Captain Artem approaching.

"You can't be out here," Artem said when he reached her.

"That's not your call."

"I'm charged with your safety."

*Nice try.* "The lord commander is to take my words as Salar's. You can tell him I'll return when I'm ready."

"I don't answer to the lord commander. I answer directly to Salar."

*Wait*, Artem didn't answer to the commander?

"Your maid will collect your things," the captain said. "You'll return to the castle now."

"I'll decide what I do," Norah told him, an anger swelling inside her. If he thought he could control her like the lord commander had tried, he was mistaken.

"See her back to the castle," he ordered the guard, ignoring her.

"I'll go back when I'm ready," she snapped, sending a ripple of tension through the air.

"Salara," Kiran said softly from behind her. "I must obey."

She pushed out a breath, shaking with anger. But what could she do? "Vitalia, get the silk. It looks like we're finished shopping for today." Then she spun on her heel and turned back toward the castle, stewing in rage as she walked. She wouldn't live like this. She was salara, and she would go where she pleased.

Norah stormed through the castle and found Mikael in the library.

He stood from his chair with a concerned brow as she entered. "Are you all right?"

"You have to choose another captain," she demanded. "Or better yet, I'll use mine."

492

He stiffened. "I've already dealt with my lord commander. Now you ask me to remove my captain of the Crest?"

"Am I prisoner here?"

His brow dipped. "Of course not."

"Yet I'm still under constant watch and command."

"For your protection."

"No." She shook her head. This wasn't about protection with the captain and lord commander. It was about control. "I've accepted the stipulation of a proper guard. If I'm a prisoner, then tell me I'm a prisoner. But if I'm salara, I'll go where I please; I'll do as I please." She held the fire of her gaze firmly with Mikael's. "Am I your prisoner? Or am I salara?"

Mikael's brow dipped in concern, and he drew closer. "You're salara. I'll speak to Artem."

Norah narrowed her eyes.

"I'll speak to him," he said again. "With a proper guard, you'll go where you want and do as you please."

"Including going to the market?"

He paused but gave her a nod. "Including going to the market."

But rage still burned on her skin.

Mikael stepped in front of her. He took her hand and pulled her closer, gently, like he feared the fragility between them.

As he should.

But as his warmth danced across her skin, she feared what was between them wasn't fragile enough.

He pulled her hand to his lips and kissed the back of her fingers softly. Something stirred inside her. He was doing more than just trying for civility, more than simply fostering an alliance. Norah forgot about the market.

"Where are you going now?" he asked.

Where was she going?

"Can I walk you?"

She nodded.

Instead of offering it this time, he simply pulled her hand under the fold of his arm and covered it with his own. Then they stepped out into the hall.

Her mind seemed to return as they walked. "I'd like to discuss my men's assignment when they return from Mercia," she said.

"Your man, Titus?"

It surprised her that he remembered his name. "Yes, and others."

"I'll see your guardsmen are named to the Crest."

"Thank you," she breathed, feeling a swell of relief. "Oh, and Caspian is a captain." She'd see him assigned appropriately for his rank.

He nodded. "We will discuss him when he's healed."

This was progress.

"I hear the Bear—your lord justice—is investigating more attacks on North towns."

"Mercian towns and those under Mercia's protection. The same as the town we saw." She pursed her lips in frustration. "We still don't know who's responsible."

Mikael frowned, and she wondered what he was thinking. "You'll let me know what he finds?" he asked.

"I will."

The muscle along his jaw tightened. "Will you send him back to the North after he returns?"

She nodded reluctantly. "I do intend to," she said.

"Good." His tone held an edge of irritation, but his face lightened as their eyes met again.

They walked the rest of the way quietly, but it wasn't an uneasy quiet; it was the quiet of comfort returning. He set a slow pace, seeming to enjoy the moment, as she was. When they reached the hall, he paused. "To the door?"

"Of course."

But that distance only gave her the blink of an eye longer with him. At the door, he turned to her. His eyes seemed brighter than they usually were—lighter, almost brown.

"I must admit, when I gave you this sanctuary, I didn't expect it to be where you'd stay. I fear I regret it now."

Her pulse quickened as a worry balled in her stomach. Would he take it away from her?

"It's a place I can't follow after you, a place I can't visit without your invitation." He paused. "I want you to know I think of you... inviting me in. Often."

Her pulse raced with each of his words. She wanted to invite him in, but when she opened her mouth, the words wouldn't come. Perhaps it felt too forward, too bold, and too soon. She didn't know.

"Can I not stay with you, just a while longer?" he asked.

It wasn't a wise idea, she told herself, but she wasn't ready to part from him yet. "Just a while longer," she found herself saying.

The corners of his lips turned up.

It certainly wasn't a wise idea. She chastised herself as she opened the sanctuary door and led him in. Now she wouldn't be able to get him out. Did she want him out?

Norah poured herself a chalice of wine and drank deeply. The wine would help.

Mikael looked around the sanctuary. He smiled as he stepped closer. "What do you do in here?" he asked.

She thought about going home, thought about Alexander, thought about *him*.

"Read," she replied.

He stepped closer—close enough to touch her. His eyes moved back and forth between hers, looking deep inside her. She set the chalice down. The wine wasn't helping.

Mikael reached up and brushed a lock of hair behind her ear. She didn't pull away. His brow creased. "Salara," he said softly. "I don't know what to do. I don't know what you need from me."

His vulnerability stunned her. She swallowed and looked at the settee. "Maybe we can just sit for a while?"

Mikael let out a breath and nodded. He stepped back and sat on the lounge, and she sat beside him. A quiet hung in the air, but she felt no need to fill it. He rested his arm between them, with his hand open and palm up. An invitation.

Norah placed her hand on top of his, and he closed his fingers around it. He was asking her for closeness. She settled against him and laid her head on his shoulder—her silent reply.

# CHAPTER FORTY-NINE

Norah woke under the rays of the morning sun, lying against Mikael with his arms around her. They were still on the settee. It was late afternoon when they'd come to the sanctuary. Had they really slept through the evening and night?

She let herself nestle into the warmth of his body. He smelled like belonging—something she hadn't felt since... ever. Anywhere.

Mikael stirred, wrapping his arms tighter around her and pulling her close. "I didn't expect myself so lucky as to wake up next to you," he said.

"I didn't expect it either," she admitted. "When did you wake?"

"The middle of the night."

She pushed herself up abruptly. He'd been awake since the middle of the night?

"I didn't want to wake you. I didn't want..." His eyes were bright. "I didn't want to leave."

Her stomach fluttered. "I wouldn't have made you leave."

He smiled as he brushed a lock of her hair back over her shoulder and drew his fingers over her cheek. "But it's morning now, and I have to go for a few days to settle trade with some of the Horsemen tribes. When I return, I'd like to... talk more. Spend more time together."

"I'd like that." She needed that.

"The lord commander will be coming with me," he told her. "So he won't be a bother to you."

There was no hiding her relief. "I'm glad to hear."

"Salara, I know he's a hard man to understand. But I hope you can come to. Eventually."

She understood the commander perfectly.

He cupped her face in his hand. "I trust him above all others. He knows you're important to me, and he's loyal. I know you don't believe this, but he'll be loyal to you as well."

He was right—she didn't believe that. "I'll keep busy while you're gone," she said, changing the topic from the commander.

He smiled. Then his brow creased faintly.

"What?"

"I have something for you," he said. "Come with me."

He pulled her up from the settee and led her out of the sanctuary toward the back of the castle.

"Where are we going?" she asked.

"A place I think you'll like." He took her through several halls, outside the back of the castle, waving the Crest guard to stay inside. She couldn't help the flutter of excitement in her stomach. She let him lead her, hand in hand, down a small embankment and toward a stone building. Mikael pushed open the carved wooden door and led her inside, and Norah's breath caught in her chest.

It wasn't a simple stone building. Once through the door, the room opened into a garden conservatory. The morning sun spilled through the wall of windows on the opposite side, kissing the greenery that filled it.

In awe, Norah clasped her hands together, walking slowly into the center of the conservatory. "What is this place?" she whispered.

"My grandmother was from Japheth. But when she came to Kharav, she was overcome with the longing sickness. My grandfather built this for her."

"The longing sickness?"

"The sickness in wanting for one's home," he answered. "We were at war back then. She couldn't return. My grandfather built this place to house the green of Japheth's Colored Valley. He and a few of his best soldiers snuck into Japheth and stole greens from the royal gardens to bring here."

"That's incredible," she breathed.

"Yes, it is." He gave a small smile.

"Did it take the longing sickness away?" she asked.

"Probably not entirely, but she had a great love for it, and she was happy."

Norah breathed in deeply, closing her eyes and letting the scents and light take her away.

"Do you have the longing sickness?" he asked softly.

She missed Mercia, but longing? It wasn't that deep. Norah's stomach knotted, and guilt tugged at her heart. She still hadn't told him she'd lost her memories. She hadn't told him when he'd asked her where she had been the years she was gone. And he hadn't pressed her more. Perhaps he felt she didn't want to tell him.

"I can't bring you the North—its cliffs, its rocks, its winter," he said as he plucked a flower from the small bush beside her and stepped closer, "but this place isn't Kharav." He held the flower out for her. "And perhaps you might look to come here instead of your sanctuary. Here, where I would be able to visit you."

Norah felt a wave of emotion at his tenderness. She took the blossom from his hand and breathed in its sweet fragrance. "It's beautiful," she said.

He smiled. "So are you."

"Mikael, there's something I need to tell you." She spun the small flower between her fingers. "You once asked me where I'd been those years that I was gone from Mercia."

He stood quietly, waiting.

"The truth is, I don't know. My memories were taken in the time I was lost. I, um... I'm still trying to figure out who I am."

His brow dipped, and his lips parted. But he didn't speak.

The words just tumbled out of her. "I don't know what happened. The only thing I remember is waking in the Wild. By some miracle I was found, but then I became queen of Mercia, betrothed to King Phillip, and was expected to war against an enemy—*you*—all of whom I didn't know."

He remained silent, and her pulse quickened. She should have told him sooner. She wanted to make this marriage work—not just the marriage, but whatever it was that was growing between them—and she didn't want secrets.

"Everyone expected all these things from me. There are expectations still." She took a breath. "But I don't know what to do. I don't know what I want. I'm just trying to figure things out as I go. And all I have is how I feel."

He only stared at her, and she shrunk inside, silently begging him to say something.

500

Anything.

He let out a long breath and took her hand. Her heart beat faster.

"Maybe that's all you need," he said finally, and gave a small smile. "Salara, the woman I see knows exactly who she is and what she wants."

His words surprised her. "You're not upset I didn't tell you?"

Mikael shook his head. "I'm realizing my luck. If you hadn't lost your memories, I seriously doubt you would have wed me."

The realization hit her that he might be right. "All this time, I thought it was a curse. But now, I wonder if it's been a blessing, to help me see past emotions that would've otherwise clouded my judgment." She raised her eyes to his. "I don't want secrets between us. Not when I feel for you the way I do now."

He pulled her closer as he reached up and brushed her face, gazing down at her. "And how is it you feel?" he asked.

Norah swallowed. Why couldn't she say it?

"I hope it's the same as I feel for you," he said softly.

"You can kiss me now," she whispered.

He smiled and brought his lips to hers.

The sun cast a deceptive warmth through the windows as Soren walked through the side hall of the castle, toward the king's chamber. He'd expected Mikael at daybreak at the stable. They were to ride to the smaller Horsemen tribes of the Shoen to renew their agreements, but Mikael hadn't come.

When he reached the king's room, he was surprised to find it empty, with only Mikael's servant.

"Where is Salar?" he asked.

Vimal gave a small bow. "He joined Salara last night in her sanctuary, my lord. He's not yet returned."

Soren bristled. He turned and strode back out of the chamber, down the hall, and through the castle, toward the North Queen's sanctuary. As he turned the corner, nearing her hall, only a sentry guard stood watch, not her Crest guard. He slowed his pace; she wasn't there.

He lingered in the cross section a moment, then he turned and left the way he'd come. He wondered where he might find Salar now. Mikael had already left the queen and the sanctuary, but he hadn't headed back to his chamber.

As he crossed the center of the castle and headed toward the dining hall, something caught his eye. Two soldiers of the queen's Crest guard stood at the end of a hallway at the back of the castle, by a door leading outside. Why would the queen be outside? And without her guard? He strode toward them. "Where is the North Queen?" he called.

"In the conservatory," Bhastian answered.

"Without you?" he asked angrily but didn't give them an opportunity to answer as he pushed through the doors and stepped outside. He stalked the short way to the conservatory, but as he reached the front step, he stopped. Through the side windowpane, he saw the North Queen. *And Mikael.*

The queen stood with her back against the stone wall. Mikael held her face in his hands, cradling her as his mouth covered hers.

A chilling burn crept under his skin and to his chest, then sank like a weight into his stomach. It wasn't the kiss. It was what the kiss meant.

He slipped around the outside corner of the castle, out of sight from the conservatory, and leaned back against the stone exterior.

Soren drew in a slow breath and forced it out. He'd seen the king with other women, with his previous wives, but those marriages had been motivated by political gain and meant very little. Mikael had never loved anyone. Until now. And that was dangerous—loving the North Queen. The one threat to him. Mikael welcomed his fate.

Soren wanted blood so badly he could taste it on his tongue. He put his hand on his dagger again, curling his fingers around the hilt to settle his fury. But there was no settling.

"I don't want to leave you," Mikael said softly as he drew back from Norah's lips. "But I've kept the lord commander waiting long enough."

Norah didn't want him to leave either, but she understood. She gave him a smile. "Go on, then."

"I'll return in four days."

She nodded.

"Goodbye, Salara," he whispered, and kissed her once more. Then he stepped out the door and headed toward the castle, leaving her alone in the quiet.

Norah waited a moment, her mind in a fog. She brought her fingers to her lips. She had never imagined this life. Mikael had woken a feeling inside her she struggled to accept. It was no longer just a marriage for an alliance. She wanted to be with him. Norah smiled to herself as she stepped out of the conservatory, heading back toward the castle.

She almost didn't feel the blade as it plunged into her belly.

The second stab came in an instant, spilling a trail of blood to the ground. *Her* blood. She clutched her stomach as the red warmth saturated the front of her dress.

Norah stumbled back. What was happening? Her legs felt like they weren't her own, and they folded under her weight. She tried to catch herself as she fell, but she couldn't feel her arms. She lay on the ground, looking up at the sky. It was so gray. No clouds, just gray. She blinked as it grew darker.

"Where's the light?" she asked the hands that grabbed her.

But there came only darkness.

# CHAPTER FIFTY

Soren heard the door to the conservatory open and peered around the wall to see Mikael stepping out, leaving the queen inside and heading toward the stables. He leaned back against the stone in the recess and waited. The king would be looking for him now.

He gripped the dagger at his side. Blood settled him. Blood created fear, and fear gave him control. But he wasn't in control now, and no amount of blood would solve that.

His skin burned with hate. The Battle of Bahoul felt like a lifetime ago, but when he thought of everything he'd lost, everything the Northmen had taken from him, it was as if it had happened yesterday. His mother, his brother, his sister. His father. His land. Now to have the North Queen in Kharav, as his salara... this he couldn't accept. And Salar had changed. He saw it—Mikael's love for her.

But Mikael refused to see this madness. Even with the visions that foretold his fall, he chose the North Queen. And he gave her everything she asked, everything he thought she wanted. He even protected the Bear, the man that would bring his own end, all because she asked it of him.

He watched his breath in the winter air. When he heard the conservatory door open again, he knew it was the queen. He delayed, waiting for her to go back into the castle. He'd rather not face her either. But it wasn't the sound of the castle doors he heard as he waited for the queen to go inside. Footsteps rang out—someone running. He peered around the corner again and saw a man fleeing around the conservatory and into the thick of trees behind.

Then he saw the queen.

Something was wrong.

She stood, looking down. From her stomach, blood spilled down the fabric of her gown to the ground below. She stared at her hands, swaying. Then she staggered forward and collapsed.

"Bhastian!" Soren thundered as he raced to her side. He dropped to his knees beside her, covering her stomach with his hands to stop the bleeding. Bhastian and another Crest guard tore through the doors at his call and looked at him in alarm.

"A man!" he barked at them. "He's gone into the wood. Go!"

They raced after.

"North Queen," he said, his worry rising. "North Queen!" But she didn't respond. He pulled her into his arms and carried her into the castle. "Healer!" he bellowed, drawing another wave of guards. "Get the healer! And Salar!"

He carried the queen down the hall and up the stairs, toward her sanctuary. The queen's maid met him halfway down and gasped when she saw them. Then she spun around and ran ahead to prepare the room.

Soren made his way into the chamber, carefully bringing her through the door, and laid her on the bed. Her blood covered him, running down his stomach and soaking into his breeches, which now stuck to his skin. He pressed his hands back over her stomach to slow the flow.

"North Queen!" he called to her again. He held pressure on her wounds with one hand as he checked her pulse with the other. Her heart still beat, but faintly. He pressed the wound tighter. Never had he thought he'd wish the North Queen to live.

It seemed to take an eternity for the healer to arrive. He was breathless from the run and started looking over the queen's body, measuring the extent of her injuries.

"Are you blind?" Soren snapped. Fuck the four kingdoms—this healer would need a healer of his own if he didn't get to it.

"I see it, I see it," the healer said quickly, and pulled some shears from his bag. He quickly cut away the gown.

Mikael thundered into the room, his eyes wide and his face etched in horror. In seeing the queen, his face twisted in anger, and his eyes burned. He rushed to her side. "What happened?" he raged.

"She was attacked," Soren told him. "Outside the conservatory."

"Who was it?"

Soren shook his head, still holding pressure to the queen's stomach. "I didn't see. Bhastian and the Crest are after him."

The healer stepped beside Soren and motioned him to loosen his hold. Soren eyed him skeptically, then raised his hands and stepped back. Blood seeped from the wounds again, and the healer quickly covered them and reapplied pressure. He mumbled some unintelligible words to his assistant, who dug in his pack for more tools. Soren's agitation grew. If this healer let her die...

"What of it?" Mikael urged the old man from the other side of the bed. "How bad is it?"

The healer shook his head. "Wounds to the abdomen are extremely dangerous. I can stitch her, but I have no way of knowing the damage inside."

"Will she live?"

"I don't know," the old man replied.

Mikael's nostrils flared. "She'd better, or you'll join her." He sank down beside the North Queen as the healer worked, his fingers on her cheek. He looked up at Soren, his eyes rimmed red. "Brother," he said hoarsely. "Bring me the man who did this."

Mikael's emotion for this woman knifed him. But he gave a stiff nod and turned to his mission. There was a man in Kharav that thought he could take what belonged to Salar. And Soren would see him dead.

# CHAPTER FIFTY-ONE

The thunder of galloping horses shook the ground as Alexander rode through the gates of the dark castle of the Shadowlands, surrounded by Shadow soldiers. He'd pushed the pace hard in returning. They slowed only to rest their horses and sleep for a short stretch each night, but Alexander hadn't slept. When the Shadow soldiers had found him, they'd said only that Norah had been injured, nothing more. It was this unknown that pushed him harder.

Part of him wondered if Norah might not be injured at all. Perhaps it was a ploy to draw him back into the hold of his enemy. It didn't matter. He would come.

He drove his mount beyond the courtyard and up the stairs to the iron-barred doors, not waiting until his horse stopped before sliding to the ground. Shadow soldiers left their mounts in the courtyard but tailed after him as he tore into the castle and raced up the stairs toward Norah's sanctuary. When he reached the alcove of the door, a sword rose to meet him, its point hitting just above his breastplate at his throat, stopping him in his tracks.

At its hilt—the Destroyer.

The dark-eyed beast of a man pushed him back into the hall with the tip of the blade.

"I want to see her," Alexander demanded.

A deep vibration came from the Destroyer's chest—a chuckle. "I'm sure you do." His face was covered, but his eyes burned with hate. "I knew you'd come."

Alexander stepped back and put his hand on the hilt of his own sword. For a moment, he dared to feel the slightest hope—perhaps it was a trap, and Norah wasn't hurt. "Where is she?"

"Let him enter," the Shadow King's voice called from inside her sanctuary.

The Destroyer's eyes darkened through the slit of his wrap. He dropped the tip of his sword and took a reluctant step back.

Alexander's breath quaked. This wasn't a ploy of the Destroyer, and now he wished more than anything it had been. Norah had been hurt. Was she inside her chamber? Why wasn't it her voice that called him?

Alexander pushed past him and pressed into the room, where the king stood at the foot of the bed. In its center, Norah lay as pale as the moon. Her cheeks lacked the color of her spirit—they lacked the color of life.

Fear gripped him. His heart dropped like a rock in his chest. He forgot about the king; he forgot about the Shadowlands. They didn't matter anymore. If Norah was gone, nothing mattered anymore.

Alexander moved to the edge of the bed, his soul cold, desperation writhing within him. His hand trembled as he reached out and grazed the bottom of her cheek. He turned her face toward him. The faintest of breaths whispered across his palm, and it flooded him with emotion.

*She was alive.*

He blinked back the tears welling in his eyes as he dropped down beside her. "Norah," he whispered. But she didn't answer. "I'm here." He cupped his hand against her cheek, silently begging for her to open her eyes. But she only lay on the cusp of death underneath his touch. "Norah," he whispered again through his teeth. His breath shook and his eyes brimmed. "Come back to me." He pulled her hand to his lips and kissed her fingers.

Her skin burned with the fire of fever, and her brow was damp; a cloth and basin rested on a small table beside the bed. He drew his hand back to her face and let his thumb graze her lips. A light salve covered them, keeping the skin from chapping. Her hair was clean and brushed, and a blanket lay over her. She was cared for. But it wasn't enough.

He was suddenly aware of the king's eyes on him. He had revealed himself—his heart—but he was too angry to care.

If Norah died...

The king's gaze was still on him. Alexander straightened and stood, and his anger grew to a fury. An all-consuming fury. He'd kill this king—for everything he'd done, but especially for this. He'd kill him.

Now.

Alexander ripped his sword free. The Destroyer lunged forward, but with a blind rage, Alexander kicked him back against the door. Then he went for the Shadow King. The king was without a sword, but he blocked Alexander's attack with the armor of his forearm. Alexander knocked him back against the wall and swept his sword to his neck, but in turn, Alexander felt the tip of the king's dagger at his own. They both stood with their blades to each other's throats.

"You were supposed to keep her safe!" Alexander seethed. "This is your kingdom. She's in your care. This is your doing!"

In the darkness of the Shadow King's eyes swirled emotion that Alexander couldn't read. Sadness? Guilt? Shame? He should feel all those things. And now he'd feel death. But before Alexander killed him, he had to know. "What happened?" he demanded.

Still, the king didn't answer.

Alexander bared his teeth, his rage growing. "What happened?" he demanded.

"Alexander," came a faint whisper behind him. He jerked his head back to Norah, forgetting the king.

Her head moved weakly, but her eyes remained closed. She inhaled deeply, wincing.

Alexander released the king and was back to her side in an instant, taking her hand and pulling it to his cheek. "I'm here," he said.

The Shadow King moved to her other side.

Her eyelids fluttered open, weakly. Then she saw Alexander. "You're back," she said with the faintest of breaths. Her face held only the whisper of a smile, but it lit the room.

He nodded. "I came as soon as I heard."

She blinked slowly. "What happened?"

"You were attacked," the Shadow King told her.

*Attacked.* Alexander's rage returned, but Norah's voice stopped him before he spoke.

"Is there water?" she asked.

The king's eyes moved past Alexander, and Alexander turned to see a back table in the room, behind the Destroyer, where a pitcher and glass sat. The beast of a man still stood with his sword in hand, ready for a fight. Finally, he turned with a protesting rumble and poured the water.

He eyed Alexander with dark contempt before reluctantly stepping to him and handing him the glass.

The king put an arm behind Norah and helped her sit up, sending a ripple of fire through Alexander. But he knelt beside her and held the water to her lips. She took a few gulps, coughing in between and wincing again in pain.

"Easy," Alexander told her.

She took a few more sips, more careful this time. When she'd had her fill, the king laid her back against the pillows on the bed. Alexander held the glass back out to the Destroyer, who scowled at him murderously underneath his wrap. But he took the glass and set it back on the table.

"Who did this?" Alexander asked the king. He would kill them too.

The king was silent.

"Do you even have him?" he asked angrily. "The man responsible?"

"Of course we have him," the king said defensively, finally speaking.

"Who is it?" he asked again.

"The brother of one of my previous wives."

*Previous wives*? How does one have previous wives? His eyes blazed at the king.

"Avenging her honor, no doubt," Norah said weakly. "Her family's honor. They've been humiliated with the annulments."

Annulments? The king had had other marriages? Alexander glared at him with an indicting fury. All of this was his fault—everything that had happened. He looked back to Norah. Her sympathy, her compassion, her understanding—they had always amazed him, even now, as she lay near death. But he couldn't find compassion within himself for the attacker or this king.

"I want to speak to him," she said. Her voice came at barely a whisper, yet it still managed to take them all aback.

"That's not a wise idea," the king said to her.

"He tried to kill you," Alexander added to the argument. "What is there to say?"

Norah turned her head to the king. "I want to speak to him," she said again.

"Your fever hasn't even broken," the king replied. "You need to rest and heal before you do anything." As much as he hated it, Alexander nodded his agreement with him.

She swallowed, struggling with her words. "Promise me you'll let me speak to him, that you won't kill him."

The Shadow King's face remained hard and disapproving. "Rest," he said, "and I give you my word I won't kill him before you speak to him."

Norah nodded faintly and leaned back, closing her eyes to sleep again.

Days fell away, and Norah finally found herself able to sit up without assistance. She didn't remember the attack, and for once, she was appreciative. Her skin was healing, but an internal ache still lingered. She forewent the drink of herbs offered by the healer to relieve it. There was something between Alexander and the king, a new animosity, and she didn't want the fog of pain medicines as she tried to understand what was happening.

Mikael sat with her often, not saying much, but his presence calmed her. He brought her books and anything else he could think of that might help her pass the time.

The cool air of morning hung around her as she sat in bed for yet another day. Vitalia brought a tray of breakfast as Mikael took what had become his regular place in the bedside chair.

"How is Salara-Mae?" she asked him.

He rocked his head back in slight surprise. "She's been worried about you."

Norah tried not to move as a chuckle escaped her.

"I think she's secretly starting to like you," he said.

"She likes me more than she likes the lord commander."

He nodded. "That she does."

"Why does she dislike him so much?" That was a silly question, perhaps. There were no redeeming qualities about the brute. Quite the opposite. But the commander was fiercely loyal to the king—had saved him, protected him—how could a mother not appreciate that?

"I don't know. She always has. From the moment she saw him."

A knock rattled the door and Alexander stepped inside. Mikael stiffened.

"Lord Justice," she greeted. His presence in Kharav brought a thick tension, but she still couldn't help her happiness each time she saw him.

"Queen Norah." He didn't acknowledge the king. "I came to see if you needed anything. Or if you wanted to write a letter. I'm sending word back to Mercia with news of your health."

"Yes, I'd like to write a letter." She moved with a start. "I completely forgot. What about the towns you went to investigate? Did you find anything? Who attacked them?"

Alexander shook his head. "We found nothing. Only the aftermath. Whoever it was, it's like they had disappeared."

His words drew Mikael's interest. "Where was this?" the king asked.

Alexander eyed him as if loathing the thought of speaking words to him. "East of Bahoul."

Mikael looked at Norah. "Not far from the town we saw destroyed. Same offenders, no doubt."

Norah felt her stomach turn, remembering.

"You found nothing?" Mikael asked Alexander.

"Same as you, I believe," he replied coolly, but there was a knife to it.

The king sat calmly, but his nostrils flared. "Did you really expect me to properly investigate an attack against the North as I launched my own?"

"What about now that you're wed to Mercia's queen?" Alexander's voice held an icy air. "Do you care? Or is your protection of Mercia the same as your protection of her queen?"

Mikael bristled and moved to stand.

"I'm ready to speak to him," Norah said, drawing their attention away from the argument, and from each other. "The man who attacked me. I want to see him."

Both men stared at her.

Mikael rose. "I'm going to execute him."

Alexander's gaze snapped to the king with the same surprise as Norah's, although he didn't object.

But that wasn't what Mikael had promised. "You said I could speak to him," she said, frustrated.

"Which is why I haven't taken his head yet."

"He attacked *me*, and it's *me* he should answer to."

"But will you make him answer?" Mikael asked, his eyes burning. "Will you punish him, Salara?"

Norah looked down at the lining of the blanket as she pleated it between her fingers. Punishing someone would be difficult for her, regardless of the crime. "When can I see him?"

"As soon as you're well enough."

"I'm well enough now."

Mikael's lips thinned, then he gave a reluctant nod. "Then you can see him in the courtyard, before he's executed."

He would force her hand. She glanced at Alexander, but there was still no objection in his face.

The knot in Norah's stomach grew. She needed to see her attacker, look into his eyes, hear his defense if he bothered to give one. She wasn't sure if she could execute him, but if she didn't, Mikael would. Would he think her weak? What about the people of Kharav?

And what would she think of herself?

Bhastian pushed Norah in a wheeled chair outside to the courtyard. Vitalia walked beside her, followed by the rest of Norah's guard. Mikael required more of them now—an army everywhere she went. They were suffocating, but this wasn't the time to complain about her guard. Things would return to normal eventually.

The sun sat low, close to the horizon, spilling colors of blood across the sky. Fitting. A crowd had gathered ahead in the courtyard, and it unsettled her stomach. "Stop here," she said.

Bhastian brought the chair to a halt. "Is everything all right?"

"Help me up," she said to Vitalia. "I want to walk the rest of the way."

"Salara," her maid protested. "You're still healing."

"I said help me up."

Her maid sighed disapprovingly but stepped to help her as she was bid.

"Let me," Bhastian said, coming forward and gently scooping his hands under her arms to help her stand. She didn't want his help. He was loyal to the commander, was someone the brute trusted, which meant she couldn't trust *him*. But she did need the help.

Norah winced in pain, forcing herself to inhale and exhale until it subsided to an ache.

"Salara," he said as he stepped around the chair to her side, trying to encourage her to abandon her effort.

"Just give me your arm," she panted.

Bhastian looked around, clearly unhappy with her decision, but he held out his arm for support. She looped her hand through it, steadying herself.

Carefully, they continued forward, arms locked, unhurried.

The crowd parted as they drew near. She spotted Alexander. His face was full of disapproval. He started forward to meet her, but she shook her head to stop him. Mikael shot her an objecting look as well, but he said nothing. Out of anyone, he knew the importance of the perception of strength with power.

Her attacker was on his knees, his arms bound behind him. What she didn't expect to see were others with him—a woman, a boy, and an older couple. The younger woman wept. Norah looked at her closer. She knew this woman.

It was one of Mikael's previous wives.

Norah had seen her at the celebration when she first arrived in Kharav, only Norah hadn't known who she was then. She suspected the older man and woman to be their parents, and the boy a younger brother perhaps. They all knelt, bound, with their heads down. Why were they here?

Norah looked at Mikael in dismay. "What's the meaning of this?" she demanded.

He said nothing, but his eyes were dark, his intentions written on every crease of his face. He was going to execute them *all*. A wave of horror flooded her.

"North Queen," her attacker called out to her. "I beg you. Please spare my family! Myral. My mother, my father, my brother. They had no part in my doing. I acted alone. Please!"

Norah found herself clutching on to Bhastian as she gaped at them. *Myral*. Yes. That was the woman's name.

"North Queen," Myral cried. "I've spoken harsh words against you. But my parents and younger brother are innocent." The woman swallowed back a sob. "Please, spare them!"

Norah could only stare at the woman. The knot in her throat choked her voice. Norah had required the annulments. She was the outsider who'd come and turned the wives away from a life they had known, a life of status and privilege. How could she fault this woman just for speaking against her?

"Please, North Queen," her attacker begged, and she turned her eyes back to him.

Mikael stepped forward, seeming to grow even larger as he readied to give his judgment. Her heart hammered in her chest. He was going to kill them.

She let go of Bhastian's arm and willed herself to stand on her own. "I'm not the North Queen," she called out. "I am Salara."

Mikael stopped, and she felt his attention on her.

Her attacker nodded desperately. "Yes, of course, Salara."

"What's your name?" she asked him.

"Amet, Salara," he said quickly.

"And you sought to avenge your sister?"

Amet fought back the tears and nodded his head. "Yes, Salara," he said. "To avenge my family's dishonor."

"It's you who dishonor your family, by attacking your salara, and without the decency of a challenge." She paused, unable to say the words, unable to speak his fate. But she had to. "I can't let you live," she managed to get out.

The man nodded, weeping.

*Quickly*, she told herself. She needed to be quick to save the rest of them. Her eyes moved back to Myral. "But you. I forgive your words, and I won't seek further justice, against you or your family."

Amet and his sister gasped in relief, crying in appreciation.

Norah glanced back at Mikael, and rage rippled across his brow. His lips parted, flashing his teeth. She'd pardoned them publicly. Would he overrule her with his own judgment?

Urgency clawed at her. "Remove them," she ordered the guards. She didn't want Amet's family to see his fate, and if she could get them away before Mikael acted on the threat in his eyes...

The guards grabbed the family and dragged them from the courtyard. Myral let out a cry but didn't resist. *Gentler*, Norah wanted to call out, but Mikael's fury grew with each passing moment, and she just wanted them gone. Away.

Mikael watched as they were dragged from the courtyard. He didn't stop them, but his need for retribution hung heavy in the air. She gave into it, nodding to the punisher. Amet resigned himself to his fate as the steel blade came for his life. Blood sprayed across the cobblestone. Even though she knew it was coming, she couldn't help but flinch.

A sickening calm settled over the courtyard.

Norah clutched her stomach tightly. Her lip trembled, but not from the crippling pain she gritted her teeth against. She had to get away from the death, away from this place, away from Mikael. She moved back toward her chair with as much calm as she could muster, but she thought she might not make it.

"Salara," Bhastian's voice came behind her. "Let me carry you. You can't walk."

She shook her head. "No," she breathed through the pain, "just help me back."

He took her arm and walked her back, and she sank thankfully into the chair when she reached it. Then he pushed her back to the castle.

Back in her chamber, Norah let Bhastian and Vitalia help her into the bed, where the healer busied himself with checking her wounds.

Mikael entered, standing back and waiting as Norah was tended to. She refused to look at him. He was angry, she knew. But she was angry too. He would kill an entire family...

The healer gave a nod when he was finished. "The wounds are fine," he told her. "But you need to be more careful until you're healed."

The healer and Vitalia gave a bow and left her to Mikael. She could feel the burn of his gaze, but she still couldn't look at him. "Those people were innocent," she said. She couldn't keep her voice from shaking. "They didn't need to die."

"They did," he replied with cold gravel in his voice. "They did so that everyone would know what happens to those who threaten you. *You* could have died."

She snapped her gaze to his. "But I didn't!"

"But now they know you're weak."

"Mercy isn't weakness!" she spat back.

"Fear is!" His nostrils flared, and his brow dropped low. "You didn't spare them with mercy! You spared them because you couldn't stomach their blood." He drew back. "And I'm weak for letting you."

He left her alone in the wake of his anger.

# CHAPTER FIFTY-TWO

"Is the pain gone?" Alexander eyed her as they sat at the small table in her sanctuary.

Norah drew in a long breath and nodded. "For the most part." It wasn't exactly a lie. Two weeks had passed since she'd been stabbed outside the conservatory behind the castle. Her flesh had healed over, and the physical pain was gone. It was her heart that hadn't yet healed. While Mikael no longer seemed angry, things were different between them. They still hadn't reconciled.

Vitalia set a tray of tea and fruits in front of them. This was how they had started taking breakfast—with Alexander stopping by each morning and sitting with Norah as the sun poured through the windows. She liked him near. While tension remained high, his presence kept Mikael at a distance, something she needed, or thought she needed.

So easily the king killed, without thought and without regret. That scared her.

He scared her.

And yet... something seemed missing without him. And his absence spiraled her further into self-loathing. Who was she if she could look past this darkness? And what would she be for her people if she couldn't?

Alexander waited until she finished before taking anything to eat for himself, as he usually did. She left the dried figs, as she usually did. She knew they were his favorite.

"This came for you this morning," he said, breaking the quiet as she chased down the last bite of her biscuit with a drink of tea. He pulled a letter from inside his coat and set it on the table. Norah froze. The folded parchment held a silver seal. Catherine's seal.

She only stared at it, unmoving. It was the first letter her grandmother had sent. "What does it say?"

Alexander shook his head. "I don't know."

Norah leaned back in her chair. She had prayed her grandmother would write. Letter after letter she'd sent with nothing in return. But now, now that she was full of self-doubt, her grandmother was the last person she wanted a letter from. Catherine abhorred her marriage to the Shadow King, seeing him as the great evil. Maybe she looked to remind Norah of that now, to tell her how this wouldn't work. And maybe she was right.

"Will you not read it?" he asked.

"So she can shame me? Tell me I've made a terrible mistake and how this will all fail?" She couldn't take it. Not when she truly felt like she was failing.

"She wouldn't do that."

Norah cast him an unbelieving eye.

"I've been keeping her informed of your health. I'm sure she's sick with worry for you." He waited for her eyes to meet his. "Read it, Norah."

She picked up the letter, feeling the heavy parchment between her fingers. "I will. Just not right now." She stood and stepped to the vanity and slipped it inside the small wooden letter box on top. "How is your brother? Have you heard from him?"

He snorted. "Yes. About how unfair it is I won't let him come to the Shadowlands."

She smiled.

"He asks of you. I've told him you're well."

She nodded. It wasn't exactly untrue. "If I write him a letter, will you make sure it gets to him?"

"Of course." He paused for a moment, then said, "There is something else. I have a task from the council. I need to leave for a while."

She frowned as she sat back down at the table. "What kind of task?"

"Nothing I want to bother you with. You have enough on your mind. I shouldn't delay, but I'll wait until Caspian and Titus have returned."

She supposed she should be thankful for the opportunity to send him away from the Shadowlands for a while. The tension between him and Mikael had only grown since her attack. She should have sent him home to Mercia, but she couldn't. Perhaps this task was what she needed to force herself into action. He needed to go. But he wouldn't leave if he feared for her.

"I have an entire army guarding me now," she told him. It was the closest she could get in assuring him to leave.

He snorted. "Of Shadowmen."

"There are good men here, Alexander." She thought of Kiran. If not any others, at least one of them was good.

"Regardless, I don't want to leave you again."

She didn't want him to leave either. He'd just returned a short time ago from investigating the attacks on Mercian towns. "I'll be here when you return."

Finally, he nodded.

"How long will you be gone?"

"Only a couple weeks."

Too long. She nodded sadly and took another drink of her tea.

Norah made her way down the long hall of the castle to the library in the far wing, with an entourage of guards behind her. While her stomach wounds had healed over, the lengthy walk brought an aching stitch deep within. At least she didn't have to go out into the winter to a separate building like in Mercia.

As she walked, she looked out through the windows at a narrow garden area with a thin pool in the center. It had wintered over, and its greenery had been cut back to the ground, but it would be beautiful when it came to life in the spring. On the other side of the garden ran another windowed hall, parallel to her own, and she stopped when she saw Mikael. He was speaking to an older man from his Circle, Kharav's council. The man noticed her, and Mikael turned, with his eyes now on her. They stood a moment, their stares caught through the windows until she broke away and started forward again.

From the corner of her eye, she saw the king part from his councilman and walk down his own hall, keeping pace with her. Norah cursed under her breath. She would see him around the corner, where the halls met and became one. She could turn back—an appealing option. But she continued.

She came to the end of the windows and paused against the stone before turning the corner. She could still turn back...

And awkwardly shuffle through the army behind her...

And make it even more difficult when she next saw the king.

*No.* She pushed out a breath and turned the corner.

Mikael stood waiting where the halls joined before stretching to the library. "Salara," he greeted her when she reached him. "I almost thought you'd turned back."

"I thought about it," she confessed.

His head gave a slight nod, and his eyes grazed the ground. "Are you going to the library?"

There was no denying it. The library spanned the entire wing; there was no other reason she'd be there. "I am."

"As am I."

She tilted her head in feigned amusement. "How coincidental."

They walked side by side under the arched hall. Columns of stone rose to meet at the center above their heads and bounced the light with a majestic air. No matter how many times she walked this hall, she never grew tired of its beauty.

"It's good to see you out," he said.

It was good to be out, but she said nothing.

They reached the carved doors of the library—another sight that always overwhelmed her. Mikael could stand a man on his shoulders, and they still wouldn't touch the top. But Mikael wasn't looking at the doors; he was looking at her.

She shifted uncomfortably, searching her mind for how to part. "Did you have something to find here?" she asked, prompting him on his way.

But he gave a small frown. "No."

She could only stare at him. "Then why did you come?"

"To be with you."

Norah's breath faltered. These were the moments that made her want him near, that made her forget about everything else.

He stepped closer. Her hand hung at her side, and he brushed it softly with his own, testing. The warmth of his touch seeped into her skin, creeping its way up her arm and through her body. So little time they'd spent alone the past several days. Her anger had been driving her mind, almost making her forget his effect. Almost.

She didn't pull away.

"I don't like how things have been between us," he said. "Tell me how to fix it."

He wanted to fix it? But she didn't know how. They came from completely different worlds.

"Please, Salara. Tell me."

She shook her head. "I can't live like this, with this violence. Or with you thinking I'm weak because I value human life."

His eyes moved back and forth between hers. "I don't think you're weak."

"But that's what you said."

"I was afraid."

She stilled.

He drew closer. "I was afraid because I'd been so close to losing you." Ever so gently, he pulled her hand up to his face, cupping her fingers against his cheek and kissing her palm. "I can't lose you."

In front of the world, he was cold and dark, threatening. He was the Shadow King. Impossible to love. But with her, the darkness fell away. He was Mikael. Impossible to hate.

She shook her head. "Don't do that."

He frowned. "Don't do what?"

"Don't make me stop being angry at you. I need to be angry." If she wasn't angry, then she would be accepting of the darkness, and she couldn't be accepting.

A low rumble came from his chest. "Have you not been angry long enough?"

"No!" Him trivializing her emotion only brought it to the surface again. These things were serious. People's lives were serious.

His brow bent. "Will it be forever?" His words came at barely a whisper. It wasn't patronizing but a question steeped in longing and worry. And it disarmed her.

"Just longer" was all she could manage to get out. Except there was no *longer*. Any anger she'd struggled to hang on to slipped from her grasp.

"All right," he whispered.

She let out a breath, and an ease came between them again. There was a rawness about him now, a vulnerability. And he was still so close. His warmth permeated her barriers and pulled her in. She found herself leaning in, and he dropped his head to hers.

But she put a firm hand on his chest. "No."

He stopped. His lips were so close to hers, but they didn't touch. Then he nodded, relenting.

"I can't trust you," she whispered. "It makes me afraid."

And while she told herself she was afraid of him, it wasn't just him. She feared herself. This wasn't about who Mikael was. This was about who she was—something that still escaped her. Could she be who she wanted and still feel for this man?

His mouth opened to speak, but no words came. His eyes searched hers. "I'm salar. These aren't easy decisions for me."

His brow stitched, and she leaned back. "Really? Because they seem to come quite easily. And I'm salara. They're my decisions too." She paused, trying to slow the sudden rush of frustration. "You don't rule alone."

He quieted again.

"You have to talk to me," she told him, "before you act. We decide together."

He nodded again. "I can do that."

*He could do that.* She softened. That wouldn't solve all their problems, but if he talked to her...

A calm returned, and her spirits rose. She'd missed him, and to be near him again, to have gained some understanding between them, relieved her. They continued through the library.

Mikael followed her, holding her selection of books as she pulled them from the shelves.

"Do you need all these?" he asked. "You can always come back for more."

She gave a small shrug of her shoulders. "Then I'd have to come back every day."

"I wouldn't mind." He took her hand, stopping her and shifting to a more serious note between them. "I want to see you every day. I want to be near you. Every day."

She swallowed back the words on her tongue, the words that would have said she wanted the same. Because she did. "I'm finished," she said softly.

Mikael waved her guard back and away as they stepped out into the hall. They walked toward her sanctuary—slowly, quietly—with him at her side, carrying her books. She couldn't deny she preferred Mikael to her army entourage.

"Your lord justice left this morning," he said, picking back up their conversation.

Norah bit the inside of her cheek. "You keep a close eye on him."

"His every move."

His tone chilled her. She silently praised the Mercian council for whatever task they had for Alexander—anything to get him away from Kharav for a while. She cursed her selfishness in keeping him near. When he returned, she'd have to send him back to Mercia.

Norah glanced outside, across the courtyard, and saw the man Mikael had been speaking to earlier still standing in the parallel hall. "Is he waiting for you?"

"Yes. But he can wait a little longer."

"You should go," she said. "I'm sure there are many important things for you to tend to."

"Nothing is more important than being here with you, right now."

She couldn't help a small smile to herself.

They reached the hall to her sanctuary, and she took her books from him.

"Thank you," she said softly.

"Of course." He brought her hand to his lips and pressed a gentle kiss against her fingers. Then he left to return to his waiting Circle.

# CHAPTER FIFTY-THREE

Mikael was waiting in the dining room when Norah arrived. Instead of at the end of the table opposite her, his plate and chalice sat to the left of her own. She raised a brow and bit back her smile. She liked that he threw out rules and proprieties to be near to her.

He pulled her chair out for her and waited.

Norah couldn't hold the hint of a smile any longer. "Thank you," she said as she took her seat.

Mikael took his own chair and set to work moving food to their plates from a large center platter.

"The king plays the servant this evening?" she asked.

"Every evening if you want, so long as you're here." The corner of his mouth turned up. "Does it win me favor?"

"Maybe a little," she admitted with a wry smile. But then her smile fell, and her seriousness returned. "But it's not what I want, you know."

His face grew solemn. "I know." He poured wine into their chalices and raised his to his lips but didn't drink. He set it back down. "I'll continue to disappoint you, Salara. We're very different, you and I."

She stared at him for a moment. "Or maybe we're two imperfect people in an imperfect world, fighting for the good of our kingdoms."

His eyes met hers. "Can we fight for each other?" he asked softly.

*Fight for each other.* Not just for an alliance, but *for each other.* She felt the soft knocking at her heart.

They ate quietly, exchanging reassuring glances. When they were finished, he stood and offered his arm, as she expected. She took it and let him walk her back to the sanctuary. The returning ease between them brought back a comfort she'd missed.

When they reached the alcove, she stopped and turned to him. Mikael pulled her closer, threading his fingers in hers. He smelled of smoky earth and lemon thyme, and she breathed him in. His touch, his warmth... "Stay," she found herself saying.

His lips parted in surprise, and he nodded.

Norah led him inside the sanctuary, where he waited for her cue. She wavered. "I didn't mean... intimately."

He nodded again.

She wondered if he could hear the lie on her lips, but she couldn't allow herself that tonight. Not yet. Her mind wandered back to what she'd once told Tahla—that she'd only hoped for friendship with Mikael, to be strong allies.

That wasn't true.

She wanted more between them.

But she hadn't given herself to him since their wedding, and they seemed to be different people now. Different people who needed to make this step forward again, as if it were the first time. But before that could happen, she needed them fully well, and for that, she needed more time, with him. She needed them to be closer.

They stood in the candlelit silence.

"Can I simply sleep beside you tonight?" he asked.

Sleep. She needed sleep. But she didn't know if she trusted him. She didn't know if she trusted herself.

But she wanted him to stay, and she nodded.

He reached back, between his shoulders, and pulled his shirt over his head and then sloughed off his boots. Then he lay on the bed under the quilts with his arm stretched out to his side.

She glanced down at her dress. A nightgown would be more comfortable, but she had absolutely no intention of changing clothes with him so close, even in the side bath chamber.

Norah sat on the edge of the bed and then shuffled back and under the quilts. She laid her head on his outstretched arm, and he pulled her close to him. The heat from his body seeped into her, quieting her shiver. She let his nearness calm her, and she closed her eyes in the warmth of his being.

Then she drifted into dreams.

When Norah opened her eyes again, it was morning. Mikael lay beside her, his breaths long and rhythmic. She'd slept deeply, feeling safe, feeling right. Was this right?

She shifted back, careful not to wake him, and propped her head on her elbow. He lay on his back, and she gazed over the patterned skin of his chest and torso. It wasn't often she was free to simply look at him, to study him. Close and unhurried.

At the base of his throat, shoulder to shoulder, spanned a thick collar of inked design. Overlapping shapes like plated spears edged the top, with hanging banners like the night sky. The color of his skin created an image against the black, resembling the peaked arches of the kingdom's architecture. She reached out and drew her fingertips across it. She liked this one. He bore the only one like it. The other designs were the same as those of the lord commander—the braided motif on his right chest and the banding that ran to his right shoulder around a ring of mountains centered by a sun against a black circle. This one she didn't like. Without thinking, she scratched at it with her fingernail.

"They don't come off," he said, his eyes still closed.

She bit her lip.

"You don't like my markings?"

"Not this one," she admitted. "It's the same as the lord commander's."

He opened his eyes and turned his head toward her, inhaling a waking breath. "It's when we fled Bahoul," he said.

She ran her fingernail over the ring of mountains.

"To Kharav," he added to his story as she made her way along the design. Her fingers grazed the sun. "And I became salar. It's Soren's story too. It's why he bears the same."

"He has a black sun. Yours is the color of your skin against a black circle."

"Because I'm salar. My skin is the sun."

Norah drew her brows together. "Why a sun?"

"That's what *salar* means."

She almost laughed. "The Shadow King is called the Sun?"

"Yes," he said, giving a small smile. "As are you. *Salara.*"

She drew her hand back to the design across the top of his chest.

"It's called a khlavik," he said. "The mark of salar."

She traced the patterned bands circling down his arm, admiring the intricate detail. "What do these mean?"

"Histories of our people, duties, my purpose," he said.

She brushed a bare space on his left chest. "There's nothing here."

"It's not finished." He was quiet for a moment. "I'd saved it for Mercia's defeat, but instead it will be the story of you becoming my salara. I haven't gotten it yet because I was waiting for the right time. I wanted you to be there."

"To get the marking?"

He nodded.

This was important to him, she knew. And what was important to her was that he was letting her in. It was more than just his words now, more than just his touch. He was building her into his story, giving her a piece of him.

"Are you sure that's what you want?" she asked. "I mean, maybe you should think about it more." She tilted her head slightly as the corner of her mouth turned up. "It doesn't come off."

He chuckled as he rolled to his side. "I've been thinking about it ever since you agreed to wed me in Aviron." His eyes shone brightly in the light of the morning. "Will you come with me, Salara?"

"I'll come," she said softly.

He smiled.

"What will it look like?" Norah asked as they walked past the gardens and toward a large temple. It had been two days since he'd told her he wanted to write their story in ink, and that was where they were headed now.

"I don't know. We go to Salta Tau, and the Gift will show her the story and give her the image for my body."

"Salta Tau?"

"Mastera of the ink." He stopped and took her hand. "This is very special. It's a ceremony, a long one. Soren will be there, and my mother."

She nodded. She could tolerate the lord commander for a time, so long as she didn't have to speak to him. Or look at him. Or acknowledge his presence.

They reached the temple, and he led her through a series of halls back to a large open chamber. As he'd said, Salara-Mae was there, as was the lord commander. They stood on opposite sides of the chamber from each other. In the center of the room stood an old woman. She wore a simple, light linen gown, with her long white hair pulled back into a thick braid behind her.

The woman bowed. "Salar. Salara."

"Salta Tau," Mikael greeted back, bowing his head.

Watching him, Norah did the same.

The old woman spoke in the Kharavian tongue, but Mikael answered so that Norah could understand. "I come for the story of my salara," he said.

Salta Tau rolled her lips together with a bob of her head and held out her hands. Mikael took one and then took Norah's. Then he nodded for Norah to take the other.

Norah reached out, taking Salta Tau's hand and completing the circle.

Salta Tau closed her eyes and spoke what sounded like a spell into the air. She rocked slightly, forward and back, forward and back, with her eyes closed as she silently mouthed the words over and over.

Norah glanced at Mikael, but he only watched the old woman intently.

Salta Tau stopped. "I see," she said, her eyes still closed. She dropped their hands, but Mikael still held on to Norah's.

"Battle. Blade. Blood. Crown." The old woman spoke in the Northern tongue now, her accent thick and choppy.

The corners of Mikael's mouth turned up, but Norah frowned at her words. Surely it didn't take a special gift to see what could describe most every story in Kharav.

Mikael released her hand. Servants in long linen tunics stepped forward and stripped him of his clothing. Norah squirmed, still uncomfortable with the unabashed Kharavian ways, although she wasn't offended. She kept her eyes on his face.

They spread a mixture of herbs across his chest, letting it sit a moment before sponging it away.

"To clean the skin and numb it," Salara-Mae explained. Norah hadn't realized Mikael's mother had stepped beside her, and the woman's voice startled her.

"Does it hurt?"

"Not much," Mikael assured her.

"It hurts a great deal," Salara-Mae said. Mikael scowled at her.

Norah swallowed.

"Sit beside me," he told her. Then he lowered himself onto the heavily embroidered mat on the floor and lay on his back, waiting.

Norah took a seat on the floor cushion to his right, and Salara-Mae took the additional cushion just behind.

Salta Tau sat on Mikael's left side. The woman picked up a long tool with what appeared to be barbed bone at the end. She dipped it into a bowl of ink and set the edge against the skin of Mikael's chest. Then she struck it with a small mallet. Blood sprang from around the edge of the tool, but the woman wiped it away and continued.

The inking felt like eternity. The constant tapping of the mallet, the bleeding—Norah felt it pained her more than Mikael, who lay motionless. She could barely make out the design forming under Salta Tau's hands—a patterned circle of some sort.

Finally, as the sun started to set, Salta Tau stopped. Mikael's chest was a mix of blood with ink, and Salta Tau spread a thick mixture of herbs over it. Then she covered it with her hands and spoke again in the Kharavian tongue. Norah bit the inside of her cheek to quell her impatience. She wanted to see the finished image. Even though it seemed somewhat unoriginal, as she had gathered through Salta Tau's words—swords, blood, something with a crown—this was their story, and she wanted to see it.

She cast her eyes around the room as they waited. Salara-Mae sat expressionless. Norah looked up at the commander to find him staring back at her, his eyes dark and cold. They hadn't spoken since her attack. Mikael told her Soren had been the one to find her, the one who'd saved her. She wondered if he would add that to his own inked stories. Under *Tales of Regret.*

Salta Tau wiped away the herb mixture from Mikael's chest, catching Norah's eye and calling back her attention. Mikael watched her as she leaned over him to see.

His skin was still raw and swollen, but very clearly now appeared the image of two crowns, mirrored against each other along a spear in the center, and bordered with layered blades to create a circle. On the top sat Norah's Kharavian crown, or rather, a representation of it in the geometric patterns of their marking style.

Then she gasped.

She hadn't recognized it at first because it was inverted, but on the bottom was her Mercian crown—her mother's crown. It wasn't a patterned interpretation like Kharavian ink images, but instead bore the crown's exact likeness.

"How did you see this?" she breathed. "Where is it?"

Mikael looked down at his chest. "What?"

Norah's lip trembled. She looked back up at Salta Tau. "Can you tell me where it is?"

Mikael pushed himself up to sit and caught her hand. "Where what is?"

"My mother's crown. I lost it." She paused, her eyes welling. "I lost it when you took me as I was on my way to Aleon." She looked back up at Salta Tau, her desperation surfacing. "How can you see it? Do you know where it is?"

"That's not how the Gift works, Salara," Mikael said softly.

"No." She pleaded Salta Tau. "If you saw it, maybe you can see what was around it. It could help me find it."

But the old woman shook her head.

And the disappointment came as heavily as the original loss. Norah let out a breath, trying to regain control of her sudden emotion.

The servants spread another mixture of herbs across Mikael's skin, and he shifted for them to wrap it. When they finished, he donned his clothing again. Then he reached out his hand and helped her to her feet.

He didn't release her after she stood. Instead, he pulled her closer. "I'm sorry, Salara."

She shook her head. "You've done nothing wrong." Her voice came in barely a whisper.

He seemed to waver on his words. "Does it bother you?" His eyes searched hers. "Does it bother you that it's on my body?"

He was worried about how she felt about it. His concern quieted the churning inside her. It calmed her mind. "No." She looked at his chest, now covered in bandaging and his tunic. "At least I have an image of it now."

He raised a brow. "Do you always do this?"

"Do what?"

"Look for the best in everything?"

She struggled for words. What else was she to do?

He gave a gentle smile as he offered his arm, and she slipped her hand into its warmth.

Norah stood in her sanctuary, looking at Catherine's letter—the letter Alexander had given her a week ago—still unopened. She should read it. But not yet. She didn't know what was keeping her, but just... not yet.

The door of the chamber opened behind her. "Salara," Vitalia said, and Norah turned. She held out a folded parchment, a wide smile on her face.

"What's this?" Norah asked as she opened it. When she saw the image, she gasped. The image of her mother's crown.

"I thought you'd want it," Vitalia said.

"Where did you get this?"

"The lord commander sent a detachment out this morning. Each soldier holds a copy. They're tasked with finding it."

Norah's eyes widened.

"There's even a reward for citizens," Vitalia added.

"The lord commander?"

Her maid raised a brow with a shrug. "I know."

This man continued to confuse her. Norah couldn't believe she was about to do this, but she took the parchment and left to find the commander.

He sat in his study, finishing a letter. Norah had never been in the room before. It looked much like Alexander's in Mercia—a large desk covered in parchments, cabinets full of books and records. When he saw her, he didn't rise. She bit the inside of her cheek. He was always testing her, always trying to show her she didn't have complete power.

She would overlook it, partly because she didn't have the energy to argue with him and partly because she was here to thank him. She was already rethinking the latter. But maybe this could be the start of a civil relationship. He was lord commander of the Kharavian army, and she was salara. They couldn't hate each other forever.

"Do you need something, North Queen?" His voice was rough and unwelcoming.

He didn't call her Salara, something she had yet to correct him on. She didn't know why she hadn't. Each time he used it, she felt she lost more ground to demand it of him. She hated it. But she still couldn't bring herself to correct him, even now. Especially now. She looked down at the folded parchment in her hand, reminding herself why she was here.

"Yes, um, I..." Why was this so hard? "I heard you sent a detachment out this morning and—"

"I do as I'm bid," he said gruffly, cutting her off.

*Of course.* Her cheeks flushed with embarrassment at her assumption the kindness had come from him. Of course it had been Mikael. And here she was, making a fool of herself, giving him more power. Her embarrassment turned to anger. "You know, a gracious person would just allow someone to say thank you. Maybe politely credit another."

His brow furrowed. "Do you take me for a gracious person?" He almost seemed offended. "And did you really want to thank me?"

"I *did*," she answered, her voice rising. "But I obviously don't now."

"Well, you're welcome for that, then."

She snorted. This man was unbelievable. "You're an asshole."

He raised a brow. "Is that all?"

Norah wasn't sure if he was dismissing her or prompting her for more insults. Her breath shook, and she had to keep from crumpling the parchment in her hand. Forcing back the words on the tip of her tongue, she pursed her lips in festering rage and spun on her heel, leaving him in her wake of frustration.

She stormed down into the great hall, gritting her teeth. To think she went in there to thank him—never again. They *could* hate each other forever.

"Salara," Mikael's voice called her.

She stopped and turned to see him walking toward her.

"Are you all right?" he asked.

"Yes," she managed, trying to calm herself. This was where her thanks were owed, and she didn't want to start by criticizing his beloved commander, his asshole brother-in-arms. "Yes," she said again, swallowing back her frustration and trying to put the commander from her mind. "I was actually just looking for you."

"Were you?"

She nodded. "I heard about the detachment sent out this morning to look for my crown. I just wanted to let you know that... it was more than I ever would have expected, and... I wanted to thank you."

The corners of his lips turned up. "It's unlikely we'll find it, but now that we have its image, it's possible. When Soren suggested it, I admit I felt a bit of a fool. I should have thought of it myself."

Wait. It *was* the lord commander's idea?

He reached out and touched her arm. "The men will start where I took you. Let's see what we find."

She nodded, her mind still spinning. Then she stopped. "My Northmen might not take kindly to Kharavian warriors in the outer reaches." She couldn't even get her grandmother and the council to accept her marriage. She certainly wasn't going to get them to accommodate Shadowmen within the borders.

He smiled. "They won't even know we're there."

Like they'd been there before...

# Chapter Fifty-Four

The afternoon sun waned as Norah walked along the windowed hall, looking out into the courtyard. The sky was alive with colors of purple and orange. It was beautiful. A smile crept across her lips. Sometimes it was easy to believe a good life could be made here, if she let it.

Her mind still churned with everything that had happened. She could let herself dwell on the hardships and the despair, everything she had lost. Or she could look to the good: Mercia was safe and fed, and the threat of war between their kingdoms was gone. Mostly. And marriage to Mikael was not as she'd expected. Maybe she *could* be happy here.

She turned back toward her sanctuary, but her smile quickly faded when she looked up to see Mikael and the lord commander walking toward her, with Artem just behind. Mikael's stride was one of purpose. One of anger.

"What business do you send your lord justice on?" he called before he even reached her.

It took her a moment to understand what he'd asked. "It's a task for the council. Why?"

"What kind of task?" he pressed sharply. His tone made her own defenses raise.

She paused, trying to remember her conversation with Alexander. "I don't know, he didn't say. It's insignificant."

"Is it, now?"

Why was he so bothered? "What's this about?"

"He rides for Aleon," the lord commander snarled.

Norah gaped at Mikael in surprise. "What? That's not true." It didn't make sense.

"Our scouts confirmed it," Mikael told her.

"He wouldn't go to Aleon without telling me," she insisted.

"Well it appears you're wrong," the commander said.

Mikael's eyes shifted to his brute, warning him. He turned back to Norah. "You didn't know of this?"

She shook her head. "No, there must be some mistake. But even if he *is* going to Aleon, I'm sure there's a perfectly rational explanation."

"What could be a rational explanation for meeting with our enemy?" Mikael asked.

"Aleon isn't an enemy," she countered. "They've been friends and allies for generations."

"Of the *North*," Mikael stressed. "And let me remind you, that was with the promise of your hand."

She felt the tension escalating. "Let's not jump to conclusions. I'll speak to him when he returns and sort everything out."

"I'm eager to hear," Mikael said stiffly.

The commander's face flashed with anger, clearly offended by Mikael's tolerance. Artem stood behind them, smug and hostile.

Norah's stomach turned. What was the council doing? Just as things were seeming to settle, this jeopardized everything.

Norah paced the winter gardens with Vitalia and Serene in tow. She sucked in the chilled air to clear her mind. Why would the council have sent Alexander to Aleon? And why had Alexander not told her? He'd said he hadn't wanted to burden her more. Perhaps he'd gone to mend the relationship between their kingdoms. The news of her betrothal to the Kharavian king hadn't been received well by Aleon, understandably. She felt a pang of guilt when she thought of Phillip. He'd have seen her decision as an insult. And he'd done nothing wrong, nothing to break their alliance. She'd just changed her mind. Mikael was the only one who could give her peace.

"Try not to worry, Regal High," Serene's voice came from behind. The Mercian title fell strangely on her ears still. Her Kharavian title felt more natural now. "Mercia and Aleon have been friends for a long time, and business between them isn't uncommon. It could be something rather trivial."

She looked back at Serene and forced a smile, appreciating her maid's effort to ease her heart. "That's what I keep telling myself, but trivial things don't require a lord justice."

Norah paced the garden until she could no longer feel her fingers, then she headed back to the castle. She walked the long hall, and when she reached her sanctuary, she froze. Inside stood Captain Artem. And in his hand—Catherine's letter.

"What are you doing in here?" she demanded.

He didn't answer.

"This is my sanctuary. You're not allowed here!" Her eyes moved to the parchment in Artem's hand. "That's my letter!"

He stood, unbothered by her anger. "Why would a letter come from the regent?" he asked. "Telling you to return home urgently?"

"You read my letter?" she seethed. She held out her hand. "Give it to me!"

But he only looked at her with an icy gaze. "All while the Bear meets with Aleon."

"Give it to me!" she demanded again.

Kiran stepped inside from behind her, his hand on the hilt of his sword.

Artem shifted his gaze to Kiran, and his eyes darkened. "Do you forget your place, warrior?"

"You forget yours," Norah snapped. "Give me my letter, and get out! You're never to set foot in here again."

Artem gave an amused snort. Then he tossed the opened letter on the vanity before leaving, giving Kiran a daggered glare as he shouldered by.

Norah stood, still in shock.

"Are you all right, Salara?" Kiran asked her after Artem had gone.

She only nodded, unable to speak.

"We'll take our post. Call if you need anything." Then he and two other members of the Crest saw their way out, closing the door behind them and leaving Norah to her rage.

Vitalia and Serene said nothing but shifted closer to her.

Norah's hands shook as she picked up the letter from the vanity and sat on the chair at the small table. For the first time, she read its words.

*Dearest Norah,*

*This letter comes without excuse for the time it's taken me to write you. Indeed, I should have sent it earlier. Much earlier.*

*The lord justice sent news of your attack. Times such as these fill one's mind with everything they wished to have done differently, everything they wished to have said. There's much to say, Norah.*

*I pray this letter finds you safe, but safety is not enough. I need to see your face, my child, to see you well. And Mercia needs her queen.*

*Come home, if only for a short time. Return to Mercia. Urgently.*

*You have my love,*

*Catherine*

Norah's mind raced. At first glance, the letter seemed a heartfelt realization by her grandmother that she'd almost died, with a plea to return home. Understandable. Except, Catherine had said *urgently*.

The letter had arrived with Alexander's order to visit Aleon. Surely the two were related. He'd told her he didn't know what the letter said. Did he know Catherine wanted her to return home? What was really going on?

Norah found Mikael in his study, with the lord commander and Captain Artem. Of course. They turned as she entered. The cold of the room made her skin prickle. Her stomach knotted, but she forced herself steady.

Mikael's eyes followed her in. "Do you know what the North is planning?" he asked her.

Now didn't seem the right time to air her grievance about the captain's intrusion in her sanctuary. Mikael obviously knew about the letter; he had to know how it had been found. Did he care? She tried to pull her mind from it—she needed to focus on settling things down. "You don't know if anyone is planning anything. It's purely speculation at this point."

"The Bear rides for Aleon," the brute snarled at her. "And the regent calls for your immediate return."

Yes, it was damning, but she needed to keep things from escalating until she could figure out what was going on. "I was attacked," she countered. "My *grandmother* is worried. She wants me to return home."

"Urgently," he added.

Norah glared at him. "She fears for my safety. Can you blame her?"

The brute snorted. "You're not in *urgent* danger." But his stormy glare swore otherwise.

Her eyes narrowed. "She doesn't know that, and frankly, neither do I."

"She sends the Bear to Aleon."

"The council sends him," she argued back.

"It's the same," Mikael said, stepping into the argument. His face was calm, but his voice brimmed with anger. And something else... Sadness? "As regent, your grandmother would be involved, even if she didn't order it herself."

*No*, her grandmother wouldn't do that. Would she?

His eyes were still on her, seeking answers. "Do you know what the North plans?"

"Mikael. Just give me some time to understand what's happening."

He stepped closer and cupped her face in his hands, quieting her. "Do you really not know?" he whispered. "Salara."

Again, she shook her head, but she could see his doubt.

"Salara," he said again, more faint this time.

She realized it wasn't Mercia he focused on—it was her, and what *she* knew. He was more concerned with her than Mercia. And his eyes were filled with more than doubt. All she could do was look back at him. She had no words. She didn't know how else to assure him.

Slowly, he bent his head and brought his lips to hers. It wasn't a kiss of passion, or of longing. It was a confession of fear. It said what his words couldn't. He was begging her not to betray him. He pulled back slowly, his eyes searching her.

"Do you still wish to escape me?" he whispered.

Not escape... but she did wish to go back to Mercia, to the people who loved her, to the only people who could help her find herself. "Would you let me leave?"

His brow dipped, and pain flashed in his eyes. "Would you not stay with me of your own free will?"

If she had the choice to leave... "Mikael." Her voice cracked.

His nostrils flared, and his brow dipped lower. He saw her hesitation. Her truth.

"Mikael," she said again. Yes, she wanted to leave. But that didn't mean she wouldn't return. Did it?

He straightened and looked to the lord commander. "We leave now." The commander handed him a belted sword.

Norah's pulse quickened as he fastened it around his waist. "What are you doing? Where are you going?" she asked. Fear flashed through her. *After Alexander.* She caught his arm. "Mikael, wait."

"I have to go to the seer," he said. "I'll be back in three days' time."

Her heart steadied a little with the relief he wasn't riding after Alexander, but she didn't understand. "The seer?"

"I have to see if the Bear plans to bring Aleon against me." His voice was cold now, and he backed just out of the reach of her touch.

The knot in her stomach twisted until it ached. "What about me?"

He paused. "I can't let you go." To the seer or to Mercia? A dark storm eddied in his eyes, and her heart dropped. *Neither.* "I'll return in three days," he said.

"Take me with you," she pleaded. If there were new visions of what was to come...

"Only Kharavian royal blood can visit the temple of the seer," the commander said.

And apparently the commander, Norah added to herself in frustration. She pursed her lips. Rules didn't apply to him.

Mikael frowned. "You'll stay here," he told her. He cast an eye toward Artem, then he and the commander strode out, leaving her with only the captain.

And just like that, she was a prisoner again.

# CHAPTER FIFTY-FIVE

Norah woke to Vitalia calling her in a panicked voice.

"Salara! Salara!" her maid cried. "You have to wake up. Something terrible has happened!"

Norah sat up with alarm, blinking the sleep from her eyes and trying to focus her mind. "What? What's happened?"

"It's Bremhad!"

*What*? "What about Bremhad?"

"He didn't come home last night. Kiran found him on the workmen's stairs, just outside the kitchens."

Vitalia's words came too quickly, and Norah was having trouble following. "Wait, but... is he all right? Where is he now?"

Her maid paused, swallowing, and then shook her head. "He's dead, Salara."

Norah clenched her quilts in her fists. A weight crushed her chest. She couldn't breathe. *Dead*? Her mind swirled around her. She stumbled from the bed and let Vitalia help her with a dress. "Where's Kiran?" she asked, her voice trembling.

"At the public mortium."

*The mortium*. She felt as though a dagger had been thrust into her chest. "W-What happened?" she stammered as Vitalia quickly finished the lacing on her dress and ran to get her cloak.

"The prefect is saying Bremhad fell on the stairs and hit his head, that it was an accident."

Norah swept out of her sanctuary with Vitalia beside her.

"But it makes no sense," her maid continued. "Bremhad doesn't even come into the castle, except to tend to the greens on your balcony when you're out. He wouldn't have been on the stairs last night."

Vitalia led the way to the public mortium, a large stone building where Bremhad's body had been taken. Norah followed her inside. The halls were poorly lit, and the smell of death hung heavy in the air. Vitalia led her down a long hall, past a series of open chambers. Pale bodies lay atop wooden tables. Norah pulled her cloak tighter. They reached a chamber at the end of the hall. Inside, a woman was weeping. Norah entered to see Kiran and an older woman, presumably his mother. They were cleaning the body of his father, who lay on a table in the center of the room.

*Bremhad*.

And it hit her.

This was her fault. Her eyes stung. It was another message from the lord commander. He was punishing her by hurting those around her, those she cared about.

The older woman wept as she worked, sponging Bremhad's head and gently smoothing his silver hair. Kiran looked up when he heard them enter, and his tear-stricken eyes widened in surprise. "Salara," he said as he stepped toward her. "You didn't have to come here, to this place."

"Of course, I did! Kiran, I'm so sorry," she cried, tears streaming down her own cheeks.

Suddenly, Kiran's eyes moved over her shoulder to someone behind her, and she turned to see Captain Artem.

Kiran bared his teeth with a ragged breath of wrath. "You did this!"

He rushed the captain but was caught by two of her Crest guards.

"You did this!" he thundered at Artem. "I know you did this!"

"Kiran!" Norah cried as her guardsmen dragged him from the room and down the hall. What was happening? She could only stand in horror as Kiran's bellows echoed through the mortium. She gaped back at Artem. "Did you really do this?"

"The prefect has ruled it an accident," he answered calmly.

That didn't answer her question, and horror struck her. Kiran's roars still echoed from the hall. "Where are they taking him?" she demanded.

The captain looked at her with gloating eyes. He didn't answer. Then he turned and left the chamber.

Norah stumbled backward in disbelief but caught herself against the wall. Vitalia stepped forward and clasped her arm. "Are you all right, Salara?"

She'd forgotten her maid was even there. She looked back at Kiran's mother, who stood frozen, still grieving her husband and frightened for her son.

The woman swallowed back her emotion to give a small nod of her head, and whispered, "Salara."

Norah's heart burst into pieces. Everything inside her hurt. "I'm so sorry," she whispered. She looked at her maid. "Vitalia, please, stay here. Help her."

"Of course."

"Anything she needs—help preparing the body, money. Anything."

Vitalia nodded. "Yes, Salara."

"I have to make sure Kiran's all right." She cast one last apologetic look at the woman. "I'm so sorry," she breathed again, then she turned and left the chamber.

It was everything she could do to not fall apart as she stepped out of the mortium. Bremhad's death was no accident. She wanted to blame the commander—it seemed fitting. But the commander was with Mikael. That didn't necessarily absolve him. He could have ordered it.

Kiran had accused Artem. Maybe it was only his grief lashing out. Or perhaps he was right. Maybe Artem was punishing her. Did he know Bremhad was Kiran's father? Perhaps Artem was punishing Kiran for his defiance in her sanctuary.

She scanned the grounds for the captain, but he was nowhere to be seen.

"Where is Artem?" she snapped back at the Crest following behind her.

"He may be in the forces office," her guardsman Sonal told her.

"Take me there. Now."

She followed him to a building beside the soldiers' barracks. Inside, Artem stood with another soldier. The soldier bowed and left as she entered.

"North Queen," Artem greeted her coldly.

"It's Salara," she cut back. She wasn't going to let *two* assholes get away with that. "Where's Kiran?" she demanded.

"He's been detained."

"Where?"

He cast her an annoyed eye. "Where we detain men."

*In the dungeon.* "He's a member of the Crest!"

Artem snorted. "No longer. He falsified his documents and attacked his superior."

*Superior.* Artem was anything but. "You can't do that!"

"I'm captain of the Crest. I can."

His cool tone infuriated her. She'd thought she couldn't loathe anyone more than the lord commander. She'd been wrong. "I order you to release him." She may be a prisoner, but she was still queen.

The corners of his mouth turned up in amusement. "I answer to Salar."

He was such a smug bastard, so confident that Mikael's attention was focused on the threat with Aleon and that it would bode unfavorably for her. She was starting to understand the want for blood. If she had a dagger in her hand...

She wouldn't let him get away with this. Without a reply, she turned and stormed from the office and back to the castle.

Night passed, and another day came, but Norah couldn't sleep. Her body was tired, but her mind couldn't rest. Vitalia had stayed with Kiran's mother, and Serene had spent the night in the sanctuary with her.

Her maid helped her dress, carefully fastening the clasps of the gown and straightening the lacing. "You look like you haven't slept a wink, Regal High."

She let out an exhausted breath. "I haven't."

"You might find it more comfortable in the villa," Serene suggested. "It's nice there."

Norah sat down at the vanity with a stoic face as the maid brushed her hair. "I don't want to talk about the villa again," she said. "Ever." If she could, she'd burn it to the ground. She'd burn everything. She hated this wretched place—it was breaking her.

"Yes, Regal High," Serene said quietly. Norah watched her maid in the mirror as she gathered the linens from the bed and swept them into a basket. She left the room just as Vitalia entered with breakfast.

"Salara," Vitalia said breathlessly. "Good news! Kiran was released. Just this morning."

Norah spun around in her chair. That was good news.

"The Crest is unhappy with his treatment. I fear Artem's mercy is temporary, just to appease them. Hopefully Salar returns soon."

Yes, Norah was desperate for his return. But for now, she was relieved that Kiran was at least free. "Where is he now?"

"Back with his mother, preparing. The burial will be this afternoon."

Norah rose from her chair. "I have to go." She had to be there.

"Salara, it would be... unconventional for you to be there. Bremhad was a servant. Only those who have died a warrior's death would be seen into the ground by salar. Or salara."

To hell with conventions. "I don't care." She paused. "Unless... Kiran doesn't want me there?" After all, this was her fault.

"Of course he'd want you there. It would be a great honor."

"Then I'll go."

Vitalia gave her a sad smile.

"Help me get ready."

The wet, muddy ground was soft beneath her feet.

Outside the city, Norah walked with Vitalia up the hill to the large public burial ground. She wished she'd left her jacket in the carriage. The sun sat high in the sky. Even though it was still winter, it was as hot as a summer day.

They gathered in a large circle around a hole in the earth, with Bremhad's body wrapped in linen beside it. It seemed such a strange thing, to bury the body of a loved one in the dirt. In Mercia, bodies were burned to free the soul so it could travel to the gods, except the bodies of the kings and queens. Their souls remained tethered to this world, watching over the people, guiding their hands to the will of the gods.

The Kharavian people didn't believe in gods or souls. They believed bodies should be returned to the earth from which they came. Norah didn't know what she believed. Neither made her feel differently about death, neither took away the pain.

More people had come than she'd expected; many were servants, and some were dressed in finer clothing. She was surprised to see so many soldiers of the Crest—perhaps all the members of the Crest—nearly an army.

"I didn't know the Crest knew Bremhad," she whispered to Vitalia. "Or knew that he was Kiran's father."

"They didn't. They only found out yesterday. But they came to support Kiran."

Her eyes combed the people to find him, and she did—standing beside his mother. He spotted her and started toward her.

Vitalia slipped away as he approached, giving them space.

"Salara," Kiran said as he reached her. "You honor us."

"It was the least I could do." She watched as he pressed his lips together tightly to hold back his emotion. It only prompted her own. "It's warmer than usual," she said, breaking the weight of the air.

Kiran's breath steadied. "It's what greenskeepers call alhilat—the great trick, a false spring." His lips held a weak smile. "My father hated it. It lasts just long enough for the blooms to start, then the ice returns and kills them all." He looked at the skies. "We'll soon be in winter again."

Kiran's face hardened, and Norah followed his gaze to see Artem at the edge of the grounds.

"Ignore him, Kiran," she told him. "Focus on your father."

"I'll see that man dead."

She couldn't object. "You really think he did this?"

"He ordered it. He wouldn't do it himself, fucking coward." He glanced at Norah. "Forgive my words, Salara."

Norah watched Artem as he watched them. He did look like a fucking coward. He was the only man who wore full armor, aside from Mikael. He probably viewed himself of equally deserved status. He wasn't.

"Are men loyal to him?" she asked.

Kiran snorted. "A few. Not many."

"How is he captain, then?"

"He was captain of the Crest for Salar's father. He'll stay captain until he's promoted. Or dies."

"Maybe that's why he wears all that armor. The latter's more likely."

Kiran snorted again. He turned and looked at her. "If you ever need anything, Salara, I'm still in service to you. I took my oath for life. I'm still a soldier of the Crest."

"Thank you, Kiran."

He gave her a small bow of his head and went back to join his mother by the body of his father. She wished Mikael would return sooner, to right this wrong. But how could it be righted? And what would he do? Now there was this distance between them, and she was a prisoner. *Again.* Maybe that's what she'd been all along. Maybe she'd only been fooling herself. Maybe what she'd felt, what she'd thought she'd felt...

Vitalia took the vacated place by Norah's side.

"I can't stay here any longer," Norah said. "I can't bear it, Vitalia. I have to find a way to get home." She watched as men lowered Bremhad's body into the earth. No more—she was leaving. Today. Tonight. She turned her eyes to Vitalia. "You know this castle. You can sneak us out."

Her maid nodded. "I could get you as far as the burial ground. Then I could return and keep them unknowing a while longer for you to get away."

Norah grabbed her arm. "No. You're coming with me. And Serene. I'm not leaving you to these monsters."

Vitalia stared at her for a moment.

"Do you not want to go?"

"No. I mean, yes, I-I do," Vitalia stammered. "I just didn't think you would... think about me."

"You're my friend," Norah said firmly. "You're coming with me. You and Serene."

Her maid gave her a teary-eyed nod. "All right. We'll go." She paused. "Wait. Even if we get out of Ashan, we still have to get through the Canyonlands."

Norah couldn't help a small smile. "I know someone who will help us."

*Tahla.*

# CHAPTER FIFTY-SIX

Darkness hung over them. A successful slip-away plan put Norah and Vitalia outside the blacksmith forge, just across the way from the stables. They hid by the walls of the forge. It surprised Norah how easy it had been to climb out of the bath-chamber window in her sanctuary, down the trellis, and to the ground below.

Serene had stayed in the sanctuary and was tasked with making occasional noises—talking, laughing—to confirm occupancy. After the guard change, she was to take a tray of half-eaten dinner down to the kitchen, *tidying up*. No other staff would be in the kitchen at this hour. She'd slip out the side hall and down the stairs to where Norah and Vitalia would be waiting with horses.

Time passed at a snail's pace. Norah's heart raced in her chest. She prayed everything would go to plan. They only needed to get the horses and meet Serene outside the kitchen.

She and Vitalia slipped along the wall of the smith's forge and silently crossed the cobblestone street toward the stables. But before they reached the side doors, a soldier stepped out in front of them. Norah stopped suddenly, and Vitalia grabbed her arm. The soldier held a spear in his hand—he was a member of the Crest. Norah sucked in a breath. Then she recognized him.

*Bhastian.*

"You need to get back to the castle, Salara," he told her. "The captain's looking for you."

"Well he can keep looking," she said sharply.

"Salara." There was something in his voice that made her skin prickle. "You'll want to go back."

But she didn't want to go back. She couldn't live like this anymore. "No." She shook her head. "I won't."

"Salar and the lord commander will be returning soon."

All the more reason she had to go now. "I'm leaving. Step aside."

But he only blocked her way. She couldn't fight him—she was no match for a warrior of the Crest. And even if she could get away, she'd lose Vitalia, and Serene. She had to try a different approach. "Bhastian. Please. I'm begging you." Was Kiran the only one with compassion?

He hesitated, but then shook his head. "I can't, Salara. I have to take you back."

"Bhastian," she pleaded. "Help me."

He motioned her back toward the castle. Fight flooded her mind, but she couldn't, she reminded herself. And, since Bhastian was here, they'd likely found Serene. She wouldn't be outside the kitchen waiting, and Norah couldn't leave without her.

Defeated, she headed back. As they walked, he waved off the guard that came running, and continued toward her sanctuary. They entered the west wing, but as they reached the main hall, Bhastian halted.

Artem stepped out from the shadows, and Norah's stomach dropped.

Bhastian struck the ground with his spear in salute and stood at attention.

"I would have thought you'd be more careful with yourself now, Salara," Artem said with a chilling tone. "All the problems you've caused, the people you've hurt."

"You mean the people you've hurt," she snapped.

"You forced my hand." Artem scoffed. "I initially took you for a sharp woman, but you still fail to grasp your situation."

Her situation. He didn't view her as queen. He didn't recognize her authority. No one did.

"Mikael won't stand for this." She didn't know if she believed her own words, though.

"I think that depends on what he sees in Odepeth."

*Odepeth.* Where the seer was, where Mikael had gone.

"You're so confident it will go poorly," she said.

"Because it's known—you cannot change fate. Salar will see nothing different."

This was the first she had heard that. Her father had changed fate. Hadn't he? His words scared her. What would Mikael do if he thought his fate remained?

He eyed her for a moment. "Where were you just now?"

She didn't answer, and he looked at Bhastian. Norah's heart beat heavily in her chest.

"She was in the library," Bhastian answered.

Her heart leapt in relief, but Norah pursed her lips in feigned anger.

Artem's eyes narrowed. "You said you searched the library."

"Not well enough," Bhastian answered.

He tilted his head, looking back at Norah. "A little late for a library visit."

"I couldn't sleep."

"Strange you would slip your guard for that. And I would have thought your maid would have given me that answer—a place so innocent."

Norah's stomach knotted. *Serene.* "She didn't know."

"So she said."

He'd caught Serene. He'd questioned her. "If you touched her—"

The corner of his mouth turned up, and he looked at Bhastian. "Take her back. And take your new post."

Norah stepped around him with a fury and stalked back to her sanctuary, the panic building inside her with each step. When she reached the door, she swung it open and let out a ragged breath.

Serene sat on the edge of the bed, trembling as blood ran from her brow and lip. Her face was swollen from crying.

"Serene," Norah gasped, rushing to her. "What happened?"

Her maid let out an uneven breath but shook her head. She couldn't speak.

Norah sank down beside her and pulled her close. "I'm here now," she said, stroking her hair.

"It was the captain," Serene managed to get out, her voice shaking. "I hadn't even left yet. He came looking for you. I told him I didn't know where you were. He didn't believe me."

Rage surged through her.

Serene glanced over Norah's shoulder and grew quiet. Norah realized Bhastian hadn't stopped at the end of the hall but had come into the sanctuary. "Get out," she hissed at him.

"I can't do that, Salara. The captain has ordered a post in your room. You're to have a guard always." Norah let out an enraged breath, but Bhastian spoke with a softer voice. "I'll take the shift until Salar and the lord commander return. They'll be back soon, and neither will stand for this."

"You can't be serious. This is all the lord commander stands for!"

The guardsman sighed and stepped to the door, turning his back to give the desolate women privacy.

Norah trembled in a maddening rage, but the only thing she could do was wait for Mikael to return. She and Vitalia pulled Serene into the bed and lay in the dark, trying to hold back the tears.

"Salara."

Norah woke to Bhastian calling her. She blinked the sleep from her eyes and sat up, careful not to wake Serene and Vitalia lying beside her.

"Is it morning?" she whispered.

"Yes, early morning. Salar and the lord commander have just returned."

"Oh," Norah breathed as she slipped out of the bed.

He hesitated. "But, Salara, it's not a good sign. The lord commander has gone straight to his study, where he's to be left alone."

That wasn't entirely indicative of something bad. If the lord commander was unhappy, it could be the seer had spoken in her favor.

She hoped.

Norah padded into the bath chamber and ran her fingers through her hair. She splashed water onto her face from the basin and took a deep breath. Mikael would listen. Things between them weren't completely broken. She just needed to talk to him.

She stepped back out into her chamber and slipped on her shoes. "Where is he?" she asked Bhastian.

"I imagine he'll be reaching the castle from the stables any moment."

Norah left her sanctuary and made her way through the castle with Bhastian close behind. What had the seer told Mikael? Would it break things more between them? She feared the answer.

She waited by the stair, pacing circles around the inlaid image of a sun on the stone floor. Her mind raced, and her stomach threatened to upheave the contents of her last meal. But she had to stay calm. She walked through the conversation in her mind. She'd tell him what Artem had done, about Bremhad and Kiran. She would tell him about Serene. She'd have to admit her effort to escape. He would understand. Or he might become more suspicious.

Her heart thrummed faster.

The front doors of the castle swung open, and Mikael strode through. He stopped when he saw her.

He looked weary. Dried mud covered the greaves of his armor. He held his helm in his hand by a single horn. He didn't speak.

Every intelligent sentence in her mind left her, every word. The silence was overwhelming between them as she searched his face for clues.

He silently walked to her, and she didn't move.

Ever so slowly, he brought his hand to her face. He brushed her cheek with his fingertips and grazed his thumb over the line of her lips. His eyes trailed his somber touch—mournful even.

Mikael pulled back, still without a word, and then turned for the stairs.

"What did the seer tell you?" she asked.

He didn't answer. He didn't want to talk about it—not a good sign, but she needed to talk to him.

She followed him up the stairs. "Mikael, I need to speak with you. About Captain Artem."

He paused. "I can't speak about this right now."

She couldn't accept that. "I'm sure you're tired and want to rest, but it's important," she pressed. "I can't tolerate him any longer. He—"

"Don't ask any more of me," he said, turning back to her. His voice was tinged with exasperation and hints of anger. "Not now."

She stepped back in surprise. She hadn't expected his reaction.

"I won't hear it," he said, and he started back up the stairs.

A heat rose in her cheeks at his dismissal. She trailed behind him, a fury growing in her core. "You will hear it!" she snapped.

He whirled back to face her. "Have I not given you everything?" he raged.

Norah stumbled back but caught herself against the railing.

His voice came low, but it chilled her soul. "I've required nothing of the North, put no demands upon you. I've given everything you've asked—peace, mercy, tolerance. I give provisions for your people. I give your army horses and weapons. Men." His face grew darker. "And I let you keep the one threat to my crown. The man who is to strike me down rides unchallenged through my kingdom, through my castle. Even now he goes freely to my enemy. Still, I do nothing."

He looked at her with defeat in his eyes. "I wed you to change my fate. But I've only brought it closer." He steadied his weight against the railing. "I won't hear it." Then he turned and continued up the stairs.

Norah took a deep breath, tempering her fury. He was speaking from fear, she told herself. And meeting that fear with anger wouldn't help either of them.

She followed him up the staircase and down the hall to his study. He said nothing as he unfastened his sword belt from around his hips and leaned the blade against the wall.

"What did the seer tell you?" she asked again.

Mikael waved his servant away, and Vimal left them to the quiet of the crackling fireplace. He pulled off his breastplate, dropping it onto the floor by his desk. He started with his left pauldron but fumbled with the small clasps and gave up. Norah watched as he gripped the corners of the desk and leaned his weight against it. He breathed heavily through his mouth.

She moved to his side. "What did the seer tell you?" she asked again, softly.

He breathed in a long breath and let it out slowly. "I die at the hand of the Bear."

She needed to walk him back from this. "That's an old vision."

"No. There will be another Great War. A powerful event. There are many visions of it now: North flags throughout the Tribelands, Aleon forces in Bahoul." He paused, his eyes burning. "You. Beside the Aleon king."

Samuel's paintings flooded her mind. But she knew things weren't always as they seemed. "Mikael, these are but interpretations of what the seer has seen. They lack context, all the detail. You can't necessarily rely on his translation."

"I saw it with my own eyes!" he snapped back.

Norah stopped as her breath hitched in her throat. *Of course*. She felt so stupid—how could she have forgotten? Mikael had a traveler, someone who could enter his mind and show him these visions. She needed to see them. "How powerful is this seer?" she asked.

"The most powerful of the four kingdoms."

Was he powerful enough to see what happened to her memories? Was he powerful enough to unlock them?

Mikael stood with a somber weight curving his shoulders. There was something more.

"He showed Soren a vision," he added quietly, "one that Soren won't speak of, even to me. It's his own demise, I'm sure." He paused, drawing in a devastated breath. "I haven't changed my fate. I've brought it to my door. And I've cursed those closest to me."

He struggled again with the clasps of his armor. She moved forward to help him, but he caught her wrist, pulling back from her touch.

The storms of his eyes eddied. "Leave me, North Queen."

# CHAPTER FIFTY-SEVEN

Mikael's anguish from the night before weighed heavily on Norah. And there was nothing she could do. Morning brought a new day, but not a new hope. This place, this kingdom of darkness that decayed the mind and heart, was breaking her.

She decided to try for a ride. She needed fresh air, and sun. How far had she fallen from Mikael's grace? Would she be denied the little freedom she'd had before?

Norah stepped out of her sanctuary to see Captain Artem personally waiting for her.

"Salara," he greeted her coldly.

His nearness made the hair on the back of her neck stand on end. Of course there'd been no retribution for his cruelty, and his smug presence enraged her. She hated this man. She praised herself for sending Vitalia and Serene to stay with Kiran and his mother—they were hidden, and safe.

"Captain Artem, what a surprise," she said, not bothering to hide her disgust.

His eyes moved over her clothing. "We're going riding, I see."

Norah pursed her lips. He was attempting to keep her in. She wouldn't let him. "Try to keep up," she quipped.

His eyes darkened.

They rode out into the morning; Norah on the mare with Artem and a small group of his soldiers behind.

Norah took them far. Her spirits rose under the sun. Artem couldn't hurt her, this she was certain. It's why he hurt people around her. And Vitalia and Serene were hidden away, protected. All he could do now was harass her directly. And she would make it very tiresome for him.

They reached Hava Lake—a deep pool below a cliff overlook. Against the dark and rocky terrain, the water sparkled a brilliant blue. Kiran had shown her this place. *The bluest water in the world*, he'd said, from the minerals in the springs that fed it.

Artem pulled off his helmet and wiped the sweat from his brow before putting it back on. He didn't wear a wrap on his head, like the other soldiers, but rather a helm that looked more decorative than functional. And like everything else in Kharav, the metal of his armor was dark, almost black, soaking in the sun. His head was likely baking in it. *Good.* She smiled to herself.

Norah looked up at the rocky overlook above, and her smile grew to a grin. She urged the mare to the water's edge and dismounted, using her hand to block the sun as she looked upward at the rock face. "A nice day for a walk," she called pleasantly. An even better day to require an overheated captain of the Crest to hike up a steep mountainside.

"You can't be serious," Artem scoffed.

She shrugged. "Stay here, then," she replied, and started up the narrow path.

Artem's annoyed grunt sang sweetly in her ears as he dismounted and followed with his guard. Petty pleasure, she scolded herself. And Artem would probably find a way to make her pay for it later. But for now, she'd give herself this small joy. It was all she had left.

It was a long climb, and despite leaving her jacket back with the mare, she found herself perspiring. Delight rippled through her as she thought of how Artem must be faring.

They were all breathless by the time they reached the top. Her legs burned, and a deep stitch clenched her side, but it was worth it. She closed her eyes, breathing in the sky and drawing life back into her body. This was exactly what she had needed. In a short while, she'd be back in the castle of shadows. She needed to remember this place—how the wind felt, how the sun hit her face. She needed it to endure the dark.

Everything was lost.

Yet something still pulled at her heart. Something small but strong. *Not everything*, it said. Not yet.

Norah stood in the sun and looked down to the sparkling blue of the water below. The light danced across its surface. Its magic smiled at her. The wind swirled around her, whispering into her ears, breathing strength into her mind. It told her to remember—remember what she was here for.

And a new strength came.

She'd almost lost herself again. She had almost resigned herself. But she couldn't. She owed it to her people. And those she loved. She owed it to herself.

Norah turned around to see Artem standing a distance away from her. He watched her with his dark and despicable eyes, no doubt thinking dark and despicable thoughts.

She raised her arms, feeling the wind underneath them. Artem's mouth opened slightly, and he took a step toward her.

Her lips peeled back into a wry smile.

And she let herself fall backward, over the edge.

"No!" he bellowed as he charged forward. But he was too far away. He couldn't catch her.

The fall was a fall into freedom.

Norah hit the water, and its chill sent a shock through her body. It took her a moment to recover, and she kicked feverishly back to the surface. She gasped for air as she battled the tangle of skirts around her legs, and her teeth chattered as she got her bearings. Looking up, she saw Artem at the top of the overlook, gaping at her but not daring to jump. She let out a triumphant laugh.

The lord commander would have jumped in after her.

But Kiran was right. This man was a coward.

Norah made her way to the bank and let out a low whistle, calling the mare. The horse found her quickly, and she sprang onto her back. Giving one last look to Artem, she urged the animal forward into a gallop.

North.

She rode until she was out of sight before she let the mare slow. It would take Artem some time to get back down to his horse, and she'd be well ahead of him. He'd never track her with Savantahla, a horse of the Wild. Norah brought the mare to a stop and looked around. Her teeth chattered in her wet dress under the wind, but she was thankful for alhilat—the break in winter. If Bremhad were there, perhaps he might not hate it so much now.

She shifted her mind to what she needed to do next. Artem had watched her ride north, toward the Canyonlands and Mercia. She smiled as she turned the mare east.

To Odepeth. And the seer.

# THE COMPLETE TRILOGY

Continue the journey with:

## ⬦— SHADOW QUEEN —⬦

For ten years, her kingdom has warred
against the Shadow King.
*Now, she's his queen.*

# ABOUT THE AUTHOR

Nicola Tyche is an American fiction and fantasy author writing romantic fantasy, paranormal, urban fantasy, and other women's fiction. Suspenseful plot twists, strong heroines, relatable villains, and melt-your-insides anti-heroes are ingredients for every book, and Nicola is a sucker for a happily ever after.

She lives in Vancouver, Washington, with her husband and three daughters. When she isn't writing, she enjoys tacos, traveling, gardening, exploring the great outdoors, and other creative projects. Visit her website at www.nicolatyche.com, connect on the Nicola Tyche Facebook reader group, or the platforms below!

nicolatyche

Made in the USA
Columbia, SC
31 January 2024

31199545R00350